CONQUERGOOD

&

THE CENTER OF THE INTELLIGIBLE MYSTERY OF BEING

A huge thanks to the Hemingway Society, to the Royal Society of Literature,
to the Royal Society of Arts, Manufactures and Commerce (RSA), to Fraser
Place and to CM+ Serviced Apartments for giving the author tranquil
places to write and work, and to everyone who gave their support at the
American Academy in Rome (Italy) while the author worked on this book,
his eighth major publication.

Reviews

"*Conquergood & the Center of the Intelligible Mystery of Being* is a captivating new dystopian science fiction novel by CG Fewston, an author already making a name for himself with his thought-provoking work. Set in the year 2183, Conquergood is set in a world where one company, Korporation, reigns supreme and has obtained world peace, through oppression… The world-building in the novel is remarkable. Fewston has created a believable and authentic post-apocalyptic society with technological wonders and thought-provoking societal issues. The relevance of the themes to the state of the world today adds an extra wrinkle and makes the story even more compelling."

~ *Literary Titan*

"C.G. Fewston creates a story replete in social, political, philosophical and psychological depth and inspections that require slower reading in order to thoroughly absorb… No pat dystopian adventure, *Conquergood & the Center of the Intelligible Mystery of Being* is intellectually challenging and absorbing. It ideally will attract the thinking sci-fi reader who appreciates not just a futuristic setting, but the moral and ethical quandaries faced by a protagonist forced to move out of his initial perceptions of his place in life in order step into the shoes of the enemy… This absorbing, engrossing story of genetic manipulation and a search for the ultimate human psyche will also ideally lend to classroom assignment and discussion for courses interested in philosophical and social dilemmas in sci-fi…

"Not your usual dystopian saga, *Conquergood & the Center of the Intelligible Mystery of Being* is highly recommended for its bigger-picture presentation of redemption and relationships that grow from adversity and self-inspection. Its inspection of the foundations of reality and the future of humans is thought-provoking and thoroughly engaging as Conquergood moves towards not only his brother, but a different vision of a new human influenced by genetic and social manipulation."

~ D. Donovan, Sr. Reviewer, *Midwest Book Review*

"Set in the far-future, Fewston's original and deeply engrossing SF tale finds a young man struggling to locate his missing twin brother. It is 2183. The post-apocalyptic world has changed: the mega-corporate and governmental entity, the Korporation, governs the law. Jerome Conquergood is homeless, roaming the abandoned and crumbling skyscrapers of Old York City when he is invited to join the Korporation… Jerome's journey to self-realization, which is hard-won, reflecting, and intricate, takes the forefront. There's palpable tension and intrigue as Jerome makes his moves and gains knowledge about both the Korporation and his identity…

"The pace clips along nicely, and the small cast enjoys transecting character development arcs. Aside from Jerome's ongoing story, Vincent's storyline and the brothers' family backstory add emotional stakes on top of the physical. The worldbuilding is authentic, and the intriguing theme, technological wonders, and spot-on relevance to present-day societal and ethical issues provide plenty of adrenaline. Fewston infuses the familiar genre tropes with raw urgency, keeping the reader guessing to the end. A must-read for morally serious readers of dystopia."

~ *BookView Review*

THREE

TWO

ONE

Author's Note

---

*Some of the spellings have been purposely altered to reflect Ernst Vollert's German book called *Die Korporation Der Berliner Buchhändler* which was published January 1, 1898.

In the following science-fiction novel, the sole mega-conglomerate of the world is known as "the Korporation."

for the
Book People

Dedicated to

Axton
&
Thor

At first we cannot see beyond the path that leads downward to dark and hateful things but no light or beauty will ever come from the man who cannot bear this sight. Light is always born of darkness, and the sun never yet stood still in heaven to satisfy man's longing or to still his fears.

C.G. Jung
Modern Man in Search of a Soul
1933

Man is, at one and the same time, a solitary being and a social being. As a solitary being, he attempts to protect his own existence and that of those who are closest to him, to satisfy his personal desires, and to develop his innate abilities. As a social being, he seeks to gain the recognition and affection of his fellow human beings, to share in their pleasures, to comfort them in their sorrows, and to improve their conditions of life. Only the existence of these varied, frequently conflicting strivings accounts for the special character of a man, and their specific combination determines the extent to which an individual can achieve an inner equilibrium and can contribute to the well-being of society. It is quite possible that the relative strength of these two drives is, in the main, fixed by inheritance. But the personality that finally emerges is largely formed by the environment in which a man happens to find himself during his development, by the structure of the society in which he grows up, by the tradition of that society, and by its appraisal of particular types of behavior. The abstract concept "society" means to the individual human being the sum total of his direct and indirect relations to his contemporaries and to all the people of earlier generations.

Albert Einstein
"Why Socialism?"
1949

The earth is finite. Its ability to absorb wastes and destructive effluent is finite. Its ability to provide food and energy is finite. Its ability to provide for growing numbers of people is finite. And we are fast approaching many of the earth's limits... No more than one or a few decades remain before the chance to avert the threats we now confront will be lost and the prospects for humanity immeasurably diminished...

We the undersigned, senior members of the world's scientific community, hereby warn all humanity of what lies ahead.

Union of Concerned Scientists
"World Scientists' Warning to Humanity"
1992

Time is but a dream of the near and of the deep.

Kebir
Anakhro Skript
2184

CONQUERGOOD

&

THE CENTER OF THE INTELLIGIBLE MYSTERY OF BEING

THREE

Conquergood was born in the year — but he does not remember the year of his birth — but he does remember that twelve years ago in the year 2171, at the age of five or six or seven, he awoke to the City of Old York, of no family, good nor ill nor otherwise. Now on the second of October that brings with it a cold mist and low fog over Old York City, Jerome Conquergood kicks his raggedy boots at a nanotube poster lying on the cracked pavement where weeds have sprouted into miniature shrubs. The last of the pigeons have died and Conquergood can scarcely recall the cooing noises those beautiful birds once made. And if the Korporate Skript mentioned anything of the Anthropocene, it might have incorrectly concluded that this day was its end.

Alongside the curb filled with glass shards and rotting pigeons, Conquergood reads the nanotube poster he has kicked —

KORPORATE PROPERTY

The caption reads and speaks aloud of its own accord from the embedded speakers hidden inside the thin frame of the e-paper. The flimsy poster swirls and dances in the miniscule hurricanes forming in the dust on the vacant street and Conquergood recounts the times he and his brother Vincent — how long had it truly been? — would flee Manhattan in Vincent's Winnebago and head upstate where they would spend the night parked next to a lake with the Adirondacks at their back, and all Conquergood can do now is recite some ancient verse Vincent had read from one of his cracked-spined books:

"You were ground in the very mill of the conventional."

What had it meant? What had any of it meant?

Every footfall Conquergood takes now is methodically counted. He has to watch his steps from then on in. Another ten blocks or so he'll be arriving at Ward One, fenced off by the mighty Korporation. Within the Jerusalem-esque walls lie Korporate Headquarters, a monolithic structure comprised of twenty immane skyscrapers bound into one seamless square structure rising higher than Babel's Tower, impenetrable, preternatural and god-like.

As super-storm clouds swell the sky, Conquergood glares up at the insurmountable seventy-foot wall, like a granite laccolith, as the generations of blue-collar workers before him had also done — whether the walls were of brick or steel, of debt or loss, or of the quiet spiritual kind; the kinds of walls the rich and powerful — knowingly or unknowingly, it doesn't matter anymore anyway — built up over the years before the Great Fall against the hardworking meek. The wall, to him, is like a fabricated Mount Whitney, beckoning the elusive climber to claim her, and even then, there are only a few who are brave enough to answer the call, as if after centuries of expectation those before him sought a treasure ship lost beneath the ocean's rolling chastity. But Conquergood knows that those who seek treasures inside Korporate walls will most surely drown — and such are the hard truths of his life.

"We are not what the Korporation makes us do," Conquergood tells himself. "Never will be, never have been."

Conquergood continues on his lone walk from the lower east ward to the upper north ward of Old York City. Today most of the streets are free from *strayers*, the scattered few men, women and even fewer children taking shelter in the maze of squalor and abandoned skyscrapers now filled with shattered windows and rats the size of giant, deformed ferrets.

The once awe-inspiring buildings stand vacant and have been so for at least thirty years or more. Brown cornerstones remain empty shells of a time where literary giants roamed bricked streets. The armored Korporate Guard, however, continue their random searches of the forsaken residences, punctuated by the Korporate signatures of transparent wisps of a flag with imbedded speakers implanted onto optical carbon nanotubes. Conquergood shoves his hands in his pants pockets and there above him — yes, there above and forbidden to be below — one of the flag-speakers beholds a uniformed black sphere with the white, immortal emblem **K** in the center; the flag is chanting — always chanting — the Korporation's shibboleth:

FROM EACH *AKKORDING* TO EACH

THE KORPORATION'S ABILITY!

TO EACH *AKKORDING* TO REACH

THE KORPORATION'S NEEDS!

Walking toward a thing no one wants is interminable and Conquergood wants now so very much to turn back and head to ten years ago — or was it twenty? — when Vincent and he had been young at their mother's bare feet at the beach. But the hard years have been far too cruel to count and now Conquergood's ears and bones ache from the continual Korporate verbal onslaught from the obnoxious flag-speakers stationed every fifty yards or so. His feet ache from the hours of walking, none to mention the years of running from the very thing which possesses all else in the world;

How can one run from Korporate-ubiquitousness?

For some reason, Conquergood, scratching at the hint of an untamed beard, believes it is comparable to Jonah running from God, that old fool's legend. Irrespective, no one really wants to choose slavery, but the choice rests either in employment with the almighty Korporation, starvation or a fate far worse than machinations devised by Korporate *Komputers*, empty meta-frames without soul and compunction.

In the distance, Conquergood sees the entrance to the Korporate compound and he readies himself to enter. There is no turning back. He was sent and now he has arrived at the gates of the most powerful entity in the world.

The soured-rolling wind picks up outside and Conquergood hears it calling his name. In a windowless room on the hundredth and tenth floor Conquergood sits idle with hands in lap where he is waiting in front of a rectangular desk of seamless black meta-plasty, a large white K swimming across the surface.

Above the e-desk, Conquergood's gaze crosses one of many patriotic and jingoistic signs — The Korporation Wants You!

He cannot pull himself away from reading the sign, as if the sign holds a magnet force fastening his skull to the direction of the message, and he reads the short phrase several times before he gives up in frustration, pounding his fists on the holes in his jeans, exposing the folds of battered knees, but he cannot resist hearing the Korporate call thrive deep in his chest, far below the firm beat of his heart.

The Korporate Kall has somehow become a part of Conquergood, imbedded in his very composition of flesh and bones. By now he is used to the speaking signs without pictures, only the letters of the *Korporate Edukated*; signboards which separate the Korporate Edukated, the KE, from all else in the natural world.

Conquergood runs a finger through the torn places of his raggedy clothes, faded, torn blue jeans and a crumpled t-shirt. He feels much the same as he normally does, which is loneliness that betrays the mind into believing one is the last person remaining alive in a world of death, despair and desolation. But he knows this time someone is watching. From then on someone or *something* will always be watching. Everything must be performed to precision. Otherwise, who knows what they would do to him.

A few more denuded moments pass by until finally — finally after all these countless hours of dreaded waiting — the repetitious sign stops speaking. Dull silence propounds beneath a constant murmur of white noise, a consistent static driving its needle into the veins of thought, much the way it has done in dull office buildings since the turn of the twenty-first century. Keeps the workers focused, zombielike, brain-dead, the strayers had told Conquergood, and it had nothing to do with soothing and comfort.

A pallid *interlokutor* marches into the room carrying a digital notepad in his claw-like hand. He's wearing a slender black *synthetik* kimono robe with a white letter K stitched on the chest for the official Korporate Seal. Conquergood knows the kimono robe is the sign belonging to a higher form of evolved society — the mud-sucking Korporate Elite — who live in splendor while those in the Outlands suffer and beg for quick deaths.

Conquergood notices the severity of the *interlokutor*'s baldness is to the point when the scalp begins chaffing off in large flaky chips, the texture of fish scales. It's as if the man is falling to pieces — piece by fish-flaking piece — before Conquergood's very eyes.

The man sits down beneath the Korporate sign and message, across from Conquergood, and directs his right hand to nonchalantly wipe his bald head clean of the fish-white flakes, as though he is covered in a corporeal layer of dense chalk. Dusting his shoulders free now the *interlokutor* settles himself in the metallic chair behind the table. The man's cheeks are bony and drawn inward to leave two dark impressions on either side of the hairless face, and his skin wavers beneath the lamp light, emitting a malodorous scent not too dissimilar to rotting dog.

Systematically and without emotion the stoic *interlokutor* begins, "Today's interview is being *kommenced* on the first of K-month-ten in 2083," recording and transcribing the conversation onto his K-pad. "Now for your first test: *kan* you tell me who said: 'Are not the pleasures of *affektion* greater than the pleasures of the senses, and are not the pleasures of the *intellekt* greater than the pleasures of the *affektions*?'"

The malaise begins to intrude. Conquergood's legs tense, feeling the impression of urination bearing down on him but able to restrict the flow. He knows the answer but cannot say — mustn't say or they'll know. Wants to scream the damn riddle's end loud and clear inside the fish-head's deflated ear.

Conquergood can see the answer before him in his mind but refuses to speak. His uncut fingernails, packed with grime, dig deep through the worn jeans and into the fleshy parts of his knees. Only one answer fills his throat.

"Was it you, sir?"

Conquergood remains passive. He knows the Korporate *kameras* are watching, analyzing, digitalizing, confirming and reconfirming his every twitch in calculated efforts to deduce his invisible thoughts. But he knows they will fail this time.

A murmur breaks from the lips of the interlokutor and Conquergood gathers it as a sort of mirthful laugh in contempt.

"Do you know why you're here?" The interlokutor speaks without inflection and his right hand, with a miniature writing utensil, wavers above the digital notepad, ready to electronically scribble down any significant remarks.

"I want what the Korporation has," Conquergood says, "I want to know who I am."

"You are who you are supposed to be." The interlokutor brings his attention fully on to Conquergood. "No more, no less. Is that not enough?"

"Have we had this conversation before?" asks Conquergood, palms sweating and heart twitching in its socket. *Have they or haven't they?* The room feels as though it is shrinking — it must be an illusion; a gas leaking in to cause hallucination — and the air is thinning.

"Perhaps we have," the interlokutor says. He taps the table with his porcelain fingernails. "But we are here now. The real question you should be asking yourself is this: Now that you are here, what shall you do for the sake of the Korporation?"

"Anything you ask of me." The words come out as an electronic statement, memorized verbatim, rather than a mournful plea, certainly believable enough.

"Anything?" The interlokutor's e-pen frantically scribbles over the flat surface of the digital notepad. "You say, anything?" He repeats the words without rising or falling upon the normal speech patterns, but in the eyes, withdrawn from the already sunken facial structure, lurks the true possession of the invitation.

"Yes," answers Conquergood, "anything for the sake of my brother."

"For the sake of familial ties *kan* certainly be a noble *kause*," the interlokutor states in a flat unemotional speech, "and simply only one position a man may take in his short, rather dull lifetime, but for the sake of the Korporation is an entirely different matter to *konsider* all together." The interlokutor calmly places down the writing instrument and interconnects his tenuous fingers into one formless shape, un-praying. "Will you serve the Korporation faithfully above all others? Will you love us as you love yourself?" The interlokutor's dark-hollow pupils twist and dig into Conquergood's direction.

Conquergood can feel his body pressing against the iron frame of the chair — how long have I been in this room? Two hours? Three? — the period of time has been considerably longer than what he originally intended it to be. He can hear the acid rain pouring, beating to be let inside, and he deems himself fortunate, away from wind and rain and hunger.

Even before entering the facility, passing through countless safety and health examinations, Conquergood had been exhausted — so tired, so tired of running —

impoverished from all the days he has spent in trepidation, a cowardliness of sensing his brother Vincent will certainly die if courage cannot be wrangled forward out of the damp enclaves of the soul — or of what little soul was left.

Conquergood has to join the Korporation. He *must* join. He has been ordered to do so.

Sitting before the interlokutor, he no longer smells the stench seeping from his own ragged garments, browned by perpetual usage, and shredded by the un-washable toils of his life. Despair rises out of the vagabond's pores. Jerome Conquergood knows his place, better than most *outkasts*, strayers.

"I will serve the Korporation above all else." Conquergood's two parched lips twitter the statement with final, dire acceptance.

For the first time since entering the room, a show of emotion in the form of a thin smile breaks the interlokutor's face, revealing rows of dental veneers.

"Very well then," the interlokutor says. "We may proceed."

Sliding to the corner of the e-desk the digital notepad, a white K-pad label resembling a one-page book, bottomless and infinite, the interlokutor pushes a button and the e-skreen on the notepad infuses itself with the top of the electronic surface of the e-desk. The interlokutor pushes a few more applications on the e-desk's top and from out of the epicenter floats up a three-dimensional holo-map of the twenty-two wards on old Manhattan Island.

"I want you to point to the ward where you've been residing," the interlokutor orders in a firm but sincere voice. "You see, the Korporation desperately desires to renovate the wards for maximum benefit to our society. With your utmost *kooperation*, we, and by *we* it's meant *the Korporation*, may better serve the *kommunity*."

The virtual map, lifting itself out of the digital e-skreen, becomes a shimmering window between Conquergood and the interlokutor. On the holo-map of the old Manhattan, facts and despair stare back at Conquergood. A quivering finger and nail, unkempt and grimy, point over to Ward 21. A large red splotch remains on the hovering map where Conquergood has just lifted his finger from moments before.

"Old China-village," the interlokutor says in his monotone voice. He retrieves the digital notepad and the map folds back into the digital e-skreen on the e-desk's surface and the swimming white K reappears in a black sea.

"Very well then. We do have an opening in our Turnkey Department." The interlokutor presses a few more applications, simultaneously sending a message to his superiors. "You certainly look the part of a Turnkey Specialist. Have you offered your DNA and RNA samples yet? Taken your necessary *vakssins*?"

Conquergood nods, knowing that the interlokutor must already know the results of the tests before the interview when sixteen *doktors* took samples of blood, hair, piss, semen, fingernails, mouth and anal swabs, and even scrapings of a back tooth — a not to mention the eight vaccine shots. Conquergood shifts in his seat and places a palm on the left side of his jaw and attempts to rub out the soreness.

"All for health purposes," the interlokutor replies without faltering. "*We* at the Korporation take immense *kare* of our employees and *we* simply want to ensure your health is '*pro re nata*' or as *we* like to *kall* it '*quid pro quo*'."

"I see," is Conquergood's answer, avoiding the interlokutor's dry attempt at Korporate humor.

"Do you really?" The interlokutor's virulent tone fills itself with a stern knife-like substance slipping between the frail folds of the man's pale lips while his ears stretch backward on his scalp, redefining the face into an even greater taut form, as though some mythical ophidian stretches its serpentine jaws to devour its kill.

"No," Conquergood replies. He bows his head and digs a fingernail into the flesh between thumb and index finger. "I suppose I don't."

"Either way, *we* have decided to grant you the position of Turnkey Specialist, as mentioned. Have you the labor signature implant?"

Conquergood turns his right wrist over to reveal a *synthetik Quik-Response Kode* grafted onto skin, veins curtailing through the e-tattoo. He touches the e-kode on his wrist and knows he is now Korporate property.

"Very well done," the interlokutor says as he checks off an item on his K-pad. "*We* will track your expenses through this personal signature and *dedukt* the purchases from your remuneration. At the *klose* of each week your wages will be inserted into your Unitary Korporate *akkount*. It is all very well done."

"How much am I to be paid?"

"The Korporation does not like to *disklose* such *konformist* details. 'Our business here is not to know all things, but those which *koncern* our *kondukt*.' You will be paid handsomely, no doubt. We like to keep *kompetition* out of the workplace. *AMAE* is a much better p*raktice* we find. Strive to do your best for the Korporation and *we* shall inherently provide all which is necessary for your sustainable living. Now, simply *authentikate* with your handprint here and we *kan* begin the process of the accession."

The digital notepad slides across the slippery surface of the e-desk. Conquergood presses his right hand flat against the e-skreen, recording his fingerprints. The interlokutor receives the K-pad and saves the signature with a delicate press of a graphic.

"Very well done," says the interlokutor. "*We* may proceed."

Conquergood digs his fingernails into his knee — *I am not the Korporation*, he thinks.

Once upon a time after having his hair cut, nails trimmed and teeth cleaned and redone directly after the entrance interview, Conquergood is bathed by the Korporate washers — young women with olive skin, black hair, and thick blood-red lips wearing constant smiles, and oh! the repeated lathering — where his skin is lavished in sweet smelling Clementine and lime body oils. Thereafter his stomach is packed with superbly prepared pork tenderloins, sirloins, filet mignons and brisket, all genetically enhanced for the best quality. Conquergood considers whether or not the Korporation is fattening him up in order to sacrifice him for a main event.

One highlight above the rest of Conquergood's extended sojourn, however, is the indulgent hours of uninterrupted sleep in a bed with *organik kotton down* pillows, a Korporate blanket with Korporate Seal, and the softest mattress he has ever had the pleasure of sleeping upon — the kind where one melts into the feathery butter of sleep — he tells himself that blessings do belong to the Korporate Elite.

Conquergood has been given a bare but adequately filled apartment with all the Korporate-appropriate necessities: bed, dinner table, chairs, sofa, etc. There is no need for cooking since Korporate chefs prepare breakfast, brunch, lunch, dinner and any desired snacks upon the ring of a *K-skreen*, a voice activated video monitor hooked to the Korporate Kontrol system. K-skreens are located by the front door, on the dining-room wall, in the bathroom, and beside his lush bed.

Often, Conquergood finds himself staring out the bay window overlooking a small counterfeit park. When Conquergood walks to the window and leans forward onto the tinted flexiglass, he silently wishes the flexiglass would vanish — just disappear and drop him down, down, down.

Providing unlimited hours of Korporate-vision, better known by all as KV, in selectable two or three dimensions, a prominent electronic skreen fills up half the wall across from his bed — and then there is the K-net interfacing. From the time Conquergood was small he has dreamed of one day watching extremely old movies and doing research on a KV. The premium luxury, however, is reserved for the KE; the ones employed by the Korporation are the only ones allowed such privileges.

Conquergood's wardrobe consists of three bare, white kimono robes hanging in the collapsible *klozet*. In comparison to his previous clothes — rags and bags more like — Conquergood concludes that the simple robes are a very intelligent choice for daily attire. He shows to the Korporate *kameras* his satisfaction by quickly adopting to his new attire and to his new way of living.

The closing recurrence of Conquergood's scheduled routine consists of Korporate *kompanionship* promptly delivered — having been confined for much of his time to the K-net on the KV — at 10:01 every night when a chime sounds a smooth, intoxicating bell.

Upon opening the door, the first time, Conquergood stepped backwards, seeing two cute and innocent Asiatic females with curls of hair — one of purple, one of green — down to their waists, in short-skirt kimono robes the color of *krimson*. The robes, absent of any official seal, had long sleeves for the arms and a short tail extending down the back.

Without speaking, and still in the brightly lit hallway, the Korporate *Kompanions* dismantled their coverings like snakes slipping from old skins to reveal their small breasts and shaved bodies. Then both *kawaii* nubiles — as nude as nude — held hands and skipped into Conquergood's apartment where they then hopped onto his bed, settled onto their hands and knees and wagged their tight bottoms back and forth, back and forth, wanting and waiting like vipers in heat. The most the Kompanions ever muttered in their meta-sibilant response to Conquergood's sly inquiries was, "For the *sssake* of the Korporation, we *ssserve* the *kommand*."

The night after the kawaii girls, blonde triplets identical in nature — down to each freckle — arrived at his door. The night thereafter, four brunette nubiles came knocking. On the fourth night, five red heads. The following night, six more kawaii nubiles stripped themselves of their coverings at his door. On the sixth night, seven mulattoes arrived at his apartment. On the seventh night, eight black women as dark as the ocean depths sought admittance to Conquergood's chambers, and for a single moment he hesitated beneath the seduction and temptation of these eight extraordinarily beautiful and enchanting women.

On each night, the Korporate Kompanions had only this to say: "For the *sssake* of the Korporation, we *ssserve* the *kommand*." Every single time, Conquergood orders the Korporate Kompanions to leave.

The eighth and final night mystified Conquergood most of all. Three dozen seductive virgins of various ethnic races in kimono robes of pink silk — rather than the usual *krimson* ones — attempted to provide their Korporate services. Conquergood, in the end, refuses them all by slamming the door in their innocent and deceptive faces.

Conquergood, however, has now grown accustomed to his comfortable days, unable to distinguish his past in Ward 15 as ever having been as real as it was.

His memories of his brother Vincent roasting sausages, eating hot dogs, and drinking cold beers by the ocean are becoming faded dreams, and he secretly begins to desire his new life at the Korporate headquarters to continue. But he is tortured by knowing he does not belong as a peg in the Korporation's attempts to pound him down with each subtle stroke of the Korporate *amae*, such pleasurable dependence which is all too inviting and manipulative.

One morning on the third week, having finished his freshly ground-and-brewed Korporate *koffee*, Pseudo-eggs ham-Benedict and two strawberry muffins topped with the right amount of genetic butter, Conquergood finds a bland-faced attendant in a green kimono robe, sealed with a white K, at the entrance to his Korporate apartment — they always know exactly where he is.

"Good morning, sir *Konquergood*," the shaggy brown-haired attendant flatly states. "A pleasure, really."

Conquergood is beginning to grow accustomed to the constant rotation of Korporate staff and the emotionless and empty speech of the KE; he chalks it up to their jealousy and vacuous spirit, but void of emotions nonetheless.

With koffee mug in hand, Conquergood confidently and suspiciously eyes the attendant. Usually at ten in the morning Conquergood treats himself to a minor nap or relaxing an hour or two in front of the KV before a brief stint in the Korporate gymnasium, followed by a hearty lunch prepared by the Korporate chefs, delivered promptly to his private quarters.

"Doing better?" asks the attendant, moving uninvited into the apartment and closer to Conquergood.

"Yes much," Conquergood replies. As he sets his koffee mug down, it ungracefully hits the small metallic dining table and lets out a sharp ding. "May I help you?"

Placing a hand on one of the two extra chairs, the attendant answers, "*We* would like to invite you to *ahr*—" — and there for the first time Conquergood notices a falter in an attendant's voice, a stumbling over of thoughts before the spoken words — the man finishes hurriedly, "*We* would like to invite you to your *edukation*. It is time to prepare for your Turnkey position. You are, after all, the specialist, yes?"

"Must I right now?" Conquergood gathers a sip of koffee on his tongue, letting it roll around in the fleshy cheeks before swallowing. Smoothing out his white kimono robe, he enjoys the fabric upon his clean skin. He is one step closer to where he needs to be. The complacent attendant is watching.

"We must for the *sssake* of the Korporation." The attendant's eyes and lips are drawn but steady, twitching and fighting almost within themselves, as two opposite magnetic forces.

"Then I must." Conquergood's words have slipped from his lungs and mouth before he knows it has happened in his bilked mind — so he must.

"Right this way, sir," says the attendant. He presents a prolonged hand toward the hallway.

Conquergood follows the shaggy brown-haired attendant down cream-colored marble floors, gleaming in their cleanliness, marked by the occasionally large black, imprinted K. At this point, Conquergood recognizes the symbol and feels a little proud for being associated with the elevated Korporate status and the KE.

At the end of the long hall, the Korporate attendant holds out a hand in the direction of two sable hover-transport slides, or t-slides. The hover-transport slides, round and wide enough for one individual, can be driven by leaning one's force in the direction one wishes to take.

Vertical transport pads, only able to navigate upwards and downwards throughout the Korporate Kompound, are located at the end of each hallway.

On their t-slides, Conquergood follows the attendant onto the transport pad where they float down and through and around several transport tubes and labyrinthine *korridors* and along one of the many transport-wells, until finally, as the attendant erects himself from the forward position on his t-slide, he halts in front of a solid white metallic door marked with black lettering:

KORPORATE EDUKATION

Conquergood sees the words and remains ignorant, forcing himself into those depths of unknowing and safety, but accurately predicts that this door has to do with his Korporate integration — the time has indeed come for him and there is no turning back now.

Conquergood jumps from his t-slide and lands onto the firm floor. The door before him slips open, releasing a gush of intoxicatingly frigid air. He has been trained for this, what is to come, but he is still not certain if he is ready. Either way, he takes a step in. He is one step closer to his fate.

VI
Edukation Extrapolates

When the metallic door slides shut behind Jerome
Conquergood, he bites his lip and plunges two sweaty
palms beneath his armpits. The temperature in the room
clings to his skin, immediately chilled, beneath the white
kimono robe. An orange fluorescent orb glows high
above creating an acute disillusionment surrounding his
senses inside the room. His once white robe vibrates a dull
orange. His skin appears as though a sickly tangerine has
enveloped his flesh. Conquergood can even taste the
orange light upon his tongue, growing icy with each
breath he takes.

A few meters away, at the foot of the back wall, an
elegantly tall woman bathes in her own orange shade,
standing beside two armchairs. She wears an orange
kimono robe — or if it is not orange, it certainly appears
that way — which ends in a short skirt on her thighs but
without the trailing cape of the Korporate Kompanions.
Her robe, however, does have the Korporate Seal.

A tele-k-skreen about the size of *The Korporate
Handbook* is fixed to the back wall. For all else, the room
remains empty. Conquergood looks back at the exit he has

just entered and says nothing. The sense of being trapped inside a freezing room with an attractive woman has Conquergood confused. His blood desires to boil but it does not. He can only hold himself as if he were a child once again squatting at his brother Vincent's feet as the two wait in line at one of the carnival rides called the Boom-Boom E-rang.

"Please take a seat," the woman says inside her orange glow with a potently delicate voice. Her hand places a citrus-colored curl behind her ear as she glides over to take her place in one of the armchairs. She moves without hesitation and without notice to the arctic surroundings — it's as if she does not feel…

Conquergood waits by the door, not having taken a step, and can make out in this unassailable orange glow the woman's lean legs crossing themselves. Her legs make impressions on both sides of her thighs and deeply onto Conquergood's imagination. He moves, as if summoned by some strange magnetic force from the woman, obediently and happily forward to his place in the armchair opposite her.

"Have you enjoyed your stay?" She says to him. "How has your *brahmacharya* been going?"

She speaks as one truly interested, and it pleases Conquergood to have some sort of conversation after a fortnight of solitude, a half month of lonely days and nights with only the K-net and KV to keep him company.

He sinks to the bottom of the suede armchair and relaxes his shoulders. Conquergood feels some warmth from the armchair as the two face each other, waiting to begin the lesson. "My what?" he replies.

"Your self-righteous *akts* of *selibasy*," she says, unenthused and direct to the point. "You haven't enjoyed the fruits of your labor, now have you, young man? This goes against our Korporate *amae*. We've been watching you and you should want to know we are not at all pleased with your behavior. Sex is a Korporate benefit, nothing to be ashamed of by that, and it is shared by all in the system. You should be grateful for what the Korporation does for you, should you not?"

"Aren't you going to tell me your name?" Conquergood asks, shying away from the subject of his personal activities. He knows *they* are watching, observing, peeping into his apartment at all hours and how he has no privacy at any time. The lecture room's orange light begins hurting his eyes and small tears form at the crevices of his eye sockets.

Conquergood, somewhat helpless, senses the woman's curving neckline, precisely slender and formulaic, and he's as a blind man who studies a lost cathedral from history upon an old non-Korporate television which speaks in descriptive nuances. But her body, slightly hidden beneath her kimono, is far more alluring than what Conquergood has seen from the Korporate Kompanions. Her perfectly shaped breasts form her partially visible cleavage at the v-line and Conquergood senses the pulsing of his growing member becoming aroused beneath the spaces of his robe. He fights the impulse — *fight, damn you*!

"Names aren't as important as you think they are," she replies, opening the robe a bit more to reveal more of her braless chest. A finger runs down the center and her unwavering gaze meets Conquergood's. She uncrosses her shapely legs, sharp as razors, and crosses them in the opposite direction. "However, if you are attached to labels, then you may *kall* me K-NE1."

"Righty-ho, then," Conquergood replies. He turns over his shoulder expecting to see someone approaching from the entrance but there is no one in the room but the *lekturer*. "So, K-NE1, why am I here? I was told by the straggly fellow outside it's time for my education?"

"You are *korrect*," she answers.

"Are you going to teach me to read?" He is testing her and the test comes out more like a tease.

A flat, sordid laugh breaks fundamentally free from the *lekturer*. Conquergood clinches a fist against his hip and that is when a faint echo, like a lost laugh from childhood, is heard from the shadows in one of the back corners of the classroom. From several vents placed all around the ceiling, more constant streams of the nauseatingly cold air rushes in, unrelenting against Conquergood's exposed skin.

"Why would *we* do that?" K-NE1 now speaks with the same flatness as the interlokutor. No rising or falling of the language can be heard, only a direct and changeless line of communication. "The Korporation's *edukation* is a different sort of *edukation* entirely. *We* mean for you to last, to grow and prosper, not destroy yourself. For you see, you are a very special individual and we're highly interested in using you to the best of *our* abilities. A Turnkey Specialist is one of uttermost necessity to the Korporation. Without you, we *kould* not exist. Shall *we* begin?"

The *lekturer*'s words fall seductively on Conquergood's ears like hot air from a hidden vent inside the armchair.

"Of course," he says. No one has ever told him of his importance in the world. He has always been an outkast, a social leper, a machine without a soul, the self without the self. But he notices that his hands dig deeper into his knees, all hidden by the excess layers of the white kimono robe — the Korporate kimono. Any sexual tension he had earlier contained within has now retreated back into its dynamic cap, an extinct tortoise withdrawing momentarily into its protective shell.

"When our Korporate database had been fully *kompleted*," K-NE1 says to Conquergood in a monotonous voice, "the database had been *kompleted* with all the *historikal* and literary data digitized, and only then did our researchers *kom akross* two *insignifikant artikles*. Do you know what these useless pieces of writing are?"

"I do not." The cold air has a metallic taste that gathers at the base of his tongue. "How could I?"

"Many, many *dekades* ago," the seductive *lekturer* says in her usual systematic pitch, "the Union of *Koncerned* Scientists *kollaborated* and wrote, almost two centuries ago in 1992, the mandate titled as 'The World Scientists Warning to Humanity' and it was some warning — so much so no one dared listen. In this mandate, however, these silly scientists of the human species, which *we* remind you that no one *kared* to *konsider* at the time, stated five *kritikal* elements to saving humankind and, likewise, the world. Let *us* edify you, young man." She pauses to open up her kimono a little more as though the room's a bit too hot for her personal comfort. "One," she begins again, "*we* must bring environmentally damaging *aktivities* under *kontrol* to restore and *protekt* the integrity of the earth's systems *we* depend on; two, *we* must manage resources *krucial* to human welfare more *effektively*; three, *we* must stabilize the population; four, *we* must reduce and eventually eliminate poverty; five, *we* must ensure sexual *ekwuality*. As you may know already, *we*, the brilliant, the wonderful, the *only* Korporation, have in *fakt* and deed *akkomplished* all of these key *kriteria*. *We* did what no one else *kould*: *we* saved humankind and the world from absolute and undeniable *destruktion*."

"You said there were two articles."

Without hesitation and ignoring Conquergood's remark, K-NE1 continues her lecture,

"And then there was the *sekond artikle* which furthered *our* global ambitions and justified *our* aspirational methods. Alan Thein Durning, the man to have granted *us* our final *direktion*, wrote in 'The *Konundrum* of *Konsumption*' that '*scientifik* advances, better laws, *restruktured* industries, new treaties, environmental taxes, grassroots *kampaigns* — all *kan* help *us* get there.' *We*, as you may already know, young man, are finally there."

"Brava." Conquergood smirks. He has heard all this Korporate garbage before, but he is surprised by how much the woman actually believes this fabricated nonsense. Even if Conquergood could prove her wrong, which he cannot, he knows his trying would be of no use — the Korporation has brainwashed all these people, and he's next.

"You do not take our *suksesses* seriously," says the lekturer. Her tone is direct and the voice neither rises nor falls a decibel. "What is today?" She asks, attempting an alternative subject from her senseless spitting out of data and information that, she must know, has been unable to persuade and convince Conquergood.

"Tuesday, I think." Conquergood is usually able to remember the days of the week, but after the long sleepless nights where quick spurts of shattered visions in brief dreams of a woman, a night, a beach and the long days he has been having he no longer is confident of anything — it is far better that way.

"Wrong." K-NE1's voice folds out between her lips unbroken, like a slap of a ruler on a desk — or on the hand. Her face penetrates through the orange light and into Conquergood's insecurities — what's she getting at?

"Wednesday?" He asks, remaining uncertain on purpose — don't let her even guess what he's doing.

"Wrong again."

The laughter Conquergood expects from the lekturer is instead replaced by a depreciative sternness. K-NE1's rather attractive facial features morph into what appears to be a more narrowed jaw and hooked nose. The figure now before Conquergood reminds him more of the interlokutor in the initial interview weeks ago than to the woman he saw a few minutes prior.

"The identifiers you use for days have long been replaced by…" — again the stumble and pause — "…replaced by far better ones."

"Have they?" Conquergood is beginning to see what she means by an education, and he believes he'll be learning a great deal before lunch — if only they would stop with that horrible orange light!

"Those *arkaic* forms used for days of the week have been replaced by a series of simpler, far easier ones," she instructs him. "For instance, Sun-day, as your ancestors and the less *edukated* phrased the day in worship of the sun, is now simply *kalled*, as you may know already, young man, as *Kdaya*. Mon-day, or that awful Moon-day, is now *Kdayb*. These Korporate identifiers abound in all places, as you must be fully aware by now. Anything to add, young man?"

"I get the point," inserts Conquergood. "And Tuesday must be *Kdayc*."

"You *are* a fast learner, aren't you?" She withdraws a miniature K-pad from a side pocket located on her armchair and taps a few icons. The ceiling vents slow the monstrous, rapid pouring of cold air by several degrees. "Let's move on to lesson two then, shall *we*?"

"Now we're talking." Conquergood estimates he's getting the hang of the education business. He, like the other outkasts and degenerates, had feared the word "edukation" but the Korporation is making it so very simple and practical — quite very natural and easy this whole business really is.

K-NE1's hands clutch themselves on her extended knee, leg flawless and motionless, while remaining in her lap the K-pad waits to ease Conquergood of his pain.

"How many days are there in one week?" she asks.

"That's easy," Conquergood says. He gives her a wry smile filled by a clever expression. "There're seven days in a single week."

"Wrong."

Once more an unbroken sound of certainty and knowledge against credulity fills the orange atmosphere around the lekturer and student.

"Wrong?"

"Yes. Wrong, young man."

"Are you sure about that?"

"*We* are," replies K-NE1. "The reality of the situation you are in is to determine whether or not you are sure."

Her shoulders are square, her back straight, her expression undivided, solid. "Are *you* absolutely, one thousand percent sure?" Her bird-like nose, neck tilting back, she breathes in deeply, as if to lace her veins with the frost lingering in the air.

"I don't really know." Conquergood's grip digs deeper into his knees — he cannot let them know, do not let them know anything about what he must know, what he already does know, in fact and shape and sound, in all that is holy, that he should know everything, and does know.

"Good, you're moving rapidly through the lessons," K-NE1 says. She taps an icon on her K-pad and the cold air slows and the room grows a bit warmer for Conquergood. "It's far better to not know than to believe you know something which is false," she instructs him. "There are, since the *Twenty-first Dekree* was established by the Korporation many many years ago, now only six days in one week, young man."

"Six! What happened to seven?"

"The Korporation, also as you must *klearly* know by now — or are you wasting *our* time," she lifts an eyebrow before continuing, "has been our *akting* president since the *elektion* of forty-eight."

"I know."

"Then you should also be kindly informed that the Free People's *Republik* of the Ameliorated States, better known worldwide as the United Subsidiaries of the Ameliorated, U.S.A. for short, the subsidiaries unanimously voted as of the year twenty seventy-five, over one hundred years ago, in a *historikal* outpouring of support in New Philadelphia, and *deklared* that the last day, *your* Saturn's day, in false worship of the silly god Saturn, was entirely useless for any business purposes. *Kurrently* the modified *Gaelik kalendar kontains exaktly* three hundred and thirteen days, minus the fifty-two worthless days and minus the *subtraktion* of a day in a leap year, absolutely worthless. The *dekree* proudly established a refurbished, and friendlier Korporate *Kalendar* at a polished eleven months instead of an awkward and obtrusive twelve."

Conquergood sits baffled, shaking his head in perplexity. He knows the Korporation has been making new laws, some of which no outkast could ever follow or understand at the exponential extent by which the laws are created, disseminated and then instituted swiftly upon society. "I've heard of people losing time, but this is absolutely insane. Imagine, all in one morning I've lost an entire month for each year of my life. How many years is that?"

"*We*, at the Korporation, *kan* assure you, young man, it is not *krazy*, as you have honestly phrased it, but absolutely *sertain*." K-NE1 uncrosses her legs and sits to one side of her armchair, leaning forward. "As you might have guessed, all the days of K-month-twelve have been abandoned, tossed, as well as all those frivolous silly little days your kind liked to *kall* holidays. There's work to be done, young man, and *we* are the ones doing it."

"What?" Conquergood matches K-NE1's posture while he slides himself forward in his armchair, his hands on his knees. "Are you trying to tell me there's no longer Christmas?"

Granted, Conquergood has been too poverty stricken to enjoy and celebrate this sacred holiday, but he has heard stories of the olden times, passed down from strayer to strayer beside trash fires in the non-Korporate wards, strayers with wild, imagining eyes as each spoke of times out of time when children awoke to a countless number of gifts beneath decorated trees, baubles twinkling against white lights. Conquergood had had dreams of himself and his twin brother Vincent opening gifts beneath a bright Christmas tree, but these had only been dreams; and even then after hearing these fantastical stories on a freezing night, he dreamed many times of waking to a cheerful house filled with the calm clamor of family, toy trains and cars being rushed about on the wooden floor, stockings hanging over a fireplace filled with happy fire playfully slapping at itself and the logs, and his mother's laughter somewhere in the background, just out of the struggling reach of his dreams and memories. But all of that had died, he knew full well, with the disappearance of the recreational trees and before the Korporation placed a tax on oxygen and secured the rights of all trees as an endangered species while forcing the middleclass in every country either into work for the Korporation or out onto the streets as the much-loathed strayers.

"You are *exaktly* right to be *shawked*," KNE1 says in her dull voice. "*We*, here at the Korporation, understand the *perfektly* natural feelings one has with a holiday like *Krissmas* and *we* do share in your sympathy for such a loss of a treasured *okkasion*; however, times do indeed change, young man, and those who *kan't* keep up will be left out, as they once said, in the *kold*. It is *striktly* business — you do understand, don't you?"

Conquergood listens to the lekturer but her speech begins to drone on like a finely equipped electrical fan from the previous century. He manages a nod of acceptance — *defeat absolute*.

A chime sounds and rings loud in the room. The melodic vibrations begin to dissipate. Conquergood and K-NE1 wait as the room settles back into silence and stillness.

"In addition," K-NE1 continues with full steam and fervor, "the Korporation, in *direkt* response to the *publik*'s loss of an overly-*kommercialized* holiday, has introduced a far superior holiday and festivity which *we* are sure you will enjoy."

"Really?"

"Oh, yes. Every K-month-eleven on K-day-eleven *we*, that is all the employees worldwide at the Korporation, celebrate *our* most famous and be-loved holiday: Korporate Revival."

"I see." Conquergood's mind begins to numb. He commences to see how hard it is to learn.

His vision, inundated by the orange piercing light, swirls alongside the lekturer's head and voice. To be frank, Conquergood doesn't even know his own birth year. Hiding in vacated apartment buildings in Ward 15, what had long been forgotten as Greenwich Village, fleeing from the Korporate Guard, scrounging for meals out of Korporate dumps in Ward 22, once called Lower Manhattan over a century ago, and all of this *"edukation* and learning" has taken a toll on him.

Conquergood has even been mindless to the fact that the world left him behind decades ago — *when exactly?* — when exactly he can't be sure.

Society had passed him by without waving, never failing to stop to consider the welfare of him or his twin brother, Vincent, orphaned and destitute. The world consumed itself with business and he knows nothing about the grand successes of the Korporation. Conquergood is even mindful to the fact that the rest of the world he believed to have known existed is changing daily — by the minute, by the second, by the millisecond — and the faith in the world he once knew, he is certain, is becoming muddled and shredded into solid, irreversible doubt — where has the world gone? — he does not know.

"Today is your birthday," the lekturer continues with a few soft celebratory claps. "Born again today in K-month-ten, in the year of our Korporation, twenty-one eighty-three."

"My birthday, huh?" Conquergood's mind purposefully empties itself of any more knowledge. The mind he has blatantly ignored over the past twenty plus years has doubled back and retreated and failed. Memories blur and fight against one another, and the mind drapes itself blank, veiled by too much knowledge, too much learning and edification. His eyelids are collapsing. His fingers starting to lose their grip on his knees and contort themselves into devilish talons. A feverish weakness in his chest shivers and pulses down his arms and down further into his aching wrists — *breathe, just breathe* — but he can't.

"If you like, it is yours," K-NE1 says, "and remember everything *we* have *diskussed* here today. Your soul depends on it."

Conquergood can no longer see; all sight for him has become a bright orange blinding wall.

"*Kom.*" K-NE1 stands to a towering position over the young man, misshapen and unmade, who is slumped back in his armchair. "For now, your *edukation* must rest." She extends a perfectly manicured hand out to him. "After lunch, *we* will begin lesson five."

"What happened to lessons three and four?" Conquergood can feel life and energy gently pouring back into his body, a slow release of lava upon ice, knowing that the lessons have halted, ceased, even though it is only for the moment.

His vision returns and he accepts her hand, himself revived, softly, and he's led away from the shrill orange of everything in the room — how long has he been learning? — and he cannot say for how long — three hours? two? one? — but he understands now that he has been *edukated*.

"As *we* have mentioned before," K-NE1 says, speaking as she leads Conquergood to the door by the hand. "You are, in truth, a fast learner. A prodigy, if *we* may say so."

The metallic door slips open to an intense light, a bright white pouring out of the hallway. Conquergood, for a moment, doesn't know whether to retreat back into the dizzying orange radiance of the classroom or to proceed forward into a new white blindness.

Suddenly K-NE1 gives him a firm shove in the back. His strained eyes fill with refreshing-cleansing tears, and he sees a green blur shimmering beside him. The next thing he knows he's in the hallway and his orange robe has miraculously turned back into white.

"We too *kried* after our first morning of Korporate *edukation*," says the green blur, the exact same green-clad attendant from before the lesson, or so Conquergood thinks. "Was it not liberating?"

Conquergood stumbles a bit, but manages a slight nod. The brown-haired servant grabs Conquergood's arm.

"I've learned so much," Conquergood mutters. He continues to wipe his cheeks and eyes dry, dark spots filling blank vision, as if he were witnessing the depths of eternity coming to a concrete end.

Back through the multitude of transport tubes and *korridors*, the attendant leads Conquergood back to the living quarters. At the entrance of Conquergood's apartment, the attendant stops and places a hand on Conquergood's shoulder, "Just wait until *Lesson Ten*," and with that he leaves Conquergood to a prepared lunch waiting on the dining room table — alone at last.

V
Lesson X

Conquergood pushes the lunch plate away. Nothing has been wrong with the filet mignon and sautéed green beans, sided by freshly mashed potatoes — those Korporate *bangers* of sorts — smothered in warm brown gravy and sided against three hot rolls mounted with creamy Korporate butter. The meal was quite palatable, but after eating three plus square meals — plus snacks — a day for over two weeks, Conquergood starts to feel his stomach seams stretch and absorb the additional food into fat, while the expansion of his inner-flesh creates an intense aversion to all things bodily. He had barely even eaten his lunch when it made him sick to his stomach and the nauseating effect sent him dry-heaving to the bathroom sink to wash his face and the back of his neck. And the relief is short lived because Conquergood's body quivers with excess and he palpates his soul and flesh and knows he is empty — ever so tired of the bounty of far too much — becoming devoid of true substance. He wonders if this is what the Korporation really is: bloated pangs of luxury.

Conquergood believes himself denigrating the bounty before him with such lack of enthusiasm, sighing as his fingers twirl the silver fork against the plate causing shrieks of friction to consume the silence in the lonesome room. Even side-tracking thoughts of the nightly female entertainers, huge piles of hot melting flesh he consistently refused but second guesses, prove futile. Within him a hole grows more abundant, yet Conquergood's flesh edges outward, flexing forward and ever beyond where before only space and time had been. He sits at the table staring into the *krimson* wine and believes himself to be a young lover who has lost all passion for his mate, disparaging her for her small breasts that he once relished with such fiery power as fresh lovers often hold in their cherished youthful vigor.

Life's sweetness drips its last few drops from Conquergood and he begins hating himself for wanting more but not having the energy or motivation to seek it out; as if he is a warrior-king who at last, after long years, conquers the entire world, climbs and builds upon the peaks of Chomolungma his blazing throne of eternal power — glory everlasting — and on that golden throne of immortality this warrior-king has nothing more to do, nothing more to live for; nothing more even despite two-hundred and twenty-two virgins exhausted each week until there can never be another memory isolated from all the rest of the warrior-king's concubines; the final page of the final book written is read and there're no more books to follow, finished, and the end does become the end. Conquergood, not too long ago, once had only himself and his free, ungoverned spirits — unbridled and untamed — and nothing remained for him to worry — but now. Now he remains unmoving in reflective isolation, as if he is chained to the chair at the table. Foremost, his brain writhes in anguish from having been *edukated* that very morning by the KE.

Three wine bottles of a hundred and seventy-six-year-old Italian Chianti stare back at the young man with the bulging waistline beneath the white kimono robe. Conquergood continues to think for half an hour — sitting and staring into space, more like — as delightful thoughts of his twin brother well up and consume Conquergood, but he catches himself in the memory when his pseudo-self wants to reach out to touch his twin brother fishing for Chinook salmon and rainbow trout there beside the lake in an early morning fog, and Conquergood stops the memory, freezes in frame because he can no longer recall his brother's name — *what was it?* — and he considers questioning the congealed gravy on his plate on the table but that proves just as useless as his own mind — *what was his name?* — *had he forgotten so soon?* Just a few days ago he had known his brother's name and now he is too weak, feels too fat despite the sessions at the Korporate gym, too tired to find the answer, to find the name above all other names — *is there even an answer?* — and that is where Conquergood finds himself, questioning and hoping that if only he could turn back the pages as if in a book within his mind and find the answer — *what is his name?* — but there is no name; for the moment the name of Conquergood's twin brother has been erased, systematically wiped clean by the overwhelming power of the Korporation — *all cannot be lost, or can it?*

The question is answered with a firm rap at the door. From the sounding of the metallic frame comes the call for the afternoon's lecture. If at all possible, Conquergood wants to stay in his quiet apartment and sleep the day away and not venture another minute into the grim orange glow of that drab classroom. A final strike sounds before the door slides open. Conquergood does not stir from his place at the table.

As the door slides away and vanishes into the wall, Conquergood sees another green-robed attendant — this one's different, with black hair cropped short — standing in the bright white of the hallway.

The fish-eyed attendant says in a bland voice, "It is time, sir, for your *edukation* to *kontinue*."

Conquergood has grown comfortable with the fact that each attendant-*eskort* is different, and yet each one still holds the distinct nature of speaking without emotion or inflection. They are all alike and never the same, an inexact copy of a broken copy that can never be duplicated just right — or so it seems — and the one thing he does not admire is that most of these green-clad attendants are honored with the official Korporate Seal, a bold black **K**, on their robes while — not that it matters anyway — his robe remains blank, colorless and without insignia, disconnected and isolated from within and from without — un-one with the Korporation and the KE. Conquergood gives out another sigh and then gathers his senses to join the attendant out in the hallway.

The attendant, in the same direction as before, leads Conquergood and they turn, after mounting a vertical transport pad, to ascend toward a few korridors higher up; the two men reach a white door and in its center are once again those dark words:

KORPORATE EDUKATION

For Conquergood, even though he doesn't need to read the words, the door appears to be the same as the earlier one. When the attendant orders the door to open, however, Conquergood can easily distinguish the difference because this new classroom holds a delicate brown lambency rather than the preceding orange glow from the morning lesson.

Other differences: two mahogany chairs and a matching desk wait at the back of the room that has a floor of smooth oak. A tele-k-skreen — one of so many throughout the Korporate Kompound — can be located on the back wall. Squatting on one of the squared-corners of a wooden desk, a balding man in a brown kimono robe, also with the official Korporate emblem, picks at his nose. If there were still monks in the world — the monks, however, have vanished, dispelled some fifteen years ago because their religious practices contrasted and challenged the Korporate belief system, and these monks were censored, banned, outlawed, made obsolete — the lekturer, however, could have easily passed for one of these forbidden monks — or even an obese Thelonious Sphere Monk, the jazz giant from the land of the forefathers. The lekturer adjusts his squared eye-glasses, as square as a dated Korporate ten-dollar *koin*, upon a smug nose of coarse red blubber.

Conquergood enters and notices the temperature contains a more moderate climate than the previous orange-lecture room, which had been arctic in nature.

"Good afternoon," calls the balding lekturer-monk in brown as Conquergood approaches. "Are you ready to begin your lesson this afternoon?"

"Sure." Conquergood eases himself in one of the wooden chairs, grating the floor as the hard legs slide back. "What's your name?"

"My name…" — again the stumble and pause — "You may *label* me as K-NE1-2. But you must *kom* to understand, appreciate and further realize that names, or rather labels, are not all that *signifikant* here at the Korporation. After all, what's in a label?"

"I'm not sure," Conquergood answers. His voice wavers then falls flat before the hefty lekturer.

Conquergood's fingers search once again for his knees, security and seclusion, beneath his Korporate kimono. When the clutch falls firm enough, Conquergood eases a little. The heart, regardless, races inward beneath the thoughts of being so very different from all the others at the Korporation. Conquergood, like all the other strayers in the deserted streets, had known very little of Korporate life when he had first entered the Korporation many weeks — how long? — ago. Knowing a trivial amount of information possesses a sense of calm and freedom, the space for creativity to ignite itself; a person cannot be blamed if he doesn't know any better.

"A name is what we call people," Conquergood mumbles, reluctant of his answer.

K-NE1-2 huffs and coughs into his fist then sluggishly moves his avoirdupois behind the desk and into his lekturer's chair.

"A label, or name as you have put it, *koms* from a higher authority," K-NE1-2 says, rolling his buttocks into place in his lekturer's seat. "*Historikally*, at the time of a person's birth the parents held the power and so the parents labeled the infant with an *insignifikant* word, which you *kalled* a name. *We* shall now extrapolate. Do you know who once *deklared*, 'Overt and apparent virtues bring forth praise; but there be *sekret* and hidden virtues that bring forth fortune; certain deliveries of a man's self, which have no name'?"

The lekturer's voice sings, unlike the interlokutor during the interview session when Conquergood first arrived at the Korporation. This lekturer's voice even dances, unlike the first lekturer K-NE1 and all the other green-clad attendants. The chubby lekturer-monk K-NE1-2 speaks with inflections and pitches in his speech — ah! an alternative to the mold can exist.

"I don't know, sir," Conquergood says as he tires of the questions he knows and the ones he doesn't care to answer. The Korporate Elite are hung up on quoting the very smart but very dead — why is that? Even the questions that Conquergood believes to know, he really doesn't know. What can he know that the Korporation does not? Or even greater: what does he know that the Korporation does not?

"I have no parents," Conquergood inserts. "A dusty old social worker named me when I was about five or six or seven years old. I believe I was born on the fourth of July in a place once called South Dakota. But I hear that place doesn't exist anymore, does it?"

"*Kwite* right, my dear boy," K-NE1-2 says merrily, "but that was before states of the *old* union were abolished sometime *bak*; the Korporation is now with you in your longing for a family. *We* are the ones here to help you. Always to aid you in your greatest hours of need. In your *kase*, the wretched social worker was your labeler. It's certainly a grand deed the Korporation has done for you by dismantling the old form of the *demokracy* and all its *ineffektive* labels and names and the such, and all by a majority vote from the new U.S.A., *we* remind you. Even the Korporation bears no such labels. It is as it will be, no more and no less; and in that state of *konstancy* and *plutokracy* success is and forever will be."

"I see," Conquergood replies. The flesh on his knees rips and tears and breaks beneath the white robe, momentarily altered brown by the false light.

"*We*, however, must digress just a bit." The lekturer pulls open a drawer and removes a silver flask. Once a few quick sips of the fetid liquor are taken the lekturer-monk returns the flask into the drawer, closing it with a thud. "A name is a word and a word is a label," he continues blithely. "If a high power *kan* grant a name, an even higher power may de-name, as it were. The same must be said for a label. Don't you agree?"

"I do." Conquergood shuffles his feet from out of the leather slippers. His bare toes, now free, explore the floor.

"*We* are becoming thoroughly impressed," K-NE1-2 remarks. When he grins, Conquergood sees the same immaculate set of porcelain veneers the interlokutor had.

Then one of the lekturer's fingers shoots into the air and digs into his left nostril, bulging round and round in anticipated discovery for a dormant ball which should be left to its cave. He wheezes a few times and coughs in a matching series. Finally, the portly instructor continues,

"*We* have been told how fast you are able to learn. *We* have never believed *we kould* find such an astute student this late in the marketing season. And for you to turn up on our doorstep and fit the *rekwuirements* for Turnkey Specialist is absolutely superb!"

The flask makes another appearance and quickly vanishes behind another thud.

"Since you are a very smart young man, let *us* move on to lesson seven."

Conquergood is beginning to like his edukation, for it appears the lekturers are skipping lessons and perhaps, after all, he is not as *unedukated* as the mocking flag-speakers in the wards used to make him out to be. Even some of the ragged strayers would claim their superiority over his intelligence and for several years in Conquergood's adolescence and on into young adulthood through his prior edukation and training on the streets, he believed he was and would remain ignorant.

One day a few months previous to joining the Korporation, Conquergood concluded that edukation would be meant for better men, more poignant men worthy of the credit.

Sitting now before K-NE1-2, Conquergood's charade allows the pride, not quite hubris but almost, to burn deep in his aching chest, frantic with constant racing of itself against the invisible power in his Korporate surroundings. He begins to consider himself a better, smarter man — yes, a *total* man.

"Now for the Five Korporate Laws," K-NE1-2 begins adamantly, foregoing Conquergood's adulation as he lifts five stubs for fingers high above his head before slamming his hand down to the desk — *Thwack!*

Conquergood jumps and repositions himself in his chair.

"I believe I know the first law," Conquergood says in a quivering voice. He wants to impress his new lekturer and to be the greatest student K-NE1-2 has ever known. "The first law is to serve the Korporation above all others."

"*By Korp!*" A wide-eyed K-NE1-2 rocks violently in his chair, banging the front legs firmly back to the floor. "*We* do believe you are a genius and not a *dunkish* pupil after all. Right before *our* very eyes, *we*'re astonished. Usually, the students *kom* in and simply take e-notes. But here, on this grandiose day, *we* have a student that refuses, refuses *we* say, to take e-notes, saving the Korporation *kountless kosts*, and instead *interakts* with the *lekturer* while doing a little research on top of all that!"

The flask reenters the space between the lekturer's thickset lips before returning to its private drawer. The lekturer-monk's three chins waddle from the tiny gulps.

"Thank you, sir," Conquergood manages to say. At first, he is unsure if the lekturer is being sarcastic or simply stupefied. He sits straighter in his chair and his hands, for the first time, relax themselves on his knees.

"The *sekond* law," K-NE1-2 reignites again, reciting an invisible script from memory, "is that no one must steal from the Korporation. For this penalty is severe."

"I see." Actually, Conquergood doesn't see, but his secret fear of being held as an ignorant sloth refuses any other answer than an affirmative one.

"The third law is to always speak well of the Korporation. Keep up a positive attitude, never slander, but rather remain silent. All for the sake of the Korporation, you know?"

"I do," Conquergood affirms. "Remain silent."

"*Kwickly* now." K-NE1-2 hurries his speech into one formless sound, helped by occasional, but momentary, visits from the flask. "The fourth and fifth laws are as follows: one must love the Korporation above all others; and the Korporation is and will always be the final judge regarding *politikal* or *apolitikal* matters."

"The final judge." Conquergood's words come out automatically and sound more like a flat-mindless repetition rather than a repeated phrase with the necessary accentual tones.

"Very good," K-NE1-2 says habitually. "Moving on, since there's an appointment which needs meeting at the spas with K-NE1 in less than half an hour; now, where were *we*?"

"The final judge," Conquergood boldly answers.

"*Kwite* true," replies the lekturer. "You *are* a smart one; one who has learned all this without any waste of e-notes or resources. Well done, well done, *we* add."

"Yes."

"*We kan* now move to *our* final lesson of the day." The flask, dulled by the mud-colored light, once more appears for an extended overture and retreats back into the desk drawer.

"Lesson Ten?"

"*We* do believe, young man," K-NE1-2 says with a full, boisterous voice, "you'll go far in this business; a *suksess* you are! You are, in *fakt*, without *kwestion*, our prized pupil. If you ever need a single thing, just let *us* know. Never had *we* such an *enthusiastik* and exceptional mind as yours. But enough of the flattery — on to Lesson Ten!"

The lekturer-monk wobbles for a moment, nearly making a dramatic dive to the floor, but is saved by a quick hand on the edge of the desk. He repositions and steadies himself while checking the seams in his robe. His hands try to smooth out a wrinkle which isn't even there. After several drunken attempts, K-NE1-2 abandons his task and draws his attention back to his prized pupil.

Conquergood observes the lekturer closely, desiring to know the truths to success as the Korporation has instilled into all peoples, into all cultures, into all nations, into the entire world, unifying the lands and races to accomplish what had only been a vague dream and that dream was called world peace.

"Do you have any siblings?" K-NE1-2 asks, avoiding eye contact, searching the floor for some invisible roving object. His head sways a few loose strands of brown strings that must have been hair on the shiny scalp. Conquergood imagines the lekturer is searching for his flask.

"Yes," Conquergood says. "I have one brother."

"What is his name?"

Conquergood has forgotten his brother's name and it is better to say there is no name rather than try and label something he has cherished. "He has no name, sir." The words come out truthfully.

The thick light, deepening in its draping brown ambiance, begins to fill the spaces between Conquergood's feeling and thinking.

Without warning jocund laughter from the lekturer breaks fiercely free, followed by babbling,

"*Kwite* true, *ya' boy*! Ha! *Howwellyou learnyourlessons*."

Settling a bit and lifting his glassy gaze beneath his eyeglasses to meet Conquergood's, the lekturer-monk continues,

"*Our* point is this: family is important and seeing how the Korporation is your family now, *we* would and will be glad to have your family join our family."

"Really?" Conquergood's interest shoots up and out. He had slipped into an obedient doze, but at the mention of seeing his twin brother again enthralls a sense of completeness within his mission. "Thank you, sir. I'd like that very much."

"So would *we*," K-NE1-2 says. "Now. Where is your family staying, by chance?"

"The last I checked it was Ward Twenty-one," Conquergood hesitates and the words cannot come out as easily as the others, "but sometimes *we* roam around. Safer that way."

"*Kwite* naturally," the lekturer says, "to be a roamer, a gatherer. *Roks* get nowhere, do they?"

"Not at all, sir." An ease fills Conquergood as he is talking with the drunken lekturer. Something is happening but he cannot place a name on it — *labelless*. "Perhaps the Korporation could try Ward Twenty?"

"The old *Tribeka* place?"

"Don't know any ward by that name," answers Conquergood. "You could try there though. As I said, *we* move around so much it's hard to say for certain which ward it was."

"*Ohwell*," the lekturer says in a defeatist tone. "Let *us kontinue*, shall *we*?"

The lekturer-monk takes great care to lift his rotund body up and out of the chair. He waddles with his stubby legs around the desk and finds his original seating, on the corner of the desk, one fat leg dangling freely.

"And since *we* are your family, *we* must remember one thing" — there it is once again, the stumble followed by the unmistakable pause — "Love others as the Korporation has loved you."

The word "love" embarks on a journey within Conquergood's mind, entering past the eardrums, shooting frantically through the gray matter of the brain, down into his beating heart, and transforming up into a deep sigh, consumed only by the innocent tears of salvation. He wipes his face but the tears come, relentless. No one has ever told Conquergood that they loved him. And then after all the years of being incomplete — selfless, unmade, absent — Conquergood accepts the words which have eluded him, haunted him, rebuked him, and even caused him to forget he has ever wanted to hear that four-lettered word in the first place.

"Yes," K-NE1-2 says, noticing the power of his persuasive speech and the fragile moment before him. "*We*, at the Korporation, do love. We are a family now. 'Out of many there *koms* one.' We must never forget the love *we* have so freely given. We must never forget all that *we* have done in the name of *our* love."

"Love," whispers Conquergood, as if it is a caged thing which needs to be set free to fly across vast endless skies. To him the word is magic, true absolute power. And certainly no one will ever call him a liar.

"*Our* time is up," says K-NE1-2, pointing a stubby finger towards the door. "And so is the *edukation*."

"You mean," Conquergood speaks softly, "I'm finished with my edukation?"

"Indeed, we are."

The door to the brown-lit classroom slips open to reveal another green-clad attendant — this one with red hair — waiting to guide Conquergood back to the living quarters. Looking out of the chocolate light and into the bright vanilla of the hall, Conquergood had forgotten how the room is masked in its own illusion. He stands, rises as if on a floating petal, to leave.

"Next time," says K-NE1-2, taking Conquergood by the shoulder, "the Korporation will grant you with the honor and freedom and *satisfaktion* of having your label removed. In the Korporation, *we* are all *ekwell. E Pluribus Unum!*"

"All *ekwell,*" reverberates the attendant from out of the diamond light of the hallway.

"All equal," Conquergood repeats.

He joins the attendant out in the hall and follows him as they glide on the hovering transport slides through the maze of korridors and transport-wells back to the living quarters. The entire time Conquergood remains silent, lost in the reflection of knowledge, absorbing the lessons, forehead throbbing.

At the entrance of Conquergood's apartment, the attendant concludes the journey by saying, "*We* took the liberty of providing some *authentik* sherry to ease the pain from finishing your lessons in one day. You must be awfully tired. I know I was, and it took me six months to *komplete* all ten lessons. Not an easy task, *we kan* assure you, sir."

"Yes, a bit." Conquergood walks in and the door is secured behind him. He enters once more the apartment's stillness; its constant silence drapes over him as a warm cloak on a very cold night and he feels once more comforted to be away from people. He locates the bottle of sherry on the table next to a newfangled book where on the white cover the black printing reads:

**KORPORATE
REKWIREMENTS
And
PRAKTICES**

**A
HANDBOOK
For
MEMBERS**

On the inside of the front cover bold words are printed:

Korporate Knowledge Base – 000

Conquergood flips over to the inside of the back cover and finds a handwritten inscription which reads:

**guard the Self,
guard the Soul,
or forget the things
the eyes See**

He tosses the thirteen-hundred-page book aside and pours a few shots of sherry into a tumbler. A swallow comes next. The liquor works its magic and numbs the constant, genitive throbbing of Conquergood's temples for a brief moment before the pain reasserts itself.

Conquergood again pours the glass full of sherry and cascades the entire contents in one smooth, rhythmic swallow. He stumbles over to lie on the bed, thoughts evanescing into futile slumber.

His mind swims, dreaming of something called a soul, and then he mutters gently, "you were ground in the very mill of the conventional." The words come out like a prayer from his childhood. A dying memory only he holds. The smell of lost lemons is the last thing he breathes in before darkness immerses and drowns him.

Because the one necessity he has never used is not present in the room at the time of his waking, Conquergood has no way to tell the time. A familiar disillusionment creeps upon his waking and so he cannot be sure how long he has slept.

The automatic shading is on; curtains drawn together over the bay window, allowing the room to be encircled with a shadowy frame of slippery darkness. But Conquergood is certain it was the sort of sleep that washes the throbbing away, filling his mind with new beloved energy, and stimulating his spirits to its previous peaks.

On the night table, Conquergood notices a large cream-colored envelope sitting on the Korporate Handbook. Opening the envelope, he discovers inside a matching card with black printing.

He knows the number well enough. "Eight," he mumbles. He is flat on his back, head reclined on the pillow, staring upward at the card and its message. He turns the card sideways to create an infinity — ∞.

"What on earth could that be for?"

As often as it does at the Korporation, Conquergood's question is swiftly answered with a firm pound on his apartment's metallic door. The call is not welcomed, nor is it inviting.

IV
A New Label

From rags to riches, from pauper to prince, from street to palace, from unkempt to proper, Conquergood likewise detects himself changing from within, compared to the first day when the nameless interlokutor had viewed Conquergood as a savage beast that had evolved piecemeal, from four legs to two. Those same two legs, having been massaged with lavish oils daily, have been drained hour by hour to the equivalent of a liquid-filled sponge — loose, not quite right. Those same two legs carry him through the dark and over to his apartment door, pounding — hold on! — with an unexpected and unusual urgency — *Dammit!*

This time a gray-haired *eskort* in a uniformed gray kimono robe with white seal stands erect in the hallway filled with an exuberance of yellow rays. Conquergood steps back — what time is it? — and shields his eyes. He has been asleep for several hours, waking only a few moments prior to the disturbance, and he needs to protect his eyes from the intensity of the hall lights shining into his darkened apartment. He is a little surprised that the usual green-robed attendants have not come, and still he cannot imagine why anyone would come to see him now.

"Are you ready, sir," the gray *eskort* inquires, once again in a flat, inflectionless tone. "Eight *o'klok* has arrived and *we* must hurry to be on our way."

Conquergood absently stares at the gray figure before him, featureless and nameless. The gray *eskort*, however, is much bulkier than Conquergood's previous attendants, and Conquergood further notices he cannot place a name on the feelings brought forth when confronted with the daily visits from the Korporate staff.

"And?" Conquergood folds his arms across his chest. "What's the big rush?"

"Well, sir," the gray *eskort* begins, lifting his dimpled chin from off his neck, lean and pulsing with veins. "Didn't you receive *our* invitation?"

"That?" Conquergood points to the cream-colored card with the bold number over on the night table beside his bed barely visible in the dark room. "Is that what *you* mean?"

"*We* certainly do, sir," the gray eskort says, rocking in his stance, checking both ends of the hall. "You hurry up and change now or *we'll* be late. *We'll* just wait out in the hall and when you're ready, *we'll* take you up. How does that sound?"

Foggy and still not quite awake and a bit put off at having been disturbed, Conquergood leans his head out into the hallway and checks both ends. Only the gray eskort is present.

"Who do *you* mean by *we*?" Conquergood asks. He is tired of the games, the rules, the lessons and the culture — and above all, the constant use of this 'we' business.

But the gray eskort stares blankly back into himself and cannot comprehend even the slightest of answers. Disrupted silence is what remains when followers cannot think for themselves.

"Take me where? I thought I was done for the day."

Without question, regarding his previous itinerary, Conquergood would have been done for the day. He often leisures himself to a few iced over Korporate beers, with a level of thirteen per cent concentration, a finely cooked dinner of the choicest steaks and potatoes by Korporate chefs, and only then to playfully reject the Korporate Kompanions each night at 10:01. Not tonight.

"No, sir," the gray eskort says firmly, but without the human connection Conquergood is seeking. The gray-haired man holds his hands close together in front of his waist, mildly rocking back and forth, assuming the obedient role of eskort. "The night is just beginning for you. Now *we* would please like it if you would go and *please* get dressed." He is emphatic and it startles Conquergood. "*We*'ll be late, that is already a certainty. But since you're the guest of honor tonight, we are allowing this tardiness to be overlooked for the time being." The gray eskort holds, for about three seconds, an awkwardly fake grin, a comical expression of one's attempt at sincerity which results in blatant indifference.

"Glad to hear of it," Conquergood replies. "Give me a moment." The door slides shut and Conquergood retreats back to the wardrobe, housing all three of the same outfit, a bare white kimono robe. He alters his clothes, identical to the ones he had on moments prior, and joins the eskort out in the hallway.

Twenty minutes later and several stories up, the gray eskort and Conquergood on transport slides search for the destination through the maze of halls. A multitude of similar doors flow by in flashes and Conquergood loses all sense of direction, becoming completely lost in this overwhelming Korporate Kompound, as one so often does. Finally, after three sharp turns right, they approach, the end of a hallway that resembles an entrance to an ancient monastery: two wooden doors thirteen-feet high wait with a nice chestnut finish. Engraved on the left door is the letter K and engraved on the right is the letter E. Two gold knockers, in the likeness of rams' heads, gleam in the gray eskort's black eyes and Conquergood shivers more from the sudden onslaught of nervousness shaking through the gray-haired man than from the countless possibilities which lie hidden behind these two doors that must conceal the Korporate Elite. After regaining his composure, the gray eskort thrusts the doors back and he and Conquergood step away from the transport slides.

Conquergood's bladder restricts and he fights to keep his composure. His right leg begins to twitch and then a roar fills his insides. Never before has he witnessed as many people congregated into one space as he does then. Once, seven years previous, he had counted eight strayers beneath a bridge during a severe super-storm which lasted for about twenty-four days, which flooded most of the wards and drowned several dozen of Conquergood's friends. Standing between the two doors marked K & E, he is then greeted by an unexpected and thunderous applause arising from no less than 613 Korporate members.

Enshrouded with Korporate flags and banners, both vertical and horizontal, like an ancient pantheon discovered, the auditorium possesses three levels, a ground floor for the Elites and two balconies for the lower-status members of the Korporation. Green-robed Attendants resign themselves to the highest gallery above and this is divided into four separate sections, with each section maintaining no more than fifty seats. At the foot of the entrance on the ground floor, nearest Conquergood, the Korporate Lekturers mumble to one another in their multi-colored robes designating their various fields of *korporadmeia* — a small sea of fractioned, chaotic rainbows whispering and smiling back. Everyone applauds and cheers and the abrupt noise deafens Conquergood for several moments until the gray eskort from behind has to shout, "Go ahead, sir! It's all for you!"

Like a lost child in a candied forest, Conquergood wanders through the roar of clapping hands, violent shakes of joyous greetings on his own limp shoulders, slaps on the back push him forward, and in waves of tranquil smiles and psychedelic colors, he makes his approach to the steps which extend upward to a stage where a thin metallic podium and *mikrophone* await his arrival. An Elder in a violet kimono robe, gold seal attached and *krimson* trimmings on the edges, meets Conquergood with a firm, boisterous handshake.

"Pleasure to meet!" The Elder's voice booms above the applause. The older man's hair is dyed jet black and the smile he presents fills the bottom portion of the face from ear lobe to ear lobe while his gray eyes twitch shut when he speaks, leaving absent crevices around the sockets. "*We* are honored to have you speak to *us* this evening."

The crowd hushes itself but remains standing, eagerness dripping off every brow, as the Elder emerges erect at the podium.

"*We* are gathered here on this joyous *okkasion* to *welkom* our newest member into the Korporation. Thus far, this young man who stands honored tonight has excelled in his studies, finishing in *rekord* time while reducing *kosts* unheard of by any pupil in the history of the Korporation."

Applause converges the rafters of the great auditorium. With a waving hand to silence the crowd, the Elder continues,

"*Our* guest of honor tonight is *our* newest member in the Turnkey *Akweesitions* Department."

Someone from the gallery heaves out a gigantic gasp. The Elder gives a short, steady gaze to security at the side of the auditorium and then another one into the upper sections of the auditorium before he continues,

"*Konker*good will lead *us* to *viktory* over *our* enemies! He shall redeem *us* and unify *our* minds to the end of time itself! He has no name and from this point forward — *we*, the Korporation — will choose to know nothing of his past. He is to be *kalled Sukarno! Eloy! Akoni!* One of *Us!* *Kebir* was sent to *us* not for the benefit of our employees but for the ambitions of the almighty Korporation! May the Korporation bless thee, son; may the Korporation bless this relation *we* have made here today." Applause again erupts and with a stern hand the Elder brings the overjoyed audience to a calm stillness once more. And much louder he finishes with the words, "*E Pluribus Unum!*"

A unified response thunders throughout the crowd,

"*E Pluribus Unum!*" shouts the crowd. Applause charges into the air and this time the Elder allows it to continue unabated.

The Elder leans back to Conquergood and adds, "Why don't you say a few words? After all, you are the guest of honor!"

Conquergood clutches the sides of the podium, his nails gripping the metal, balancing himself despite his twitching leg. Slowly he scans the auditorium in an attempt to examine the crowd when he notices the members are all seated as maintained by the color of their robes. In the highest gallery, the green-clad Attendants shuffle in their seats. On the second lower level, consisting of ten rows of ten seats each, the Virgins — males and females — giggle to one another in their pink kimonos, and seated beside them — in the middle — are more Korporate Kompanions. Alongside them on the second level to Conquergood's right, are the professional Entertainers, also comprised of males and females, in their *krimson* garbs. Down on floor level, Conquergood notices the lowest section is partly maintained by a few hundred Korporate Lekturers and Laboratory Officials in their black kimonos.

Conquergood looks from the Elder to the *mikrophone* to the countless obscured faces with their eyes darkling aglitter and back to the eskorts to the lekturers, and over to the guards waiting by the exits. Conquergood sees absolutely no method of retreat nor escape, and finally he fixes his vision back on the transparent *mikrophone* lit within a circle of blindingly bright light.

"I've never —" Conquergood says, faltering.

"Just say what's on your mind, young man," the Elder adds. He staggers over to the stairs and passes out of sight, back into the shadows, swallowed by the multitude. The Korporate members appease their applause and fix themselves into their cushioned and adjustable seats, white with a printed black K stitched to the back, and wait for the guest speaker to make his approach to the podium — and in their minds they seem to shout, "*Entertain us!*"

Sweating profusely, Conquergood's heart races between violent thumps and brief stops when he meets the gaze of the most important participants in the entire array of Korporate members still waiting for him to speak.

Occupying the lowest middle section of the auditorium, Conquergood studies the rows filled by the Elders in their violet regalia. Some of the members appear extremely young while others are closer to the opposite end of life. Behind these Elders, gray robed Examiners are seated. The gray eskort that had led Conquergood to the celebration is found seated among these Examiners. Over by the exits and by the stairs leading to the stage are hulk-like men and women — *Korporate Sekurity* — in navy-blue kimono robes, seals intact.

Conquergood turns behind him, gathering his bearings, and encounters a tremendous white poster, some forty-four feet in height, hanging from the ceiling and sprawled with those immortal words:

KORPORATE STRONG

The guest of honor turns back to face the audience of inquisitive faces, all masked by complacency. He breathes gently and utters a few words into the transparent *mikrophone*,

"I do not belong here," Conquergood says. The crowd leans forward. Even he does not know what he will say next.

"As a boy, I grew up seeing the almighty Korporation as a New Haven, a wondrous paradise, and to find myself speaking to all of you, here now, is an unfounded honor I cannot claim alone. Tonight, *we* are indeed one."

Roars of automatic cheers fill the air. The clamor of acceptance carries on for several minutes. Virgins and the Korporate Kompanions snicker and nudge their peers. A Lekturer seated near the stage states to a *kolleague*, "Kebir's a genius! What did *we* say? A genius!" The word "genius" faintly lights Conquergood's ears like lust upon wet cartilage, emboldening him as the room gives way for the guest of honor to continue his speech.

"As said before," Conquergood adjusts with his right hand the transparent *mikrophone* closer to his mouth, "I do not belong in a room filled with the greatest minds and bodies in the world. Who can compare with *us*? The Korporation stands alone and unchallenged. Enemies cower in the gutters of the Korporation's shadow and drown in the Korporate streams of unmatched power. To further add, what little can be done, *we* will do *our* best to make the Korporation proud. It is true I was raised as a strayer-dog on the streets, bathing in barrels beneath bridges, eating scraps from the filthy pavement, cut off from the grand luxury of Korporate society, as *we* see and feel here tonight."

Conquergood pauses and moves his right hand across the heads of the audience. He knows he is a born leader.

This is what he has been trained to do, what he has waited to do for years. The Korporate Elite are anxious to hear more, but Conquergood stretches the pause before adding in a lower, more commanding voice, "Still, that was my own fault, a serious personal decision to regret and to have to live with. I did not know any better. But when I came to my senses and made the correct choice, the same many of *us* here have made, *we* found more than a job with the best *kompany*, our beloved Korporation, *we* found the *only* family in the entire world welcoming *us* home again."

"The only *kompany* in the world," mumbles an Elder in row three, seat five. "Absolutely *perfekt*." The surrounding Elders offer a laugh and settle back to listen to the Turnkey Specialist.

"*Our* delightful stars," Conquergood continues, tightening his grip on the podium. His leg calms from its shaking. "*Our* glorious stars moved and *our* futures changed right before *our* very eyes. The Korporation is a life-giver, a changer of destinies, and *we* will devote *our* lives to the future of the Korporation. *We* will not fail."

Four of the female Virgins in pink kimonos from the middle gallery simultaneously shout down: "Kebir's home!"

Conquergood's senses blur by the eclipsing noise of approval promulgated by the standing ovation that comes roaring up to embrace him on stage. Throughout his first speech to the Korporate Elite, Conquergood has failed to remove his left hand from the podium.

Then after the sound of frantic applause drowns beneath its own ferocious climax, Conquergood comes to realize there is a distant throbbing in his hand. As he looks down now at the left palm, he perceives deep impressions filled by small droplets of his own unique blood. The blood fills each crevice in his palm.

The blood speaks in silent ignorance of his pact, and that delicate suppression of pain fueled by a refusal to be abated rises upward and forward into Conquergood's consciousness. He stumbles, falls backward violently, head hitting stage, and he lands beneath the Korporate poster, now upside down and floating above him as an angel might hover above the dead. All light instantly vanquishes itself in an opaque darkness. Conquergood does hear, however, the crowd roaring on in dramatic applause and shouts mad with feverish hope for their Korporate *Kalling*.

III
A Mad New World

All too familiar streets, barren and god-like, surround Conquergood once more. With head lifted and pointed skyward, neck leaned back, his eyes grope past the abandoned skyline of Old York City and up into the brilliance of the blazing sun. Blue birds — things that are no longer and should not be — dance beneath a rainbow. A lone hawk, preying and gliding, etches itself across the azure of the backscreen, once more untarnished by smoke or smog. The crisp air — a new, welcoming sensation — pours into Conquergood's lungs in massive breaths.

Just as he begins to feel at home in the isolated streets, the two competing noises of silence and chaos clash violently upon his mind. The blue birds scatter. The hawk vanishes above. As a twelve-year-old boy, Conquergood learned the distinct and provocative sounds the Dark Shadows made; the champion-noise hums barely above a whisper. As silent, but ever evident, the predator can be heard drawing closer, closer and even closer still. Considerably smaller than the outer-limit drones, this aerial drone rounds the dormant Empire State Building, or the building that had long ago been known by such archaic terms of names and labels, and aligns itself directly ahead of Conquergood.

The predator's front emerges forward like a narwhale, the extinct unicorns of the garbaged seas. Its body spans 13.5 feet long and its wingspan stretches 24.35 feet wide. Strayers call the lightweight machines KUDs, for Korporate Unmanned Devices. Conquergood calls them the *Dark Shadows*.

Standing in defiance of the KUD bearing down on him, instead of scrambling for cover within the belly of the industrial skeletons, Conquergood stands his ground, feeling himself more of a man than ever before. Mad and patient and articulate as a timeless Spanish bullfighter, he faces the Dark Shadow without fear, knowing full well that the drone will not alter its course or retreat from its trajectory.

The KUD whizzes by at only fifteen-feet off the ground before lifting its orbed-horned face upward toward the reign of unlimited space. Heart racing, pounding to be set free from its prison, Conquergood watches as the Korporate drone grows fainter and fainter — No more. Let it be. Let the world be as it should.

His spirit has changed, and in that spirit, he believes himself one with the Dark Shadow. Reborn. He no longer remains an individual lost in the mire of his own solitude. The Self has been established. The man has become one with the Korporation.

Conquergood exhales as he awakes from the tangible dream.

The KUD is barely visible in his memory now; it is the sun, however, which ignites his heart with violent, torturing beauty, and as he lies in bed, having slept all night and all morning, he knows the sun will wait for him like a lover who on the edge of a shore will be wishing, calling her heart's affection homeward as though he were Luis Alejandro Velasco, abandoned at sea to die. Suddenly, Conquergood becomes aware of the sweat profusely pouring from his body. His face, neck, and back are layered in thick pools of perspiration and he does not want to move from his position on the bed.

At lunch, instead of privately dining as he has done on every occasion beforehand, another green-robed attendant, this time a woman, comes and guides Conquergood to the Korporate Kanteen.

The *kanteen* buzzes with constant murmurs the moment he enters. Every head turns to the Turnkey Specialist, who stands in the entrance with sweaty palms waiting for the crowd to turn its gaze away.

The attendant departs to her own lunch and leaves Conquergood in the thrust of several hundred pairs of eyes fixed only on one object — the white robed man glittering like a full moon in a dark sea at night.

Frozen in the deluge of whispers and stares, Conquergood finds himself being pulled by a stranger's soft hand.

He looks ahead to find a woman with blonde curls pulling him through the *kafeteria*. Her freshly laundered yellow kimono robe ends on her thighs in a short skirt, flittering upon her body like enraptured daffodils in one of Wordsworth's enchanted fields. Her eyes — eerily blue — flash back to check on him and then faces forward to maneuver through the *kanteen* traffic. Her face contains a commonplace nose above two well mounted lips — a face that is untraceable, concrete.

Conquergood soon notices their winding path, in and around chairs and motionless employees with trays in their hands wanting to get a glimpse of the new Turnkey Specialist, is heading for a queue.

"You have to keep moving," she says, head presented forward toward the lunch queue. "If you stop, they'll bury you with questions. Believe me when I say you don't want that. They'll never shut up — a billion questions about life on the *outside*."

"I see," is all Conquergood manages to sputter out of his vocal folds.

"Not yet, you don't," she replies. "But you shall soon enough. Just wait."

"No, I believe you."

At this word, the woman in yellow offers a wry frown as if he had contracted a deadly dose of unpopularity from walking into the room naked and covered in Korporate pistachio butter.

"You have a lot to learn, newbie," she says.

"I do."

It has come out as a statement, a proclamation of fact, but she takes it as a question.

"*You do*, you know that!" Her vivid pronunciation and intonation come out spectacularly clear and surprises Conquergood.

But it is her robe that has caught his immediate attention — a robe like the golden butterflies in the treeless Ward 7 Park.

"What's your name?" he asks. Of all the members he has met at the Korporation, the fair-headed goddess has been the first to exhibit any sort of natural emotion and the natural speech patterns that he is so familiar with on the outside in the streets and under bridges.

"You may refer to me as Klaire," she replies without hesitation. "My label has been known to be K-NE1-2-U, but don't bother with those silly and insipid formalities."

Klaire looks down to find her hand is still in Conquergood's. For a moment he thinks she may leave it there but then she lets it go.

"I was beginning to wonder," he says.

"Oh sure," Klaire goes on, handing Conquergood an empty lunch tray and edging him forward in the queue. "We only use labels in more formal settings like the Korporate Edukation Senters or the Korporate Labor Kamps. Do you want simulated lamb or ostrich steak? We also have simulated swordfish and grilled kangaroo?"

"Don't know," Conquergood says. He stares down at the buffet table, thirty or more feet long. He has never seen so much food in one place before and he is uncertain as to where he should begin. "Anything will be fine."

"The Korporate chefs have been choosing your meals for you, haven't they?"

"I suppose so."

"What do you like?"

"I like peanut butter."

"Try these," Klaire says. "They'll fatten you up." She flops down a genetically enhanced tomahawk steak and a breast of roasted chicken. Next, she piles on mashed potatoes with cream gravy and grilled bell peppers with green beans and sautéed onions. The final touch is a hot roll smothered in Korporate butter. "Anything else, dear?"

"No," Conquergood absently replies. He can feel the weight of the food bearing down on the tray in his hands. "I'm sure this will do nicely." His cheeks flush and betray his affection for Klaire's take-charge attitude.

She grabs two bottles of mineral water and leads Conquergood down to a scanner. She waves her labor signature — much like his own — on her right wrist beneath the neon light and a light on the scanner turns from red to green.

Klaire then leads him over to a circular table in the corner where two other men sit reflectively.

Conquergood stands holding the tray of food and observes a rather strange pair of Korporate members, both wearing black kimono robes with the Korporate white seal stitched in fine detail. To Conquergood's left, a small obese man with mustache is eating a bowl of vanilla *ice-kream*; on Conquergood's right, a thin man with an extended chin has only a teacup in front of him. The two men have finished their lunch and are now enjoying their desserts.

"This here's Mister Know-It-All," Klaire says, pointing to the plump balding man with an overgrown brown mustache. His dark eyes appear like a beetle rolling back and forth, forth and back, back again, and then forward again.

"Kin," he jocundly announces with a chubby hand, a bit greasy, out-stretched. "It's much easier to remember, I *kin* assure you."

Conquergood doesn't get the humor nor does he understand Kin wants to shake his hand and it ends up looking like Kin is groping for some foreign object on the table. From his nose Kin puffs air through his mustache and settles back in his chair and resigns to enjoy a mug of hot Korporate koffee with his *ice-kream*.

"Or why not refer to him as a fat-over-grown sesquipedalian," Klaire says. She stands on her tippy-toes and lets out a small squeal of laughter.

Kin scoffs and buries his mustache back in his Korporate koffee.

Klaire motions over to the next fellow who is lean and dangly like a praying mantis.

"Happy to introduce without the frivolous and resplendent monikers," the man wearing thin eye-glasses injects before Klaire can arrive at a zany anonym. "You, son, young Turnkey Specialist, may refer to me as Sir Windsor the Sixth. My family has belonged to this fine institution long before the days it was a super-*konglomerate*. Berkshire Hathaway, China National Petroleum, State Grid, UnitedHealth —"

"Here it comes," Klaire inserts to Conquergood as she takes a seat and leans back in her chair. She bites on a green apple and waves for her friend to continue. "Let's have it all again. Let's hear it."

"Before the Metaverse arrived and changed the world ever after, Alphabet — with its pre-born Google — Amazon, Apple, BP Oil, Daimler, Exxon Mobil, ICBC, Meta — which was born after Facebook — Royal Dutch Shell, Samsung, and Walmart — just to list a few of the ancient ones," Sir Windsor VI continues, "had all been some of those great fierce bulldogs of our ancestor's age… before the Korporation arrived to save us."

"That's about enough of that," Klaire inserts between a bite of her green apple. "Don't bore us to death."

"Let's digress in such a lengthy history lesson as this," Sir Windsor VI says. "Please sit and join us. Any friend of Klaire's shall be a friend of ours. Would our new *kompatriot* like some hot poppy tea with Lagavulin?"

"Not today," Conquergood says, cautiously placing the tray of food down and sitting between Klaire and Kin. The newcomer's hands begin shaking and he slides them under the surface of the table.

Klaire's eyes, projected downward, are watching as Conquergood's fingers dig into his knees. She smiles and lets out a sharp-squealing laugh. Half of the employees in the *kanteen* turn and look at her. She shrugs them off.

Conquergood settles himself in his seat. Kin huffs and puffs because he has spilt some of his koffee on his robe. Sir Windsor VI appears unfazed by the unexpected display of Kin's crudeness. Lost in thought, the thin English-esque-man delicately fingers the teacup in front of him.

"What's the laugh for?" Kin questions, his mustache twitching like a large broom sweeping across his face. "Amused, *are* we?"

"Kin appears to have been smooching with the wrong monkey again," Klaire replies. Her blonde curls bounce against her shoulders in light frolicking play.

Three pairs of eyes dart over to Kin's auspicious face and mustache layered with vanilla *ice-kream*. Even his own eyes attempt to make the journey beyond the plump cheeks and nose to see that hilarious debacle residing stubbornly on his own face.

"By Korp!" exclaims Sir Windsor VI. "A tissue shall do much justice to that hedgehog beneath that monstrous nose. Aren't we looking the grand jester today?"

Kin huffs and puffs and sneezes, which causes the layer of *ice-kream* on his mustache to spray all across the table. His cheeks are boiling as he cleans the froth from off his mouth.

"What happened to the giant bulldogs?" Conquergood's voice quivers across the table to Sir Windsor VI, who is examining the remaining amount of poppy tea left in his teacup.

"What's that, me boy? Bull-who?"

"You spoke of your ancestors and the bulldogs," Conquergood says, much stronger and firmer. "*Alpha Gobble*, was it?"

Kin scoffs at Conquergood's remark and ignores the others and returns back to his mug of koffee.

Klaire giggles and reaches for a drink. She unscrews one bottle of water and swigs. Her cheeks puff out wide and she relaxes back in her chair watching the boys make nice.

"Google. They were Alphabet and Google, young son." Sir Windsor VI releases a heartfelt chuckle before sipping his loaded poppy tea. After patiently clearing his throat, he adds, "Either way, it makes no difference now. They're all the same as one."

"What do you mean?" Conquergood asks. "How's that?"

"What *does* he mean?" Kin says. "Please tell us. What *do* you mean, you English muffin?"

"Play nice," Klaire says in a low voice, calm but direct.

Kin turns away from the conversation, crosses his stubby legs, and retrieves a K-pad from his briefcase located beneath his chair. A three-dimensional *krossword puzzle* rises from the e-skreen.

"The meaning," Sir Windsor VI begins again, eyes shining beneath his silvery spectacles, "is *merkantilism.*"

"*Merka*-what?" Conquergood asks. His hands have not moved from their position on his knees beneath the table. The mountain of food remains untouched on his tray. He doesn't have an appetite today, in front of Klaire.

"During the sixteenth and seventeenth centuries," Sir Windsor VI explains, "nations began doing business in a very special manner. What happened was that one nation, which was a designated area with similar minded people grouped under a single flag, very unlike the Korporate unity we now find among us here today, and these nations would export more than they would import, having the merchandise paid full in gold."

"Everyone knows that," Kin says without looking up from his three-dimensional e-puzzle. "All old news."

"The Korporation was the first to reignite this form of lost business," Sir Windsor VI says, ignoring his laboratory partner. "Now what we had was a grand fine specimen of achievement for all of humanity. Petty rivalries were bought and silenced in the very thing they often fought wars over — authority through gold. Murky manipulative business models — *Asa' al-Shay'* — were squelched through the purchasing of subsidiaries. Maleficence has not existed in the business sphere, let's say, for at least two or three generations, if not longer. We are all one in the Korporation and the Korporation tends to its own; frankly speaking, *one* is enough."

"You see —" Klaire breaks off. "What would you like to be referred to as? You never told us?"

"You never asked," Conquergood replies.

"Well, I'm asking now."

"Jerome."

"Well, you see, Jerome Conquergood," Klaire says, placing her gentle hand on his more tense hands beneath the table, "When the world's existence became threatened by Global Warming, a few dozen *kompanies*, organizations and what was left of the few learning institutions, all of them joined forces and started the Global Allianz Movement. By transforming into a single but much larger transnational organization, the Korporation managed to pave a new way forward into the twenty-second century. The Earth's natural resources and eco-environment were *gravid* business back then, like gold or diamonds and other raw gems when they were first discovered by primitive minds, and these same dull minds back then placed value on meaningless worthless trinkets."

"The Green Movement?" Conquergood repeats.

"Like talking to a child," Kins says.

"Environmentally friendly, young son," Sir Windsor VI asserts. "Our beloved Korporation, with its newly built funds and resources, helped to lead progress by reducing CO_2 emissions, slashing wastes, etcetera, etcetera, and thereby reducing sixty-five per cent of pollution in its first twenty years. Due to the supreme might of the Korporation, we now have a much healthier world to enjoy and live in."

"And then there was the Great Water Shortage," Klaire adds. "In twenty-one twenty-five, two-thirds of the world's population did not have access to potable water."

Conquergood watches her lips move as one might watch the ocean tide increase and reside back into its depths. He wants to know what tongue, what kraken, holds its secrets from him.

"The Korporation," Kin interjects, no longer being satisfied with his e-puzzle and the outskirts of the conversation, "stepped in and privatized the whole mess. With one sweep of the hand, all was tidied and more efficient. Ocean water, river water, rain water, bath water and the like were bought up, purified, made clean and holy and all that *ditty-fitty* business minds do, and all this water was collected and made new and distributed equally to the masses by the Korporation alone. But everyone knows this. Except for someone like you, that is."

"Then we must teach him the path," Klaire continues as if the three Korporate members are one and the same when citing a log of scrutinized history.

Klaire continues: "The Korporation did what no government at the time could do. In twenty-one fifty-seven, the Korporation purchased the remaining stakes in a highly profitable venture, Environmental Commodities. Sunshine taxes and oxygen taxes were enforced by the Korporation, and these profits in turn were used to decrease pollution to almost nothing. Over time, the natural world became clean once again. The world made new. A new heaven on a new earth, if you like."

"But a few years later," Kin says, rolling his finger around the edge of his mustache and taking up the mantle of reciting and impressing history upon their guest, "the Korporation successfully lobbied to pass new laws which would find *kompanies* guilty and dismembered, and also stripped of the long held 'personal status' granted by the old America's fourteenth amendment, which was then under the abolished constitution — if any organization was found guilty of committing violent acts of aggression against the Earth. The Korporation, *fatty-full* and proud, alone helped to prosecute over a few hundred thousand cases and in a matter of three years the number of corrupt businesses decreased by seventy per cent worldwide. A year or so later, the Korporation again successfully lobbied to remove public services once and for all, deeming them to be ineffective, poorly managed and simply a waste of allocated resources. All services were then privatized. Back then it was the democratic and the very capitalist thing to do. But that was all before society evolved to *Korporatilism*. The world needed a change and it got one."

"I told you he was a know-it-all," Klaire remarks to Conquergood.

Kin, having said his piece, maneuvers back to his three-dimensional e-puzzle on his K-pad.

"Incredible," Conquergood says, enthralled at the history of the Korporation. And although he is not able to eat his lunch, he manages to relax his hands and remove them from beneath the table. "So, all the *kompanies* became this very one?"

"Not exactly," Klaire answers. "You see, darling, some *kompanies* were either too slow to accept the new change or were resistant to change. A great many *kompanies* were dissolved due to their inability to change. Many just didn't want to abide by the new mandates."

Kin stops doodling on the e-puzzle for a moment and listens. Sir Windsor VI appears to be nodding off in a light sleep.

"Do you know what those thirteen black banners on the *kanteen*'s front wall represent?" Conquergood asks.

Each portrait, solid black, is approximately twenty feet in height and six feet in width, all lined in a neat row. "I don't have a clue," Conquergood adds as Klaire and Kin turn to examine the black banners, "and I've been wondering about what they could mean."

"Each one symbolizes the Thirteen," Kin states with extreme certainty, as if divulging a long-held secret. "These Thirteen are the original owners of the Korporation. Our Korporate forefathers."

Conquergood's interest draws him back to the blank banners. An emptiness fills him as he stares at the banners hanging against the wall. They look as though they are darkened doorways or windows, mysterious portals, leading into the unknown. At one point, Conquergood imagines that he's seeing thirteen illuminated faces glowing within the dark blankness on the black banners — phantasms filled with ultimate wisdom of all times, all races, all societies, and all cultures — all of which had been shaped by these immortal Thirteen.

Klaire forces the trance away, shaking Conquergood by the arm.

"You shouldn't stare, darling. Try to eat."

Wiping his eyes with his thumb and forefinger, Conquergood concentrates back on the table and its occupants. Kin and Sir Windsor VI, now wide awake, are watching, expecting, and half-hoping to witness a spectacular event — an eclipse of the soul, perhaps.

"What line of work are you in?" Conquergood manages to ask Sir Windsor VI.

The teacup in front of Sir Windsor VI has been drained and the man, after having a short nap, has moved on to the final stage of his dessert, a thin opium cigar. The process of inhalation causes soothing sounds of pleasure while downward-spiraling flumes of smoke pours out of his long nose like steam. "We're employed in the GRL," he finally says. "Top of the line kind of work. Ever heard of us?"

"GRL? No." Conquergood looks confused. "Could you tell me a little about it? Sounds fascinating."

"Now there's a polysyllabic word," Kin says. He huffs and puffs and scoffs.

"The Gene Research Laboratories." Paying no mind to his kolleague's humor, Sir Windsor VI continues, "Certainly some truth wouldn't hurt. Wouldn't we agree, Kin?"

"Why not blather it all out now, why don't we," Kin replies, face firm in his K-pad. "As long as we don't go and give away our multi-trillion-dollar secrets. That's if we still had any *kompetition* left." Kin chuckles, and through the air scribbles a word into the e-puzzle with his e-pen.

Klaire provides another giggle, covering her mouth with a few finely manicured fingers. She washes down the green apple with some water.

Just about that time a man in a black kimono robe encroaches Klaire. "Hello," he says. "Do we know each other?"

"No." Klaire shrugs and waves the man off. "Never." Her eyes drop to the center of the table. "Impossible."

"Never a komp—"

"We told you NO," Kin roars, voice rattling as his fat fist slams down upon the table, bottles and cups and mugs spilling over. Conquergood jumps in his seat and has to reposition himself. He is not quite comfortable with this unexpected element among the Korporate members in the kanteen.

"We see," the stranger says. His face becomes baffled, his eyes widen, and his hands shake. The ears on the sides of his head bend back and low like a scolded ass. "We do apologize. Yes, that's right. We remember now. The former kompanion we're looking for has purple hair. We're mistaken. We beg forgiveness."

"Idiot." Kin growls to himself. His face resembles a bulldog's as he focuses on the quivering intruder. "Moron."

"May the Korporation bless us," the man says. He retreats back into the array of Korporate members in the bustling kanteen just as swiftly as his arrival.

An elephant-sized silence muzzles its way upon the lunch table and over its four occupants until Sir Windsor VI continues speaking. "As we were saying… where were we again?"

"Grand mysteries of the human rats," Kin replies. "We're going to give away the keys we've been working so hard to shape. Like any of it matters anyways." He buries his face back to his e-puzzle.

"True indeed," Sir Windsor VI says. From the opium cigar a drag is stolen and he casually releases the fumes from his nostrils. "Our research duties… well, we might explain it or we might as well show it. Show, don't tell, as they say. Why don't we take this little party to the labs?"

"I'd like that very much," Conquergood replies. He looks over at Klaire, chin down on her chest with her collapsed hands one upon the other in her lap, folded like the wings of a dead canary. Her eyes flitter up and find Conquergood looking at her.

"What a novel idea," she says with a quaking voice, trying to find its cheerfulness and command once again. "I've a few errands to attend to. Do you mind?"

Conquergood isn't sure who she's speaking to.

"Young Quixote here doesn't mind a bit," Sir Windsor VI speaks up. "Do you, Jerome?"

"Not at all," Conquergood replies.

"Settled then," Klaire says. She rises from her chair and trips over one of the chair's legs. Conquergood, lightning fast, grabs one of her arms and steadies her.

"Thanks," she says. "Young Quixote here is left to the charge of the expert *doktors*." Without another word, Klaire's yellow robe flitters through the crowd and out of the kanteen. She is gone.

Conquergood's eyes follow her and then dart between the two *doktors* closely watching him. A calm comes profoundly as the three men bounce a gaze from off one another, waiting — oh, how he hated waiting.

"Our sorrows are our teachers," Sir Windsor VI says, quoting Lord Veralum. He then pulls from his vest pocket a gold chain attached to a digital-pc pocket watch and checks the hour, room temperature, *atmospherik* pressure, and weather. "It's about that time. Shall we?"

"Sorrows are for the babes," Kin replies to his *kolleague*'s lovelorn remark. "How about we go find out what those damn mice are saying about us *this* time."

II
The God Gene

The *k-line* is a moniker often used for the Korporate Portal reserved for the higher-ranking members of the Korporate Elite. The Korporate Portals transport Korporate members vertically and horizontally to any destination within Korporate Headquarters at a much faster speed than the transport pads and wells which are meant for those who are in no special hurry. The *k-line* is much faster than the much smaller t-slides, designed for shorter distances. Conquergood, since his arrival and the early days of his employment with the Korporation, has only taken the more obvious and easily accessible t-slides when he's alone roaming through the vast Kompound. Slowly and surely, Conquergood is learning the interior maze of the Korporation. Timing, however, must be everything. And so, he waits, plays his part, acts the role the Korporation has created for him and then, after all, there is Klaire to consider.

Next to the door of the *k-line* a tele-k-skreen with standard face and voice recognition is mounted. Conquergood is impressed when Kin has merely to speak into the monitor and say, "L88-13-6."

Sir Windsor VI explains to Conquergood that the destination is *adequately* labeled with the level of the floor first, here labeled L88, followed by the row, 13, ending with the room number, 6. Destination: L88-13-6. Simple.

"It's rather dull," Kin says, "to be taking the turtle slides all the time."

Inside the *k-line*, moving at a remarkable speed, Sir Windsor VI and Kin comfortably enjoy the ride while Conquergood holds his arms close to his stomach. The *k-line*, on magnetic rails, whizzes upwards and then sideways through the immense group of buildings forming the Kompound. Conquergood nods in the affirmative to what is being spoken, and he is barely able to listen. He cannot respond and manages only to hold his stomach in desperate hope of relief.

"First time, eh?" Kin remarks. He lets out a modest chuckle that makes his dense mustache bounce between his upper lip and chubby nose. "I recall my first time in a *k-line*. I'd been only a lab-flunky, acne and all, back then. Dr KJD was the one who took me up to the Korporate Labs. I nearly exercised my right to express my lunch all over the good *doktor*'s sandals. Can you imagine that?"

"The *k-line* does take some getting used to," Sir Windsor VI adds. He chews on the end of a new, but unlit, opium cigar. "The speed, though, is exhilarating, once mastered."

"Easier than staying on those blasted-floating circles," Kin remarks, busying himself by checking notes on his K-pad. "The *k-line* is the best way to get around."

Conquergood looks up and again nods, barely without a word, in the affirmative.

Eventually the *k-line* whirls to a gradual halt. The tele-k-skreen, much like a human voice, sounds, "Have a wonderful experience, *doktors*. Make the Korporation proud!"

Kin bursts through the doors first with his briefcase, followed by a stumbling but grateful Conquergood. Sir Windsor VI contentedly chews on the end of his slender opium cigar while he gracefully steps with one long leg out of the portal as if he is setting foot on Mars for the first time.

(Verily, it must be inserted for absolute transparency in the *Anakhro Skript* that Dr Windsor VI followed in his great-great-great grandfather's footsteps by setting foot on Mars twice. Once was when Sir Windsor VI was in his prime at age thirty in 2155, and the second time happened when he explored the effects of Mars' atmosphere during the Human Genome Project, put simply as HGP, a decade later. At that time, HGP was still maturing, having first started ages ago in 1990. During the time of Sir Windsor the First's initial research, the project had just begun to evolve into a generational endeavor.)

The k-line drops the three men in an antechamber where twenty-two black lab *koats*, all lined in neat rows, hang along the wall. Over their daily black kimono robes, Kin and Sir Windsor VI slide into their black lab *koats*, *holographik-koded* badges dangling from their belts.

Kin slugs over to the tele-k-skreen and blasts a few impatient words, "Let us in, dummy!"

Immediately the flexiglass doors glide apart. The three men step into a smaller room, *sekurity* doors closing them inside.

"Sometimes I wonder," Kin says — he scoffs, huffs, and then puffs — "They act like this is a holy fucking temple and it's starting to rattle me a bit."

Still queasy from the trip on the k-line, Conquergood nods and holds his stomach.

"By Korp!" Kin grumbles, "We'll wrangle that squeaky little lab-flunky yet — regardless of which family he had the generosity to hatch from."

"*They* are now going to detoxify *us*," Sir Windsor VI inserts between Kin's frantic remarks over to Conquergood.

A systematic spray covers the three men in a fine layer of a purifying mist.

"All for health purposes," Sir Windsor VI clarifies. "*We* simply mustn't allow any foreign impurities into the lab and ruin our research."

Noxious, Conquergood shakes his head in the affirmative once more in a vain attempt to understand and in every attempt to avoid the speech which would embarrass him.

"Don't worry about that weak stomach," Kin says, slapping Conquergood on the back. "When those blasted church doors open and we're in the real holy grail of it, we'll have some special remedy."

"Watch out," Sir Windsor VI says. A sly grin curves itself above the English-esque-man's protruding chin. "The last time *the remedy* was offered, Johnson, our lab partner, found himself in Korporate *Rekovery* for two weeks. Doubtful Johnson ever got over it."

"Johnson's a wimp, a sniveler, a moaner, a damned grumbler," Kin rattles on. "Now don't go scaring the poor chap. Let us men have our fun."

The purifying spray ceases and the three men, wiped clean, are ready to leave the enclosure.

Two more flexiglass doors systematically open to reveal an incredible windowless laboratory that is longer than its width. In the middle runs a row of stainless-steel lab tables, matched with others set along the side walls. On each table are beakers, bottles and test tubes in various shapes and sizes filled with a variety of colored chemicals. The lab chemicals, for Conquergood, resemble rainbows in bottlefuls.

Down at the far end are five stainless-steel pods, sixteen feet in height, each one about eight feet in width. At the opposite end of the room, and by another set of *sekurity* doors, are countless stainless-steel repositories.

Near the entrance to the lab, Johnson reclines with his feet up on one of the tables.

"Johnson, get those stinky feet off *our* tables!" Kin shouts, flabby cheeks bouncing along the sides of his famous mustache. "We've work to do, regardless of which great-granddaddy coughed and spat you out. Now, where's your K-pad?"

"Yes, sir," Johnson says. He peels his feet from off the table and fixes his thick set of eye-wear properly back to his nose. "Have you seen" — the young lab doktor rushes through the aisles looking for his K-pad. "Oh, here it is."

Conquergood watches quietly from behind the shoulders of the two doktors.

"You'd lose your legs," Kin says. He scoffs and huffs and puffs. "Lose them, I'd say, if they weren't attached to that lanky-danky torso of yours."

Johnson, with K-pad finally in hand, mulls back over to his desk in front of the assorted chemicals he's been working on all morning.

"Leave the boy alone," Sir Windsor VI says. He moves to the back of the lab where the five stainless-steel pods reside, consuming most of the lab's back space. "It's his first year on the job and all you've done, Kin, is manage to get the boy ill. That frat boy drink sent him to KR for a few weeks."

Johnson buries his head in the K-pad, lights bouncing back and forth between the e-skreen and his thick eye-glasses. Formulas, charts and diagrams flash by in repetitive cycles every three to four seconds.

"Johnson," Sir Windsor VI calls from the end of the room. "Have we got those results yet from K-623?"

"Not yet, sir," Johnson answers. He remains focused on his K-pad. "We're still going over the xenon issue, and it may be another few hours before we have the results."

"Very well," Sir Windsor VI replies. He strolls over to a tele-k-skreen on the back wall near the five pods. "Lift shields."

Kin adds with a fervor, "Let's see what those blasted mice have to say now." He stuffs his hands in the pockets of his black lab *koat* and joins his kolleague in front of the five pods, shields rising.

Conquergood steps away from the *sekurity* doors and walks down the aisle leading to the five pods at the back of the lab. He can feel something stirring behind the shields. As the shields slide up, revealing the contents inside, Conquergood feels his eyes bulging from false expectations. His balance grasps frantically to hold solid to its surroundings, but fails as he tries to stop the strange female voice inside his own mind, but he can't, and so he clutches his head and falls hard against the side wall. The two doktors remove their eyes from their five specimens inside their pods and look in the direction of their forgotten guest of honor.

"That belly still upset? Absolutely forgot" Kin asks. He waddles over to a repository where he bends down and opens a drawer removing a brown bottle with a white top and no label. "This will make things better."

Conquergood meanwhile fixates his blank stare on the contents of the pods through the flexiglass barriers. Inside each of the five pods, sitting isolated and resigned to waiting in their own pod are five young females: four who are white — a shade more akin to pale ivory — and one, Number Three, who is black — a remarkably beautiful ebony sheen.

Conquergood estimates their ages to be five or six or seven but perhaps they are younger. Each female is bald and hairless and shrouded in a kind of cerecloth garment attached to their frail bodies as if the *e-kloth* is a second skin. There are no mice, no rodents, no monkeys, no primates of any kind. The five girls sit motionless, sitting with their legs folded inwards, hands resting on their knees, seemingly in patient reflective thought.

The five children remind Conquergood of an old photograph he had seen once as a strayer in one of the abandoned buildings on Fifth Avenue. The apartment hadn't been lived in for several decades but the place remained semi-furnished. The floor was strewn with magazines and newspapers, yellowed and worn and torn. The dates of the artifacts were from various decades over the last two centuries. Conquergood had sat for countless hours in that dusty and mildewed apartment scanning every letter of every word and memorizing every picture he came across.

From one of those magazine pages a colorless photograph now bursts into his mind as he sees the children enshrined and enthroned in their pods. The image is of a robed monk sitting peacefully in the street. He's surrounded by curious onlookers and soldiers — and all are waiting for the monk in the street to move, to yell, to scream for water, to do something, anything. The remarkable attribute which burns the image into Conquergood's thoughts is the single fact that the monk is on fire. At first sight, when the shields glide open, Conquergood has, but for an instant, seen the infernal monk once more appear in each of the five pods.

"Drink this," Kin says, handing Conquergood the brown bottle with no label. "It'll ease that baby's stomach. You know, we should mass produce and market this stuff. Call it 'Kin's K-line Solution' or something of the other. Our slogan is: every swallow gets closer to God."

"Suppose so," Sir Windsor VI responds. "But it all depends on which god we are chasing." He turns back to his calculations much to Kin's chagrin.

Conquergood, absent of his own presence, receives Kin's remedy and gulps down as much of the concoction as he can fit into one healthy swallow. The elixir bites into his tongue, sears his throat, burns his esophagus and boils his insides with a new hell-fire all its own. An arid heave of blazing fumes evades Conquergood's belly and lungs and throat and bursts free as a mighty belch.

"That moonshine tequila has a powerful kick, huh?" Kin retrieves the brown bottle with no label and returns it to the drawer. "Only in times of true emergencies. But that belly will be brighter by day's end, more so than a budding rose in blossoming springtime."

"We'll say," Johnson says, glancing up for a moment from his formulas on his K-pad, "but we're no Turnkey Specialist now, are we?"

Kin shoots Johnson a stern frown and menacing glare, just as he did in the Korporate Kanteen with Klaire's strange admirer.

Twitching his mustache and wiping his balding scalp with a firm-straight palm, Kin rejoins Sir Windsor VI beside the five pods. The latter is busy at work, scribbling on his K-pad.

"Still not a word, huh?" Kin asks. He fixes his gaze on the third pod in the middle of the five. "Not even a single peep or squawk."

"Seems to be that way," replies Sir Windsor VI. "The research appears to be precise. *We* have been over every strand of their DNA and RNA formations and sequences no less than nine hundred times. These specimens are flawless in every bodily trait known to the species. No impurity what-so-ever. What the *scheol* is wrong with them?"

"We'll figure it out." Kin shakes his round head, stray hairs flying freely to and fro. He tucks his hands into his black lab *koat* pockets and rocks back and forth on the balls of his feet. "What about a possible misfiring of the cerebral electrodes? Is there anything wrong with the STN?"

"STN?" Conquergood asks. He hasn't moved since drinking the remedy but chooses to pull himself up to edge alongside the two doktors standing in front of the five mysterious pods.

"What he's referring to," Sir Windsor VI explains, towering over his kolleague, "is the *Subthalamik Nukleus*, or more easily known as the STN."

Conquergood nods and studies the five statuesque lab subjects imprisoned in their pods. Inhuman these children all appear — as if God-magician-scientist cupped hands together with wet sand and formed a living being only to then abandon the creature to the rolling sea. The children seem dormant and dead from within.

"As to the answer, Dr Kin," Sir Windsor VI says. "STN is at a phenomenal percentage of over eighty-eighty — the highest *we* have achieved to this very date."

"And still not a sentence, not a word, not a sound."

"The neuro-exams also returned negative," Johnson adds from the front of the laboratory. "We're still running through the dozen or so other tests though."

The five feminine faces, lips, eyes, remain lifeless. One has to pay extreme attention to their nostrils to even notice that the five females are still breathing. But as Conquergood looks closely, an immortal appearance drapes itself over the five mysterious beings — living shrines to their own perfection.

Kin taps a few fingers on the flexiglass surface of pod Number Three. "Did we quadruple check the spinal taps?" Kin asks, lifting his head upward to his kolleague.

Inside the five pods, the ten eyes don't even blink. The ten eyes simply stare outward, detached, towards forever and anon — what once had been called "the Thousand-Yard Stare."

"Certainly," Sir Windsor VI replies. "We've even examined their original donor embryos — all pure and excellently enhanced. We gather it must have something to do with the STN."

"Why is the STN so important?" Conquergood questions. He stands off to the side of the two doktors. His knees are gaining strength and his stomach becomes stronger than before the ride on the k-line. The remedy, still haunting Conquergood's mind and stomach, is a huge success. Kin's K-line Solution, he reflects, is the elixir of miracles. "What do you suppose happened to all of them?" he asks.

"Nothing *happened* to them," Sir Windsor VI says. "We designed their STNs to magnify their aggregate inputs and outputs. This sort of manipulation to the central atoms allows for the reception of information from a designated source domain. The layers of such an anatomy span through many kinds of species, not only the human kind; however, we've tested rats and monkeys and snakes, and in previous human trials a plethora of living results were spoiled. We'd say, a little flaky-shaky. But these five, in our minds, are going to alter the future of our world, the future of our species, and the future of our beloved Korporation."

"What for?" Conquergood asks. "I don't get why all the trouble."

"What for?" Kin scoffs. He huffs and puffs. "We're going to solve the issue of senescence. We're going to *perfekt* humanity, Mr Turnkey Specialist. What do you think we're doing here — twiddling our thumbs? Evolution's the key that turns the Wheel of *Kommerce*. There're loads of money to be made. We're going to establish everlasting youth and innocence and peace in the world. Imagine: no more battles. Sure, the Korporation has solved the problem of major wars among the lands and peoples. Yes, minor skirmishes still pop up here and there. Just imagine, yet, all of humanity, though, in a blissful peace with the Self, Soul, and Other-selves. Now that's something we have no price tag for."

"You see, Jerome," Sir Windsor VI begins, "the Korporation has eliminated many of the diseases and viruses in our world. Much of it was done under Dr Ringmeier in his famous Bluebird Program, many-many years ago. Individual skirmishes, however, are prevalent world round and are responsible for over sixty-six percent of fatalities, thereby dropping overall Korporate input and output. By altering the STN, *we* should be able to enhance any ability to behave without the necessity of forethought."

"Enough of all this funky-lab pseudo-talk," Kin injects. "In other words, Jerome, we've altered their DNA and RNA so that these five beings might transform the symbol of perpetual bliss and peace within the mind and body. We refer to it as the God Gene. It's the next stage of evolution."

Again, Conquergood nods methodically. "Powerful stuff." He doesn't know what else to say. Never did he imagine such wonder, such awe, such horror in an attempt to maximize profits and to further subjugate the human species into genetic complacency. But the proof is in the seeing and he is seeing it before him in the form of five young girls, all perfect and beautiful and pure.

"The Korporation has been working on it for," Kin says, "what must be, let's say, at least three or four generations now."

"The general notion," Sir Windsor VI adds, "lies in the *Theory of Reflexivity* and *Kritikal Rhetorik*. Long before any of *us*, MkKerrow had been one of the first to denote that '*absence* is as important as *presence*.' By improving the absence of forethought, inner peace may thus be achieved. Premeditation may be replaced by *skripted aktions* — much like programming one of those old *komputers* from the twentieth century."

"Brilliant," Conquergood mutters. "And you can't figure out what's wrong with these children?"

"Nope," Kin replies. "The blasted mice won't say or do a thing."

"We believe the problem lies in the nervous system, a sort of paralysis of speech," Sir Windsor VI adds. He dictates a few e-notes into his K-pad. When he finishes, he places the hand-held device into his lab pocket. "But tests thus far have proved fruitless. We'll have to do some additional examinations on them later this week. But we are, after all, on a deadline. We only have a few weeks and we need to have something to present to the Korporate Ministers."

"Perhaps," Conquergood mumbles. But when the doktors turn their heads to face his, he has to steady his voice to be heard clearly. "Perhaps these children are thinking. You know — in deep meditation."

"*Thinking?*" Kin stutters. "*Kognitive reflektion*, do you say? Is that right?"

Johnson belts out a few seconds of laughter, bends his neck slightly about, and then immediately desists, retreating back into his work.

"Yes," Conquergood replies, "thinking."

"Now that is a novel idea," Sir Windsor VI says. He abruptly removes his K-pad and begins scribbling on the e-skreen. "We haven't done any neural tests for higher brain performance."

"Johnson!" shouts Kin.

"Yes, sir?"

"Order up five jumbo-sized neuroimages — *pronto*, our *amiga!*" Kin grins wildly at his young kolleague who simply frowns and continues writing on his K-pad. "Thinking," Kin mutters to himself. "Thinking before speaking? Might it be possible? That simple?"

"Don't know," Conquergood replies. "I could be wrong. When it comes to science and biology and medicine, I'm clueless. I just figured 'man is the helper and interpreter of nature.' Thinking makes the most sense to me."

Kin and Sir Windsor VI glare over at the new Turnkey Specialist.

"Turnkey Specialist, ha!" Johnson belts out.

"Johnson, shut your trap!"

"Where did you learn that piece of philosophy?" Sir Windsor VI asks. His brow turns downward to Conquergood, who takes a step backward.

"From the K-net," he answers. "I've been doing some research in my free time. Fabulous thing Korporate knowledge is."

"It certainly is," replies Sir Windsor VI, eyeing the Turnkey Specialist with a newly undecided interest. "Haven't you had any desire in the millions of virtual games able to be instantly linked to the mind and senses?"

"We are," Johnson inserts, his eye-glasses with endless formulas flashing upwards to Conquergood. "Add us as a friendly kolleague and we'll play the brand new multi-hundred hook-up where the goal of the game is to —"

"Johnson?" Kin says. "Enough of that voracious prodigality. Jerome is the preservation of integrity, so don't go and ruin our Turnkey Specialist with those mindless games."

"Yes, sir."

"Oh, and shut that trap! Another word and, *by Korp*, it's over for that little heritage!"

Johnson buries his acne covered face back to the e-skreen and loses himself to the research found on no less than twenty-two three-dimensional multi-layered e-skreens.

Conquergood winces, slightly embarrassed. "Can't say I've had a chance to play any games yet."

"No fretting," Sir Windsor VI says as he pats Conquergood on the shoulder. "We find the fifteen-level chess relaxing with two other participants, especially over a nice bottle of Società Gin. We believe the number of maximum players stands at seven players simultaneously, but soon to be upgraded to thirteen. The other games seem, well *uhm*, downright frivolous. The puerile still play many of the virtual games they have nowadays. Why, just the other day, we witnessed that twenty-player gardening game famously known as *The Green Thumb of Tomorrow* in the substandard three dimensions, and believe this, they were planting daisies and tulips and the like of all things earthly. Simply treasonous! We simply mustn't afford sympathy with such venal employees. Mindless workers lost in the habits of gardening and planting by the flutter of their eyes upon the new e-skreens."

"Better than using thumbs," Johnson mumbles.

Kin stands staring at the five females with his fists firmly rooted in his pockets. "Johnson!" he shouts once again, breaking from a hole in his cryptic concentration, "Why didn't we think of thinking?!"

Johnson wobbles, nearly falling from his stool. Without an utterance, the lab technician pushes up his spectacles and dives back into his research without losing a thought to the e-skreen.

"That's enough of these five little mice for one day." Kin steps over to the tele-k-skreen and orders, "Lower shields."

When the five girls are once more hidden from view, Conquergood eases a sigh, holding his head and stomach.

Kin turns and moves back to the Turnkey Specialist. "You must be exhausted with all that thinking you've been doing. Your lekturers, though, always said you were brilliant, Jerome."

Sir Windsor VI raises a thin eyebrow, hand firmly attached to his Korporate *Mountblank* e-pen.

Kin continues speaking. "Turnkey Specialist, by Korp! The rumors are certainly unquestionable, bona fide and veritable. Johnson, the rumors are true. Kebir *is* a genius. He's the one who's going to save the Korporation. And on top of all that, after all is said and done, he might make you an unemployed *strayer*. You need to step up your game a bit, Jo-Jo Johnson."

"Yes, sir," replies Johnson, without realizing he has said anything at all, more of a reflex than a forethought.

"As for you, man-wonder, brain-child," states Kin unwaveringly, taking Conquergood by the arm and leading him down the aisle and back to the *sekurity* doors to the k-line, "Let's get you back to your apartment for a nice rest. Because of you, we now have some real work to do tonight."

As Conquergood steps back into the k-line to return to his living quarters, he suddenly realizes that the weight of his years was heavy enough to keep him from soaring free of the Korporation and all its kin.

I
The Gift

Two or four days, who is to say for how long, slink by for Conquergood in his isolated apartment. He does not go to the Korporate Kanteen. Instead, he eats alone in private. The Korporate chefs prepare his meals and there is no satisfaction as the time in the kanteen with Klaire. He wants to see her again. But after the incident in the Korporate Lab with Kin and Sir Windsor VI, he cannot go about risking another mistake. He has lost count of his steps. There have been many steps to count from the moment he stepped into the Korporate Kompound, and Conquergood knows the kameras are watching, studying his every action. Even though it was but for a moment, the pride and vanity which so often fills, blindingly, the self and eyes with deceitful practices had taken control. He faltered. He out moved his own maneuvers. Conquergood isn't a genius. He is not the Korporate savior. He is not their chosen one. Nope. He can never be that. The days in his darkened apartment, away from the Korporate members and entertainers, allows him space and time to gather his senses, to refocus, possibly to reduplicate.

Conquergood stands at the edge of the large bay window; his forehead perched against the flexiglass as he stares downward into the enclosure created by the four inner walls of Korporate Headquarters. The tele-k-skreen comes alive with the concurrent image of Klaire. She does what she has been doing for the past few days she's trying to reach Conquergood.

Remaining by the bay window, he listens to the smooth inflections of her language, the sincerity driven by compassion within the confines of her communication. The context is clear, regardless of the content. She does not resemble the others. To him, Klaire is alive.

"Jerome," Klaire states from the tele-k-skreen. Her blonde curls fill the e-skreen. "Why won't you speak to me? I really want to see you again."

Why does she try so hard? Conquergood knows relationships, especially between Korporate members, never last. The Korporation owns everything. They own the world, and even, as it seems to Conquergood, they own the souls of men and women. And that is what has become of society.

The world became the very thing that Conquergood feared it would become. The world is no longer made of beautiful things — except for Klaire, perhaps she alone is beautiful — but the world is an ugly world filled with tele-k-skreens, rudimentary jobs, the draconian Korporate Guard, and the endless supply of Korporate nanotube posters constantly muttering the Korporate shibboleth that the almighty KE is supreme and that they alone are holy and faithful. And the world continues to spin around that great fire ball ninety-three million miles away and no one does a damn thing to change. *We* have allowed ourselves to be driven into automatons with machine hearts and machine minds. *We* have allowed ourselves to be manipulated into cyclical causes and effects. *We* have been molded into the image of *our* new god — and it is not at all what he had wanted for himself or for his twin brother.

He wants a world, a truly free world, whatever that means, to be united in the desire of self-actualization. Where a babe can be born into any family, rich or poor, receive equal edukation and be allowed to shape his or her own destiny. That is a global culture worth living for.

But now Conquergood knows that is not the world he lives in. He lives in a Korporate world where the Korporate Elite control the very thoughts and desires of the population — and *destiny*, well if there ever was such a word to describe the ability for men and women and children to choose their own paths of progress in their lives — there is no longer such a word in the Korporate vocabulary. Destiny has become obsolete. Vanished — poof! Dust and stardust. Yeah — that's what destiny has become: the ashes of dead dreams.

Furthermore, the Korporation has been right about one thing, however. The world has changed, is changing, and if you don't keep up, then you'll be left behind. The matter of business precedes all things material and spiritual. The Korporation demands absolute allegiance.

"Come on, newbie," beckons Klaire's voice, filling up the insides of the motionless apartment. "How about we take a walk in the Garden?"

Conquergood's palm presses against the flexiglass and he gazes downward at the arboretum, a lush green garden filled with trees and bushes, and then his gaze reaches up to the sky. Cumulus clouds roll by without notice; images present themselves as though they are a herd of extinct elephants standing frozen — no more hills like giant elephants; no more poets to preach of Nature; no more Walden's Pond. He wants to consume the freshness of the air and devour the intensity of the sun's rays through his skin, a flesh now paled by countless hours in his apartment watching KV or searching through the K-net for answers to an endless array of questions. Outside, Nature had been the key which once unlocked the doors inside the soul. Conquergood dashes across the room to the tele-k-skreen by his bed.

"Hey there," he answers. "Don't go. Please."

"For a second there," Klaire speaks back, "I thought you were unemployed." She's smiling and her blue eyes grow bigger in favor of Conquergood's strong jawline and full lips. He refuses to be shaved and has a slight beard forming. He feels as though she is admiring the presence of hair on his manly face.

"Not unemployed," he says. He feels glad to see her before him now. Klaire's face. Granted, over the last several days, Conquergood has replayed her video messages to the point of absolute memorization, but there is nothing like the immediate moments before him on the tele-k-skreen. "I just needed some rest. I plan to start work today in the Turnkey Department right after lunch."

"We can go out now, if you like?"

"I'd like that very much."

A romantic pause of mutual acceptance comes to a flutter between the two tele-k-skreens.

"I'll be up in about five minutes," Klaire says. "Then we can go down together."

"See you soon."

The tele-k-skreen blanks itself for a moment when the call ends but is immediately replaced by the Korporate Seal roving from corner to corner on the e-skreen.

Roughly five minutes later, Klaire, in her bright yellow Korporate Edukated attire, appears at Conquergood's apartment door. Together they step over to the k-line, hop into the portal, and descend to ground level. The ride lasts for eighteen seconds but it feels much longer.

Out in the open, Conquergood and Klaire stroll freely side by side. Conquergood has not been out of his apartment in some days and it dreams true again, home in a word, relief.

The Garden of the Gods has a multitude of trees: cedars, cypresses, elms, junipers, oaks, poplars, red maples, and willows, to list but a few; and there are a variety of rose hybrids — blue roses, *krimson* roses, lavender roses, pink roses, violet roses, white roses, yellow roses, and dozens more.

"Roses are the official Korporate flower," Klaire remarks. "We find them extremely delightful."

"Truth is beauty," Conquergood says. "So, these roses must be full of truth, unlike the Korporation."

"We shouldn't say things like that, dear. *We* should be grateful for what the Korporation has given us. *We* should be thankful for knowing what our lives are like here on the inside, safe and sound, compared to what our lives could be like outside these walls. And such thoughts, of the outside world, frighten me. You should know this better than any of us."

The two Korporate members meander a moment in quiet thought around some orange grandiflora roses.

Over by the four walls are iron trellises, completely consumed by tea roses. Several stone benches encircle an artificial pond with a rose fountain in the center. Everything seems to be in its geometrically precise place.

Conquergood looks up to discover a transparent dome enshrining the warm Garden in its tropical climate, and outside the firm, relentless hand of what used to be October blanketing itself over the surreal and docile Garden in eternal springtime.

"What're you thinking about?" Klaire says.

Conquergood sees his shadow intermingling with Klaire's on the ground in front of them, and he tells her, "The shadow attached to me is a reminder that I am here — here now with you. This shadow can only be if I am. Without me, there is no shadow."

"I never thought about shadows in that way before," Klaire says, holding onto Conquergood's hand. "Tell me something else. Something that means something special to you. I want to know what inspires you."

From Pope's essay, without really thinking about what he's saying, Conquergood recites to Klaire:

> Hope springs eternal
> in the human breast;
> Man never is,
> but always to be blest.
>
> The soul, uneasy, and
> confined from home,
> rests and expatiates
> in a life to come.

Conquergood continues to walk side by side with Klaire, this stranger who seeks his company. He's wearing his sandals and is careful with each step he takes over the lush lawn. Klaire's sandals dangle in her hands while her bare feet crunch the green blades of grass, singing the songs of themselves as unified and natural; and her toes, like baby elephant teeth, chop a path below.

"What have you been doing lately besides resting?" Klaire asks. "Dreaming of me?"

"I've been doing a little research," he replies. He believes he sees a robin in the bushes but it has been only a stray rose fluttering in the artificial breeze.

"What kind of research?"

The two make their way to a stone bench, Korporate Seal engraved, and sit. Conquergood takes the liberty of removing his feet from his sandals and allows his bare toes to mingle in the crisp lawn beneath him. At either side of the stone bench are Cherokee roses — *rosa laevigata.*

"Oh, I've been doing a little of this and a little of that," he answers. He enjoys the cold grass blades between his toes. He cannot say what he is doing. He has never done it before.

"I need to tell you something," Klaire says. Her hands clutch the stone bench as she leans slightly forward, face downward watching her toes gently and playfully removing the flora.

"No, you don't," Conquergood says. He doesn't want to know. "I don't need to know. Ignorance is a beautiful and powerful thing sometimes."

"Don't you care others will know something about me that you don't?"

"Why?" Conquergood replies. He doesn't care to know anything more. He knows enough of the world, of the Korporation and of himself. He turns and stares off at the surrounding four walls covered in sprawling roses and then he fixes his gaze on the above dome, imprisoning the sky above.

"Knowledge can distort truth," he says. "At the time we don't know it's happening, or even if it does or will, but it does without us having to know. Ignorance has a sort of power, too. What others know about you or about me isn't everything there is to know. It isn't truth. It can't be. I don't need to know anything more about you. I don't care to know."

Klaire lifts her head from the downward position, eyes ablaze against Conquergood's adamant refusal of knowledge, and stares at him as if truly seeing the man for the first time, as though chalk has been wiped from a blackboard to erase the answers which had been there the whole time riddling her life with too much information.

"Just because we say we *know* something," Conquergood says, as though listening to the flora surrounding him, "it doesn't mean we know what should be known. The natural world around us knows things we can never come to know, no matter how long and hard we try to study it. This happens mostly because when we know everything, we can't take the time to know anything else." He pauses for a breath. He turns and faces Klaire, cheeks flushed with red splotches. "The only thing I want to know is how you truly feel and what you truly think in all that flesh which hides it from me."

Klaire's eyes drop from Conquergood's and onto his well-rounded lips that have become wet and plump from too much oratory. She leans inward and kisses him, and he automatically draws her into his arms. Knowing, for them, has become much more than words in a language of communication. Wisdom is the seeing without seeing, the feeling without feeling, and the believing without believing.

Klaire and Conquergood break the embrace when they hear a portal door of a k-line open. At the opposite end of the Garden, three Korporate members — two red-headed women and a gray-haired man — step from the portal door. They have on black kimono robes and they linger for a moment by the portal door as they take in their surroundings. One woman offers the other two the usual thin opium cigars. After a brief ceremonial lighting of their *poppy tears*, the Korporate members walk and smoke with a constant chatter among them.

"I must be going," Conquergood says. "I don't want to be late for my first day on the job."

Klaire uses her thumb and forefinger to wipe Conquergood's lips dry. "Go ahead," she says. "We'll see each other tonight for dinner."

"How about we meet about seven?"

"Let's make it six, darling."

Promptly at one an eskort, who's wearing a black kimono, arrives. Conquergood is mindlessly staring out the bay window once more thinking of Klaire. The KV is turned off and the bell tolling at the door spreads loosely throughout the apartment like liquid mercury. Conquergood has waited for this moment all his life and now it is happening and he is ready.

"Ready yet, Jerome?" the eskort calls from the doorway. "Today's our big day. Are we up for it?" The sentences are flat, unlike the way Klaire and Kin and Sir Windsor VI speak. Conquergood has grown more aware and accustomed to the transitions between the hard and soft voices, the transitions in dialect, of the Korporation and its deadness.

"As ready as we'll ever be," replies Conquergood from the bay window.

"Just follow," orders the eskort. He turns and proceeds down the hall. Conquergood manages to catch up to the eskort with a few hurried paces.

"Are we another doktor?" Conquergood asks. "We mean because of the black robe and all?"

Heading for the nearest k-line, the two men's strides are hurried and equaled in proportion.

"No," answers the eskort in an abrupt voice. "*We* are in the Turnkey Department. *We* will be working together for the next few weeks."

"Working together for the next few weeks?" Again, Conquergood has meant it as a question but the eskort fails to catch the rising intonation.

"Exactly," the man replies in a drill-like voice. "After that we won't be working together anymore."

"We hope that's not true," Conquergood says, half to himself. Both men step into the k-line portal.

"T166-38-13," the eskort says methodically into the tele-k-skreen. "Remember the *kode* for next time."

"Certainly." Conquergood wishes some noise can rise from inside the portal, but only silence fills the small confines of the k-line. "Do we have a label?"

"*Kall* us the Superior," the eskort says. "But *we* will have too much work for any chit-chat. Labels are for the babes. Names are for the under-*edukated*."

The Superior's voice unexpectedly deepens and it surprises Conquergood. The eskort, his kolleague, his manager, his superior is immensely serious and Conquergood is surprised he didn't notice it sooner. Or if he had noticed it, he believes it was a case of *passionlessness*. The mood thickens in the portal, going from a lackadaisical feeling into an intensely focused energy.

"*We* have a *projekt* to finish in less than one month's time and there's no time for silly games. The projekt was handed down from the top with the utmost urgency. *We kannot* fail the Korporation. At any *kost we* must *suk*-seed. Understood?"

"Understood," replies Conquergood obediently. The inward steps Conquergood is counting are becoming shorter and faster. He keeps counting, paying closer attention. A chance, he knows, will come and he must take it when it does.

The portal door to the k-line opens to an empty vestibule. Above two large *sekurity* doors in front of Conquergood is a white sign posted with the bold black lettering:

KORPORATE KONTROL

The Superior marches through the vestibule and commands into a tele-k-skreen mounted next to the *sekurity* doors,

"Turnkey — Alpha ends Omega, K-11."

The *sekurity* doors slide open. The two men step through the doors and into the main egg-shaped work area, approximately sixty by forty feet.

Surprisingly, unlike the brightly lit Korporate Labs, the Turnkey Department is considerably dark. The lights are off and Conquergood grows uneasy as he walks inside. The *sekurity* doors shut behind with a solid thump.

In the epicenter of the room, a holo-globe replicating every minuscule detail of the Earth rotates three feet from off the floor. The e-globe is six feet in diameter and about as high. The e-sphere glows bright enough to light the center of the room and causes a penumbra to fill the rest. At the corners of the room, one cannot tell if someone is standing there or not. Conquergood becomes, however, instinctually aware of someone watching him from the dark hidden places.

The Superior faces the e-globe and stares at North Amerika.

"Freeze rotation," he says.

The spinning e-globe halts. Conquergood joins the Superior next to the e-sphere.

"Do we know what we are seeing?" the Superior asks.

"We do," Conquergood replies.

"Then *kan* we find and point to the *lokation* of Korporate Headquarters?"

Conquergood points to the north-eastern portion of the United Subsidiaries of the Ameliorated.

"*Korrect*," the Superior says, satisfied with his new Turnkey Specialist. "Now, show us where New Philadelphia, our nation's *kapital*, is *lokated*?"

Conquergood correctly locates and points a finger to the area on the hovering e-globe.

"Good," says the Superior. "Now let's get ready to alter the face of Korporate earth."

"Alter?" Conquergood looks over at the Superior, whose eyes reflect two small e-globes, brightly lit. "We want to alter New Philadelphia?"

"The Korporation has an agenda, Turnkey," the Superior says, not heeding the Turnkey Specialist's misguided confusion. The Superior folds his arms across his chest and continues to analyze the e-globe with an acute sense of awareness of the agenda. "For a *krisis* such as this, we would normally and gracefully use *biologikal* weapons, like the infamous koronavirus of 2019. Much the same way we did when we later *suk*-sessfully wiped out over four billion living in a bloated world of poverty. In our hallmark and memorable achievement, we brought the employment rate to ninety-seven per cent worldwide, and we did it almost overnight. Now that is business we are willing to live by."

Staring at the e-globe and remembering a few words from an ancient book still rarely read, Conquergood mutters, "Ashes to ashes. Dust to dust."

"Now listen up, Turnkey," the Superior says. "Do we see those red e-dots moving in a pattern similar to migration heading for our nation's kapital?"

Walking around the motionless-hovering e-globe, Conquergood sees hundreds of the red e-dots from all over the e-globe trudging toward U.S.A and amassing at New Philadelphia.

Large red e-blots appear in the regions of NATO, a nomenclature once known for the 1949 North Atlantic Treaty Organization but which later evolved in 2147 — after the Korporation was elected President — to represent the New Amerikas Treaty Organization, comprised of the North and South Amerikan territories.

More of the red e-blots also appear across the Eurozone — which controls the territories of Europe and Afrika, but now most often understood by the acronym NERO — the New Eurozone Reunified Organization — since 2149.

Finally, a few of the red e-dots are spotted in the regions of Indoasia and Oceanika, the latest addition to the Korporate Unified Lands since 2152.

The four Korporate Kommonwealths are handsomely displayed on the e-globe in front of Conquergood and the Superior. The Korporation did what none other could: the Korporation conquered and unified the known world.

"What are these yellow e-dots?" Conquergood asks. The red e-blots are far outnumbered by the yellow ones to a count of sixty-three to one.

"Oh, the yellow ones," the Superior says. "Nothing to worry about. The little yellow e-dots represent the lokations of each subsidiary the Korporation owns. Just touch the hologram on the lighted e-dot and there is all we need to know."

The Superior touches one of the yellow e-dots within Indoasia and immediately a side e-skreen illuminates out of the e-globe. The image resembles a tele-k-skreen and one only has to speak directions.

"Open source in," the Superior says, "let's see, how about the kanteen?"

"Fine," says Conquergood, watching closely to every maneuver the Superior makes.

"Open source — Korporate kanteen," says the Superior. Then he reads a number on a list on the top right side of the floating e-skreen. "Open source number sixteen thousand, four hundred and six."

Immediately another *holographik* e-skreen pops up over the pre-existing one.

Through a live feed, Conquergood spies a handful of Korporate members in Indoasia sullenly eating their dinners.

"There's not many there now *bekause* of the late shift." The Superior reads the digital e-klock running on the e-skreen. "Yup, past three in the morning over there. But as they say, the Korporation never sleeps. *Klose* source e-skreens."

The command is instantly carried out and both *holographik* e-skreens zip back into the yellow e-dot in Indoasia on the e-globe.

"We follow every detail to insure proficiency. The Korporation is a prime model for minimum waste and is highly *effektive* when it *koms* to maximizing profits."

"We're flummoxed," mumbles Conquergood. "Who knew such proficiency was possible."

"And rightly should be," the Superior says. "Now let's remember, New Philadelphia is our primary target. As we have noticed, Turnkey, the red e-dots are of extreme importance. The red e-dots represent the opposition. Traitors to our beloved system. In just over ten days the opposition known as Grassroots will be gathering in NATO's kapital. There are reports, however, of a separate faktion — The Lighthouse — will be attending as well. The opposition believe they will be immune and safe in New Philadelphia bekause of the Treaty Akkords of seventy-three. Wrong are these fools. They won't even know what hit them."

Consumed by the e-globe's sinister incandescence, the Superior releases an unexpected grin of pleasure and sadistic satisfaction.

Conquergood never once considered the Korporate agenda as the one revealed now before him. Eliminating the target means eliminating the Kapital. Eliminating the Kapital means total domination. Total domination means an even greater world peace than what the Korporation has already achieved. The here and the now, the beginning and the end, Korporate Kontrol demands supreme allegiance and absolute power.

"Turnkey," says the Superior, turning his face from the hologram and over to Conquergood, who has stepped away from the e-globe and into the shadows of the room. "The Korporation needs us now more than ever. We are at the verge of *komplete viktory* or it will be our arrant defeat. Are we ready to serve the Korporation for the sake of the Korporation?"

Conquergood believes his inner spirit — the one which apparently belongs to the Korporation — is growing and shrinking, fighting itself, in uttermost turmoil of itself. He no longer holds any question as to what a Korporate Turnkey Specialist does; all that is clear to him, as clear as the darkness that thrives inside this room of planned horrors.

"We are," Conquergood replies to the Superior. "We are ready to serve the Korporation for the sake of the Korporation."

"Then let us get started, shall we?"

TWO

VIII
A Korporate Rally

Upon his order, at precisely 20:05, the ancient Hindu *Aum* — the king mantra, the cosmic sound — begins playing through the auditory system connected to the KV. Conquergood reclines upon pillows propped against the headboard of his bed, where he stares at his white robe lying disheveled in the hall alongside the yellow robe. But it is the coolness of the white sheets across his lean muscular body — Klaire has been a motivating factor to get himself into shape through many hours in the Korporate gymnasium — that have given Conquergood a confident feeling of repose, reminding him of a time when he once visited the beach many years ago — *how long?* — he does not remember — it feels like ages.

The frothy surf that day had climbed high as he dove beneath the crashing waves. For him, swimming was a battle fighting for a power of control often difficult to master and sustain — *it came down to instincts*. Afterwards, he remembers collapsing on the clean wet sand, the small waves flowing up and around his exposed body, nude and exhausted. There were never any of those Dark Shadows out that far from Old York. Conquergood, free and reflective, lay exposed to the world and to the universe.

Lying in bed with Klaire now comes close to that experience on the beach; but with the woman, unlike the bathing from the ocean waves, he feels guilty, tarnished, dismantled from all that was naturally holy in the self. He has made love to this woman and as her lips come together in her sleep and she puffs out soft gasps of air in the sounds of *ppeewwhh*, steady and constant and rhythmic, Conquergood holds her close and he believes she has been destined to his arms alone. Her past no longer matters. His past no longer matters. They lie alone and the world continues to spin — *and he's the better man for having her by his side*. Conquergood holds Klaire close and the two heartbeats are swiftly becoming a unified rhythm as old as the song of love itself. Old tunes, however, are old for a reason.

Conquergood's chest heaves upward, with Klaire's mounted head firmly planted, and then his chest cascades downward. Her head weighs heavy over his heart. His breathing is slightly contracted but he doesn't dare disturb her. He wants to continue to watch her sleep. And he so does. He watches her sleep as he listens to the great Aum.

It was his first time, and for him the experience they shared remains endless, as though there would always be more of her to the end of time itself. He holds her warm body tight to his. A few hours ago, each of them had cried out in uncontrollable pleasure and moaned for more, for the ecstasy to go on and on and on until their bodies felt like breaking into wonderful pieces, egg shells of collapsed delight. The passion, he recalls, surged and surged into a final exhaustive defeat. When they had finished, something was added between them, made complete; Conquergood feels somehow more of a person. Yet, he still has not told her about the Turnkey position and what is to become of him or of New Philadelphia or of the Korporation. The world, he believes, will learn once more to take care of itself — *just as it always has had to do in the past.*

When Klaire, divinely young, had come to his door at six, he became overwhelmed by the sight of her golden hair upon her bird-like shoulders. Her blue eyes and curved hips spoke of something new to him — *something feminine and delicate and raw.* She flew into his arms and he caught her and kissed her as though her body had no end.

Sitting up in bed now with Klaire in his arms, he listens to the *elektro-akoustik transducers* in each of the four corners fill his bedroom with the ancient mantra of the long-ignored Buddhist Aum. Conquergood meditates on whether or not he should tell Klaire about the Korporate agenda that will soon be carried out — *should she know?* Motionless, he wrestles with the idea against the eternally-sacred Aum — the symbolic sound that Joseph Campbell had centuries ago explained could be "the message that God is within a person and without." Klaire's chest, meanwhile, settles itself to his stomach and their interwoven legs wind more tightly as one — *not quite a ouroboros, but close enough.*

"You awake?" he asks.

Klaire's head lifts a little and a few mashed curls untangle and fall and tickle Conquergood's tightening abs.

"Yeah, sure," she says. "Why?"

"No reason," he answers. "I didn't feel like being alone."

"I'm here," she says. Her moves back to his chest. "You'll never be alone as long as we're together."

Conquergood can feel her eyelashes blinking against his skin. It reminds him of another time outside the Korporation — *another time dripping to the forefront of wet memory:*

In Ward 7's Old Central Park, Conquergood had encountered a swirling multitude of monarch butterflies. Only for a few seconds, the butterflies had gathered around him and formed a whirling cocoon. He had stood entrenched by their silky wings — *like in bed with Klaire* — and he dared not move. He often recognizes when a special moment comes to his life. When Time — *or the energy and flow of that intangible but ever poignant system illustrated by ruin and decay* — becomes fragile and still, Conquergood knows he should pay closer attention to the natural world around him. One of those times happened in the Old Central Park with the monarch butterflies. The other time is happening as he remains holding Klaire, uncertain of their two fates — *and all the steps he has counted have become lost, muddled and gathered as one.*

And it is Klaire who, head upon Conquergood's chest, sighs and says, "I can feel your heart beating."

All Conquergood can do is reply in earnest, "I cannot. I cannot."

Both of them soon drift off into a solipsistic doze and do not wake until the morning.

On *Kdayf* at seven in the evening, the Korporation holds a rally in the main auditorium. Excluding the Kompanions, all the Korporate members are there. Each member is coordinated once again by the color of the departments they work in, and everyone mumbles with fevered anticipation as the energy builds in the great Hall.

The amphitheater is abuzz with gossip because a handful of members are the only ones who know what the rally is about. On center stage, where Conquergood had a short time ago been de-named and had given his acceptance speech, a black velvet drape with a white Korporate Seal covers a large domed object.

Murmurs are growing in the galleries, especially among the green-clad attendants. The Korporate Rally is one of the first since the highly expected delivery of the newest edition of the Korporate required K-pad, which in only a few well remembered minds had been the seventy-ninth version of the device.

Down in front, the Elders appear pleased with the upcoming attraction. Conquergood and Klaire sit nearby in the section for honored guests, three rows from the stage. A nervous pit in Conquergood's stomach grows as the ceremony delays itself for the most revered of the Korporate staff, the holy *Kleriks*.

Conquergood knows what's coming. Kin and Sir Windsor VI have not stopped talking about it during lunch sessions in the Korporate kanteen for the past four days.

"Marvelous!" Kin would exclaim across a bowl of vanilla *ice-kream* and a mug of hot Korporate koffee. His mustache would dance a little livelier than usual. "She's spectacular!"

"Who?" Klaire had asked. "Does Kinny have a new lover?"

"Wait and see, dear girl," Kin would spout. "Just wait and see. In a few days, miracles will happen. Grand miracles! Never before seen. Just wait and see!"

"That little advice the other day, Jerome," Sir Windsor VI had said, "proved to be most helpful. Spot on."

"Advice?" asked Klaire. "Advice about what?"

"That's right," Kin had answered. He twirled his mustache with one hand and extended the mug of koffee in the other, a kind of toast to fame. The mug came to meet the mustache, brisk greetings were made. When Kin finished taking a drink, he continued, "Mister Turnkey Specialist over there did what *we* doktors couldn't do. Mister Sherlock once again has risen from the grave, tested time immemorial and solved the mystery of the two lummoxes who failed the Great Sphinx's riddle."

Klaire beamed from within and slid a hand under the lunch table and onto one of Conquergood's quivering hands.

"Don't be so hard on yourself, Mister Know-It-All," Klaire responded to Kin. "You two would've figured it out sooner or later."

"Later is probably nearer to the truth," Sir Windsor VI had replied. "Either way, we are indebted to Jerome here for the role he has played in the development of the Korporation's latest advancement. Here, here!"

The good doktor raised his small teacup with hot poppy tea and warm Lagavulin, as did Kin and Klaire with their respective drinks of koffee and water, and all three had toasted with sincere admiration their Turnkey Specialist.

Now in the buzzing commencement, Conquergood remains silent while Klaire huddles alongside, her arm around his. Reverberating deep within his mind and out before his eyes are the words spoken by Sir Windsor VI: "indebted for the role he has played."

What had Conquergood done? How will a few choice words spoken with pride in the Korporate lab turn out? *What does it matter?*

He, like the four hundred plus Korporate members gathered for the unveiling of the new Korporate product, wait for answers.

After about another sixteen more minutes of restlessness, Kin and Sir Windsor VI step up and onto the wide stage. Following them are thirteen hooded kleriks, dressed in sky-blue robes that drag upon the floor. The kleriks' robes have a *krimson* rose emblem stitched on the back and a white Korporate Seal on the front. From beneath the thirteen hoods, gray masks can be perceived — *Conquergood would later report in his skripts* — as though the masks hid the faces of his forgotten fears.

The thirteen silent kleriks position themselves in a semi-circle around the domed object covered by a red velvet drape at center stage. Kin and Sir Windsor VI approach the front of the stage where twin transparent *mikrophones*, thin as wires, are ready for their grand announcement.

Kin, a duplicate of some forgotten Roman philanthropist, waves frantically to the audience. Cheers rise and surge and Kin urges the hoopla to grow louder. *More!*

Sir Windsor VI holds himself silent and perfectly erect, hands clasped before him, face drawn in a dignified right triangle. The tall, thin doktor comes across as an odd sculpture more than he does a living, breathing man.

"*E Pluribus Unum!*" chants Kin heroically. "*E Pluribus Unum!*"

With great applause, the crowd returns the Korporate motto, "*E Pluribus Unum! E Pluribus Unum!*"

"Welcome, my dear, affectionate, humbled Korporate members!" shouts Kin. The blusterous voice rings in everyone's ears. "Welcome! Welcome all to the Oasis of the Real. *Annuit Cœptis!*"

One of the Elders in the front row gives a few hand signals to advise Kin to lower his volume and enthusiasm and move the *mikrophone* away from his mouth. Kin nods in understanding, mustache booming around two bright red cheeks.

"The Korporate sesquipedalian is at it again," jokes Klaire. "We'll be here all night."

Conquergood nods but remains focused on the veiled dome and its hidden contents, where an intense energy draws his vision inward into its mystery of being.

"Excuse me," Kin inserts into the *mikrophone* with less volume than before. "We are gathered here on this grand eve to rectify past mistakes and failures. For hundreds of years our brothers and our sisters have attempted to achieve what the Korporation has *finally* achieved. Philosophers and sages through the ages — Plato, Aristotle, Erasmus, Lucretius, Quintus Ennius, Cicero, and on and on — until tonight — and prophets, such as Jesus and Mohammed and Buddha and scores of forgotten others — all have endeavored to bring peace to *ourkind* and to alter the warring soul and shape it into a peaceful one without limits. As we well know, for the most part, these simple-minded beings before our time failed us; the Korporation, however, our beloved and most honored benefactor, has taken the liberty to set ancient principles to work in the modern world. How, we might ask?"

"*When* is more like it?" Klaire mumbles to Conquergood.

They share a brief laugh, and he squeezes her hand which rests in her lap.

"The future of business is no longer the beloved ecosystem," Kin rattles on. "The Korporation, all by its lonesome, cured global warming by removing cars from off the streets, and by planting wind-farms out in the oceans, and also by our sheer brilliance to make the world a better place for us. The Earth has healed itself through the guidance and great understanding of the Korporation. However, the world shall go on living when we shall not."

As Kin speaks, thick bolts of saliva shoot from his lips and across the stage and down into the front aisle, where his spittle lands at the feet of the Elders. Sir Windsor VI shakes his slim head in embarrassment.

"The future of business is the salvation of the Korporation," Kin says. "With a cleaner world before us, we must learn to change and to unleash our mortality and our eternity within. A new heaven is now among us, but our eternity still eludes our feeble grasp."

He pauses to take a breath, his flabby stomach heaving. The enthralled audience hangs upon every syllable as if it will unlock their bodies and allow their souls to fly away into everlasting glory.

"Tonight is the night," Kin bellows, with renewed steam, "that shall change the Korporation for the next millennia, if not beyond all times. Tonight, the Korporation will reveal what none has ever accomplished in over sixty thousand years. Tonight is the beginning to it all. Tonight is the Alpha to our Omega. Tonight, we shall be born anew! Now has arrived the final era of our Korporate song. Tonight, justice and honored rules return. The almighty order of the ages is born afresh. Now a new lineage is sent down from heaven on high. *Novus Ordo Seclorum!*"

One clap sounds from an Elder and then a tidal wave of applause follows, cheers building upon itself and echoing and reverberating off the walls of the auditorium. Confidence rises in Kin and he manages to silence the crowd with a few exaggerated waves of his hands.

"Let us not postpone our revelation any longer," Kin roars, his hands high above his head now covered with huge drops of sweat. "Let us not postpone what we have waited our entire lives to see." He turns to the thirteen kleriks standing alongside the veiled-domed object. "Please do us the honor and remove the veil from our eyes so that we may truly see our future."

The thirteen kleriks simultaneously step up to the red velvet drape and pull thirteen gold cords. The covering cascades to the stage floor while gasps snowball throughout the Korporate members, with only some weak-scattered applause.

Just as Conquergood predicted, inside the dome of flexiglass, breathing holes at the top and out of view, is one of the five subjects from the Korporate Lab sitting with legs crossed, hands on knees, as if in suspended meditation.

Conquergood's mind fills with running images of the black-and-white photograph which holds the inflamed monk — *ever burning, burning, burning* — no more to suffer the heartbreaks of this world.

When Conquergood's mind settles, he witnesses subject Number Three — her flawless black body still wrapped in *e-kloth* — unaltered from the time he had first seen her in the lab until now during this hallowed moment of revelations from the two Korporate doktors.

In awe, the audience looks back and forth between Kin and Sir Windsor VI, who both rather foolishly allow several uneventful minutes to pass, draining the energy and excitement into a dreadful pit of lethargy.

An attendant finally erupts and shouts down from the gallery, "Why won't *the mouse* move?!"

Before anyone can reply, a lekturer yells out and adds, "Make the black mouse say something!"

Kin stands aghast, baffled, huffing and puffing. He stares over at his retreating kolleague. Out of range of the *mikrophone*, Kin tells his friend, "Why don't you say something. You've said about as much as a dead horse. Speak up, twig legs!"

"Lady Lemming in need of help once more," Sir Windsor VI replies with complete composure. He glances from Kin to the crowd to Conquergood and Klaire. "Very well, then."

Sir Windsor VI moves closer and starts speaking into the *mikrophone.* "If we may have our undivided attention once more for just a few moments," he says, quieting the audience. "The Korporate experiment before us is a prime model of harmony. Nothing may deter It from the immeasurable depths of Its endless meditation. To answer the obvious — why doesn't It speak — is that It is processing data at speeds unheard of in today's Korporate Komputers. It does not speak since to do so would mean It must cease Its cerebral ponderings, even if but for a slice of a milli-moment. After six dozen examinations, we assure us that Number Three has not only the highest ever mapped brain system ever, at over ninety-nine per cent, whereas, we remind all, most of us have only as high as thirty-one per cent of brain processes, and furthermore, Number Three has extended life genes, adding to her life span somewhere in the thousands of years rather than our one hundred. We've been able to solve the issue of *senektitude,* and that's just the beginning." He has the audience's full attention now and he pauses a moment longer to hold the suspense. One wrong word and the doktors are finished, exiled into unemployment. "In addition, Number Three has also been exhibiting a state of euphoria and, what some might refer to as, a state of extended enlightenment for time improbable. Number Three is the ultimate illustration of our future, of our potential possibilities. We have touched the God Gene, and we have been made glorious."

Sir Windsor VI turns back to a frozen Number Three in a groggy state of perceptive stupefaction. The audience remains disinterested, dissatisfied, disgusted. Most Elders believe *It* is another grand failure like all Its predecessors — a monstrous waste of Korporate time and resources.

Then from behind the Elders someone howls, "The newest K-pad was *way* better!" Huge squeals of laughter erupt throughout the audience.

Many Elders begin removing themselves from their seats and congregating out in the hallway. Grumbling, the thirteen kleriks depart the stage in systematic file.

In a last-ditch effort to salvage, rather foolishly, some attention from the scattering audience, Kin bellows absurdly into the mikrophone,

"Blasted imbeciles! Wait! Wait and see!"

Some offended Korporate Elders stare back in disbelief as they exit the auditorium.

"Wait, wait damned simpletons! We haven't heard everything yet!" Kin cries out. "Her name is *Zawadi*! *Zawadi*! She's the future of our Korporation!"

At this point only a few Korporate members by the back exits remain in the emptying auditorium shaking their heads and huddling and conferring with one another. Conquergood and Klaire join their friends on stage. No one dares say a word.

Kin stares blankly at the emptying auditorium below and says to himself, "*Et tu, Brute?*"

Sir Windsor VI steps over to his kolleague and drapes a consoling arm around Kin's slumped shoulders. The taller doktor retrieves a thin opium cigar from his pocket and places it in the corner of his mouth and gently gnaws the tip. He confides to his stubby little kolleague, "Better going next time, eh?"

Conquergood walks over to the dome and looks at Number Three's inactive pupils. She's an empty shell, filled by more empty shells. Conquergood reaches over to touch the surface of the flexiglass dome when one of her eyes rotate to meet his.

In Conquergood's mind he hears her beautiful voice speak:

"My Fathers have not failed me. I am whatever has been, is or shall be, and no mortal has taken off my veil until now. I am Nature, the Mother of all Things, and the Mistress of the Elements, the Beginning of Ages, and the Queen of the Departed Spirits born anew."

Conquergood reacts with the voice still echoing in his mind and he tugs Klaire's arm.

"Did you hear that?" he asks Klaire. "Did you hear what she just said?"

"Hear what *who* said?" replies Klaire. Her eyes shrink into narrow slits, deepening the brow a bit over her eyebrows. Klaire's shoulders shrug and the lips on her face tighten.

"Don't give me that," Conquergood, pointing at Zawadi, blurts back. "Did you hear her? Did anyone else hear what she just said?"

One by one the lights in the auditorium dim and flick off. Klaire looks questionably at Zawadi, unmoving as a glacier, and back at Conquergood's distraught expression.

Kin, having noticed the disturbance, retreats from his fellow doktor and stretches a short arm upward in an embrace around Conquergood's neck and pulls the Turnkey Specialist closer to him.

"Quit pulling our legs, old chum," Kin says. "We've been humiliated and it's time we admit our defeat."

Kin is now awkwardly attached to Conquergood as he leads Klaire and Sir Windsor VI towards the stairs at the end of the stage.

At the top of the stairs, before descending, Kin concludes, "Let's go and enjoy some of that famous K-line Solution. At least that'll be a smashing hit."

All the lights in the auditorium have been shut off, wrapping the four friends in awkward shadows as they pass into the bright white of the hallway.

Meanwhile, still in her flexiglass dome, Zawadi is left to the dark stage where she yearns for the light.

VII
Ministry of Konklusions

"We've found," says Kin, who is now a little drunk and mournful from his famous K-line Solution in Conquergood's apartment, "that a nail standing out from all the others is only going to be pounded down all the more."

Conquergood and Klaire recline on the bed pillows while Kin and Sir Windsor VI sink themselves with reflection deeper into two leather-synthetik chairs. Soft neon-blue lighting shades the room as the four enjoy a bit of *the remedy* after the colossal failure at the Korporate Rally earlier that night.

"It's not the first time we've failed," Sir Windsor VI explains. He sits straight, not touching the back of the chair. One of his legs lie slumped over the other while he enjoys an opium cigar. "We always do better the next time. Have faith in the Korporation."

"Better?" replies Kin, dumbfounded. "Better than perfection? How the hell is that possible?" The chair is turned towards one corner of the room, and he allows his head to fall back and his arms to slump over the sides. "How better than our beloved Zawadi? Not a single flaw in all those precious little genes. The cells of the others rapidly deteriorated, which we must admit, resulted horribly in a shortened life span, and that was before any duplications could be made. Hell, we solved that problem. And now Zawadi, in all that glory, will outlive us all. Zawadi is the future of the Korporation now."

"We should call a private meeting," Klaire says. "The Four Ministers should hear this directly and then we could try and explain things a bit better." She curls over onto Conquergood and wraps her arms like the fabled koala did once upon a time to the eucalyptus tree. "Maybe the Korporate Ministers will listen and the problems worked out. Zip, zap, zam — all better!"

"We wouldn't dare," Kin responds. He lifts the unlabeled brown bottle filled with the remedy and takes a swig. He twists the white top securely and tosses the bottle over to Conquergood. The bottle lands on the bed next to Klaire. Kin continues on in despair, "They'll have our heads if we go to them and try to reason out this mess. Zawadi is a disaster in their *nescient* minds."

Conquergood is adrift in his own thoughts and not really following the conversation. He thinks back to the auditorium and when Zawadi had spoken to him through telepathy. Such a side effect is purely accidental, but she has somehow established the foundation for the future of *genetik* research for the next two hundred years, beyond the twenty-third and twenty-fourth centuries. The doktors and the Korporation don't even know it yet — *not a clue to what humanity will become and what they'll soon be capable of.*

"*We* will have no choices," Sir Windsor VI remarks, the opium smoke from the thin cigar mushrooming up and permeating out through the neon-blue shadows. "We'll have to begin again. We must never give up."

Even Conquergood feels a little high from the second-hand opiate smoke as it continues to billow from Sir Windsor VI's lungs, out his inverted chimney of a nose to spiral downward across his pointed chin and outward across the room.

Sir Windsor VI's two fingers dangle the thin opium cigar as one might loosely hold a rapier. His body is evidently there in the apartment, but as Conquergood will one day recall in his official *Skript* he kept daily:

"With his eyes unrecognizable, the good doktor's consciousness touched the fourth dimension by dreaming of the next realm, hidden by a thin veil of thought, no doubt brought on by the opium's effects."

The lanky doktor clears his throat through the opiate haze, the rich aroma filling the room.

"Shortly after the rally," Sir Windsor VI says without emotion, ashing his opium cigar into a flexiglass tray on the table next to him, "while we were in the k-line, the Four Ministers sent a sekured message to Johnson in the lab. The meeting has been arranged for tomorrow morning. Eight sharp."

"Off with our heads!" Kin exclaims, quite drunkenly. He takes one of his thumbs and draws a horizontal line across his throat, which is more chin and chest than any throat Conquergood has ever seen.

"Doom! Doom! Doom!" Kin continues to lament. "We're doomed! The Four Ministers will disperse us into the wilderness, stripping us of our edukation and ranks. All our research will be handed over to imbeciles, like that flunky Johnson, and we'll be... we'll be... we'll be —"

"Unemployed," Klaire interjects. "That would be horrible."

Conquergood is now listening intently. He's been sipping in the remedy and it's been gradually altering his consciousness, a mind attempting to create clarity through a distinguishable point emanating out of Kin's drunken outbursts. Conquergood knows the wilderness that Kin fears, and Conquergood further knows the Korporate Edukated and the Elites do not belong among the strayers, the wild outkasts. Exile would be a death sentence for Kin and Sir Windsor VI.

Conquergood remains quiet and absorbs the spoken speech around him, the remedy, and the movements of Klaire's body upon his own. Her eyelids grow heavy with each word and she uses a free hand to pull a blanket across her tight, well-maintained body.

"Doubtful they'll un-employ us," Sir Windsor VI remarks. "Highly unlikely."

Conquergood flings the brown bottle back to Kin, who catches it and finds greater lows to swim in.

"We'll have to wait and see what happens," Sir Windsor VI remarks. He taps the gray remnants from the thin cigar into the flexiglass tray beside his chair. "Old *fata* has reasserted herself. If we are to be *eradikated*, then we will be so. If the Korporate Ministers order our demise, that shall be so. Our hands, as we used to say long ago, are tied and we just might be taken for a small ride outside the Kompound to be dropped off and left all alone."

"How morbid," Klaire says with closed eyes. Her voice groans more than vocalizing these two words. She's fading to a sleep filled with solemn forgetfulness — *a remedy all its own.* She breathes heavy and Conquergood pulls her closer — *sleep now, sleep away these nightmares found in the living.*

"Morbid is right," Kin replies, along with a grumble. "Twig legs stood there on stage like a dead fig on a dead branch on a dead vine on a dead wall on a dead —"

"That's a bit rough," Sir Windsor VI says, "wouldn't we say?"

"No. Better. Like a...a... oh, why bother?" Kin's stubby chin settles to his chest. "We are doomed to the ends of the earth. They'll strip us both of our Korporate Seals and we'll be nothing but savage strayers. Not to offend, Jerome." He swings the tail of the brown bottle upwards once again and with a full gulp drains the remaining contents of the powerful remedy.

Through his haze of opium-induced visions, Sir Windsor VI notices Klaire fast asleep and Kin inebriated beyond recourse.

"We must be going," Sir Windsor VI says to Conquergood. "We have a big day tomorrow."

A little drunk from the remedy himself, Conquergood nods in understanding and relief, thankful to be alone with Klaire and away from the doktors.

Sir Windsor VI sticks the stub of opium cigar into the side of his mouth and holds it in place with clamped teeth. He erects himself and proceeds to help Kin to his feet. In trying to stand, however, Kin finds his legs are numb, fast asleep, and he drops to the floor as fast as three sacks filled with purloined onions and potatoes from the outer limits. Sir Windsor VI, unbelieving in what he is witnessing, glares down at his fallen *kompatriot*. With a foot, he softly nudges Kin in the ribs.

Conquergood laughs low to himself.

After several moments of squirming around on the floor like an overturned beetle, Kin finally rights himself by using the edge of his chair. He is then able to stand upright to allow blood to cascade down through his legs, pricked with sharp-tingling sensations akin to a hundred now extinct sea urchins stabbing his flesh and bones. Kin groans in agony from the painful misfiring of nerves.

"Shall we see you tomorrow morning, Jerome?" Sir Windsor VI asks Conquergood. "The support would be greatly appreciated."

"Happy to help." Conquergood nods, and then adds, "Think nothing more of it."

Sir Windsor VI — the thick opium smoke pouring up around his face as though breathing fire — nods his lean head and chin in return. He then manages, with extreme effort, to support Kin over to the door. The two doktors wave farewell and vanish into the bright hallway. The door seals shut.

"Lock door," Conquergood says in a passive voice. The automatic locks secure the apartment door from any more outside intrusions. "Lights off," is his next command and the neon-blue lights vanish to create a gentle sleep-assuring darkness.

"KV on," orders Conquergood. The KV rises from its hidden place in the floor at the foot of the bed and flicks on, presenting the Korporate Seal. "Film — *Kasablanka*, the Bogart original — play minimal audio," Conquergood says with a firm voice.

The commands are carried out. The film showcasing Humphrey Bogart and Ingrid Bergman begins playing on the KV in three dimensions, the sound barely audible. Conquergood doesn't need to hear the dialogue. He knows the words by heart, he tells himself, closing his eyes from all the pain of seeing too much and knowing even more — *but such is life in such a world as this.*

At night on a beach eight wooden poles are erected into the sand and create a large circle. The beach is lit by the fires burning at the top of each of the eight poles, each twenty feet in height.

In the circle's center, Conquergood stands gazing at the multitude of stars above with a full moon dominating the night sky. He can hear but cannot see the surf crashing — where beauty swims in its infinite sweet madness and he knows he is asleep and deep in another one of his many dreams — and he hears the waves crashing upon the shoreline. A forested land rustles behind him with a feeling of that allusive unknown.

Out of the blackened waters, a wet figure steps from the ocean as a prophet had done ages ago. The wet figure is a woman striding up the beach to Conquergood. She approaches through the shadows wearing a saddle-tan bikini of leather forming to the contours of her slender body, which has been deeply tanned by a benevolent sun. As she draws closer to the circle of flames, Conquergood sees that her black hair contains streaks of blonde braids, as though they are streaks of moonshine in the dark.

As she joins Conquergood within the circle of the eight illuminated poles, he hears trumpets playing a familiar melody, one he is unable to name.

The strange woman's delicate hands embrace his muscular arms. Her chestnut eyes stare up and lock with his. He turns away from her to look for a strange sound coming from the crashing surf, but she pulls his face back to hers. She speaks but he cannot discern her words over the roar of the ocean, growing louder with each wave finding its way to shore and to their bare toes.

Conquergood feels that he should know this woman. That he has known her his whole life. But her name is absent from all the other names in his heart and memory. He wants to speak to her, to ask her for her name, but his voice comes out silent and she only smiles knowingly. She places his hands on her bare hips to take her in and she rocks beneath his touch, the muscles in her neck and throat throbbing. The woman on the beach isn't Klaire, not even close. Then a cracking of a branch in the shadows over to his left splinters his attention.

He turns away from the wet familiar woman to see Zawadi, that once caged experiment now set free, standing outside the circle of light. The name of the familiar woman comes to him, and when Conquergood turns back to the familiar woman within the circle of light next to him, she holds an expression of love-longing; he feels he has always known her, and that they had always belonged together.

Suddenly — as though he has broken the cruel surface of a sea drowning him like mad, able to breathe again — he gasps out in waking relief to call out her name, "Leona!"

Conquergood is immediately ripped from the *santarin* image of the familiar woman and awakes in bed to Klaire shaking him. (We must insert here from the Skript that Conquergood's own definition and use of the adjective "santarin" means "a beautiful, yet sweet sadness.")

For a moment or two Conquergood stares at Klaire wildly because he is unsure of who she is anymore. He pushes Klaire aside and gets out of bed and steps over to the bay window. Still in that dream now lost and no more, he leans against the shaded flexiglass to allow the waking to come. He wipes tears from his eyes and cheeks and doesn't know why he is crying so.

Klaire sits upright on her knees on the bed. She is without shirt, and her ivory breasts and dark nipples are perfectly proportioned and stiff in the cold morning. Alert, she readies for her attack.

"Who's Leona?" she asks.

Conquergood, likewise nude and free, stares for a moment poignantly down at the arboretum below. A few Korporate members are having an early pre-dawn stroll and smoking their *poppy tears* in the soft light, and then he remembers Klaire's kiss from earlier and weighs it against the heavy vision of his dream of Leona.

"I don't have a clue." He faces the sullen and jealous woman on his bed and adds, "I honestly don't know."

Conquergood lies on his bed listening to Wagner's "As the Gods Enter into Valhalla" and thinking of the memories he could not be sure were memories as the sun rises over the Korporate Kompound.

After all, the video-like images he keeps seeing in his mind's eye could have been dreams, and these dreams might have been with him for as long as he could remember. Ultimately, he does not know the memories from the dreams, and the uncertain dichotomy within his being causes him to question his reality even more: Is he the being he was yesterday? The being he is today? The being he might never be tomorrow?

These kinds of questions (on Time and Being) concerns Conquergood deeply, and he decides to reflect, instead, on the dreams of his memories. In the end, he doesn't care if the memories are real or not; the memories come from somewhere deep within himself and, for him, that is real enough.

What could the memories even mean? he wonders. Does it even matter?

Conquergood closes his eyes and he sees his mother brushing her long, golden hair before a vanity mirror. In the memory, he clutches the doorframe watching his mother moving the brush one hundred and one times down through her hair, like a waterfall of liquid gold, that stretches to the three-legged stool she sits upon. Cotton pajamas clothe his mother and to him she looks innocent and young, too young, to have had two toddling boys.

Even so, Conquergood notices himself and his twin brother (the name is now lost to him) being hugged by their mother — this far too young woman who appears to be in her early twenties or late teens — in a photograph being eyed by his mother in the top right corner of the mirror. In her eyes, Conquergood sees and feels all the love and affection she had for him and his twin. She seems to be thinking of them when she bends her head to the side and smiles for no one other than the thought within her being.

She brushes and brushes in her little zone of contentment and comfort for as long as Conquergood needs the memory to last. He lets the images of his mother brushing her hair play many times over before moving on to let the memory end. When ready, Conquergood lets the memory finish. His mother turns to him and calls him away from the door.

"Come brush my hair, son," she says. "You have such strong little hands."

The moment when Conquergood touches the brush the memory ends and vanishes into nothingness, like water into water.

A few of these data-memories can be suspended in his mind for hours, like the one with his mother brushing her hair, or the data-memories can flash by in an instant with a severe flashpoint:

His twin is digging in the wet sand and sweeping his yellow curls away from his face; his brother is jumping into the waves crashing to shore; his brother is shouting to Conquergood to come join him in the water; Conquergood's mother is walking alone on the beach; two sets of footprints trailing his mother; the gulls are low among the clouds and blazing sun; flies are buzzing near the thick sweat on his neck; the twin boys, like Romulus and Remus, are chasing after their mother; Conquergood is winning the race to first cling to his mother's leg; a family of whales blow their spouts; a sheepdog bounds over the sand and into the surf; his brother is calling the sheepdog "Shenandoah" as Conquergood falls upon the wet sand; Shenandoah is licking his face; a man in the distance on a high hill is waving to the twin boys, waving for them to come, sheepdog and all, to come and to hurry home.

A few of these data-memories, like this, flash by too quickly and Conquergood would have to play at least fifteen times before he feels satisfied with his grasp on the specific data-memory. But when he does, the order becomes jumbled, out of place, from the time before, and the meaning of the memory would often change.

For a second time, still in his bed with eyes closed and listening to Wagner, Conquergood plays the flashing memories again in his mind:

Shenandoah is licking his face; a man in the distance on a high hill is waving for them to come, sheepdog and all; the twin boys are chasing after their mother; Conquergood is winning the race to first cling to his mother's leg; two sets of footprints trailing his mother; the gulls are low among the clouds and blazing sun; Conquergood is falling onto the wet sand; flies are buzzing near the thick sweat on his neck; a family of whales blow their spouts; his brother is calling the sheepdog "Shenandoah" as the sheepdog bounds over the sand and into the surf; his brother is shouting to Conquergood to come join him in the water; Conquergood is digging in the wet sand and sweeping his yellow curls away from his face; his mother is walking alone on the beach.

Conquergood could play this memory-set over fifty times and each time the order of events would be different. There should have been more memory-sets of his family, but there was only a dark mysterious void. Conquergood, long ago, had learned he could no longer trust these memory-sets. What truly frightens him now is that one day he would be unable to trust his own thoughts. Conquergood needs to find his twin brother. Yes, he needs to find his twin. Then and only then would Conquergood be able to find his truth.

Klaire is snuggled once more within Conquergood's arms as they lie in bed among the pillows waiting for their breakfast to be served by the Korporate chefs that morning. Neither one can sleep, and for a long time they listen to one of Klaire's favorite selections: Chopin's Nocturne in E-flat major, Opus 9, Number 2. The legato melody fills the bedroom with a profound ease.

Conquergood imagines the individual notes of music are actually letters forming whole words into phrases and sentences that shape themselves into a story found in a book that no longer exists and would never be read again. Only the music remains of that story now.

"What're you thinking about?" Klaire seems to ask this question a lot. "What's going through that mysterious mind of yours? I really want to know."

"I was thinking about my mother," Conquergood says. He rubs the bridge of his nose. "I was thinking how she used to play the piano for me when I was a baby. I'd cry and she'd play, and we'd both laugh at the silliness of it all."

"You can remember that?"

"There are memories, yes."

"I can only recall my mother's name," Klaire says, "which is strange because at times, like now, her name feels like a familiar abstraction, like it is my name, and I know that can't be possible. I can't even remember her face but I can remember her name: Kimberly Klark. How odd a name can be: so much meaning packed in one or two words."

"Do you feel that you loved your mother?" Conquergood asks. An e-display on the ceiling plays a muted holo-video of a waterfall, and he watches this as he speaks, "Does it feel like she ever existed?"

Klaire remains silent and keeps her eyes closed with her nose breathing in and out on Conquergood's chest.

Her legs tense and wrap themselves around his legs just as her arms cling tighter around his body.

"Klaire?"

Her whole body falls limp and she relaxes back into a half sleep. A short time later, Klaire's tears drop one by lonely one onto Conquergood's chest. He had never before seen a woman cry, not even out beneath the bridges in the Outlands.

"What is it?" Conquergood asks. "Lovers shouldn't be afraid to tell each other everything."

"Nothing," Klaire says. She wipes her eyes and rolls away from Conquergood. "I remember nothing."

Conquergood leans over and holds Klaire in his arms, and they both continue to listen to Chopin while they lie on their sides as one. The piano seems to want to draw the emotions ever outward, and Conquergood can feel his chest swell from a deep breath that almost doesn't want to leave.

Conquergood thinks Klaire has fallen asleep when suddenly she speaks,

"Shouldn't I remember? Something? At least one thing? A face. A touch. A word. A kiss. One kiss. Why can't I remember?"

"Not everyone can remember their childhood. Very few can remember their infancy."

"But why can't I remember?" Klaire shivers and grows more agitated the more she speaks. "Why can't I remember my mother? My father? Shouldn't I remember? What if I have brothers or sisters? Is something wrong with me? There should be something, but all there is inside is nothing. The deeper I dig for some shred of memory the darker my caverns of thought become. Do you think it's strange I can't remember?"

"Do you remember anything about the place you come from? A street or a building? Did you have a dog or a cat or a bird when you were a child? Something like that?"

Klaire, in the nude, rolls out of bed and paces the room with her hands squeezing out the pressure in her knuckles. Conquergood shifts his back against the pillows on the headboard and motions with his hand for the piano music to decrease in volume. The sensors monitor and capture his gesture and the piano music recedes into the background. With each step, Klaire continues to deliberate.

"Horses. I remember horses. How funny is that. I can hear them breathing in the dawn hours. I can feel their coarse manes between my fingers."

"Horses?" Conquergood asks. "Real horses?"

Klaire stops pacing, puts her hands on her hips and says, "Yes, *real* horses. Why do I even bother?"

"I see."

Klaire continues her nervous pacing along the foot of the bed where the KV had been earlier that night. "I've always had a memory about horses running in a valley. Until today, I never had any reason to believe my memory with the wild horses had anything to do with my parents, but when you asked about a place and I thought about my mother and father, the memory of running horses came to me. What do you think it means? Am I being odd?"

"It means your parents were horses." Conquergood can't help but to laugh at his joke. And laugh he does.

Klaire stands with her hands on her hips and a scowl on her face.

"I'm sorry," Conquergood says. "I couldn't help myself."

Klaire calmly walks over to the side of the bed, picks up a pillow, and slaps Conquergood with the pillow across the side of his head.

"I open up to you, really open up to you," she says, "and this is what I get? You tease me?" She tosses the pillow at him. "Bastard."

Conquergood settles his laughter enough to rise out of bed and he takes Klaire in his arms. He kisses her shoulders, her neck, her cheeks, her temples, her chin, and finally her lips.

Klaire pulls away, her hands on Conquergood's chest. "Do you think I'll forgive you so easily?"

"Not at all," Conquergood says, and he falls with her to the bed where he begins kissing her as though to map out her body for all of eternity.

At a little after seven that morning, Conquergood is greeted at his apartment door by Kin and Sir Windsor VI. Vivaciously, both doktors have been restored to their previous-professional selves. Klaire has decided to remain in bed to get some much-needed sleep.

Without a word, the three men march down the overly bright hallway and toward the k-line. And as the portal door opens, the three kolleagues believe they are ready for anything.

"Four Ministers," Kin speaks, voice barely above a broken whisper as though echoing back from a seashell. His shoulders lift themselves for a brief moment and then settle to relax. He breathes deeply before a long sigh comes quivering out.

"*Korrection*," says the meta-voice from the tele-k-skreen. "Please verify destination."

"Take us to the Four Ministers, dim-witted machine," shouts Kin. "Now, half-witted komputer! Before it gets ugly."

"Most assuredly, Doktor Russell," says the meta-voice. "Destination — the Four Ministers. And Kinny, *ganbatte*!" The k-line promptly starts, zipping ever upwards to the very top of Korporate Tower.

After riding for several silent minutes in the portal, as sound and silent as a coffin thirteen feet below vegetation and rock, the three men are soon released into a vestibule that leads them to a long-solemn corridor, where at the end are large double doors with the Korporate Seal and the words:

Korporate Ministry of Konklusions

In front of the entrance, eight Korporate guards — four on each side of both doors — are wearing full body armor consisting of heavily plated e-helmets, torso and leg padding with heavy duty boots. The modern gear is highly resistant to fire, ammunition and toxic chemicals. Each of the guards, silent as the thirteen kleriks, wield readied *Korosu* batons across their chests. If necessity requires the guards to do so, the *Korosu* batons can release a high-power voltage, enough to disintegrate the victim into instant ash. The *Korosu* batons are also capable of squirting a paralyzing sleep-inducing toxin into the air to neutralize the enemy. Beneath their e-helmet visors, impenetrable and interlinked to the Korporate Komputers, the guards record and monitor the three kompatriots with extreme precision and suspicion.

"Here we go," Kin says. Bravely, he takes the lead, forming a V as they step past the eight guards and into the chambers most feared by the Korporate staff. The double doors slip shut and secure, heavy bolts locking solid as the Korporate Bank vault.

The three men walk up to the center spot and stand where a large black Korporate Seal is engraved on the white marble floor before and below the Four Ministers, who are silently and patiently standing behind elevated e-platforms. Conquergood finds the vast quasi-pious *kourtroom* — making the three men feel tiny and insignificant — is lit on either side by polished cathedral-like windows twenty-two feet in height and eight-feet wide.

Each window — eight on each side of the kourtroom — tells a story through colored mosaics illuminating and illustrating the history and symbols of the almighty Korporation. On Conquergood's left — ordered from the entrance to the four judges' e-benches — the eight symbols are as follows: the Wheel of Dharma, the Triskelion, the Jain Emblem, the Cakra Bhawana, the Eye of Horus, the Abeir-Toril, the Khanda, and the Taijitu. On Conquergood's right — also ordered from the entrance to the four judges' e-benches — the eight symbols are as follows: the Unicursal Hexagram, the Flaming Chalice, the Faravahar, the Lotus Motif, the Bodhi Tree, Twins, Footprints, and the Dream of Maya.

Lit by a rainbow of colors streaming from the sixteen windows, the three men face four raised metallic e-platforms — the judges' e-benches — separated from one another by a distance of four feet. At each of the four e-benches sit a Korporate Minister, each varying in ethnicity. The Ministers are shrouded in long black robes which have a Korporate rose emblem in red on the back and a white Korporate Seal in front. Behind the Four Ministers, the Korporate Seal in black is protruding from the white-washed wall giving the illusion that the seal is floating in midair. At the two back corners of the kourtroom, behind the four e-benches, two large Korporate flags hang firm and motionless, as though the flags are made of meta-plasty.

The first Minister on the far left has rugged wash-worn features upon his darkened face, wrinkles consuming much of his brow and cheeks, while his full head of silvery hair gleams from the sunrays cascading and splintering through the colored windows. The front of the e-bench holds a golden plaque with the caption:

He who knows not, and
Knows not he knows not —
He is a fool — shun him.

Below this quote is the symbol of the Endless Knot. Beneath the symbol and in front of this Minister a placard is posted with the name:

INDOASIA

The next Minister has a slightly reddened face and a plump neck well-mounted on two bulky shoulders. She hunches forward presenting a slight hump on the back of her neck, allowing her black hair to fall along the sides of her ogre-like face. She presents a stern frown directed at

Kin. Her e-bench has a similar golden plaque posted at the front, but the caption reads:

> He who knows not, and
> Knows he knows not —
> He is a child — trust him.

Below this quote is the symbol of the Jeweled Umbrella. Beneath the symbol and in front of this Minister a placard on her e-bench displays the name:

OCEANIKA

The next Minister is also a woman but she appears to be the liveliest and happiest of all the Four Ministers. She isn't quite smiling but she isn't frowning either. Curly red-hair twists down the sides of her face, giving off a warm quality to her presence in an otherwise cold and menacing kourtroom. On the front of her e-bench the caption reads:

> He who knows, and
> Knows not he knows —
> He is asleep — wake him.

Below this quote is the symbol of the Conch Shell. Beneath the symbol and in front of this Minister a placard on her e-bench contains the name:

EUROZONE

The final Minister, resembling the long-forgotten John E. Hoover, is seated on the far right. He's an elderly man, like the Indoasian Minister, and he has silver hair encircling a bald scalp. Archaic bifocals on his protruding beak causes his nose to bulge crookedly to one side. His pale mouth is imbedded between two hunks of cheeks and followed by no less than three flabby chins. The Minister's ears are strangely pointed at the tops and bottoms, created by a rare mutation commonly known in the Korporate world as Elfism. In self-glorification, he slouches forward over his e-bench. The front of his e-bench has the caption:

> He who knows, and
> Knows he knows —
> He is wise — follow him.

Below this quote is the symbol of Six Victory Banners. Beneath the symbol and in front of this Minister a placard on his e-bench has the acronym:

NATO

Also on each of the four e-benches and beneath each of the four golden plaques a black bifurcated eagle stands out remarkable and poignant against its stale background. The single avian body features two heads, facing in opposite directions much like the ill-fated god Janis. With its wings spread wide, one set of talons grips a set of thirteen anachronistic pen quills while the other set of talons clutches onto eight scrolls rolled tight and tied by a single red ribbon.

Kin, Sir Windsor VI, and Conquergood stand in a straight line, the Korporate Seal above and below their heads and feet. A green-clad attendant appears from behind the e-benches and gives each of the three kompatriots Korporate translators to help mediate the following meeting. They promptly insert the miniscule devices into their ear cavities.

The Eurozone Minister — her red hair dangling freely as she peers down at her K-pad — speaks in French. In English, Conquergood synchronously hears her opening remarks:

"We all know why we've gathered here this morning, and with extreme *reluktance*, we might add. However, we must *reflekt* the *kase* presented before us by the Korporate Elders last night at twenty after twenty."

The three other Ministers, no doubt preparing their arguments, scribble into their K-pads. Kin's knees quiver. Sir Windsor VI, half in an ill-inspired and elusive daydream, nods along. Conquergood remains attentive but unattached.

The Eurozone Minister continues in her native French, but for Conquergood her voice comes out instantly in English:

"The Korporation has provided both Doktor Windsor and Doktor Russell with unlimited funds and excessive opportunities to achieve the ultimate Korporate *Kalling*. The floor is now open for konsideration."

The Indoasian Minister speaks in Mandarin, but the insta-translation etches itself out in English:

"We would like to thank the doktors for their diligent efforts thrust upon them in the Korporation's efforts to generate a Utopia for all humanity. We should also be reminded that these doktors have thus far exceeded and excelled in their research, regardless of any failures they may have had recently and unfortunately *enkountered*."

Kin mistakenly and mindlessly interrupts,

"Zawadi *isn't* a blasted failure!"

In French, the Eurozone Minister rebukes the doktor, "Doktor Russell, we should be reminded not only of the standard business procedures but also of the etiquette. *Konsider* this as the last warning. Please kindly kontinue, Minister."

"As we were being reminded," the Indoasian Minister says in ancient-scholarly Mandarin, staring down at his e-notes on his K-pad's e-skreen, "We should reflekt not solely on recent failures but we should also reflekt on past *suksesses* as well. One last thing, the Korporation owns one hundred percent of the world's patents, including *mekanikal* and, more importantly, *biologikal* patents partly due to these two obedient and loyal doktors. We should hold these two doktors in the highest regards of respekt. The floor is now open for further konsiderations."

Kin nods in full agreement. "Now that," he whispers to Conquergood, "we agree with."

"The Oceanika Minister would like to add a few words," the bulky woman says between fattened lips. In a sluggish form of English, the Minister continues, "While Doktor Windsor has in the past few *dekades*, and even further back than most of us remember, labored to promote the Korporate image and *akkomplished* several inspiring feats of loyalty; to name a few: the *suksessful projekts* on Mars, more recently the *atmospherik* alteration tests on Jupiter, and the high regard to his esteemed *genetik* bloodline, and lastly, might we rekall, his humble achievement at winning the Korporation's highest honor, the Korporate Peace

Prize. Instead of keeping the reward, however, he donated the esteemed and enormous prize money to the Korporate Re-Edukation Department and to the Korporate Perception Management Department. We, the Ministry of Oceanika, are unable to find any faults in Doktor Sir Windsor VI. His less admired kolleague, however, Doktor Russell, in the past few dekades has led failed projekt after failed projekt that repeatedly led to low produkt placement in the Korporation and resulted in a waste of produkts and a loss in profits and an overall dekline in produktivity. Some of us do not have eternity, Doktor Russell. Let us also not fail to mention the lab teknician, Doktor Johnson, who was sent to Korporate Rekovery for six weeks due to Doktor Russell's *neglekt* and poor decision making."

The three other Ministers nod in agreement to the Oceanika Minister's remarks.

"Three weeks," Kin grumbles to Conquergood. "It was three not six." Kin further mumbles something about having once given the Oceanika Minister some of his special remedy during a late-night dance party and something sinister about a weasel named Johnson. Sir Windsor VI places a hand on Kin's arm to steady his kompatriot. Conquergood is uncertain as to what he must do, and so he watches and listens as most great leaders are required to do at some point in their journey of self-discovery and self-fulfillment.

The NATO Minister, tri-chins wagging, concludes the remarks of the Ministry in hoarse, semi-audible English,

"The Korporate *rekords* have been updated and no additional remarks are necessary on this Minister's behalf.

Does Doktor Russell, Doktor Windsor, or the Turnkey Specialist have anything further to add at this time?"

"We'd like to add a few things, Minister," Conquergood says, stepping forward, away from his kompatriots. He looks into each pair of the Four Ministers' eyes, while they receive him in great interest.

"Last night, Zawadi spoke," Conquergood says. "Her formed communication is not like ours. She has the unique ability to cast her thoughts into others. Zawadi is not and we repeat *not* a failure. These two doktors have achieved a miracle and long-lasting praise should be their only punishment."

"No one has yet mentioned any kind of punishment," the Eurozone Minister, with an effulgent charm, says in insta-translation from her French. "We are merely here to evaluate the two doktors' progress and determine a *satisfaktory* outkome. Thank you, Turnkey. That is all for now. These remarks have been entered into the official Korporate Skript. Does anyone else wish to add to these remarks?" Her eyebrows rise in expectation of someone accepting her challenge.

Sir Windsor VI and Kin shake their heads in the negative while avoiding eye contact because they know it is futile to argue against the almighty Korporation. The Korporation possesses supreme power. To speak with self-assertiveness, or in an effort to defend one's individual self ultimately separates the Korporate member further from the Korporate Hive. It is far better to remain silent, to the bite the tongue, than to assert individuality. One is the Korporation or one is none. We are all or we are nothing. Such is the Korporate Path.

Conquergood steps back in line with his kompatriots.

"All remarks have been updated," the NATO Minister says in a firm-throaty voice, erupting more from his large gut than his tarred lungs. "Ministers, please proceed and rekord the findings in the K-pad and we shall kontinue momentarily."

The Four Ministers scroll feverishly upon their K-pads. Conquergood glances over at Kin and sees his plump cheeks paler and more shrunken than normal. Sir Windsor VI remains unaltered in appearance and Conquergood half-assumes the doktor might be under a powerful opium trance, disconnected from his immediate surroundings.

After a few short-intense minutes of deliberation via their K-pads — better known by the Korporation as E-Deb — the Eurozone Minister nods her head at the other Ministers in final majority acceptance of their agreed upon Konklusions. The Four Ministers stare down at the three kompatriots.

Once again in French the Eurozone Minister begins her concluding remarks, insta-translated into English,

"We first would like to begin by thanking everyone for their welkomed participation here today, and the Korporation must reminds us now that it always takes kare of the little people, even if the little people choose to be ungrateful of the Korporation's services. The Korporation loves the little people and the little people must love the Korporation. With that said, the Korporation, hereby, finds Doktor Windsor VI a rekommendable member and no less than ten percent of his kurrent salary shall be inkreased and added as a raise to kongratulate him on his suksesses. In regards to the Turnkey Specialist, who boldly spoke to the Korporate Ministers in good faith of his fellow Korporate kompatriots, we find him suitable for a pay raise of fifteen percent of his kurrent salary to be deposited into the First & Only Korporate Bank no later than by seventeen post meridiem today. As for Doktor Kin Russell, the Four Ministers have voted in a three to one ruling to unemploy him for a period of not less than one year but not greater than five years, when at approximately every year from this date, *Kmonthten* on *kdaytwenty-seven*, a re-evaluation will take place before the Korporate Ministers to rekonsider Doktor Russell's status and rank with the Korporation. Effektive immediately, Kin Russell shall be stripped of his Korporate Edukation, Rank, and Titles and he will remain on Administrative Leave until the Korporation deems necessary for the safety and progress and good of the Korporation and its Korporate Branches."

A green-clad attendant comes swirling around the Indoasian Minister's e-bench, stepping over to Kin and violently ripping the Korporate Seal from Kin's robe. Next, the attendant politely gathers the earpieces and vanishes back behind the four e-benches of the Ministry of Konklusions.

Conquergood stands frozen, stupefied by what has just happened — *Has he been on trial? Was that even a trial?*

The Korporate Trial lasts a few rapid minutes longer and then it is over. Finality comes over the three kompatriots — two are receiving promotions while the last is unemployed and banished from the Korporation.

The double doors to the kourtroom slide open behind the three men. Four of the eight Korporate guards march assertively into the kourtroom. The four guards then proceed to drag Kin by the arms out through a back passage located somewhere behind the Four Ministers' e-benches. Meanwhile, the Four Ministers have promptly dispersed from their *holo-projektions*.

Conquergood and Sir Windsor VI stare blankly at one another. The last remaining four guards direct them to immediately vacate the kourtroom. And so thus ends Kin's residence at the Korporate Kompound.

Back in the k-line, Sir Windsor VI speaks solemnly, "Purely unavoidable. A truly sad state of affairs, don't we think so, Jerome?"

Conquergood repeats the words absent-mindedly, "Purely unavoidable."

What would become of Kin? Would he ever be seen again? Conquergood knew then that there's cracks even in the finest of palaces.

"Take this. It'll help," the doktor says. Sir Windsor VI removes two thin opium cigars from a pocket and hands one to Conquergood. "As sweet as glory, it'll make everything right as rain."

Conquergood mindlessly accepts the doktor's thoughtful *preskription*. The opium will most certainly help.

Then the doktor adds, "By the way, kongratulations on the promotion — purely unexpected." He jabs the unlit cigar between his teeth and secures one end with a clinch. "A little extra dough never hurts, does it?"

"Purely unexpected," Conquergood says in disbelief as the k-line zooms downwards and sideways. "Purely unavoidable. Sad state of affairs. There was no other way. Was there?"

VI
Kommunikation

Sweet, perfumed darkness envelopes the apartment, sealed shut into silence. At the edge of the bed, Conquergood sits smoking the opium cigar Sir Windsor VI had given him. Night has fallen over the Korporation.

The intoxicants from the opium cigar smother the Turnkey Specialist into a mind-numbing euphoria. Objects in the dispirited room loosen their firm hold on reality, blurring fine shapes and the exactness which binds things to their places. Loosely holding the ghost of Kin, a single chair morphs into one impressive block of stone before Conquergood, and Conquergood imagines Kin locked somewhere deep inside the stone block.

On the bed, the Turnkey Specialist reclines disjointed from the rest of the apartment as though he is surrounded by a sea of water: the nightstand and tele-k-skreen float; the thick curtains over the bay windows float; even his mind floats in a tranquil fog of smoke and opium.

Conquergood believes, however, his thoughts to be enormously coherent. He sees the bald interlokutor from the very first day he had arrived at the Korporation for the job interview. In his recollections, Conquergood knows the audacious interlokutor is dying, or rather rapidly wasting away — one flake at a time.

It is not a natural death like the many natural deaths Conquergood has seen in strayers who succumbed to the forces found in gutters or beneath bridges or within the vacant but crumbling high-rise apartments during extreme winters and blistering summers. No, the interlokutor had been disintegrating before his very eyes, and Conquergood sees it as plainly and as clearly as one who comprehends two plus two for the very first time: the large chunks of skin shedding itself; the false teeth hiding the fact the originals have fallen out one by one long ago; and, the flat-dull voice absent of its very own heartbeat.

Conquergood, in his opium induced vision, sees Zawadi caged in the Korporate lab: she sits with legs crossed in repose as her arms, like enormous wings, flap, and this causes the pod to hover beneath her small frame of a body. Zawadi then speaks using her lips and mouth and tongue and not her ingrained ability of telepathy, but regardless Conquergood fails to hear the young woman's words. He strains his ears, pulls the vision closer with his mind, trying to grasp subject Number Three. And as he comes face to face with Zawadi, she speaks a single word and Conquergood receives it perfectly as if she is sitting beside him on the bed. The vision of Zawadi bends low to Conquergood's left ear and whispers the name again,

"Leona."

The vision folds upon itself, collapsing and retreating into the confines of Conquergood's unadorned self. The opium cigar has run its course and only a drop for a cherry remains between his forefinger and thumb, burning mad in searing pain.

He stumbles to the toilet and flushes the cigar remains. From the neon sink, aglow in neon-blue, he washes his face with cold water, several splashes worth, and he blinks into the holo-mirror, burrowing into the reflected eyes and beyond the fleshy pulps of sight, into that part of self no one could ever come to know because if someone revealed the secrets of being, then all would be unmade in the universe — or so Conquergood would have liked us to believe.

Conquergood starts to see not one lifetime but two, three, and then a fourth and fifth. His eyes grow heavy and weightless with too much concentration. Another cold splash of water hits his face, breaking the holo-mirror's power of foresight. He has to see Zawadi. Conquergood breathes the name out of his mouth and onto the images, fogged. *Zawadi.* It hangs ahead of him in the neon-blue darkness. *Zawadi.* And the word curls back at him through the haze of opium smoke, lingering in the dark apartment. *Zawadi.* He sees the holo-name printed on the walls, chairs and even on the KV. *Zawadi.* The name penetrates and procures Conquergood's deep-self, further down than the name Leona. *Zawadi. Zawadi. Zawadi.* The daze breaks and Conquergood finds he is talking to someone who is no longer present in the room. He is alone and only the name of Zawadi keeps him company. He has to see her. Must. No point in waiting any longer. The time has come.

A Regal *holo-klok* holds Time prisoner the moment the hands begin to tilt. We are trapped in the *holo-klok*'s endless wheel, burdened more by the constant repetitions of the never-changing cycles from sunrise to sunset. It's not that we can't get Time back; we have plenty of it to go around. The problem arises when we've lost a person or a thing so extremely loved or valued, we beg and plead for Time itself to disrupt the forward-intended flow of God, of the Universe. It's then that we fail and fully know we are powerless and mortal, that we are not a god.

In the dust of the land, hunched over by countless wars, fields of blood upon blood, hoping to hope no more, in the sweet sweat of our sacred flesh we have so diligently learned to duplicate, becoming our own mortal masters over the immortal, while in this never-ending sway of Time there's an inviolable knowledge of how pure and valuable life really is — or should be, and still is not. The Arcanum of our own mortality sets us apart from all other creatures under sun, cloud, heaven. We are free in time; if only we could understand the holy energy which sustains us.

It's not in us to count each hour of the day; such madness snares the spirit in vines of suspended turmoil — if one may call what we hold within the decay of flesh and blood a spirit, a soul, a cognitive awareness of the subconscious, a shrouded darkness of the never more; it is, however, within every being to lie back and attempt to count the multitude of stars, where beauty jets the thing unnamable within to fly, formed anew throughout the endless and uncountable galaxies in formless pleasures. We should know. We were created from these images.

Yet humankind is counted by its days upon the Earth, shaped by all deeds which construct and destroy — waiting for the end, the final day of the Anthropocene. Then in the failing light of another day we, Jerome Conquergood, will witness the birth of a universe in our children's faces, glowing in a smile of pure-innocent radiant fire-star joy, unfathomable to the heartache and loss, which ages the mortal mind of women and men.

We want the soul and everything in between.

The Korporate lab is abandoned to its dark secrets. Once inside, Conquergood locates the five pods at the back of the long room.

"Lift shields," is softly spoken into the tele-k-skreen, slightly lighting the shadows on Conquergood's face.

The stainless-steel shields lift to reveal the five subjects, identical in every way but one. Conquergood finds Number Three sitting in the exact same position as their two previous encounters. When he looks through the flexiglass barrier, he can see her eyes remain closed while the other four subjects' eyes stare outward in a state of lethargy — not quite alive — but open. Conquergood places his right hand on the surface of the flexiglass. Number Three raises her hand in a similar fashion to meet his. He can feel an energy surge between their two hands.

Conquergood thinks, *Who or what are you?*

Number Three replies without speaking and Conquergood hears it clearly in his mind,

I've told you who I am. As for what I am, that remains a mystery, but I can tell you this much: I am the past. I am the present. I am the future. I am the Alpha which ends the Omega. I am not you, but we are the same, we are one. Do you not know this?

Conquergood has heard the last part before but he cannot place it. He thinks to Zawadi, *What do you want from me?*

I want what the Korporation wants, Zawadi communicates. *I want for you to see what I alone see. I want for you to want what I alone want.*

What is it you want?

Jerome Conquergood why do you ask such childish questions? I have taken all knowledge to be my province.

How do you know my name?

How does a parent know the name of their unborn child? How does a tree know that it is a tree? How does a squirrel know how and when to forage? How is it you are able to think, to learn, to know, to reason, to remember? How can you ask me foolish questions?

Conquergood watches Zawadi closely. Her outstretched hand is no bigger than an autumn leaf ready to fall. Her fine-spun body remains constant and uniformed in every minute action.

How shall I, Conquergood asks by his thoughts, *forfeit my life for the sake of the Korporation? How can I willingly kill for a greater good?*

Finally, replies Zawadi in thought, *you are asking the difficult questions. How can one take the life of another?*

The voice in Conquergood's head sounds soft and sympathetic, like wet rosebuds gliding down a slow river.

But I owe them my life, Conquergood confesses. *I owe everything to the Korporation. Without them, I cannot be.*

What about for the sake of your brother?

Who?

Have you forgotten Vincent already?

The name comes rushing back to life in Conquergood's being along with countless memories of his twin brother. Conquergood sees images of him and Vincent at the waterfront fishing and laughing in the rain.

He had forgotten. He had allowed himself to forget. He had allowed the Korporation to take many of the memories in exchange for his allegiance. He had allowed one loyalty to replace another.

Conquergood searches the black hole inside himself where he knows there should be more memories — recollections of a life already lived long, long, long ago.

What price has Vincent unwillingly paid? Zawadi asks.

Conquergood has already sacrificed so much for the sake of the Korporation.

Zawadi, Conquergood communicates with the speed of his thoughts, *Please tell me where Vincent is. I must know.*

If I tell you where your brother is then I must ask a favor from you. It is one simple task you must follow.

Anything.

Why are you so willing to do anything for something you want? You forgot your brother and yet you are willing to do anything to find him?

I've no choice. I've never had any choice. The choices have already been made for me. Fate is the controller of my destinies. Fate is —

The choices are yours alone to make, communicates Zawadi, through her thoughts alone.

Either way, I need to know where Vincent is. Will you help me or not?

As you wish, Zawadi thinks. *One task for one brother. Are we agreed?*

Agreed.

The pact is final and everlasting. The contract is made, whole and complete, regardless of the consequences. Unto the end, Conquergood will faithfully keep his word.

You must deliver the Korporate ampule to New Philadelphia. You are the Turnkey Specialist and you must carry out the Korporate assignment. Do as you've been instructed to do.

But they want me to carry God-knows-what right up to the steps of the nation's kapital during a conference filled with innocent people. Is that what you want? Do you want me to wipe out an entire city?

I've asked you to complete the task already set before you. You have already made the promise. I'm simply asking you to keep your promises. Do you still agree or not?

As I said before, I've no choice but to agree. Tell me where Vincent is and I'll fulfil my oath to you and to the Korporation. My honor binds me.

You will find your brother at the House of Morgan.

What?

You may find Vincent if you follow the signs to Forty Wall Street. Now you must hurry before he ends what you have already started.

What do you mean?

If you take the k-line down to Tier Two, you will find an open vent in the lower east corner. Follow the tunnel and it will take you outside the Korporate Kompound. Do not hesitate. Do not delay. You have only a twenty-minute window before the night maintenance comes and reattaches a new shield for the vent. Move quickly and you will save your brother.

Conquergood's mind drops blank as if a curtain has fallen. Zawadi's hand lowers to come to rest back on her knee. Her eyes, with long lashes, remain shut as if in REM sleep. In the gray light — on the authority of the restored Korporate Skript — her cheeks appear to hold a ghostly glow not too dissimilar to St. Elmo's fire one might witness while lost at sea beneath a full moon and an endless sky of stars. Conquergood sees her chest moving in calculated breaths. A change, albeit a minor one, is overcoming Zawadi.

Hurry! Her voice screams inside his head. *There's no time to waste. Go now!*

Conquergood turns and leaves the Korporate lab.

Down in Tier Two, a vent is open just as Zawadi had said it would be. He climbs into the tunnel without difficulty and before he knows what has happened, he's outside the Korporate Kompound.

For the first time in weeks, Conquergood breathes in the cold fading October air. He can smell November on the horizon. Stars are clearly visible above. When Conquergood breathes a sigh of relief, a tension lifts from off his chest and shoulders. The pressure vanishes. He is outside and his skin comes back to life, rushing with forgotten exhilaration. His whole organism makes the self within pulse alive once more. Then he runs with mindless urgency and only when Ward One is far behind him does he bend over, holding his knees in swirling exhaustion, and vomit onto the cracked pavement.

V
Ward 22

By the time Conquergood reaches the outer edge of Ward 22, his sore knees and blistered feet ache with an extreme anguish duplicated to that of someone having a severe varicose ulcer on their shinbone. Notwithstanding, the pain biting from within his legs is the least of his worries. The last October night deepens into its bowels of cold. Having to wear the thinly layered kimono robe with sandals inside the moderately controlled climate of Korporate Headquarters is ideal, but as Conquergood jogs along the Old Hudson River he considers his Korporate dress to be highly impractical and unnatural. The low temperature breezes come easily beneath the garment and it is the driving force which compels Conquergood forward and not the idea of seeing his twin brother, Vincent, again. Looming high above the dark and deserted Old Canal Street, skeletal buildings appear as though the Greek and Roman Titans have fled to Old Manhattan, where they wait in exile, in steel, in oblivion.

Conquergood attempts to recall what the abandoned wards must have been like a century or two ago — Could there ever have been enough traffic and communion to fill the roadways and bridges? Could the multitude of restaurants and shops ever have accommodated enough people? — To some extent, against the rationale and logic and history, the vacant skyscrapers and apartment blocks seem to have been built for a future generation of goliaths to come and once more make use of these facilities. Conquergood believes the shell of Old York City to be an empty city clinging on to an old hope for a new people to come and begin again. However bright the dreams might have been in the past, the lightless reality is that the Old Yorkers have vanished and only the crumbling city's structures were strong enough to remain, regardless of their centennial decay.

Breathing in deep, Conquergood allows the stars and the cold and the fresh air to feed him. The darkness beneath the monstrous buildings — like frozen titans standing motionless in a wasteland — increases the magnitude by which the stars above across Space and Time journey to meet him. Despite the emptiness all around there is a sense of clarity, and Conquergood knows how life should be shaped beneath the unobtainable heavens glittering with uncountable possibilities. He trudges onward through Ward 22.

Conquergood cuts across side streets and finds a larger street with rusty, corrupted signs reading Broadway. As he walks along, he looks for anything to clothe his exposed body away from the raw elements. Glancing through the broken shards of windows prove fruitless. Everything in the lower wards has long been looted and burned because of the '49 ban, turning Old Manhattan into the Hazard Zone. After the '45 Transonik Offensive — which destroyed most of the cities once known as Los Angeles,

San Francisco, Portland, Seattle, New York, Boston, and the District of Columbia — citizens were forced to migrate and move away from the east and west coastlines. Following the advice ordered by the Korporate Guard — which became the privatized military in 2137 — citizens migrated and spread themselves to the safety of Korporate Kontrol, one that squeezed softly at first, only to become a death grip to individual freedoms across the globe. Once they gained the power, the Korporation refused to relinquish it.

The official *historikal* Skript teaches us that the Korporate Guard blockaded both coastlines off at a maximum distance of six hundred miles, and only those who had special visas were allowed to enter into the *sekured zones*, such as New Philadelphia, the restored *Kapital*. Long ago, the survivors in Maine, New York, Pennsylvania, D.C., the Carolinas, Georgia and Florida were displaced into Mississippi, Kentucky, Tennessee and Ohio.

A Korporate-funded analysis showed that California was in real danger of further falling into the sea, and this led to the massive relocation of the west coast. Citizens who had been living in Washington, Oregon and California eventually dissolved into Montana, Wyoming, Utah and parts of Arizona. Special temporary visas of no more than thirty days were allowed for those entering Hollywood or Las Vegas. Many of the lower and middle-class citizens who could not afford to relocate became homeless strayers — the dreaded and forgotten outkasts.

On the authority of the K-net, Conquergood had also learned that in 2145 the transonik blasts across multiple key mega-cities had been carried out by extremists, who had been the poor meek of the old lands called America — the long silent majority who had had enough from the elite and exclusive trillionaire class — and the silent majority had existed for far too long on scraps tossed down by the overly corrupted wealthy minority.

Shortly after the concerted attacks, the ones who survived — known as the Fallen — were strongly advised to relocate — to where, no one knew — only to then be banned from ever returning to their homes.

For the *Gentrifikation Projekt*, the almighty Korporation cited safety concerns for the displaced citizens as a major influence. In case of possible future attacks, *Preemptive Safety Prekautions* — decreed by the Korporation — were of the utmost importance to restabilize and to return peace to the nation.

Because of the intense participation by the Korporation lobbying in politics and its superb and timely actions taken to assist the Fallen after the transonik attacks, the Korporation — which was entitled by the 14th Amendment to hold the same rights as a human individual, in addition to trillions of dollars and years of lawfare and dogged persistence — the Korporation managed and weaseled itself into the presidential election and was elected as the acting President in 2148.

By that time everything in the old Republic had been privatized and it made complete sense to WE — officially the Wealthy Elites Party — after the recent Korporate response during the years of the Great Tragedy that people, country, God had to hand over power to the Korporation in exchange for economic protection — freedom was traded for sound auspices and additional securities.

The "votes" proved to be the most terrific decision the outdated democracy ever made or would ever make again. The Korporation was able to swiftly eliminate terror cells all across the country, and, later, the world. The Korporation alone abruptly ended the several decades long War on Penury, the feat previous administrations were unable, or at times unlikely or unwilling, to accomplish.

The world looked to the Korporation as the modern-age Leader, new steps in a novel direction. The War on Indolence had ended in 2139, mainly due to the Korporation's successful lobbying to legalize many of the mainstream drugs for the benefit of the employed. The Korporation had cited several health benefits and huge profits that would undoubtedly flow into the pockets of politicians — more or less, the Korporation — and the profits would he combined with higher new taxes.

By 2151, the War on Pedagogy also came to a final and much needed konklusion. One highly intelligent tactic the Korporation implemented to bring the terror cells to their knees included the kreative use of an evolved system of Under-Kover Marketing. Citizens signed secret *kontrakts*, which freed most of them from edukation and debt, but forbade them to reveal the true Korporate agenda. Global citizens — employed by the Korporation and its subsidiaries — utilized *Under-Kover Marketing*, which responsively became a success. In as little as nine months, terror cells were detected and eradicated. Citizens cruelly and effectively betrayed one another in hopes of being accepted in the Korporate Kollektive.

After the War on Insolvency in 2152, during the last presidential election — Conquergood reflects as he scrambles through the wastes of Old York City — the Korporation bought the World Bank out right, taking control of the world's finances as a kampaign strategy, and soon thereafter eliminated all debts, both private and public. Developing nations all across the globe hailed the Korporation as the one who would bring World Peace out of somnolent dreams and childhood fantasies and into stark, blinding reality of the sophomoric adults. The Korporation was then elected to a second term as president but after a unanimous vote by Congress, which progressed and evolved years later into the *Final Kongress*, the two-term presidential law was removed and the Korporation was granted presidential status indefinitely.

In 2155 — three years after freeing the world from debt — the Korporation announced a new and emerging conflict: the War on Social Vokation. Global citizens once again hailed the Korporation as a savior. The employment of the poor masses began with the slogan:

KORPORATE KNOWLEDGE IS POWER

The Korporation cited the Prophet Mohammed in regards to the two 'mercies' in life: the first, bring water to the thirsty — the Korporation accomplished this in 2125; and the second, educate the ignorant.

Ilm, for Knowledge, became the war cry for a modern-day conflict. Nations were no longer fighting each other; they were fighting *Ignorance*. In doing so, "Islamophobia" vanished worldwide. Global citizens finally came to possess the three States of Being they had always needed and longed for: Edukation, Power, and Equality. Edukation brought Power and Power brought Equality.

Truly, in the minds of the global citizens who joined the Korporation and became official Korporate members all three States of Being were amicably resolved. The Korporation never failed to take care of its own. The chasms had been bridged — seemingly for the good of all humankind.

Conquergood is becoming one of *them*, and the word "them" comes to him at both times strangely *absurd* and *powerful*. He needs to be one of *them*, he wants to be one of *them*, but the more he knows about *them* the less he knows why he wants to be like *them*.

Waking from a mindless-nonstop trance of being on autopilot, Conquergood smells the piles of garbage located at the far side of Ward 22. Rot and sulfur drift up from the disjointed piles of smoldering rubbish and fill the insides of Conquergood's nostrils and lungs.

As he walks, with each heavy and calculated step, he can see smaller lots of refuse stacked against the walls of the disowned and abandoned buildings. Like a throne without a king, a three-legged chair mounts one such heap. The closer he comes to where he needs to be, the greater the intensity of the odor. The foul smell wrenches his insides into six knots and the new pain momentarily distracts him from the old pain, numbing sensations caused by the cold clinging to his exposed skin.

Then Conquergood spies what he has hoped to see for the past few excruciating hours. A small fire blazes in a grove once called City Hall Park now called the Burning Meadow.

Lonely Woolworth, another empirical monument of a lost era, can be seen toppled on his side in the shadowy depths of night.

Conquergood knows who will be waiting by the fire, because a few strayers could handle the terrible and tyrannic odors of the Korporate dumps. Sure enough, his three friends huddle in large overcoats, a faint resemblance of the Lost Ivans, and these three men have stationed themselves around a blazing fire, burning one of the many trash heaps.

"Ritz!" Conquergood calls out. The shadowy figures by the fire turn their sunken heads, dark as coal dust. "Ritz, is that you man!"

An arm shoots into the air and waves from the man seated between the other two.

Ritz, a bald man in his late fifties, stands over six feet eight inches, while his wild, gray beard falls to his navel. Beneath a large, tattered overcoat he wears a dirty-red sweater. As Ritz walks to meet Conquergood, he tosses a stray metal pole out of his way, wipes his hands on his raggedy jeans, while his boot kicks away the crumpled frame of a discarded baby's stroller from a time of babes lost now to the wolves of progress.

"Conquergood? How the hell are you?" Ritz says rhetorically and shoots a hand toward Conquergood. "Thought you were dead. Eaten."

Each man grabs the others' arm and pulls the other in for a hug. Upon closer inspection of Conquergood's kimono, Ritz adds,

"Are you a madman? Is that what those Korporate-devils dolled you up in and danced you out for the show?"

"Shut up," says Conquergood, shaking profusely as he stumbles over to the fire and seats himself to warm. "I'm freezing. Can barely stand."

Ritz gathers in another scan of the Korporate garment and then shouts, "Hey, Dodd!"

"What?"

The reply comes from the man who has been seated on Ritz's right. When Dodd stands, his bulky overcoat drops to the ground, masking his legs. His face of fifty years appears ten years younger and a lone scar drags from his right ear lobe down to a robust chin of prickly hairs. In his left hand he wields a bowl and in the other a spoon, which he playfully jabs upwards and says, "What took you so long, Conquergood?"

"Get our prodigal boy here some real clothes," booms Ritz, taking his seat back by the fire. "You can finish eating when he's started."

The last man, Otalp, speaks in a child-like voice. "Conqygood?" He isn't as tall as Ritz or as short as Dodd, but he's just as wide, and his cheeks shine like two round lanterns whenever he smiles. He is smiling now.

"Conqygood, is that really you?"

"Yes, Otalp, I'm back."

"I think you go bye-bye for a hundred thousand million years or more."

"Pipe down, Otalp old boy," Ritz belts from out of his broad chest. His eyes gleam beneath a protruding brow and his nose digs deep into his beard, as though an owl seeks haven in an old oak during a thunderstorm.

Dodd carries over some spare grimy clothes and, in a few minutes, Conquergood dresses beneath a large overcoat, jeans and woolen socks full of holes, and when

Conquergood gets a chance, he warms his hands and boots by the fire. Otalp brings him a bowl of onion and potato soup, heated in a tin pot with a lid. All four men sit around the fire, reminiscent of countless other nights.

"So, tell us," says Ritz, holding up the white kimono robe in his hands. He breathes in the fabric's lemony-sweaty smell and then thickly spits across the trickling yellow and blue flames. "What was it like in there? Did they do tests on ya'? Did they examine ya'?" A quick grin perches itself upright on the old man's lucrative texture.

Upon the broad and loose usage of the word "examine" does Dodd break out into a potent laughter which carries over to Otalp, who has not fully understood the insinuation and jape.

"I bet it hurt," Otalp says. His eyes are wide with curiosity imagining all the sharp instruments the Korporation must have used to examine and study Conquergood from the inside out. "I bet it hurt and hurt and hurt until you beg them to stop and you say stop and you tell them that you are their favorite friends and that you love them, yes?"

Conquergood leans his head sideways towards Otalp with a few fiery words of correction dangling on his tongue, but seeing once more the toddler face in the firelight upon the body of an overgrown teenager, he retreats, docile, and nods.

"It did hurt, Otalp, old friend. Hurt and hurt. Couldn't stand it anymore."

"I knew it," Dodd says. He waves the spoon around before dipping it into his bowl and shoving his mouth full of undercooked potatoes. He chomps with his mouth open and his eyes never retreat from the fire. "I wouldn't beg them no how to stop no matter how much it hurt. I'd die first before I give in to those Korporate bastards!"

"We all know you're a fighter," Ritz says amusingly, "and we also know full well that you'd squeal your balls off the moment they walked through the doors with their magic batons. Open your arse, ya' might." Laughter follows.

"Yeah, open for a spit," Otalp says playfully. "You'd squeal like a cute baby pig."

"Hey, Otalp," Dodd says.

"Yes, Doddy?"

"I hear there's some chocolate in the fire over there. If you give me some, I'll let you have the rest. Kay?" The lack of compunction in Dodd's voice can be counted by truck loads.

"Kay, Doddy," says Otalp, a grin lighting his face at the mention of chocolate. He had eaten chocolate only once before when Dodd found some in an abandoned shop, Geneva or something it was called. Otalp stands up awkwardly, having early stages of arthritis, and starts to reach into the fire before Conquergood leaps up and stops Otalp's hands at the fire's edge.

"There's no chocolate, Otalp. Go ahead and finish your soup." Conquergood helps Otalp sit back down on a stray log. "I also need you to listen in case we forget something. Can you be sure to remind us later?"

"Kay," replies Otalp, voice sweet with innocence. "I'm glad you back. You're my bestest friend. Not like Doddy."

"What about me?" asks Dodd, holding a chagrined expression. His arms are propped down over his knees and the soiled overcoat. When he looks up from his slouched position, he resembles one of those extinct hyenas Conquergood had researched on the K-net. "I was the one who gave you the chocolate in the first place, remember?"

"Pipe down, Dodd," Ritz orders. "We need to do some serious debriefing. So, Conquergood, what the hell happened in there?" He throws the Korporate kimono he has been holding into the fire. All four men watch as the kimono catches flame, turning from white into thick black and vanishes into dark smoke. "Did you find out anything?" Ritz says, adding to his friendly interrogation. "Anything? Anything we should know about? After all, we're your comrades and what you know I think we should all know too."

"Without question," Dodd adds from his slumped position. "Confess, or else!"

"Me too," adds Otalp, beaming. "Me too. Let's play."

Conquergood holds the bowl of soup out in front of him, elbows resting on his knees. He is warm again. While Ritz's words sound vaguely familiar, the image of Zawadi trapped inside the Korporate Labs comes back to haunt him as she seats herself hovering above the flames. From her meditative state, she silently watches Conquergood from her position above the fire. And then without a word she vanishes into the rising smoke.

"They told me," Conquergood says in a straining voice, "that I must to find my twin brother Vincent."

"What?" Dodd blurts out, pieces of onions and potatoes shooting from his mouth. "Has he lost it? What's he talking about Ritz? He's gone mad. They've must've done something to him."

"Pipe down!" Ritz waves a hand to quiet Dodd. "Speak up, boy, and tell us about this Vincent fellow. You can believe us when we say we're all very interested."

"I don't know," Conquergood replies. "I'm not sure if I even remember him. My memories are all blurry. But I remember one thing clearly: they said I could find him at Morgan's House in Ward Twen—"

"They've got to him!" Dodd yells to Ritz. "He's lost his mind or they've taken it from him. Either way, we've been compra-compra-*mized*. We can't stay here."

"Pipe down!" Ritz bows his bald head and rubs a hand over the rough skin. "If I have to tell you again, Dodd, I'll come over there and shove both that spoon and bowl nicely into that cute little arse of yours. Now go ahead Conquergood."

"They… They…" and Conquergood wants to say: they were not the enemies we thought they were; they are our saviors. Instead, he says nothing.

"They?" repeats Otalp, believing he has missed some important information. He is doing his best to follow the conversation. "Are they monsters with three eyes, four arms and a creepy tail?"

The three other men snap Otalp a what-in-the-hell-are-you-talking-about look but Otalp grins in return of the aspersion.

"No four arms, Otalp," answers Conquergood, biting on a piece of onion from the soup. Then he adds, "No tails and certainly no three eyes either."

"That's a relief," Dodd says. "I was beginning to worry for Otalp over there, because maybe the Korporation could come and give him a cute little pig's tail to match that face of his." Dodd lowers his scowl and touches the boundary of the fire with his outstretched hand, feeling the burning balance between cold and heat. Dodd closes his eyes and accepts the sharp stinging sensation, his face glowing red and wild in the white light of the fire. After a few moments, he retreats and leans back away from the flames and back into the cold night air.

Ritz strokes his long Tolstoyesque beard and watches Conquergood beneath the extended brow, eyes like spying men hiding in caves situated in high cliff walls: they can see you, but you cannot see them. Ritz finally leans forward,

"Tell us more about this Vincent fellow."

"I know I need to find him. He's my twin."

"Brother?" Otalp questions. "Our brother? Who?"

"He's going to do something terrible," Conquergood adds, "and I have to stop him."

"Like what?" Ritz asks.

"Not sure, but tomorrow morning I'll need to…" and Conquergood ceases because he is unsure of what he needs to do. Certainty has left him and now doubt pours into him with the sharp sting of the night's dropping temperature. "I'm not sure of anything anymore. The Korporation's…"

Ritz and Dodd share a look filled with questioning confusion and dark suspicion. Otalp can only look between his two friends and wonder what he has missed in the rather simple words from Conquergood.

"Conquergood," begins Ritz in a voice which rustles like dried tree leaves clutching their branches before the final great fall sweeps them into oblivion. "You have no brother," says Ritz slowly. "I've known you for fifteen years and I'm the closest thing you have to a brother. So, tell me: who is this Vincent you continually speak of? We don't know him. As long as we've known you, you've never known anyone by the name of Vincent."

Conquergood looks from Ritz's concentrated brow to Dodd's scowling constitution to Otalp's nodding head of child-like knowing. Within his own memories, Conquergood can plainly see Vincent with his blonde curls on the beach. Vincent is there in Conquergood's mind, very plainly; in the faces of his three friends, however, Conquergood knows there could not have been a twin brother in this lifetime.

Then Conquergood scans through the countless Vincent-memories, like a slideshow on a K-pad. Every single memory, albeit few and distorted, has a clear background different to the devastated wards he has known for the last two decades. The places in the Vincent-memories are unfamiliar and unreal, unlikely. The timeline is all wrong. Conquergood holds no other memory outside of Vincent which contains the backdrops of a clear and sunny farm, bright days of fishing by the river, or even the mountain they used to hike on the weekends. At times Conquergood sees himself inside the Vincent-memories and he is the same age as he was then, sitting by the fire in Ward 22.

Conquergood becomes aware of two distinct *faktions* of his memory: one is of the strayers, Ritz and the Lighthouse squad, in the abandoned city of grime and waste once called Manhattan; the other is of Vincent always in the countryside or on the beach, reflective and perfect.

How can both sets of memories be true?

Conquergood turns to look wildly at Ritz, as though he has seen a ghost trapped in the pages of a book or on the glossy surface of water.

"What's my last name?" tests Ritz.

"Don't give me that," replies Conquergood. "I haven't lost it."

"What's mine?" Dodd asks. "Time to answer up."

"I don't have one," Otalp says, "but can you give me one? I really really want one."

Conquergood places the bowl on the ground before his boots and stands to move to the other side of the fire. He turns to his three companions, faces alight with fearful anticipation. Conquergood is being tested and he hates being tested.

"Ritz," Conquergood says patiently, "Your last name is Ringmeier. Dodd, you scoundrel, your last name is Reese. And Otalp, dear friend, I've told you this several times before, you can have my last name."

"Otalp Conqygood!" Otalp shouts to himself, cherishing the sound his own name makes against the shadows of leaping flames and the piles of rubbish encircling them.

"Now that you all have your names back," Conquergood says, "I can't tell you who Vincent is. Maybe he doesn't exist, but he lives up here." A finger jabs into his right temple. "Either way, we're going to Morgan's house tomorrow to see what we see. Agreed?"

"All righty," Ritz says. "Why don't you take a seat and we can all finish out our supper in a little peace and quiet. Silence never hurt anybody as far as I know."

At that moment, coming from somewhere behind the four seated men, a suffering sound springs to life from within the shadows outside the reach of the fire's penumbra.

Conquergood stops and listens. "What's that noise?" He indistinctively hears what sounds like an animal groaning or a person moaning in terrific agony.

"I catch him," Otalp says joyfully. He turns and points behind the seated men into the dark edges of the fire's last light. "He was lost and I find him."

"We caught us one of those k-bastards this afternoon," Dodd says. "The coward didn't even put up a fight."

"He was lost all righty." Uninterested, Ritz turns in his seat to face the noise. Next time Dodd here finds some chocolate, Otalp will be the first to take his share."

Upon hearing Ritz's words Conquergood walks several yards behind the group to where a man is chained to a large stone block half-buried beneath a trash pile. The plump man, wearing raggedy jeans and boots and a shabby coat, lies with a loose potato sack over his head. Conquergood pulls the bag off to find a ruffled mustache severely in need of a good trimming. The disheveled captive huffs and puffs.

"Kin!" shouts Conquergood. "You're alive!"

"Jerome? Barbarians... plan to eat me... for dinner." The prisoner holds his aching head while he mumbles within a stupor. "How did you manage to find I out here? Where those mad brutes? Those imbeciles with no manners? Have they gone? Me wish I had my special remedy. O, Jerome. You saved me."

"I'll explain all that later." Conquergood turns back to the three men, who are now standing curious and frightful. "Otalp, come and help free this man. He's one of us now."

IV
Koded Messages

"Two fiery sticks placed together will burn themselves away." The reflection of the fire bulges in Ritz's eyes. He speaks low and mournful as one delivering a eulogy. "Man grows bright by the side of man, and alone, he remains stupid."

Kin, having been fed a bowl of onion and potato soup, remains quiet over by Otalp, who attempts to count the stars with an ear to the ground. Dodd smokes his pipe with rusty tobacco, minus the opium.

"After the tongue has got a skill for lying," Dodd says between puffs of thick smoke masking his distorted face, "it's almost impossible to stop it."

Conquergood looms on the opposite side of the blaze as he warms his hands and observes the other four men. The night grows darkest. He's being tested again.

"Only you can bring yourself peace," Ritz replies. He frenetically rubs his old hands with firm authority. He is barely moving any other part of his body, but if you were to look deep into the wells of his eyes, you would find activity abound. "And nothing can bring you peace but the triumph of your own principles."

A spark of recognition ignites in Kin's eyes as he's stargazing. He knows that last line quoted by Ritz. He glances over at Conquergood, who is watching Ritz and Dodd exchange verbal barbs of wits and wisdom.

"Compulsion repels," replies Dodd, "impulsion impels."

"Friendship," Ritz returns, "is the highest degree of perfection in society."

"The simple fool believes every word," Dodd answers. He opens his small mouth like a whale gulping in great pools of water and fish and out comes curls of thick smoke. His scar stretches and tightens along his jaw. "But the prudent man looks well to his going."

Kin turns from Ritz to Dodd to Conquergood seeking to recognize any form of understanding between the men. The conversation at first had struck him as depressing, if not utterly bizarre, but now he realizes they are speaking in a strange cipher system using specific references from pre-Korporate philosophers and sages. Kin cannot be sure, however, if the cipher is meant for him or for Conquergood, but he doubts little if Otalp — who is with a juniper stick violently slapping the shadows on the ground before his feet — understands any of the ongoing dialogue. Having never heard a discussion quite as intriguing, Kin decides to play his role in grandiose fashion. He rubs out his famous mustache, as one might sharpen a sword before battle, and readies himself for the War of Wits.

"Your sole contribution to the sum of things," Kin exclaims with confidence, "is yourself."

Ritz and Dodd turn their heads from the fire and release a slight chuckle at the untimely addition of Kin's insertion. Otalp claps his jumbo-sized hands in furious enjoyment as if a parent has just heard her infant speak with cognizance for the first time. Conquergood allows a brief grin to pass toward his former kompatriot, who nods in acknowledgement of his latest joust in words.

"If there is any person to whom you feel a dislike," Dodd replies with a low mutter over to Ritz, "that is the person of whom you ought never to speak."

"A fool speaks his mind," replies Ritz, looking over at Kin, "but a wise man keeps it in 'till afterwards."

"It's better to decide a difference between your enemies and your friends," Conquergood says over to Ritz — their eyes connecting across the leaping flames.

Conquergood finishes the thought, "In the former case, you will certainly gain a friend, and in the latter lose one." Conquergood nods back to Kin in affirmation of his loyalty. Conquergood, much like the ever-faithful Otalp, has chosen to remain faithful and true as he defends his long-lost friend.

Kin sinks into his seat and attempts to hide behind Otalp. Kin's face, once shining with a surge of adrenaline and courage before battle, flounders cowardly into his hands. Otalp places a giant comforting paw on Kin's shoulder. The conversation is in fact not about Conquergood.

A few days ago, Kin had been on top of the world as one of the most celebrated and elite doktors of the century and then he had unexpectedly fallen to a prisoner among the trash heaps of Burning Meadow.

Now by a wasteland fireside — "O you who turn the wheel and look to windward" — Kin is being judged, yet again — and such judgment is never an issue of justice but one of formality.

"There is such a thing as the intolerance of the tolerants," says Dodd, wanting to be fully heard. He rubs his legs and chews on the end of his pipe. Then, almost as an afterthought, he adds, "As well as the violence of the moderates."

"Esteem a worthy friend," replies Conquergood without drawing a hesitation, "as your greatest blessing."

Otalp stops attacking the shadows with his juniper stick and turns the stick in Dodd's direction and speaks with an authoritative voice, "And a good man, though troubled on every side, is not distressed; perplexed, but not in despair; persecuted, but not forsaken; cast down, but not destroyed."

Otalp has finally joined the War of Wits with a commanding voice of a spoiled-demanding child. He quickly adds, "A bad man is wretched inside every earthly advantage." Otalp's voice and body come alive as a thing bewitched and haunted, becoming detached from the man and earth, as if a Phoenix carries itself into flaming-soaring flight.

"I've never had any pity," Dodd replies to his friend, "because I think they carry their comfort about them."

"*I am* a good man!" Kin stands and huffs and puffs. The others freeze and watch Kin for a moment to determine his next move. He then falls back to his seat and proceeds to bury his face back into his proud, shaking hands.

"The most miserable man," Dodd says low to Ritz, "is he who cannot endure misery."

"Form your plans with deliberation," Conquergood says over the flames toward Dodd, "but execute them with vigor."

Silently Ritz nods and strokes his beard, as one might stroke a snake's back, for a long deliberative minute.

Scowling, Dodd continues smoking his pipe. He attempts to blow rings but only broken clouds come spurting out of his mouth. Otalp has once again taken up the activity of battling with his juniper stick the shadows on the ground as if swarms of fire ants marched upon his castle.

"Why are you hitting the ground like that?" Kin suddenly asks, breaking Otalp's concentration.

"Because no stay still," Otalp replies. "Slippery little devils. Elusive and quick."

"What are?"

"Shadows," Otalp says. "Shadows."

"That doesn't make any sense. No sense at all."

"Exactly my point. Why won't they stay still?" Otalp says. "Tell you another thing that makes zero sense." For a moment, he refrains from slapping the shadows. He turns and meets Kin's slumped shoulders and perplexed mustache, drooping along the crevices of Kin's cheeks.

Otalp adds, "We only accept our fantasies if we are able to reject them later. Can you make sense of that?"

Unable to figure Otalp out, Kin hunches to one side. "I'm not sure what to make of you, Otalp. You're as tricky as those damn shadows there." On the ground before the two men, the shadows dance and twirl and blink as though they were playful pixies.

The men wait for the final word from Ritz, pacing up and back in steps of twenty. He stops in mid-stride after several minutes and says for all to hear, "Yield rather to persuasion than to compulsion." Ritz turns to Kin and adds, "In prosperity, be moderate; in adversity, be prudent. Pleasure is fleeting; honor is immortal."

"What the hell does that even mean?" Kin blurts out in frustrated stupefaction. "Will someone please speak in proper English? Preferably in the old American style."

"You are," says Otalp, the voice retreating back into its calm innocence, "our friend now."

Ritz, limbs aching from too much cold, hobbles over to Kin. He puts out a hand and it is accepted by the latter.

"We are honored," Ritz tells Kin, "to have another worthy mind among us, despite the present circumstances of your ostracism. Forgive us our rather dull formalities, but we've come across Korporate spooks before. You can never be too careful these days."

"You could have done without the rhetoric," replies Kin, taking back his hand. He wipes the palm on his grimy jeans. His head collapses down further between his shoulders as he crosses his arms over his chest for additional warmth. Where a neck should have been a large mustache rests on top of his overcoat with an obtrusive nose and two languid eyes peering out.

"Again, our apologies," Ritz says. "We've found it necessary at times to be cautious of newcomers. Not everyone can be one of us, you see. The Korporation is the world, and if we are to exist in *their* world then we must, at times, be leery of strangers." Ritz concludes by taking back his seat between Dodd and Otalp.

"New friends are best!" Otalp exclaims with trusted acceptance. He slaps Kin's back with such a force that

Kin is knocked to the ground. As Dodd laughs through a haze of smoke, Kin gathers himself up and dusts himself off.

"Well, thank you for your hospitalities," Kin says. "Thank you for saving me from this dreadfully harsh and unforgiving environment, regardless of how barbaric your rituals may be. Me can assure you my ties with the Korporation have been unfortunately severed, and this is without any fault of my own. Innocent! In-no-cent!"

"None more monkeys jumping on the bed!" Otalp shouts. "Give them breads! Give them circuses!"

"Righty ho," Dodd answers. "I'll take some of that."

Hysterical laughter bursts out of Conquergood and pours into the other four men. Despite being taken aback by the sheer absurdity of Otalp's remarks, Kin joins in unison with the merrymaking. The fire burns brighter as the night softens its grip on the five friends.

Conquergood and Klaire face each other in the darkened room. The only light penetrates from a glow in the kitchen around the corner. Face to face, eye to eye, each one thinking of the other, alone and alive.

Staring at one another as though they are foreigners with tongues of a different language, communicating without vocalized speech, with the absolute touch of both hand and soul, or like two children upon the edge of a mature discovery their infantile vocabulary cannot yet voice its meaning.

Conquergood believes himself lost among her delicate cheeks, her hair braided back and falling to the center of her back, and the nude shoulders exposing simulated, stimulating flesh. Her perfume wets his lips for the moment and he caresses her breasts with gentle kisses, living and dying into another — a love making reincarnation.

Klaire trembles from nervousness and from the cold pouring into the bedroom from the vent above the bed. She kisses Conquergood's firm chest, her hands placed around his biceps.

Conquergood allows Klaire to take control. She becomes dominant and moves his head down to the pillow with a lasting kiss which separates and binds a few of her words to complete the silence:

"I love you. I want you. I need you."

Time slows. Time halts. Time ceases. Time betrays itself with heaving sighs of satisfaction for the purpose of lovers. Time is endless because it is absent.

When Time springs back to life, jolting delightful movements forward into a few clandestine hours, Conquergood is forced into waking, eyes popping wide, knowing by the sounds of his own heart vibrating from off the frozen ground, and the breathing of his own two lungs, solid and consistent, he is alone. He, Jerome Conquergood, is indeed alone — without Klaire.

His loneliness, however, is only a thought from within. But such a powerful thought it is. The thought, unspoken, can inhabit physical form, carrying the weight of the world. He is fascinated by how an abstract thought, an emotion, may have the power to cause physical, concrete pain in a person. And as he lies on the ground shivering from the wet, pre-dawn cold, his thoughts drift back into his lucid dream where he had once shared a bed with Klaire. The other half of his waking mind tortures himself for having left the Korporate Kompound, his luxury apartment overlooking the arboretum, artificial and fake as it may have been, and, without question, for having left Klaire and the warmth of her body.

Still, Conquergood has been alone for most of his life, or most of what he can recollect of his life — this lifetime anyway. Even around the Korporation and its Elite, and even among the Lighthouse Faktion, something unseen penetrates the core of his being. He is somehow different and in moments of silence and in moments of observant meditation he notices an absence in another person's eye or breathing, performing perfectly the necessary daily functions to a fault. And Conquergood, half in sleep and half in wakefulness as his head lies on a smooth rock, once again considers Aragon: "The marvelous is the eruption of contradiction within the real." Apparently, a contradiction boldly exists in all things surrounding Conquergood: in bodies and buildings — *But what is it?* And pondering this question, this coruscation, upon every hour brings back the dubious thought, the action, the movement of loneliness, eternal but not infinite,

Who am I?

Now watching the dawn buttering itself across the horizon, Conquergood stands vertiginously on the edge of half a bridge, broken and unmade. The connection had once unified Manhattan and Brooklyn before the Korporation severed the island's linking artery.

Conquergood stares downward into the waters and believes it is easy to jump, to fall, to let go of everything that the Korporation and the world tie him down with. And then Conquergood mumbles another quote — or part of one — from Louis Aragon: "The apparent absence of contradiction must be reality."

Another thought comes to Conquergood as he dangles over the side of the crippled bridge, a quondam vein snipped away — perhaps people can truly-verily fly and they have just forgotten how. The sun creeps up across the time-worn Old East River like liquid gold swimming through the gray hairs of a dead man.

Conquergood will need to get back soon, but he wants to see it through to the end. To finish what he has started long ago, but he decides once more to trod back into his thoughts of relativism. He is more involved than Otalp, even more so than Dodd ever will be.

Conquergood clings to a steel bar and leans over almost parallel to the Old East River below and he wishes it were the Old East Sea. Down below its surface, large mysterious shadows swim. Swim they do upon his soul.

The sun is coming and nothing can stop it from coming. When the sun wants to come, it comes. When it wants to go, it goes. Despite all the power of the Korporation and its machines, the sun does what it has always done before. And so, it will do the same tomorrow — until the sun expires, heaving one final-bending inward pull only to immediately reverse into one final-spreading outward push of powerful-unstoppable energy. Then the world — all that Conquergood sees and feels around him, and so very much more — will have just enough time to contemplate its unjust but natural end.

The fabrication of perceptive reality consumes the inner workings of Conquergood's mind just as much as it does the materialistic soul of the Korporation — what is *real*? What is *truth*? What is *real* illusion?

Without definitive answers to these allusive questions, Conquergood believes that *Beauty* cannot exist. Nothing matters afterwards, only names written in Keats's forlorn rain — a watershed of mawkishness. This fabrication exists in the very core of human beliefs and endeavors — *we* or *I* or *they* or *anyone* remain in the undying and unforgiving Now of the One telling the Story, the Myth — the undying center of the intelligible mystery of being.

The World and the Korporation belong as one and it consists, comprises itself, of rare individuals taught to systematically integrate their unwavering values and faith, despite language or religious differences, into the folds of the One — *E Pluribus Unum*! Everyone shares a common interest and it is the Korporation. All cultures, all religions, all peoples are deemed equal by the Korporation — have *we* not longed for peace on Earth and equality among men? Women? Children?

The Earth, his planet — Conquergood considers — has peace, and no matter how hard he tries he fails to visualize a time on this beautiful-thriving planet that has not known such tranquility and prosperity than the time at hand. Poverty surely existed, but with each new willing strayer being employed, and with each *outkast* dying from starvation and hubris, global citizens are becoming unified beneath the One World Order, and these global citizens have been made equal in finance, kommerce, and status. It is only a matter of time before *Korporate Kurrency* becomes obsolete. The ancient concept of money is but a trifling dilemma if one belongs to the mega-meta-organization that possesses all things in all places — is this not the new heaven on the new earth?

Conquergood once heard of a mysterious-prophetic strayer — known as the Soothsayer — who had long ago roamed the Outlands preaching-screaming about a land, a reality to some, where the One who controlled all things in all times provides all to all, and Conquergood feels such a time is imminent.

Conquergood knows the Old East River — taking only a few minutes to do the job — will be nice and freezing. Once the job is done it is done for good. An end to an end and that will be that — no more games, no more jobs, and no more of anything. For all he cares, the end can consummate a thousand new beginnings.

Dangling within the precipice of splintered bars, the morning breeze lifts Conquergood and he knows he is ready to meet and join the river. His mind has been filled with too much and still it is not enough — "I am older at twenty than a lot of people who have died."

As it has done every day since 1624, the sun rises and glorifies itself throughout the clear skies and over the forgotten boroughs. Another unimportant day in the lives of women and men has come to Old York City.

When Conquergood hops off the ledge and onto the pavement, Vincent's name is on his lips. He breathes and the name hangs lifeless in the vapors. One thing remains for Conquergood to do. There is no other way. It must be done. The river must wait.

Having been led by the hand by a boy to his spot before the tens of thousands in the crowd, the blind man's two worn palms press firmly against the two pillars on both sides of his body. The structure feels strong and resolute. His resting shoulders wait for the final moment. Blind, but with holy power, he can understand the weakness found in humanity, and such truth finds its way upon his own fractured soul. His thighs tighten but remain flexible and ready for the great push that is to come.

Finding the prayer he needs, he begins to push outward into the center of the marble pillars. Through his back, his shoulders, each sinew exerting unfathomable amounts of pressure and power out into his arms and deeper into his hands and palms and fingertips until the energy finds the pillars breaking, splitting, snapping, shattering, crumbling, cracking down-down-down among the frantic screams from the motionless crowd watching the horror of their own demise. Vanishing in the quake, the countless voices scream in one instant and are forever muted in the next.

As though he's a faithful sentry, Otalp is sitting in the same place he had been sitting the night before. No sign expresses that he has slept.

Kin uncurls himself from beneath several canvas bags and he watches Otalp pushing a juniper stick into the glowing embers. Looking around the campsite, he realizes that Dodd and Ritz are absent. Kin drags himself out of his earthly bed, dusts his clothes clean as best as he can, and retreats from the aches in his joints and neck by taking a seat next to the growing fire and to Otalp.

"Good morning," Kin says. "What a night that was." He rubs his face to smooth out the mustache and it appears as though he is in considerable want of a hot shower. The sun has not been up for very long and it appears white. "What's the time?" asks Kin, searching the area for Dodd but to no avail.

"No time out here," Otalp replies. He pushes the juniper stick into the small side of a flame and lets it fall. He bends over and gathers a tin cup and fills it with simmering koffee. Otalp replaces the koffee kettle alongside the fire, next to the pot of onion and potato soup from the night before, and silently hands the tin cup of koffee over to Kin. Resuming his seat, Otalp retrieves his juniper stick and begins inciting the tiny flames and glowing embers.

"That'll do nicely, Otalp," Kin, inhaling the fragrance, remarks into his steaming tin cup. The koffee tastes bitter but violently strong, and in Kin's mind it is of a superior quality, much higher in *kaffeine* levels than he had known back at the Korporation. To get a proper buzz, Kin had to drink at least six mugs of Korporate koffee to start his workday. Kin's beginning to feel nice and cozy after a few sips of Otalp's koffee, and Kin begins to forget the aches and pains in his back and legs from having slept on the cold-hard ground.

"Where's Jerome?" Kin asks.

"Gone bye-bye," replies Otalp.

"Really? Where to?"

"Maybe he going home."

"Where's home?"

"Where's your home?" Otalp asks with receptive interest.

Kin starts to answer the question out of reflex, but the morning haze of first waking halts him. He was going to say that his home is the Korporation but there are two problems with that answer: first, he wasn't born at the Korporation, nor if he had been born, then did that necessarily classify it as his home? What is a home?

Second, he never considered having a home. Everything that was necessary, vital and substantive had been provided to him by the Korporation. Why would he want anything more? What is a home anyway?

"Well done, old boy," Kin states. He sips his koffee and wishes it to be a little hotter. "Perhaps people should listen to you more, Otalp."

"Why? What can I say that another cannot say for himself?"

Kin's eyes freeze in place on the koffee in his tin cup. It is far too early in the morning to be doing any real thinking — that certainly cannot begin until at least ten. "What's the time? Can you at least tell me that?"

"The sun's the time. See there?" Otalp points one of his stubby fingers at the fully formed orb. "It's morning and not afternoon, nor is it evening."

"I'd say it's seven-fifteen on the dot," replies Kin, carefully observing the sun in the sky. "Yup, that sounds about right." Contented with knowing the time, Kin moves on to the next order of business. "Where're your two buddies? Did they get eaten by wild tigers?"

"I like white tigers. Tigers are soft but fierce. They will eat you if you don't watch out. They're like giant cats. I'd like to be a giant cat."

"Me too," replies Kin absently. "The felines have always attracted me more than canines." Kin stops suddenly and glances at Otalp suspiciously. "No tricks and games, Otalp. I'm on to you now. I don't care a thing about felines or canines or marsupials or mammals for that matter. Where are your two pals?"

"They are mammals, aren't they?"

Kin is about to take a drink of koffee but the tin cup remains suspended before his furry mustache and quivering lips. His heart beats a little faster and he grows a little livid.

"Are you playing the funny man with me this morning? Because I'll tell you something, old Otalp old boy. I have seven doktorate degrees and countless awards for excellence. You won't get by this deductive sleuth and my keen prowess for long. I tell you this as truth."

"Deductive?" Otalp remains attentive to the fire. "What's de-ductive?"

"I'll ask you one more time." Kin swivels in his seat and places the tin cup on the ground between his boots. "Where are those two ruffians you call friends?"

Without looking up from the ground, Otalp raises the juniper stick and extends it over Kin's shoulder. Kin turns a hundred and eighty degrees to see Ritz and Dodd trudging up between two large piles of garbage. Ritz's face is drawn lengthwise, extending it farther with his gray beard. Dodd moves erect, still not as tall as Ritz, and glows with a feverish joy erupting from the ego who knows he knows.

Ritz nods to Kin and takes his seat next to Otalp. Dodd walks by the three seated men and plops down into a slight shadow created by another large pile of trash. Taking tobacco from a small personal pouch, Dodd methodically lights his pipe and lies back with one arm behind his neck.

After things settle a bit, Dodd remarks, "Otalp, tell your best friend over there that his boy's gone — again."

"My best friend is Conqygood," replies Otalp, turning to face Dodd.

Curls of fresh smoke slip and twirl upward from Dodd's crooked mouth and into the crisp morning air.

"I mean," clarifies Dodd, "tell the man sitting to your left that Jerome's gone."

Otalp changes directions to Ritz and says, "Dodd says Jerome's gone — again." He returns to his duty of jabbing at the birthing fire with the juniper stick.

Ritz nods without a word. He kneels down and pours himself a semi-fresh cup of koffee.

"Is that true?" Kin asks. He has started on a second cup of koffee after Ritz and Dodd walked up, and he is beginning to feel partially awake.

"As true as that tin cup in your hands," Ritz says, "and that koffee in your gut." He stands up and takes a few lengthy steps around the side of the fire pit.

Kin imagines he sees a few of Ritz's thoughts swirling above the top of Ritz's head, or it could have been hot vapor rising.

"Where's he gone to?" Kin asks.

"He's gone bye-bye," Otalp replies grimly. "Already said that. Time to wakey-wakey."

"Back to work," Dodd adds. "Bending the knee, no doubt. Never thought it possible."

Ritz remains as silent as a king does before a final verdict of execution is handed down to a quivering peasant ignorant of his own crime.

"Before dawn," Ritz explains, "we followed him to Morgan's House — what had been formerly known as Wall Street a long-long-long time ago."

"So far away," Otalp says. "Street Wally."

Undeterred, Ritz continues, "We followed him to Fortieth, to a place where the First Washington was sworn in as President way-way-way back in seventeen eighty-nine. There was a message, likely a cipher."

"That history is before the Korporation," Kin adds. "Back before the Civil War."

"Inconceivable" Dodd remarks. "Unbelievable."

"On the side of a building there was a message," Ritz explains. "Could've been Korporate, but who the hell knows. As best as I can recall this was the message…" His voice grows cold and emotionless as he recites:

> *Vincent,*
> What is *death* we all so dread?
> Is it the *termination* of a life that has fled?
> Or is it a *transition* from kares on earth
> To the *realms* of bliss and *perpetual* mirth?
>
> If *death* is a transition from earth to bliss;
> The *meeting* of loved ones long *we have missed*,
> *Why should we* dread the narrow span?
> The narrow *divide* to *the spirit land?*
>
> *The reason is plain when you kome to think*
> That the *laws* of God are a dividing link,
> And he who *transgresses the laws* that were given
> *Stands* aghast *at the thought of the transition.*

"Then we lost him in the ruins," Ritz says. He sips his koffee lost in a meditative reflection.

Dodd smokes with a furious delight.

Otalp cuts at the fire with his favorite juniper stick.

Kin rubs his eyes and wishes he were dead.

Each man is thinking about the message, its clever riddle, and the answers which escape their wits.

"What the hell does that even mean?" Kin inquires after a few exacerbated moments of silent deliberation.

"It likely means," returns Ritz with a voice abounding in firm finality, "that Conquergood has gone into the Outlands to polish off another mission."

"Outlands?" Kin asks. "Mission?"

"He goes to kill," Otalp says in a low-mournful voice. "To desolate. To destroy."

Dodd is heard laughing in the background.

"Not possible," Kin says, stupefied at what he's hearing. "That's not like him."

Kin turns from Otalp to confirm the statement with Ritz. Their eyes meet and they understand one another, much in the same way a child's eyes of innocence come to meet his father's eyes of experience to better know a truth behind some horrible act.

Ritz's eyes do not waver, however, or look away. When Ritz finally gives a slight-confirming nod, Kin retreats back to Otalp, who is now violently thrashing-jabbing at the heart of the flames sparkling with a complete-final-perfect-blue madness.

III
Keystone Killjoy

Exhausted from his time on the outside and after taking an hour-long hot shower to remove the grime and the feelings of filth in every crevice, but before crashing to his bed for a much-deserved sound sleep, Conquergood shaded the optically intelligent windowpanes and closed tight the brown curtains which conceal the smart-fabric, which is able to apply images on command. The room has been waiting for two days in pitch darkness when Conquergood awakes in his apartment at Korporate Headquarters.

For the first few moments of waking Conquergood imagines seeing Leona's bare body by the windows; her perfectly formed buttocks, edging out from behind the curtains in one corner of the room, is rounded like a whole moon split down the center. Her body, playing with the light as though her hips hold the universe within, curves in the shadows.

Conquergood raises himself onto an elbow, rubbing his face with the other free hand. He has had a long last few days. He releases a terrible fit of coughing, the congestion rising into his throat while phlegm scratches and tears its way outward onto a waiting cupped palm. When the coughing ceases, Conquergood pulls himself onto the edge of the bed, chest burning, and he tries to remember how he got back to his Korporate apartment. *Absolutely blank*. He glances into the corner only to see the air vent blowing the curtains a little to the side. He had imagined her. If she had been there, then she'll always be there, but he'll have to wait for her to come again — *whenever that might be no one can know for sure*. The coughing erupts once more and he spits out more of the yellowish-purplish phlegm onto his hand. He manages to make it into the latrine when his throat tears open into another spastic sixty seconds of gagging.

Lit in blue-neon the automatic faucet comes on and excretes blue-neon water while Conquergood washes his hands clean and then his face and neck with cool waves of calm which seep into his hair, cheeks and the cool water continues to stream down his face and neck and over his bare chest.

When Conquergood looks up from the Korporate *lavabo*, the beach from his dreams is in the holo-mirror before him. Flames open bright once more — as they do in his dream — and in the reflection of his eyes Leona stands in the spaces between darkness and light — between nothing and everything. Conquergood spits into the wash basin and then places his head back beneath the free-flowing blue-neon stream.

Too much of not enough for so very long has taken its toll on Conquergood. His body shakes as he collapses backwards and there he remains against the wall with the faucet running continuously as ocean wave upon ocean wave slip to the silky shoreline inside the digitized holo-mirror where Leona stares back from that great darkness of the unknown but possible. Entrenched by her familiarity and the look of longing and searching on her face. In her augmented reality, she holds him captive. Conquergood cannot look away.

At first introspection, when growing up, Conquergood had no way of knowing people felt the way he did. There hadn't been a family around to show him the greater affections of a human bond. He didn't even know what to call the emotions he had experienced; but at other times, standing alone on the broken bridge as the dying sun set, Conquergood believed he somehow knew from within the names of his lost ancestors. Not having a family was his foundation of normalcy and any deviation from his norms came across as odd and as unfamiliar as a suffocating goldfish flopping madly upon dry land — like the time Vincent punished his pet fish named Clement for Conquergood's crime of taking too much time in the bathtub — but that cannot be a memory — *can it?*

A family — Conquergood thinks with his back still against the bathroom wall, the cold tiles beneath him, his elbows on his knees — is more or less like having a wet dream in cyberspace with a meta-lover, and thereafter when the man is all alone and knows the waking of such guilt and pleasure all intermixed in those wild-lurid fantasies, he will also come to believe — perhaps falsely or misguided in his belief — that a family is nothing more than one big-fat-giant delusion, a holo-desire.

He has been hurt and this hurt has stayed with Conquergood for far too long — *a decade or more, no?* Regardless of the anguish and spite within, Conquergood knows for a thing to be absent and missed it must first be present and in one form or another it must be experienced, real — *yes, solid and true.*

Since Conquergood has never had a true family, there is no authentic of genuine emotion to allow him to understand what it all means to have a family. There is no longing but the pit found in his aching stomach for food and potable drink, the only reliable scope of his desires — no dignity but that of survival; but now he desires a new veritable thing, unnamable, that cannot be eaten or drunk but can be had and refilled or even lost without ever knowing.

Never having felt such an emotion, Conquergood is uncertain of how to proceed. He wants it but doesn't have it. On occasion it has been found in Klaire's eyes but never his. Never his.

Remaining on the bathroom floor, exhausted yet spurned on by the greater mysteries waiting in the dark deep of the digitized holo-mirror, Conquergood spends countless minutes, entrenching decades to him, staring up into the photographic-conductive holo-mirror that takes up most of the entire wall space, locked with his own eyes and his own being — an essence true and raw — and he tries to determine if love could really exist within him — deep down beneath flesh, blood, bone.

His brown eyes — every time — explain to him the exact story, and it is like a true mythology that he cannot allow himself to believe. The blank spaces are only large crevices where some of his memories and love should be — bottomless, endless, eternal. The deeper he dives in search for some familiar point of reference, the more he uncovers a nothingness within himself holding tight to more of itself, more of nothing and nothing. This nothing is much the same to a sweet-sticky substance that embodies itself in the places of his brain, locking away the electrodes of love he believes he deserves to one day possess — as all people once did, long ago before the Great Fall of Society.

Nevertheless, Conquergood is comfortable about the fragments of his memory because, unlike many things in the world, these mental notes and severe fractures remain constant. He cannot count on love, but he knows, staring into that real-time display of his own image, that he can count on the emptiness — a kind of peace and ease without the awe — to be there waiting for him. This holo-mirror-mirage is found also in his projected death where he imagines seeing his full life come to an abrupt end and he knows the meaning for his being and his end isn't what he wants it to be.

Later in bed Conquergood awakes refreshed.

"Open curtains, lift shade."

The darkness splits and from the bay window he can see an overcast of super-storm *klouds*, gathering above the transparent dome.

Silence has stretched itself thick throughout the room as he tries to determine how he made it back his bed. Slowly he goes over and pulls down one white kimono robe of many from a hook attached inside the collapsible *klozet*. As he dresses, he releases a short cough while moving to the bay window.

He places a palm on the surface of the flexiglass window and can slightly feel the weather dropping from late autumn to winter. Loose and fluttering down, snowflakes rest on top of the dome's flexiglass surface high above. Below the dome, the interior of the Garden remains untouched in its sublime immortality of spring. A man and woman sit together smoking opium cigars on one of the stone benches near the center fountain. From behind Conquergood — breaking his concentration on the Garden's tranquil scene below — a chime erupts from inside his apartment.

"Open," he orders without looking back.

Klaire enters. "I thought you were gone."

"I am." Conquergood stares upwards toward the falling snow. "Gone."

"What?" Klaire joins Conquergood's side by the bay window. Her breath smells of strong mint, and a trace of opium hits his nostrils.

"I mean," Conquergood counters, covering his mouth for a cough, "I was gone. But I'm not sure how I got back."

"I'm glad you're back." Klaire wraps her arms around Conquergood's waist, her head on his chest, and her essence falls into his being. "You scared me."

A tremor comes from Conquergood's thoughts: images of a warzone interspersed among flashes of smoke and fire when several explosions blind him before causing him once more to erupt into a fit of dry coughs.

When the pain subsides in his chest and abdomen, and Conquergood has caught his breath, he says,

"It *is* good to be back home."

Klaire leads a feverish Conquergood to bed — and taken from the bottom of the *klozet* — she covers him with an artificial-wool blanket, embroidered by a giant **K**. He sits upright against the headboard with pillows supporting his head and back. Klaire tucks the edges of the blanket around Conquergood's legs and leaves the bedroom to enter the digital kitchen to prepare some Grand Earl Korporate tea for the both of them.

Conquergood reaches over to the night table and pulls the Korporate Handbook onto his lap. No longer caring because of the sweaty tremors rising and the pain in his mind and lungs, he flops open the book to a random page. The book settles on to page one hundred and seventy-three. Conquergood begins to read semi-silently, only a mumble can be heard:

"Chapter Four: The Fundamentals of Korporate Ideals by Doktor Keystone Killjoy."

Because Conquergood can hear Klaire in the kitchen working, he relaxes his tensed shoulders a bit and shifts to a more comfortable position against the pillows. To himself he begins to read,

"The power of the Korporation does not lie with its ability to *kontrol* all *materialistik* goods and all environmental necessities. The true nature of the Korporation's prowess to sustain faith within its members is distributed equally through the seven Korporate Ideals of Ownership: Dignity, Freedom, Fame, Integrity, Justice, Love, and *Respekt*."

"The tea will be ready in a minute, darling," Klaire says from around the corner. Her voice resonates upon thin wisps of vibrating streams. Conquergood glances up for a moment to see Klaire's shadow crossing the side wall; back and forth the dark shape goes in a frenetic pace to prepare the hot tea, a remedy from one's own stress.

Conquergood's eyes then shift back to the solid page of hemp paper, quite unlike the digital e-pages the Korporation in its mandatory readings. He releases a short cough and begins reading where he had left off:

"Dignity is the first of the seven Korporate Ideals of Ownership which must take root in a member before he *kan* transcend the paradigm of true Korporate ownership. If one is to take part in any substantial *praktice* involving self-worth, especially the worthiness of the Korporation's goals and *expektations* of its Elites, dignity must be established and allowed to *bekom* the foundation of all the other Korporate ideals."

Conquergood, with book resting in his lap, glides his thoughts to the bay window. In many ways Conquergood believes himself to be more dignified than ever before. It has been the Korporation that has given him the ability to grow and manifest into one of the much-respected Korporate members — regardless if he wears the official Korporate Seal or not — and with such responsibility Conquergood believes he has indeed found his dignity. He no longer sleeps alone in abandoned buildings, open to the climatic hands of chance. He no longer needs yellowed and mildewed books for pillows. He no longer requires a stark trepidation which had filled his most basic forms of survival. He no longer has nightmares of being found by the Korporate Guard and thrown into one of the many Korporate Kamps, where it has been legend that *outkasts*, out of sheer desperation and starvation, consume one another for pleasurable sport and fresh meat. Now, however, Conquergood has changed his fate, dear old mother *fata*. He is now, at this moment, in a warm bed, a beautiful woman on the first day of winter prepares hot tea in the next room, and, most importantly, he no longer contains the suffocating anxiety which has kept him prisoner of his own mind for so very long.

Klaire enters the bedroom carrying a silver tray with a plain white teapot and two matching saucers with cups, rimmed with blue Egyptian hieroglyphs. She places the tray on the night table and sits prostrate next to Conquergood on the bed. As she pours the tea into cups, she says, "Your digital kitchen is really bare. All I found were some Grand Earl and saltines with black olives."

"I didn't know I had a kitchen."

"Every apartment has one. It's hidden in the wall near the ordering pad. Like most appliances, it needs a voice order to work. If you want, I will show you how to operate it tomorrow. But I have a feeling you won't be using it very much, will you?"

"Please do." He carefully handles the saucer with one hand and the cup with the other. He sips a little, the hot tea slightly burning his tongue. "Still too hot." He places the saucer and cup on the bed beside him.

"Blow on it a little," says Klaire, leaning next to Conquergood. "Like this." Her lips pucker and she begins to blow the tea to cool. Then she notices the book, open and mute, lying beside Conquergood. "I didn't know you could read." She motions to the Korporate Handbook.

"Can't you?"

"Some, but not very well," she replies. "Just mostly audio, which is way easier."

"I thought *all* Korporate members could read."

"I *kan* read," Klaire barks back. She hesitates before allowing her head to come to rest on Conquergood's shoulder. "Just not all that much. We're taught to read up to the K-Five Level and after that, reading's no longer mandatory. Besides, you shouldn't believe everything you see and read."

"I see." Conquergood enjoys another drink of hot tea, the liquid loosening his throat, relaxing under the remedy — *why does it hurt so?*

"Go ahead and read me some," Klaire says. She points to a spot on the opposite page from where Conquergood has ceased his reading for deeper, more tangible thoughts.

"As you like," says Conquergood, knowing the price his throat will pay for reading aloud. But he does it anyway. Sometimes that's the way the cards are played — doing things simply because someone asks nicely.

"Read to me. Read so I'll fall asleep to the sound of your voice," she says. "I've missed you ever so much."

Picking up the handbook, Conquergood continues reading in a soft, but rather hoarse voice:

"Fame must be evident if a Korporate Elite is to remain loyal to the *kause* and to the mission. Without the fame of the individual or Korporation, there *kan* be no willingness to *konsistently* achieve an ever-greater status than before. Likewise, the loss of fame, being stripped of one's popularity and *suksess*, despite achievement and *akkolades*, is just as important as having people applaud the inner-workings of the Korporate member."

"You're a smooth reader," says Klaire, her body becoming supine, "but that's all too *philosophikal* for me." Her voice comes out barely above a mumbled whisper and Conquergood can feel her breathing slowing and her body giving way to sleep — like a Korporate Komputer shutting down to hibernation mode.

Conquergood turns a few pages and allows for a brief moment longer for the words on the page to be voiced to fill the deadness of Space and Time:

"Love for the Korporation *kannot* be achieved if Korporate members are not able to love one another. By loving, members *kan* be given one of the greatest Korporate gifts and benefits there is to propagate. Love, in its very essence, is pure *dedikation*, honorable *kommitment*, and extreme *satisfaction* — even in the most mundane of events and situations. Love is the key to developing the Korporation into a *konkrete* entity which is able to *konstrukt* its own omnipotence and ubiquitous *inkarnation.*"

Klaire has fallen into that sweet-slumbering pit of Reality Retreat. Conquergood closes the handbook and tosses it to the end of the bed. The teacup wavers and then settles. He picks the teacup up by the handle and finishes the concoction in one gulp.

Love — Conquergood thinks — is the key.

"K-News on," Conquergood commands in a low but firm voice. "Silent mode."

The KV flicks on to an aerial image. Images of a burning building, smoke churning skyward, stream in live. At the bottom of the three-dimensional projected e-skreen are the scrolling words:

BLESS THE ALMIGHTY KORPORATION!

ASSASINATIONS OF THE TOP LIGHTHOUSE

MEMBERS HAVE BEEN SUKSESSFULLY

KARRIED OUT AS OF LAST NIGHT... IT IS

ESTIMATED THAT EIGHT OF THE TOP ELEVEN

OFFICIALS WERE ERADIKATED BY THE KG IN THE ONGOING ATTEMPT TO DISPERSE AND END DISSENTION AMONG THE RENEGADE STRAYERS… MORE TO FOLLOW IN THE HOUR.

Conquergood tenses, causing the teacup to roll over spilling small remnants of foreboding tea leaves onto the artificial-wool blanket. He recognizes the burning rooftops and a large wall with the words "Kilroy was Here" e-sprayed in neon-orange — *"When a man cannot choose, he ceases to be a man."*

The neighborhood is found in Ward 15 and it flashes once more across the K-News. Conquergood, however, glimpses a recent vision of the building engulfed in flames from a different angle.

He has been there at that exact spot. The knowing haunts him, and it is not because he recognizes that his presence had recently been at that building, but because the knowing is incomplete — unmade but not forgotten — unfinished and somehow undone.

Klaire opens a single eye, looking towards the dying destruction of what had once been the meeting quarters of the Lighthouse Faktion.

"What happened?" she questions, almost mumbling.

"I'm not sure exactly," Conquergood replies, his expression filling with a sense of bedlam. "But I'd like to know. I'd really like to know."

On the authority of the Official Skript, Ritz leads the other three men down a darkened path with wire-meshed windows in the abandoned and debilitated Stonewall Inn, scrawled with centenarian graffiti and detritus.

Ritz trudges forward in the absolute blackness as though he is Shakespeare's King Lear among his beloved daughters. He instinctually and sharply turns left through a doorway without any attached door, then a right through another much smaller doorway, and then he follows a poorly made rubber-treaded wooden-staircase spiraling hellward into a mixture of leaping shadows and ascending merriment from below. After several minutes of descending into the bowels of the building, Ritz finally emerges into a large warm chamber lit in a shade of soft amber. Moments later Ritz is followed by Dodd, Otalp, and lastly the ex-*Korpatriot*, Dr. Kin.

The room's five patrons are of the Lighthouse Faktion, and they are all speaking and joking in a frenetic-jocular vernacular. But as the frigid entourage of the four arrives through the front entrance, the warm conversation immediately ceases. The five partisans hesitantly accept the four newcomers with a nod and a wide expansion of uncertainty as the incoming group finds seats on a few scattered chairs and wooden boxes.

Encompassing the side wall above and behind the tattered sofa, six rare box jellyfish pulse like intoxicated sprites in their incandescent aquarium. The light from the tank casts long shadows out across the subterranean room. One man and two women drink a greenish liquor — not unlike the legendary Absinthe — and recline on the tattered sofa which sits along the wall below the jellyfish tank. In one back corner of the room sits a man sharpening a huge hunting knife.

On the adjacent wall behind the man with the hunting knife hangs askew a single tattered oil painting of a lone lighthouse situated on a cliff rising above crashing waves. This towering symbol of hope which gives sailors the direction to a safe port beams its xanthous glory into the oncoming darkness of a volatile tempest.

Directly beneath the lighthouse painting, a lone man sits in a lone chair. "Were you followed?" Jonathan Miller questions from his armchair as he pets the lily-white head of a bald eagle, thought to have been extinct decades ago; the size of two footballs, the bird perches next to Miller on a wooden stand.

An unthinkable rarity among the city strayers, the Eagle blinks black ovals and bends its neck towards Kin. Miller's malicious eyes are buried beneath trenches of sleepless nights, wrinkles filling his gritty oil-based skin.

"Not in a million years," Dodd inserts before Ritz can answer. Near the tattered sofa, Dodd has taken a seat next to Mayhew, who sits at one end of the sofa. Mayhew is two times as large, and as hirsute, as Ritz or Miller.

"Then who's this Korporate filth attached to Otalp here?" William Mayhew asks.

Mayhew wears an anachronistic British bomber jacket with the astrological scales as an emblem for justice stitched to the chest. In his left hand, from which he sips, is a half-empty liter of Società Vittoria Gin. A scar, much like Dodd's, stretches from Mayhew's left ear and up over his brow from when a drone's heat-guided laser at twilight whizzed by less than five feet away and struck a deserted deli. The explosion thrust metal shards and all-manner of concrete debris and metallic shrapnel into the air. Ritz had been the man to pull Mayhew free of the blast's untimely mayhem on that evening thirteen years ago.

"None to fear," answers Ritz, taking a loaded pipe filled with fresh cannabis mixed with peyote from Sibley Herberg, who sits at the opposite end of the tattered sofa.

Sibley's tartish eyes glisten on Ritz, and her long straight raven-tint hair reaches to her hips. She has on a red knitted V-neck sweater, exposing beads of sweat glistening on her cleavage. Her hair falls over her partially exposed bosom and comes to rest on her taught stomach.

With one mature eye on Sibley's bountiful chest, Ritz inhales a few hits of the pipe and leans his head back on the top most part of the chair he sits in. His muscles ease and Sibley curls over the edge of the tattered sofa and begins stroking Ritz's matted-gray hair.

In the middle of the tattered sofa — sitting between Mayhew and Sibley — Mary Crook, a petite blonde with short cropped hair, is eyeing Kin with curious amusement and navigated suspicion, as a mouse might sniff around a baited trap in dire hopes of stealing a piece of cheese.

Kin, meanwhile, huddles next to Otalp's looming frame on two wooden boxes. The good but exiled doktor quivers in unexpected fright near the front entrance. He knows he is certainly out of his element here among the renegades known to Korporate members as the Lighthouse Faktion.

Gregory Barron — the fifth member of the Lighthouse Faktion — bounces between darkness and light as he stretches himself out on a chair next to Miller and the Eagle. Half of an unlit cigar drapes itself at the corner of Barron's mouth, between two full-purplish lips.

Barron's deeply toned skin resonates the profound knowledge he shares with many worldly things left unknown. The whites of his eyes stay on Dodd, not having forgotten the odious insults the last time they had shared a conversation. Dodd had blithely mouthed that Barron's mother had been developed in a Korporate test tube. Now in Barron's hands, the hunting knife's blade sparks against a thick brick.

Smoke slithers up to a ceiling fan, moving at a crawl. In the center of the room, a ruby colored shisha hookah is strategically placed on a shredded Indian rug. Embroidered on the rug three elephants decorated in war regalia march in battle against a small hoard of invading European infidels. It is this battle scene which draws Kin's attention the most.

Like the victimized rug, the tattered sofa and battered walls bear testimony to a silent profanity of misuse and dusty tribute exemplifying the tragedy of a glamorous age filled with splendor and simplicity, forgotten by all but a chosen few. Spiderwebs hang loosely in each of the four corners but remain hidden from view by the shifting shadows spawned by the jellyfish in their glowing tank.

Coquettishly, Mary dangles the hookah's hose tip to her blueberry-painted lips, inhaling the empyreal herb. A distracted Kin eyes her as she eyes him beneath her thin slits of eyelids.

Kin is worn and tired of trudging through the snow — all without a mug of koffee. He is, however, happy to be in a heated basement, escaping the intensity of the night and the deepening cold.

"Did he make it?" asks Barron, turning his gaze from Dodd to Ritz. A few sparks fly outward from the brick.

"He made it all right." Ritz, being petted by Sibley, answers without opening his weighted eyelids. "He made it in and right back out again. How he did it, we'll never know. But he did it. Or they let him do it. Those Korporate monsters may have let him in just to get their grubby hands on him. Whatever they did, they scrambled his gray-matter where he doesn't know up from sideways. He thinks he has a twin brother named Vincent. Imagine that! We should've never sent him inside. Damn those Korporate savages!"

"That was his choice, babe," Sibley says. Her long black nails rub against Ritz's arm.

Ritz appears youthful next to Sibley and he also looks to be asleep but his cogitation is ever evident. He releases a heavy sigh against his thawing limbs. To himself he says, "What the hell were we thinking?"

"A twin brother?" Barron asks while taking the pipe from Ritz. Barron's dark brow tightens and his heavy beard judders and glistens when he breathes in and out. Thick with the scent of cannabis and peyote, a smoke funnel lifts itself up and over Barron and out over the other members of the Lighthouse Faktion. "He doesn't have a twin brother. None that we know of, and we've known him longer than anyone. We've never seen him to have a twin. We're the only family he's got."

"Not the only one," Otalp says. He fumbles with his malformed stick of juniper that he has carried from the campsite. "Our brother has two families now."

The portent does not pose well on Mayhew's countenance. He turns to Miller with a searing expression of forewarning. The Eagle blinks back, slick white and brown feathers waving beneath the slow churn of the ceiling fan from above. Shades of light and dark from the box jellyfish and glass tank sink and rise on the lighthouse painting as the jelly-creatures flitter freely in their watery habitat — untouchable and godlike.

"What do you think they're up to, Ritz?" Miller questions. He brings one of the tubes from the shisha up to his mouth and watches the bubbles gargle in the base of the bottle. Delighted by the herbal enchantment, Miller jets out rings of smoke with a caricature of a hollowed-out face and ghastly orbs for eyes and a disparaging mouth in the center. Mary shudders at the rising, fuming skull sluggishly drifting into oblivion.

"Something big and heavy," Dodd sounds. His eyes are already beginning to close. The warmth of the room wades over the gelid muscles, easing them into tranquil repose. How tired he is of cold nights and snowy days.

"Something infamous," Otalp prophesies. The members of the Lighthouse Faktion, including Kin, tense up when the heavy-set child-like man speaks of holy and mysterious portents. Rarely is Otalp known to be wrong. All but Kin know Otalp's track record with omens. Mary, shivering, wraps herself with a blanket.

"There are all types of ways," Sibley states in a disinterested manner, "that we know of for altering a man's mind and mood, right?" She crosses her long, lean legs over while the faded blue jeans scrunch against each leg. She places a bare hand on a raised knee. "For one, the Korporation could've used atrocity accusations on him. Or they could've done hyperbolic inflations, polarization, and meta-propaganda we've all seen before. Then there's dehumanization. And let's not forget my all-time favorite mind control technique: Divine Sanction."

"I wouldn't be surprised," Barron says, "if they did all that on the poor boy, and then some." He wipes his brow with the back of a large hand fit to strangle two men's throats. "But the real question is why?"

The room grows silent in contemplation. Then Ritz conjures a thought aloud,

"The conference is ten days away."

Mayhew clears his throat with a swig from the Società Vittoria Gin. "New Philadelphia's going to be a hot spot. I, for one, am glad I'm not going to be there. It's a sure thing for the KG to denounce the truce and wipe us all away like memories from one of their ultra-meta komputers. What are we to them? Really? I want to know. What?"

"We're dolls to them," Miller says. "We're a nasty bug inside their righteous meta-komputer. We're nothing more than an enigma to their utopia."

"I hate political jibber-jabber," Mary says. Her motherly breasts, partially hidden beneath the blanket, jiggle and further attract Kin's attention. She notices him admiring her, and as she acknowledges his look with a wink, Kin nervously turns away.

Dodd, now gently sleeping, offers up his usual flaccid snoring, which is easily ignored by the ongoing palaver.

"In our time and age," Ritz begins, "there can be no such thing as keeping out of politics. All these issues we are faced with are nothing more than political issues. These issues of politics and Korporate whoring are nothing more than a mass of lies. They are evasions and folly found in a den of hatred and schizophrenia."

"Who said that?" asks Mary, turning her attention back to Ritz. "Sounds vaguely familiar."

"It was old George," Miller quickly answers. The Eagle nods in agreement. "The Prophet Orwell."

"But from where?" Ritz counters. "After all, knowing a name is never enough. We must know where the origins can be found. Facts do, and can, matter."

Kin twiddles his dense mustache searching the medical libraries of his feigning thoughts, and still, he has nothing more to offer to the elusive riddle. The Lighthouse Faktion looks at one face to another without any hope of answering Ritz's savvy joust.

"Do you remember the Year of the Dead Peasants?" Barron asks rhetorically, changing the subject. Everyone, as well as Kin, knows of it.

A multitude of major *kompanies* cashed in on secret life insurance policies they had taken out on their employees. The eager act of desperation came from the economic crash and the turmoil to regain profit margins.

"When the Jove virus was released," Barron continues, "it wiped out over eighty percent of the key industrial zones and their populations."

"There's no proof of who actually ignited the germ warfare," Mayhew inserts. He grips the neck of the gin bottle tighter. "But we do know," eyeing a silent and cowering Kin closely, "that all those major *kompanies* cashed in big when the J-virus hit."

"True," Miller says. He thrusts out two trails of smoke from his nostrils. "But we do know that the insurance policies those *kompanies* collected were their last gasp before the death plunge. The Korporation bought them out after the profit margins crashed into bankruptcy. It appeared foresight was not in the repertoire of the head execs. The Big Suits saw the bottom line only in that fiscal quarter. Their stocks soared to incredible record-breaking heights, but like the son of Daedalus, they did not know how high or how far their creation would go."

"Then there was the government admission in the early part of the twenty-first century," adds Sibley, her taut hands tensing against each other, chest drawing inward and outward heavily as if reliving an atrocity. "The government admitted to using blood from new-born babies in experiments. They wanted to enhance, and I quote, 'to improve the quality of human life.' Honestly. Didn't our ancestors have any standards? A moral compass to guide them?"

"Let's play this game a bit deeper and go further back in history," Mayhew inserts. He grimaces and his head falls back so he faces the decrepit ceiling with its shadows and holes. Then he continues, "During the Second World War scientists endeavored to improve human genes, transgenic and eugenics. A *bloody mess* that turned out to be. Humans and their twisted desires for knowledge."

"Joyce knew a thing or two," inserts Kin, once again untimely. He has been thinking of Daedalus but was too slow to respond. As the words slipped from his mouth to the tune of the literary reference, he knew it had been a drastic and gaunt error, a good deal too late.

"I doubt Joyce would be proud," Sibley says. From her seat beside Ritz, Sibley storms up scowling mad and proceeds to march over to Kin. A long forefinger with a silver ring in the image of a twirling ophidian, rubies for eyes, extend itself nearly touching Kin's disheveled mustache. "James could never be proud of murder, especially murdering babies, you Korporate goat!"

With that she stamps off into an adjacent room where the cooking is usually done. Ritz, amused, belts out a laugh, followed by the rest of the Lighthouse Faktion.

Kin, cheeks bursting like a volcano, lowers his eyes and clasps his hands and wishes he had some of his special remedy to pass around, or to swallow it all and forget he had ever known the glory of the Korporate Elite and the depths he now finds himself in, as though he were one of Lucifer's fallen kinsmen after the Great War Above — *better to love in Hell than to hate in Heaven.*

"But what is the Korporation planning to do?" asks Miller, looking over at Ritz. "Another air-born attack, you suppose?"

Lights from the box jellyfish tank flicker twice then shut off completely, shrouding the room in unexpected darkness. Shuffling is heard and Mary shrieks.

"Who shut the power off?" Mary asks into the emptiness confronting the dark space before her. She can vaguely make out red and blue and yellow beams flashing in splinters ahead of her.

"I'll go and check the generator," Barron says. "Damn it be those monstrous rats again. Those beasts are getting hungrier, and bigger."

"I'll give you a hand," Mayhew adds. He places the partially empty gin bottle on the floor. "I know that generator inside and out."

Rustling and lifting and shuffling are heard briefly and next comes firm footsteps resonating to the back of the den where a wooden door is covered by a large quilt stitched together by pieces of gray tattered clothes: blouses, halves of long-sleeved shirts, corduroy pants, sweatpants, parts of coats and several pieces from woolen socks with holes makeup the old quilt.

The quilt is pushed aside, offering a muffled flap to the void. When the concealed cellar door closes, it bangs against a rusted nail which keeps the door in check and prevents the it from swinging back inside the room.

Otalp feels Kin jump when the cellar door, much smaller than the frame, slams back to its place. Miller's eagle pipes a dry screech through the pitch black and the man calms the bird with smooth strokes of his hand over the ruffled feathers.

"Electricity's getting expensive?" Ritz jokes to no one. "Who forgot to pay the bill?"

Otalp and Mary laugh toward each other and the jovial quality in the sounds make the room lighter and not as scary. Their eyes adjust and determine shapes in mysterious forms. An additional human shape outlines itself at the front entrance but no one takes any notice but for a quivering and uncertain Kin.

Sibley voice erupts from the kitchen. "Ritz," she says in a flat but resonating voice throughout the stillness of the dark room, "where did you put those oil lanterns?"

"Bottom left," he replies without hesitation. "Do you need help?"

"It wouldn't hurt you none, now, would it?"

"As you please." When Ritz stands up, he trips over a shisha hose and the hookah flips over, spilling ashes and dirty water across the rug. "Damn," he mutters. A few moments later the others can hear the rummaging of metallic pots and pans from the next room.

From the opposite side of the room, the cellar door can be heard banging shut, ousting the other sounds coming from within the kitchen and the sound of the six box jellyfish slipping through oil-colored sublimity.

"Barron," calls Miller, tensing in his seat. "Mayhew, don't be messin' around down there! Ya' damn fools."

"I thought I saw someone go out. Not down," Mary answers Miller. "Who's missing? Sibley and Ritz are in the kitchen. Barron and Mayhew are in the basement checking on the generator."

"Otalp, say here," Miller tests. He grips the sides of his armchair.

"Here, here," Otalp cries with glee. "I'm here, says Old Mickie Donald." Enthusiastic clapping can be heard from Otalp. "This is fun. No more shadows on the walls. Look!" He points a stubby finger no one can see to the adjacent wall where the lighthouse painting still hangs.

Miller and Mary cannot make heads or tails as to what Otalp is pointing at, but Kin can see dark shape of a fat arm suspended directly in front of his face.

"Is that Korporate *sonofatube* here?" Miller says.

"I'm here, bird man." Kin scoffs and huffs and puffs.

Mary slips a giggle. "Glad to know it," she says back into the darkness and in Kin's immediate direction. She cannot see Kin when he blushes.

Dodd can still be heard snoring from his chair near the tattered sofa.

"Ritz and Sibley," Miller shouts towards the kitchen, "You guys still in there?"

"Yeah, we're here," Ritz yells back. "Where else would we be? Say, where are those old oil lamps?"

"Oh, I forgot," rejoins Mary, louder than her usual voice. "I moved them over to the right bins near the corner wall. They always got in my way when I wanted to get to the pots and pans for supper."

"Could've mentioned that sooner," Sibley is heard saying from out of the depths of the black portal between the kitchen and the main den.

A cabinet door slaps shut, a flick of a flint follows, and soon after a warm glow of tangerine light from two oil lamps melts its way from the kitchen into the first third of the den.

Ritz and Sibley each have an oil lamp lifted to their chests. The soft shades of light reveal Mary's face, shadowed with a hint of playfulness and despair. Ritz maneuvers the beam over to Otalp and Kin. Kin has buried his face in his hands and when the light catches him, he erects himself with distinct composure often found in the Korporate Elites. Otalp is mindlessly playing with his juniper stick, waving it to and fro as if he is the heroic Don Quixote fending off invisible windmills and warriors. Miller's strained countenance parallels the Eagle's robotic movements of the neck, each turn being very rigid and coming from the tightened nerves of the bird's fatigued system.

Followed by the banging of the cellar door, Barron and Mayhew emerge hastily from the basement and out from behind the quilt.

Sibley adjusts the oil lamp to face the two men who are sweating profusely and somewhat out of breath.

"What happened down there?" Sibley asks the both of them.

"The generator," says Barron, heaving his gut in order to catch his breath, "has been destroyed. It's hard to know for sure, but we thought there was someone else down there with us. Did any of you go down there?"

"None," replies Ritz. "All here. Even that Korporate mutt over there."

"Destroyed, my ass. Someone smashed it to bits," Mayhew adds. "The damn thing's in a hundred pieces."

"Don't look at me," pleads Kin, sensing the thoughts of the others before they're spoken. "I've been sitting here all night. Right next to Otalp."

"I can verify to that," Mary states with tempting pleasure in her soothing voice. "I've had my eye on him ever since he arrived."

"What's going on?" Dodd asks, wiping drool from off his face. He's finally managed to wake from his nap.

"Someone's busted the generator," Miller says. He places the Eagle onto a leather strap attached to his right forearm.

"What do you think, Ritz?" Barron asks, hands on his hips. He's still trying to catch his breath. "Someone was down there with us."

"We'd better get out of here," Ritz fires back. "Leave nothing to chance. Someone or something knows we're here. And I'm starting to get the jitters."

"Grab what you can," Sibley orders. "Without delay!"

The Lighthouse Faktion instantly erects itself from a group of lounging, stoned privateers into a finely tuned mechanism which wastes no time in collecting all the essential necessities, leaving nothing to haste. In as little as seven minutes and twelve seconds heavy coats have been placed on and bulging backpacks have been filled and put on the backs of the men and women. Ritz with one oil lamp leads the Faktion up the winding staircase while Barron brings up the rear with the other oil lamp.

As Barron departs the subterranean den, he swings the oil lamp back inside and catches sight of the lighthouse painting and the six box jellyfish still swimming in happy ignorance. Then by the cellar door he spies flames catching hold of the old quilt.

"Move it!" Barron screams as a wild man. He bolts up the stairs. "Move it or we're gonna' burn!"

The members of the Lighthouse Faktion run up and out of the old forgotten remnants of Stonewall Inn and into the freezing night.

A minute later a drone soars by overhead and the KG's footfalls are like an earthquake tramping ever closer. For the Lighthouse Faktion, there is no place to run. But run they do. Run they must.

II
Lesson XI

Listening to acute directions, Conquergood follows the familiar voice in his head. The tonal derivations tug at his sinews, forcing him from a deep sleep. The melody of the spoken words only he can hear stirs his limbs to stretch and causes him to pull himself away from Klaire on the bed, and this voice that he knows too well further compels him to dress and step out into the hall and proceed over to the k-line portal where he repeats the access pass-kode,

"Nil — Nil — Nil."

"Welkom, Jerome," the meta-voice in the portal says, almost seductively, "Are you ready for this?"

"I am."

The k-line descends rapidly below any known floors into the deepest and most forgotten subterranean levels of Korporate Headquarters.

When Conquergood is released from the portal, he finds himself standing before double doors of solid pine twenty-feet in height with two Illuminate bulbs on either side. Conquergood reads the golden words embedded in a wooden plaque suspended and arched above the doorway to the Korporate Knowledge Base:

A good book
is the precious lifeblood
of a master spirit,
embalmed and treasured
up on purpose to
a life beyond life.

John Milton
Areopagitica
1644

With both hands Conquergood pushes the double doors open and he immediately retracts in awe upon entering the chambers far below the Korporate Kompound and the Korporate Tower.

Floating near the walls and ceiling, illuminate bulbs ignite the windowless chamber into a soft amber which gradually reveals endless rows of shelves, as high as three stories and as long as four city blocks, housing an untold number of books.

Books. All neatly stacked and organized. Those curious and mysterious artifacts from before the beginning of the Metaverse and the full-adoption of e-skreens over paper.

The sight baffles Conquergood. In the Outlands, he often heard people speak about these objects — sometimes saw them in tatters in the abandoned buildings — but he'd never seen so many in perfect condition collected in one place. Now, he is overwhelmed by the sheer volume of books and how he is outnumbered by so many dead writers and unread pages.

Intimate-pullulating knowledge and wisdom oscillate among the archaic literature. Conquergood remains breathless for a time. He sighs against the enormity of the vision — *books should be the treasured wealth of the world as a fit inheritance to the generations to come.*

Conquergood moves through the ancient library with a new found energy, known to the scholars of another generation as *vim*. Minutes pass slowly and for a time he traces with his feet a large compass engraved on the copper-toned marble floor.

In one corner of the biblio-mausoleum, he sees a set of hover-slides and he boards one. The hover-slide rises up to the fifty-third level where he begins to peruse the leather volumes in unrestrained visual undulation. He cannot resist but to reach a finger out and to touch the spine of one of the well-preserved books.

Out of the many, one book Conquergood carefully slips away from its brethren, opens to a random page and he silently begins to read:

"We have everything we need to be happy, but we aren't happy. Something's missing."

Conquergood, a bit confounded as to the meaning of the sentences, closes the flap and reads the author's name as if it is a sanctified word, holy and consecrated,

"Ray."

As a child might do upon a newly discovered seashell, Conquergood fondles the book in his hands, rolling it over and over ever so gently. He wants to feel the eternal life inside this book. He smells the cover, the pages within, and the glue that binds.

After a short time, he reopens the book and reads the words from off the page as though evoking some divinely-mystical magic — a spell to change the world for the better — which has long been forgotten and caved in beneath ignorance almighty. His forefinger follows the imprinted text, fearing to disconnect the life line of touch and message. He believes the ancients are speaking to him. Perhaps they are. Perhaps they are.

Floating high above the library floor on his hover-slide, Conquergood continues to read from the book:

"You're a hopeless romantic."

Conquergood agrees. He is hopeless and a romantic. How can he thus be saved?

"The magic is only in what books say, how they stitched the patches of the universe together into one garment for us."

Faber is right. Must be.

"Patches of the universe," Conquergood repeats aloud.

His voice echoes across the Halls of Knowledge, and the sound it makes startles Conquergood. He peers around to determine if anyone has heard. Then he realizes the books from history and time immemorial have been hidden in a tremendous vault beneath the city and the Korporate Tower. Like him, these books have been secured and locked away from any natural or man-made catastrophe. Only a small fraction of these books has been digitized into the K-net. Conquergood knows, because he has searched for weeks trying to find the one book he had lost over eight years ago.

It must be here.

The KV and K-net exponentially strengthened the person's desire for faster and easier entertainment, faster and faster until the human mind found its zenith, leading inevitably to another Dark Age. This Korporate Age of

Darkness collapsed onto humankind a leviathan swimming amongst digital-meta philosophy, foreign languages, creative fiction and virtual communities and personal narratives. Overtime, the printed literature was gradually forgotten. People drowned in information overload inside the Old Internet and the New Metaverse. The world had grown grandiose and had been consumed — swallowed whole — in unlimited knowledge — minus morality and wisdom — and was eventually suffocated by its own twisted sophistication and sexual perversions.

Thus came the beginning of the Second Dark Ages — yet, the early Founders of the Korporation hailed civilization as having entered an Age of Light.

In Conquergood's hand, the book — yellowed and cracked, crinkling its fragile spine and emitting dust spoors — forces Conquergood to look upward.

In the ceiling, upon first glance, is the open sky, relinquishing heavenly splendor. On closer examination, however, the window is actually a virtual moving holo-painting of a grand summer sky in blue, bordered by purplish clouds. Heavenward, he visualizes the multitude of redolent books evincing a memory into re-existence.

"I remember," Conquergood whispers into the limitless virtual holo-sky. "I do remember."

He drops his gaze from off the digital ceiling and in a state of fervid alacrity Conquergood recasts the first library he had ever been in.

"Fifth Avenue," he says to himself, spinning inward in the silent erudition of self-discovery.

In his mind's eye, still hovering high above the compass imprinted upon the library floor, he witnesses the entrance to the Fifth Avenue Library: a staircase with a prostrate stone lion on one side and a stone vase on the other.

Mentally, Conquergood moves through four towering columns into the effulgent New York City Public Library. His vision catches sight of a similar sign which now hangs on the entrance to the Korporate Library. And it is the name — John Milton — which halts the memory.

"Yes, I do remember *Paradise Lost* and a great many others." Conquergood struggles into the depths of his eternal soul. "But that can't be. That's impossible. That was so very long ago." *How long?* He does not remember.

Uncomprehending, he struggles with the memory as his frantic mind races with meta-calculations. In his memory, he continues seeing rows of long wooden tables with entrenched readers intent on unlocking secrets away from the pages before them, before the time of the World Wide Web and the virtual environments, separating humanity from the natural world of touch and taste and smell. Chandeliers of such exorbitant sunshine reflecting its clean light upon a white floor and its brown walkway in between rows of tables. Buttresses lining the walls, windows giving ease to the artificial glow from above. And Conquergood is seeing it all — as clear as any memory from five minutes ago.

Conquergood remains embodied in both libraries, being two places at once, propagating between both worlds, the real and the recollection. He welcomes the exotic sensations the journey carries, admiring his own awe of what libraries had been, before the Era of Digitization conquered them; the rules of being forbidden to speak above a whisper cascade back onto his memories, as well as the mustiness of age and wisdom being on free display, and he remembers how these holy sites often went un-used and became under-valued over the generations.

Conquergood can now recall how he had behaved on his first visit to the library. As a small boy he had been nervous with polite reverence, uncertain of which way to turn, of which aisle to discover, and which row to select from, of which bookshelf to choose from, of which book he should pull from its everlasting hearth, of which pages he should read from in order to breathe in its fiery passions to fill a dulled boy's heart, igniting a mind to inspire upon 'a life beyond life.' The books had held lives of their own back then. But now he also knows that these books had made up a whole body, as though each book was a cell in a living organism in a state of repetitive meditation and waiting for the hand to pluck them from the tree which bears endless fruit. Feeling overwhelmed, Conquergood reluctantly leaves his memory-vision.

After selecting several more books, Conquergood glides down on the hover-slide and locates one of two old-fashioned Georgian style leather armchairs next to a small table and banker's lamp with bronze base and an amber mica shade. Above the two chairs is an oil painting, "Still-Life of Books, 1628" by Jan Davidsz, and Conquergood sees in the painting a violin placed on a wooden desk among scattered manuscripts.

Starting from the beginning of the first book he chose, and savoring each morsel of each word on his lips — as a dehydrated man does in a desert when an oasis can be found just in time to save his life — Conquergood finishes the book in under three hours.

Each phoneme grasps and wets his tongue in unexpected new language and cognizance. He finishes the book, places it down on the side stand, and in a fit of bedlam and clarity, juxtaposed with his soul, says aloud,

"I'm the ghost that's always around, but nowhere to be found. Why is that?"

Out of the decades of change and virtual globalization, Conquergood can hear the author's voice echoing concrete certitude from the page:

"Without the library, you have no civilization."

A quondam voice from another era, another universe perhaps, sounds from behind Conquergood, "You are quite right, Jerome."

A centenarian with a long gray braid down his back and a silvery beard down his chest emerges from behind the reader's chair and walks a few patient steps and then turns to face Conquergood.

"I am Logos Godse," says the old man, wearing a vintage navy-blue haori jacket and hakama pants. Stitched in white on the back of the haori jacket are the ancient words 理解 — *Rikai*, meaning understanding and comprehension. "In the old days, they would have called me a bibliognost, a bibliothecary, a librarian — one who is a keeper of knowledge." His tanned face is without wrinkles but carries with it a stern remembrance of another time and another age where copulation and not test tubes had once created imperfect-mortal copies of the parents. "How are you enjoying the books?"

"I had forgotten there were so many," Conquergood replies. "I do remember that once, sometime I can't be quite sure, I studied from a handful of books from an old friend, much like you."

"We all tend to forget from time to time," says Godse, taking the empty chair beside the stand where the book rests closed and drained but ready to be filled again. "But in forgetting we are allowed the ability to remember. And in recollection a brighter joy may spring within us, nourishing that which needs to be nourished, no?"

"How long have you been down here, God-see?"

"A long time, but not long enough," Godse says in an iron-like voice, polished but adequately tested over time. "Take the Korporation, for example. No one remembers to visit this place anymore, but it does make my job easier." A smirk quickly appears and then vanishes beneath his beard. His patient hands are folded in his lap and he breathes with strict regulation, basking in each simple breath as if it could be his last. There is a soothing intoxicant in listening to Godse's breathing, as if he sits beneath the Bodhi tree upon the edge of the world and remains, like many before him, unmovable.

These men and women, if Conquergood had known them and their influence on the world back then, would have lent something to this conversation with Godse. But Conquergood has begun his quest and he is bound to meet many mentors along the way, if he hasn't met a few already. Still, the memories or visions — can't be sure which — of the ancient library as new and modern as the Korporate Labs upstairs stay at the edges of Conquergood's speech. He does not want to reveal too much nor too little with Godse.

"Am I allowed to be down here?"

"Of course you are," says Godse, absorbing the smells of all the stories floating around him. "What a silly question to ask." With sweeping movements of his hands to his face he closes his eyes and takes in the air, as though it is burning incense before an altar. He does this once more and then adds, "You, Jerome, are in fact a respected member of the Korporation, are you not?"

"Yes. I am."

"Were you not recently given a distinguished promotion for your services to the Korporation?"

"Yes. I was."

"Then you are allowed, and I should know, because I was the one who gave you the Korporate Handbook," Godse says, a twist of the cheeks inscribes themselves on his lean facial frame — not quite a smile but not quite a frown either. "Are you enjoying the book?"

"Some of it yes," replies Conquergood, rubbing the small stack of closed books in his lap while he reflects for a moment. He is thinking about the memory or the vision that should not be. The times have changed and he cannot place any of them against the outline of his own being. "Do you know who wrote in the back of the handbook?"

"Actually, I do," says Godse, his eyes aglow with a fertile fire. "He was a member of the Korporation much like you many, many years ago. Andrade was his name. He was a brilliant young man and he loved to read and he soon became one of my most prized pupils. Over the years I taught him how to think and reason, to use common sense in all matters required, and I shared with Andrade the wonders of logic. But I am afraid teachers, or even stewards, cannot be students or masters for very long. My blood is not your blood, as some have said."

"Will you teach me all that you know of this world?" Conquergood asks. "Everything you taught Andrade?"

"If you wish it," Godse says. He bows his head and rubs his long gray beard along his chest and stomach. "If that is what you wish, I will teach you much more. I will even teach you about Time and Space and the Mysterious Infinite Beyond. But such things carry little importance in today's world, I know."

"Do many people come here?"

"Few venture down to this part of the Tower anymore," Godse says with a mournful exhalation in his words. "Not in several decades at least. But we manage on our own, don't we? Surrounded by all these great minds."

A moment of sparse silence fills the gap between the young and the old.

"Do you know by any chance," Godse asks, "of the Greek philosopher Dicaearchus?"

"Sorry, I don't. Did you know him personally?"

"I do," says Godse, who lifts a judicious hand up toward the innumerable books surrounding both he and Conquergood. "He was a wise man in his time. Oh, but that was a very long time ago, now, wasn't it? Still, in the aeonian recollections, many of such minds no longer exist. We have solved the riddles of the universe, or so the Korporation would like us to believe. Dicaearchus once said, 'men originally lived in a state of nature… for them it was a happy state, a golden age.' Now, what do you think of that? *A happy state.* One can only imagine these days, imagine such a golden age."

"Did you?"

"I did," says Godse, shutting his tired, elegant eyes to awaken an image of a pagoda in the mountains of Japan.

The scene is from a time in his youth, and even he has lost the fragrance of the flowers that had grown nearby. "From a time when man lived in harmony with the earth, I too lived," Godse says. "Life was different back then, and we lived closer to Mother Nature. We sat on the grass and soil as they recoiled their antediluvian forces giving life to life up into our flesh. We belong to the earth, Jerome. We were made to belong. I know this may sound strange, but the natural world is a part of us, binds us to one another. And if you take the soil, the trees, the clouds and the sunshine away, you take the biggest part of our humanity away."

"I feel like I am missing something," Conquergood says. "Missing something inside myself."

"Do you know of the word Hiraeth?"

"I'm sorry?"

"Hiraeth comes from the Welsh," Godse explains. "A word that cannot be translated very well into our Korporate English. But we have tried. Hiraeth may mean and express a spiritual longing that which now pulls you forward, Jerome. Hiraeth is likened to a homesickness, a deep longing for home."

"Can you teach me the ways that are lost? I feel I'm lost in a maze and I do feel like I'm searching for a way home, a home I have never known but have lost."

"I must," says Godse, reemerging from the mirage of his homeland. The last thing he sees of Japan is his young wife standing on the cliffs next to the ocean and the shooting sprays of water slapping playfully at the wild seagulls overhead. "To begin my young educatee, another great man said long ago before technology was technology and people learned from each other, 'Reading furnishes the mind only with materials of knowledge; it is thinking that makes what we read ours.' Do you know this man? Can you tell me who he is?"

"Give me a moment," says Conquergood, delving into the recesses of his scholarship. "John. I think his name is John."

"Many great men were named John," Godse returns. "Do you know any more of him than that? Do you know his ancestors?"

"It's incomplete."

"Then allow me to complete you. His name was John Locke, but many have also forgotten such words and such philosophers. Such sages do not matter much anymore."

"What does Locke mean?"

"What does anything or anyone truly mean?" Godse asks without seeking an answer he does not already know. "What do you think he means?"

"I imagine Locke means that to read a book is simply not enough. The reader has to consider for his own, from his own time, from his own experiences in order to gain a more complete understanding."

"Yes," Godse says. His frail chest exhales beneath the navy-blue haori jacket.

Conquergood can make out a gold aura lightly enshrined in fringes of silver around Godse's body and a brilliant glow of white upon his cracked knuckles.

Godse asks, "Would you like to share something?"

"You're covered in a strange light," Conquergood says. "I've never seen anything like it before. It's extraordinary."

"What you see is nothing new to the human race," Godse says. "But it is foreign to the Meta-races. They do not have such light from within." His hands wave around his body as if outlining the light which belongs to him and to him alone. "This is my *chakra*. It is one of attunement and connection, a spiritual force which binds us to the forces of the earth. You have one, a very unique chakra I can see, faint but it is there."

"Why can't I see it then?"

"You haven't learned what you need to learn about yourself. Something's missing. There's a lack you must fill."

"I know," says Conquergood, staring down at his hands as if they belong to someone else. He sees no light, no chakra of his own. "For the past five years I've been trying to figure that out. When it dawned on me, I was surrounded, draped in a swarm of butterflies, and it felt like they wanted me to fly away with them, but I couldn't. But when I was inside their hollow, I heard them whisper to me. Does that sound crazy to you?"

"Not crazy at all. Not at all," says Godse, appearing as though he is floating on the chair rather than implanted onto its leather. "Tell me, what did the butterflies whisper to you? What secrets did they tell you?"

"It wasn't just the butterflies," Conquergood says. Looking at the counterfeit sky overhead, the rows of books, he continues, "The trees, what few there are, the rocks, the seas and the rivers, the living things we do not take for living at all… they told me… they said to me… how can I say it without sounding crazy? They had said I was special, that I was different, and that I had a golden path to take. One that was going to change the world."

"Sounds promising, Jerome," Godse says. When he stands, his movements are immensely quick yet smooth — like a hummingbird's wings, invisible but piled with force. "Alas, we all have a journey to take in life. Mine ends here with you."

"Can I see you again?"

"As often as you like, until it is time to change our seasons. Sometimes seasons guide our paths."

"May I stay and finish reading these books?"

"As you like," says Godse, hiding his hands inside the opposite sleeves of the haori jacket. "But on one condition. And that condition is that these treasured books must remain here in the Korporate Library."

"May I ask one more thing?" Conquergood asks.

"Please do."

"I'm looking for one book in particular. You might know of it," says Conquergood, standing to face the glimmering Sage, his mentor. Fearful respect fills Conquergood and he does not stand too close to Godse, nor to the bodily aureole surrounding Godse.

Conquergood lowers his head when he speaks,

"Do you know of a book called *Why do Bells Toll?*"

"No man is an island," Godse says as if to himself, enjoying the sapidity the words behold. "You should try the fortieth row, under the name Hemingway. He is a great one, and you have chosen a remarkable book to read. When you get to the end, you'll be right there with Robert Jordan and Maria on the Spanish hillside."

For Conquergood the writer's name flows from Godse's mouth like rivers merging and rushing powerfully off a cliff into a scenic waterfall.

"Thank you," says Conquergood, backing away.

"No," replies Godse, momentarily bowing his chest and head, "Thank you for the delightful talk. I haven't had one in a very long time. The Korporation doesn't like old men, truly old men like me, to be seen, or heard for that matter, but I have enough company as I like, here in these books. Many happy returns, Jerome."

And with that, Godse departs on a hover-slide, sweeping away and out of sight behind massive columns of books. Conquergood rejoins the armchair, picks up a new novel from the stack on the stand and reads the title aloud, "*Look Homeward, Angel*," and Conquergood methodically opens the cover carefully as not to create damage to the worn book, taking in the light-brownish page and the dirt-worn smells of locked time escaping, and then he reads the first sentence to himself, "A destiny that leads the English to the Dutch is strange enough; but one that leads from Epsom into Pennsylvania, and thence into the hills that shut in Altamont over the proud coral cry of the cock, and the soft stone smile of an angel, is touched by that dark miracle of chance which makes new magic in a dusty world."

Conquergood continues to read until the book by Thomas Wolfe has unveiled most of its magic and secrets, even in a dusty world such as this one governed by the almighty Korporation.

I
The KAVE

In a starfish position Klaire sleeps on her stomach beside Conquergood. With a gentle finger, he follows her spine from neck to buttocks and up again. The spine and the vertebrae are much different than bone as it should be but close — extremely close — and he can hear her pulsing heart, a fabrication — he now knows what the machines — the Meta-races — as near-humans sound like — pumping the simulated veins and vessels, pounding up and out of her back and into his ear as he continues to stroke the frame of her life-like synthetik skin.

For days, Conquergood has had his brief suspicions, his incertitude, but never fully certain. An hour later while Conquergood reads the Korporate Handbook, Klaire awakes from her hibernation mode — asleep but not quite asleep — and she appears refreshed, rejuvenated, renewed.

Klaire stumbles into the bathroom for a hot shower and forty-five minutes later emerges joyfully in a bathrobe back into the bedroom. A pearl white towel wraps her hair up in a swirl. She is real in every way but one.

Conquergood, already dressed in his prole attire, stares out the window. He feels betrayed. Betrayed by the

Korporation that has groomed him. Betrayed by Klaire and her automaton shell — does she even dream? Hope? Love? — and Conquergood also feels betrayed by the winter storming outside the dome above and the false shade of spring stored upon the Garden's surface below. He says nothing, unable to say anything, knowing only part of what he was sent to expose — *to destroy*. Returning to the bed he begins to search through the censured research articles in three dimensions on the K-net displayed on the KV. His diligent research, however, remains fruitless — unattained.

"Good morning," says Klaire, heading into the dining area where she has stocked some groceries for the two of them. She pours herself a glass of guava juice and pulls from a metallic bowl a fresh orange. The genetically-enhanced orange is bright and large in her hand and when she tosses it into the air, she gives a squeal of delight at how heavy the orange is. She catches the orange ball, sets her glass of guava juice on the night table, and plops herself down on the bed. Conquergood joins her on the bed as she asks,

"Do you want to come with me today to see what I do?" It's the first time she has offered this invitation — one step closer. "It should be fun. You never seem to care."

"Sure," he replies. "Sounds like a ride."

"What are you looking for?" asks Klaire, peeling the orange with intense precision. "All you ever seem to do is read."

"Nothing," he says. "Just doing some light research about how we ended up here. Don't you ever wonder about things like that? How we are who we are? How the

Korporation came to own everything? To possess every man, woman and child? The entire world?"

"We?" Klaire has finished peeling the orange, the juice cascades down her fingers, and while she eats and feeds some of the orange slices to Conquergood she places the rind in the pocket of her bathrobe. "What do you mean by 'we'?"

"Yes, we," he says to her, "as in *we* the Korporation."

Her delicate hands are soft, becoming sticky beneath the citrus juices, and her neatly trimmed nails tear into the flesh of the orange. She feeds Conquergood a slice.

"Don't you ever want to consider the possibilities?" Conquergood asks. "The answers to the riddles?"

"No. Not really," she says, and she eyes him as she places an orange slice between her plush lips and into her mouth, savoring the flavor. "What would it all mean anyway? What good would it do?"

The towel covering her hair topples to one side and falls against the headboard and Conquergood's left shoulder, where she allows her head to come to a rest. He hadn't heard it before, but now the clicking of miniscule, pre-ordained parts are clearly and unmistakably audible in the cavities of his ears. Conquergood can hear the faint beating of Klaire's machine heart.

"They teach us what we need to know in Korporate Edukation." Klaire sighs and Conquergood can sense she doesn't want to discuss any more on this topic, as if a firewall blocks her vocal folds. "They teach us no more and no less. Why do you have to ask?"

"Feeling misplaced," he says. "Feeling lost is all."

"Then come join me in the PMD." She lifts her head off his shoulder and then bounces to her knees in front of

Conquergood on the bed. Her breasts are exposed, the bathrobe straddling her waist and thighs, but all he sees are her amazing eyes staring with reckless abandon back at him. "It will be loads of fun," she says. "We're not like the stuffy research labs. We are more or less another branch of employment, an off shoot of the less refined positions. You needn't worry. Nothing to be taken too seriously, I can assure you, darling."

"PMD?"

"Yes." She widens the gap in her bathrobe so Conquergood can fully appreciate the perfection of her breasts. "The Perception Management Department."

Conquergood can also sense she enjoys teaching him something about her daily labor routine. She wants to show him something but he isn't quite sure what it is.

"Haven't you heard of us?"

"When do you want to go?" he asks.

"Oh, we don't usually follow any fixed schedule. We go when we want to go." She removes the towel from her head and dries her wet hair. "It's much better for the morale. Or so we say."

She collects the remnants of the orange from her pocket and returns to the dining area to dispose of the rinds in the recycling bin located in the wall. Conquergood can hear the water faucet pouring for a minute and then when Klaire returns to the bedroom, she allows the bathrobe to trickle down her hips and legs and down to the floor. Her perfectly shaped shoulders compliment her perfectly shaped breasts which in turn compliment her perfectly shaped hips and thighs. Perfect in every way but one: Klaire is not Leona.

"Give me a minute or so to get dressed and we can go up. It'll be fun." Klaire twirls herself on a single toe, like some ballerina alone before a practice mirror, and in one flawless motion with the other foot she uses her toes to clutch her yellow kimono on the floor and tosses it up into a free hand. "We have a great view from our department. You'll love it."

After she dresses in her matching yellow-silk bra and panties and her short yellow kimono, Klaire leads Conquergood out into the hallway and over to the k-line portal. Inside she gives her command, "P-136-17."

"We are looking especially lovely today, *KLAIRE*," the voice from the tele-k-skreen says. "It might also be said that you and the Turnkey Specialist make an exceptional *kouple*." At the finishing of this sentence, the k-line accelerates upwards. "Have an enjoyable work day for the sake of the Korporation."

Conquergood blushes a little but Klaire shrugs the flattery off.

"We work in unison with the Korporate Knowledge Base," says Klaire, changing the subject. "Our primary function is to streamline bits of datum and decide which alterations are most likely to succeed for the needs of the Korporation."

Twenty-six seconds pass before the k-line glides to a gentle halt. The portal doors slide open and Klaire and Conquergood pass through a frenetic anteroom of men and women amusing themselves with anecdotes, opium cigars and reclining comfortably on floor-level couches and pillows.

Conquergood overhears one of the members lounging on a floor-sofa ask a small crowd gathered around,

"What's the difference between a wealthy Korporate employee and a pathetic strayer?"

"We don't know," one woman says. "A whip and a tail?"

"A fat bank and tons of *kash*?" one man asks.

"Fangs?" another quips.

"Why do we have to say such silly things, Robert?" a second woman replies. "Honestly, darling."

"Nothing," the jokester named Robert says. "They both do anything and everything to help themselves."

The laughter sounds loud and real while not one Korporate laborer makes notice of the two new arrivals.

Klaire and Conquergood leave the anteroom-lounge and turn a corner into the main room where they are faced with rows upon rows of Korporate staff interlocked to each other and to the Korporate Kontrol System, all interlaced and integrated within a virtually simulated meta-world that had long ago first began as the Metaverse.

Several dozen workers are reclining in massage chairs wearing holo-masks that are imbedded with mikrophones, speakers, and holo-skreens which provide the audio and visual displays. The holo-masks cover the faces and heads of the Korporate employees while their bodies are also dressed in touch-sensory e-material which deludes the wearer into believing the virtual meta-environment is the only environment worth experiencing.

"How many staff members work in this department?" asks Conquergood, absorbing the multitude lost in dreamlands — countless and infinite meta-worlds.

Klaire leads him by the hand down row after row, approximately four dozen or more workers in single file hooked into the Kontrol System.

"Oh, who knows?" she says as she bounces along the center path between the rows. "The KAVE has around four divisions of, say, if I had to guess, of about fifteen hundred or more."

"Cave?"

"Sorry," she says. She prims with an overloaded joy at arriving at her own personal superiority. "KAVE stands for the Kore of Automatik Virtual Environments."

"I see," Conquergood sees. "Extraordinary."

"Over in that far corner to the right is the Truth Projektion Division." Klaire points to the division, and Conquergood listens. "I might say it's a dreadfully boring meta-unit. I try to avoid them because they have some of the more outdated equipment. But they're expected to get some huge upgrades next year."

She leads Conquergood by the hand down the various rows and points out the different divisions and sections to the Perception Management Department.

"Down at the end to your left is the Psykhologikal Operations where I work with the most advanced tools to date. Back behind us is the Operations Sekurity Division, and next to them is the Kover Division. Some of the more experienced staff are promoted and move on to become lekturers or, if they're really talented, Korporate Elites. But that takes time, decades even, and all promotions depend on the group performance ratings. Some of the groups are designed *holistikally*, meaning the best are paired with the best and the worst employees with the worst. Imagine how difficult it is to try and move ahead in this business."

Conquergood nods along with Klaire's soothing voice and he drifts into a slight doze when he begins hearing a white noise buzzing in his veins running along his right arm. He turns his wrist over and can see the Korporate signature pulsating. The vibrations in the room invisibly bounce from wall to wall.

On each of the three walls — save a tremendous window overlooking Old York City down at the end of the center row — a silent nanotube e-sign displays the PMD's laconic motto:

TRUTH IS WISHING TO BELIEVE

Below the PMD's shibboleth, the nine strategies of the department are listed:

9.   **EXKOGITATE**

8.   **BELIEVE**

7.   **REINFORCE**

6.   **ASSURE**

5.   **SEKURE**

4.   **ADAPT**

3.   **DISTRIBUTE**

2.   **OBLITERATE**

1.   **FABRIKATE**

The words say it all. The Korporation seeks a deeper, more profound *kontrol* over the world, over humanity.

The Korporation has the land, the food, the water, all the environmental commodities, the wealth and the power, but having these key instruments to mortal absoluteness remains practically non-essential without altering and dominating a person's Free Will. Choice persists in the hands of the people — how many people Conquergood is unsure of. But by manipulating selected information to inherent, pre-described audiences the Korporation can influence, manipulate and ultimately redirect emotions, reasoning and even the motives behind the opaque screen of thoughts.

Klaire, meanwhile, skips ahead of Conquergood — lost in his thoughts — as Robert the Jokester floats by on a motorized hover-slide.

"Robert's one of our most senior supervisors," Klaire whispers over to Conquergood. "His label is KJ Dee. But we usually just *kall* him Robert. He likes that. But no one really knows why. Then again, no one cares to give it another thought either. There's some real *psykos* around here. Hurry up. I want to get to work."

Conquergood follows Klaire down to the end of the center row, where he finds himself standing against an entire wall of flexiglass overlooking Old York City. The degraded skyscrapers appear as toothpicks beneath Korporate Tower.

Far below Conquergood — once upon a time — Emma Lazarus, Chloe Anthony Wofford Morrison, Jerome David Salinger, Edith Wharton, Ralph Waldo Ellison, Herman Melville, James Baldwin, Thomas Wolfe, Maya Angelou, Henry James, Edna St. Vincent Millay, and

Walt Whitman had long ago resided in these now broken shells of Old York City, where rusty gates of iron now guard fragmented-empty exteriors — *"As for me, I am tormented with an everlasting itch for things remote. I love to sail forbidden seas, and land on barbarous coasts."*

Conquergood watches as the sun struggles to spread a few rays between massive super-storm clouds, and there in the distance is the unsounded lightning clashing over the far ends of the Outlands. He knows what it is like to be cold, hungry, and alone out there in the forbidden realms, the holes and crags desperate men and women and a few children — the Outkasts — call home.

And then Conquergood's thoughts drift to the Korporate Guard. No one ever refuses to obey the KG or their orders — not since the passing and full adoption of Korporatilism, which privatized the military and all other governmental services.

"We have an amazing view, don't we?" says Klaire, breaking Conquergood's concentration. "Sometimes I stand here for hours just looking out over the old city."

When Conquergood looks away from the Outlands that he too had once called home, he is confronted with a small dark toned woman with a wide industrious face. Her Korporate kimono is the color purple and her ebony hair is braided down her back in two fine pigtails.

"Come here and meet my good friend," says Klaire to Conquergood, her hand open in the direction of the strange woman in the purple kimono. "Her name is Jaine Ramesha. She'll help you into your virtual suit. Today, we have a big surprise for you."

"Hello, Jerome," Ramesha says. "*We* are most glad we joined this meeting today. Let's get suited up, shall *we*?"

Conquergood watches as Klaire slips off her yellow robe in full view of Ramesha and the other department staff, but they're all locked away in another space to take any notice. Klaire is garnering the same touch-sensory fabric as the other seated laborers lost in their own personal meta-dreams, and the touch-sensory e-material is tight and clings to her as an ultra-thin layer with a dangling hood on the back.

Conquergood unties his belt and drops his white kimono to the floor. He stands nude in the sight of Ramesha, who moves her sight intently over his hairless-muscular body and down to his exposed groin — shaved as required by the Korporate Manual.

Ramesha hesitates on this lower bald spot for a long moment before breaking her concentration. "Just slip this on," says Ramesha, handing Conquergood the virtual meta-suit. "When it's time, just slip the hood and mask over the head and step onto this platform here." She points down to moveable sections of the floor, hovering and divided into twenty-by-twenty slide pieces, much similar to the transport slides found in the hallways. "These V-slides will instantly arrange and rearrange themselves beneath your feet allowing you the ability to walk freely or run or jump or roll and you'll never know the difference between the real world and the virtual meta-world. You'll be able to move as you please. Even fly. Are we ready to begin?"

Having mounted her V-slides, Klaire appears like a faceless phantom with the hood and mask in place. She's enshrined in her virtual holo-suit, and soon she'll be mentally and emotionally enveloped and lost in a meta-domain filled with meta-wonders. Conquergood does not dare imagine what awaits him.

"As ready as ever," Conquergood tells Ramesha. He dresses in the virtual holo-suit and steps onto the V-slides. He pulls the hood and mask over his head and face, breathing comfortably through the slits for nose and mouth, and is enclosed in a brief moment of silent darkness. Then a blinding white flash — akin to that of a betatronic explosion — disorients Conquergood and he must kneel to regain his balance and composure.

Suddenly, inside the virtual meta-world, Conquergood finds himself alone on a grassy hill and dressed in his white kimono. His virtual meta-skin is a duplicate of his real flesh and he feels that his senses have been enhanced.

Soft-violet skies filled with golden clouds transcend above him in 360 degrees as a moist breeze, smelling of light rain, hits his face and it is real enough — undeniably lifelike and tangible.

"Someone could get lost in here," Conquergood says into the empty meta-world before him. "Where shall I begin? How does it work?"

"We need to open the Gateway first," Ramesha says, the voice coming down from the rolling clouds above Conquergood. "Speak 'Gateway' aloud, and from there we may either verbally or manually manipulate the environment to where we wish to go. Anything else?"

"I think I can handle this," he replies. "Better now or never. Won't know until I give it a try."

"Then we must be leaving now," Ramesha says of herself, and Conquergood understands the third-person hint. "We are assisting Robert over in Truth Projektion in twenty minutes. Nice to have met you, Jerome. It is truly our honor."

The soft-violet skies grow calm, and the breeze sweeps through redwood trees in the far distance and across the lush meadows immediately below Conquergood's hill. He watches the sparrows and hummingbirds dart to and fro and he waits a few minutes longer before speaking,

"Gateway open."

A multi-colored florescence of neon orbs immediately cascades around Conquergood like virtual fairies flying in a swirling hurricane. When they come to a halt, surrounding Conquergood, each neon orb is labeled with a verbal *deskriptor* and a *graphik* leading into another realm within the virtual environment. Each neon orb, almost of a liquid texture, floats systematically and life-like within their designated spaces.

Conquergood takes his time and scans over each neon orb in order to decipher their meanings. Several of the neon orbs have the individual images of astrological signs: a Goat, a Ram, a Water-Bearer, a Crab, an Archer, a Maiden, a Scorpion, a Lion, and Scales. These signs are not two-dimensional images at all but appear as authentic creations, swimming, growling, baying, turning in tiny minuets within each of the neon orbs. The other effluent orbs have links into movies, songs, role-playing adventure scenarios, land destinations, virtual sex, space travel, and data fields, among countless other data fields.

Soon, one orb strikes Conquergood's attention the most. A single aureate K, sparkling and golden, floats poignantly behind all the other link-orbs. A familiar voice — that voice that has been with him in the background of his own thoughts — guides him to this curious link-orb.

Conquergood moves his legs to find he is walking smoothly across the hill. Pushing aside the floating-drifting neon orbs — which fade away as they are pushed aside — he continues pushing these link-orbs aside until he has cleared a path and reaches the watery link-orb marked with a single **C**.

Conquergood lifts his hand and places it in the center of the link-orb marked "C" and is instantly pulled inside a virtual meta-databank of countless memory-orbs, each silver in color. These specific memory-orbs hold Conquergood's own memories.

Each memory-orb displays an active, projected scene he has considered countless times in his own mind. Memories of Leona on the beach. Klaire in the Garden of the Gods. Kin by the fire in the Outlands. The Lighthouse Faktion. There are even memories of his time in the Korporate Knowledge Base with Godse, and all these memories stare back at him through an array of ascended memory-orbs floating like silvery moons, high and full. And still, there are countless more memories.

Out of the many, Conquergood spots one particular memory-orb which draws his attention away from a memory-orb of Leona. The memory-orb in question holds a frightening image, and the image is of Klaire in the arms of Sir Windsor VI. With a quivering finger, Conquergood reaches out and touches the link-orb.

Conquergood's surroundings dissolve until he finds himself in the doorway to a bedroom. The apartment is an exact duplicate of his own, but a sense of Klaire's presence is before him. Her yellow kimono robe is on the floor beside a black one. Fake sunflowers stand inside a Grecian urn on the bedside table. A pungent smell of opium and lilacs stagnate the air. And there embraced on the bed are Klaire and Sir Windsor VI.

From Klaire's mouth come pleasuring moans as Sir Windsor VI emits and excretes sweaty grunts of his own. These volatile lovers — friends of Conquergood — do not notice him as he watches every thrust. Klaire rolls onto her stomach and shifts her buttocks upwards to be received while the doktor settles on his knees from behind — the same position Conquergood had had Klaire only the night before. Conquergood clinches his fists and his jealous anger rises against his purloined affection crippled by deceit and manipulation — *"I have lost the immortal part of myself, and what remains is bestial."*

Klaire turns and catches Conquergood out of the corner of her eye. She quickly pulls herself free.

"Conquergood?" she says in a state of dualism — one of surprised shock and the other of negated contempt. "Conquergood?" she says again, as if seeing a ghost. The name holds little meaning to the stunned observer, cuckolded. "Conquergood?"

Conquergood forces himself to step backwards out of the bedroom, down the hallway, and even further back until he is free of the painful and disturbing memory-orb that could not have been a memory — *yet.*

Soon Klaire's apartment dissolves and Conquergood is once again faced with a purplish horizon and dozens of other memory-orbs on the hill.

If it wasn't a memory, he thinks, *then what was it?*

Conquergood is about to place his hand in a link-orb where Leona's inviting image beams back at him, but the familiar voice in his head stops him.

"Not a memory as of yet," the friendly voice calls to him and says, "but a memory all may become."

Within the virtual landscape, behind the memory-orbs and other various link-orbs, Zawadi is there staring back at Conquergood. She has flowing auburn hair down past her shoulders and her skin and robe vibrate a pinkish aura, her chakra. Metallic wings of silver, tinged in copper tones, unfold from her back.

"I thought you had forgotten me," Zawadi says. Innocence commands her ancient expression. Her eyes, healthy and alive with active thoughts, sparkle like transparent cherries. Conquergood hears her voice and words not in his mind but before him as another might speak in the real world. "You have come to the right place, Jerome, my friend."

"What place is this?"

"This is *your* place," Zawadi says. With a few flaps of her wings, Zawadi sails and up over the rows of memory-orbs and lands beside him on the hill. "These links before you are who you really are... or were... or shall become."

"Shall become?" Conquergood says.

"Yes, your future," says she, the Mother Gift to All, and she points to a memory-orb over to the side. "Do you see? Can you see?"

Inside the virtual liquid of one memory-orb, a scene floats from a history that has already been lost to the decades of ecological and economic reconstruction. Conquergood glimpses a solitary boy, much like the one he faintly remembers, playing on the white sands of a calm beach. "Vincent," he says.

"Come." Zawadi takes Conquergood by the hand and they enter the memory-orb to find themselves observing from a hilltop a boy of five years playing with sandcastles on the white slopes of the beach, empty of travelers save the mother and her son. "Do you remember any of this?"

"Faintly, yes. I've had dreams." Conquergood can smell the salt from the ocean and the salt fills the pores of his skin. He can also feel the sand beneath his bare feet and he can hear the shrill cries of the seagulls in the distance. Of these sights and sounds he cannot distinguish whether these belong to his memory or the virtual meta-banks of data inside PMD and Korporate Kontrol. "Is that Vincent?"

"It was you."

"What happened with Klaire back there?" says Conquergood, pointing over his shoulder. But when he turns, he sees an old wooden fence in need of repair and he does not see Klaire's apartment. "Was that real? What happened in her bedroom?"

"Reality expressed in your humanistic definitions, Jerome, cannot purge itself against the reality of the meta-world the Korporation has created, in this place and in the next and in the ever beyond." Barefooted, Zawadi walks along the beach and she enjoys the wind in her long hair and the water rushing up over her ankles and away again. "The past, present, and future are all real at some point in time, regardless if an event has transpired or is waiting to produce itself, to become 'real' as you put it."

"Then what I saw about Klaire," Conquergood grabs Zawadi by the hand and turns her to face him, "what I saw, then, will happen at some point in the future?"

"History does have a way of repeating itself," Zawadi says. Her metallic wings from the virtual world outside the memory-orb flutter as real feathers here on the beach while her skin remains the color of a cool summer night. "You must wait and see. We must all wait and see. Destiny is a puzzling character once you get to know her."

The setting sun, heavy and low, gives way to a crescent moon out over the dazzling waters. The beach begins to turn from its hard white into soft mild grays while the small boy continues to build his sandcastles. The roll of the waves on the wet sand releases an intoxicating rhythm, soothing and refreshing against the static noise found in the background of the office.

"I do remember some of this," Conquergood says, "but I don't remember ever having experienced any of it. Does that make sense?" He turns to Zawadi. Her expression is one of grief and loss. He asks her, "How long ago was this?"

"So long ago that none are sure how long it's been," she says. Wind lifts her hair and her hair stretches horizontally, streaming like a flag in the tides of the wind. "Before the turn of the twenty-first century, that we have estimated. But how long is still a guess."

"How old am I?" Onto the wet sand, Conquergood collapses to his knees. "How old? Tell me. I must know. Who am I?"

"You are as old as you are now," says Zawadi, lowering her face to meet the discomfited man's. She bends to a knee and places a hand on Conquergood's cheek. He is beyond perplexed and quite unable to understand. Then Zawadi adds, "You are as old as any one of us."

"My brother?" Conquergood lifts his face and eyes to see the moon rising. "What of Vincent?"

"You have no brother," Zawadi says with a hint of sympathy consuming the empty spaces from within

Conquergood's memories and spirit. "Vincent is a projection of who you used to be. You are Vincent. And you are not. You are Jerome Conquergood, and yet you are not."

"Who am I?" Conquergood stands and walks out into the water until the waves meet his knees. He points into the distance, into the unknown. "I want to know who I am. Where do I belong in this world? In this time?"

"I might ask the same of myself."

"Then who are you?"

Zawadi gives no answer.

After several minutes of contemplation, Conquergood treads back to shore and looks Zawadi in the face.

"Surely, you can answer me that."

"I can," Zawadi says. "I am much like you."

The small boy who is named Vincent, still playing down on the sands of the beach in twilight, has built a moat around his sandcastle and the waters spill up and in, surrounding the structure. A Labrador's bark sounds from beyond a sand dune and Vincent waves to Conquergood.

"Still, I am not like you," says Zawadi, now watching Conquergood watching the young boy he has known as Vincent. Zawadi continues, "I am not like you. I am not of human origin. Instead, I am a creation of spliced genes, copied, and copied, and recopied beyond repair, and these genes were added to copies of other copies of prefabricated embryos. You, Jerome, are pure and untainted. You are holy. You are one of the few who remain of the lost humankind. The ones who have not been soiled by scientific experimentation and exploration. The Korporation wants to destroy you, and still, they cannot. They are you, and you are they."

"They cannot?" Conquergood is no longer looking at Vincent, but instead at Zawadi who is dissolving before his eyes. "Why can't they?"

"You are the life-blood of all that remains sacred in the world," she says. Her wings lift her up into the darkening skies. She hovers thirty feet or more above the man who remains standing on the beach.

"I must be going now," Zawadi says. "My stay in *this* world has finished. I came here to do what I had to do. I have shown you the truth. I have done what I promised. I have given your brother to you, Conquergood. Now please remember me. Please do not imagine me. But rather remember me as a friend, as a beloved, as a companion."

"I will," he says. "I must."

Conquergood watches as Zawadi's wings gracefully carry her toward the silver moon until her figure dissolves in old Luna's forgiving glow — a luminescence so often meant for young-rebellious lovers.

Retracting from the memory-orb, Conquergood — alone and unsettled — re-emerges on the hill inside the meta-vault of memory orbs, back in the Gateway as the meadow glistens from a brilliant sun. He is about to remove the virtual hood from his face, tears dripping between the mask of the virtual meta-suit and his own skin, when he hears Klaire's voice,

"I've been looking everywhere for you," Klaire says. "Where were you? Where did you go?"

Klaire's figure is not of human flesh but of a well-designed titanium alloy, perfectly shaped as her human form had been shaped. Her once golden locks have been transformed into swaying silver, metallic in nature.

"Don't be afraid," says Klaire, floating closer to Conquergood on the hill overlooking a newly formed river — formed by his own tears — and the river is lined with cherry blossoms. "I wanted you to see me for who I really am," she tells him. "This is the only place I can do that. What do you think? Of me? Of the *real* me?"

"What are you?" he says, wiping away the tears.

"Even I don't know exactly what I am," Klaire says from behind the metallic face which copies her human frame. "Does anyone ever truly know?" An imprinted **63** is stamped on the upper portion of her left arm. "We are a lot alike, Jerome. We're searching for our true identities, as all intelligent beings must, I suppose. The Korporation made me as they made you. But I am more machine than I would like to admit. I am not like you... who —"

"Is this a joke?" Conquergood takes a step back. "Is this another illusion? Another Korporate deception to mess with me? What is this? What's going on?"

"Afraid not, darling," she says. Her scintillating meta-eyes of cobalt search and analyze Conquergood's daunted expression. She adds, "the Korporation has labeled me as a Konstrukt Lover Adapted for Interpersonal Relations Enforcement — or KLAIRE, which is much simpler."

He stands aghast. "How many more like you are there?"

"No one knows for sure." Klaire reaches a metallic hand out to Conquergood, who remains unsure if he should touch it. She lets her hand fall and continues, "If we're lucky to become *aware* of what we are, we are sworn to secrecy... or sworn to oblivion. The majority here at the Korporation are as I am. I've wanted to tell you this for so very long. I just didn't know how."

"Were you sent to spy? A decoy? What?!"

"Yes, among many other orders." Sympathy crosses the meta-machine's face, Klaire's own would-be countenance. Her head bows when she says, "I'm sorry."

"Impossible." Conquergood's chest tightens, unable to adequately gain the breath he so desperately needs to make sense of the unfolding axiom before him. "Can't be."

Lies, lies, and more lies — those decrepit prevarications which breed mistrust — suffocate him. The virtual meta-world hacks at his natural order until he frees himself by ripping away the mask and hood — "*How I did thrive in this fair lady's love, and she in mine.*"

Within seconds, Conquergood re-enters the office of the Perception Management Department where all is as it was when he had left — if he ever left at all.

ONE

IV
Korporate Kopies

Thou,
whose exterior semblance
doth belie thy soul's immensity;
thou best philosopher,
who yet dost keep thy heritage,
thou eye among the blind,
that, deaf and silent,
read'st the eternal deep,
haunted for ever
by the eternal mind,

Mighty prophet!
Seer blest!
On whom those
truths do rest,
which we are toiling
all our lives
to find…

The clouds that gather
round the setting sun
do take a sober colouring
from an eye
that hath kept watch
o'er man's mortality;
another race hath been,
and other palms are won.

Thanks to the human heart
by which we live,
thanks to its tenderness,
its joys, and fears,
to me the meanest flower
that blows can give
thoughts that do often
lie too deep for tears.

William Wordsworth
"Intimations of Immortality"
1804

"The Universe is inside each one of us," the old man told the boy seated next to him on the cliffs facing the Mediterranean Sea. "Your mother, God rest her soul, wanted you to know that."

The boy stood to follow his father down the hill, but the boy stopped and looked out over the sea to where a ship was passing across the horizon. The boy thought of how he had lost his mother to the Black Death and what great sorrow it brought him. When the boy was at the bottom of the hill faced with the pastures of his father's sheep, the boy knew he had lost his great joy and doubted if he could ever find it again. Nevertheless, he knew that the Universe inside him was divided by a great sorrow and a great joy.

A few years later the boy buried his father next to his mother on the same hill overlooking the same sea. His father had followed the sadness each bottle provided and the boy believed on some nights his father might one day be happy again. But that had not been the case and the father died a broken man leaving the boy without a family.

The boy sold his father's land and sheep and a week later was hired to work a merchant's ship. He dreamed of faraway lands and peoples and the great joy he had lost years ago.

Decades later the boy, now grown into a man, returned with his wife of many memories and their two teenage sons and infant daughter. He and his family stood on the deck of the ship and looked up at the graves on the cliff where his father and mother were buried.

"Where are we?" the eldest son asked.

The father leaned down and gave the boy a kiss on his head and said to his family, "At last we are home."

Holy, thy art! Thy sacred body is cherished as the angels who kneel before the throne of God. You — the one who reads and comprehends — are as loved as those who willingly obey. *Who are you without me?* Zawadi demands.

Conquergood heads out of the Perception Management Department and into the k-line without so much of a glance at the laborers toiling in their interlocked virtual state of extended lethargy. At first, staring at an expectant tele-k-skreen, he is unsure of where to go.

Back to his apartment? Into the Korporate Kanteen? Into the arboretum? Meet Godse in the Korporate Knowledge Base?

All the questions are instantly rejected. Conquergood wants to see one man in particular:

Doktor Sir Windsor VI.

More questions, paradigms unsolvable, are needed to be asked and the doktor is the only one Conquergood knows who can answer them, now that Kin has become a strayer, an outkast.

"L88-13-6," Conquergood commands.

The k-line rapidly descends over and through the Kompound to the Korporate Labs.

Inside the lab Conquergood finds Johnson analyzing test tubes. The cages that once held Zawadi and her companions at the back of the lab stand open and empty.

"Where's that bastard Windsor?" says Conquergood, firmly positioned across the metal table where Johnson focuses on his work. "Where's that snake?"

"Not here." Without looking up or taking notice from his efforts at pouring liquid from one test tube into another, Johnson's eye-glasses fill with the colors of volatile rainbows as he adds, "Try the private quarters. Our good Windsor has been on leave since yesterday. There might be an illness going around. Hope the virus doesn't spread too much."

"Where would that be exactly?"

"K — Forty-three — Six," Johnson says, carefully pouring a reddish-liquid from a beaker into a test tube filled with a mossy-textured substance.

"K — Forty-three — Six?"

"That's the prize." The liquid combination inside the test tube begins to gargle frothy bubbles. "Now are we allowed to resume our work? Deadlines are at hand."

"Where's Zawadi?"

"Who?" Johnson is intent on recording the chemical reaction upon his video-eye-lenses. He cannot look away even if he wants to.

"The test subjects." Conquergood points to the opposite end of the lab. "The ones that were in those cages back there."

"What? The *mice*?"

"Yes, the damned mice!"

"Oh, the Korporation shipped them out a few days ago. Nothing to worry about. It's all up to pro-te-kall."

"Where to?"

"Don't ask, don't tell," Johnson says. Disappointed, he stops his recordings of the chemical reactions and erects himself. He pushes the frame of his eye-glasses up the sleek ridge of his elongated nose. "Several of the KG dropped in with newly updated orders. Something about a Safe Haven. Don't know what that means, but they said something along those lines. Now, if we do mind, we need to politely ask to give us some peace and space. These experiments aren't really privy to outsiders, to non-doktors, anyway. There's work to be done and since that over-inflated *maniakal* ass is unemployed, who is left to do it? That doesn't need a valid answer."

"Johnson," says Conquergood, fighting back the temptation to knock the spectacles clean off Johnson's pimpled face, "You can have all the space you deserve." Conquergood leaves Johnson's chagrin to settle itself among the beakers and test tubes.

The k-line gradually rises to the doktor's private quarters and Conquergood stands outside, afraid to knock, fearing and knowing the event in the memory-orb will likely be waiting on the other side. Conquergood pauses an unnatural pause. He hesitates another moment longer, then bangs his fist on the metallic surface of the door.

The first few attempts go unanswered. He waits.

Conquergood's chest tightens at the thought of Klaire in bed with Sir Windsor VI, but after all she is only a machine. She's not Leona. Another few bangs on the door do the job.

The doktor emerges as the door slides clear. His black hair, singed with streaks of gray, is disheveled. His black kimono hangs crooked and have been quickly thrown on to his lean frame. Something is not quite right about his jerky movements and the dirty whites of his eyes. Conquergood watches the doktor closely.

"May I help you, Jerome?" Sir Windsor VI ties the belt around his waist. "What's the fuss?"

The inquiry sounds as though it is posed to a complete stranger. Conquergood despises the distance found in the doktor's guttural tones.

"Who am I?" Conquergood forces out the words, the question burning and haunting and dangling before him more than all the others. "What did the Korporation do to me?"

Sir Windsor VI leans out into the hall and briefly glances from side to side before retreating back into his apartment with the words,

"They're watching. Follow so we may have a little chat. They're always watching and listening anyway."

Conquergood enters the apartment and follows the doktor down the small hallway.

"You seek dangerous answers to riddles from someone in a position of the utmost importance to the good of the Korporation. But you're beginning to ask the right kinds, Jerome. And that is progress."

The apartment is banal and sadly interchangeable with Conquergood's own, formulaic and dull, except for the pungent odor of opium lingering in the stale air. Four empty bottles of Vittoria Gin lie scattered on the silvery polish of the dining room table. There is no sign of any other person having been there.

"Give an old man a moment to get washed up. We'll only lose another minute."

The doktor vanishes into the back bedroom, a shower can be heard, and Conquergood takes a momentary seat at the table. He gets up, paces, and then steps lightly to the bedroom and finds a velvet curtain. Conquergood pulls one corner to the side, and he thinks he sees Klaire asleep, worn out and sweaty, lying on her stomach, facing the shaded bay window where the domed Garden waits below. She must have gone to Sir Windsor VI after he left her, she needing comfort from her distress — as if machines need such things. Her banana-colored hair is strewn across her naked back. Her face is turned away from him. Her breathing is heavy.

The shower abruptly stops and Conquergood lets the velvet drape fall back into place. He returns to his seat at the dining room table and he waits another ten minutes for the doktor to return.

Sir Windsor VI eventually slips out from one side of the velvet drape in a newly pressed black kimono. Conquergood can clearly see the doktor's eyes blazing with too much opium and gin. The doktor smiles a crooked but perfect smile.

"Vermin!" Conquergood rises from his place at the table, fists clinched, and smacks the doktor forcefully on the left temple. "Scoundrel!"

Sir Windsor VI stumbles back, hitting the wall. Conquergood steadily approaches and lands two more firm punches to the good doktor's jaw.

"Degenerate filth!" Conquergood screams.

The doktor's false teeth — much like the interlokutor's from the entrance interview — plop out and slide across the floor as blood spurts from the doktor's elongated nose. Knocked off balance, Sir Windsor VI falls back and lands on the floor with a painful thud.

With clinched fists and a mad heart racing in all its power, Conquergood towers over the cowering doktor.

A cry comes from the bedroom, "Windsy!" And the voice does not sound like Klaire's at all. The velvet drape is flung aside and a strangely-familiar woman emerges wearing a red kimono robe and lands on her knees beside the injured doktor. "Poor Windsy." Her hands trace the old man's swelling face. "What has happened? Are we all right, my dear sweet? Who is this madman? What has he done to us?"

"We'll be fine, Kate," Sir Windsor VI says. He calms her with a stroke of his hand against her chin. "Just fetch us our teeth over there." He points to the dentures on the floor resting against a chair leg. "But help us up first, dear."

"Kate?" Conquergood steps back in shock. "Kate?"

"Yes, Jerome," the doktor says. "Kate is a Korporate *kompanion*. We should've introduced her sooner. Much, much sooner, it appears."

"Here, our darling sweet," says Kate, handing the dentures back to Sir Windsor VI, who washes them at the kitchen sink before slipping them back into his mouth. The doktor takes a seat in the chair Conquergood had previously occupied. "Aren't we the *trukulent* one today?" Kate says to Conquergood.

Kate retrieves a clean washcloth, wets it, and wipes the blood from off the doktor's face while Conquergood sits opposite the doktor.

"Do you really want to know who you are?" The doktor says, rubbing his jaw. "Most of us want to know such answers to these kinds of perplexities about ourselves, don't we? These intelligible mysterious of the Universe — ever within our grasp — such riddles, however, never have the answers we want them to have. Yours — if we're allowed to make a wager — is a much more arduous issue to interpret — webs within webs. Rather, let us show you. We have, after all, been the doing and the showing type, haven't we?"

"Show me now," says Conquergood, rising from the chair. "Show me everything you know."

"Kate, dear, how about hibernating for a spell," Sir Windsor VI says. "It's been a strange morning and it's only going to get stranger."

"As my sweet demands," Kate says. "For the sssake of the Korporation, we ssserve the kommand." With her face showing the distrust she holds for Conquergood, she bows and retreats back through the velvet drape without another word.

"Let's get to it then," Sir Windsor VI says. "There's no time like the present."

Conquergood follows the doktor out of the apartment and into the k-line portal down the hall in an awkward silence, no man wanting to speak. Conquergood's breathing begins to slow while Sir Windsor VI continues to nurse his jaw.

"IF — 232 — 111" is the command Sir Windsor VI gives into the tele-k-skreen.

"Please verify the destination's *atomik* number," the raspy, feminine voice says inside the portal. "Then we may proceed at the pleasure of the Korporation."

"Verify sypher," the doktor says firmly. "Nine — six — nine."

"Thank the Korporation, Sir Windsor," the meta-voice returns. "May the workday prove fruitful."

The k-line whisks sideways, around the Korporate Tower and Kompound, and then darts upward, upward, upward.

"I didn't mean, I mean about Kate. I thought…" Conquergood says. "Never mind what I thought. Tell me why, why are you doing this?"

The doktor stares blankly out in front of himself, lost in a heavy daze. Then he forms the words, "The memories, most often, are too much for us to bear. Too heavy even for the immortal gods — if they do exist in some place and time. And you, our beloved Jerome, have left us little choice. After all, we're born in fits of rage and hope, are we not?"

When the k-line comes to a gentle halt, after a long silence between Conquergood and Sir Windsor VI, the *komputerized* voice says methodically,

"Greetings to Safe Haven. Have a wonderful moment."

Sir Windsor VI and Conquergood enter and they are immediately faced with large steel doors. The doktor presses his right hand upon an anachronistic palm reader, and after a few brief scans, a red light blinks green in confirmation, unlocking and opening the vaulted doors.

"Please don't judge us, son," says the doktor as the steel doors to Safe Haven rotate open. "What the Korporation did was done in order to save humanity — the human species from annihilation. Now follow, Jerome. And try not to touch anything. You're about to see the most valuable and priceless possessions in the world — esteemed above all else. Gifts to us all."

Sir Windsor VI leads Conquergood through the massive steel doors and onto a platform overlooking an exhibition room several times larger than the Korporate Kanteen and Labs combined.

On the main floor, sixty feet below the two men, thirteen meta-plasty tubes stand twenty-five feet in height and ten feet in diameter. The clear tubes contain smoky gases — the colors of old limes, of old plums, and of old lemons. Shadowy figures float inside these immense tubes, standing as gods once did in marble along ancient Athenian and Roman streets and halls.

"Inside these preserving shells," Sir Windsor VI says with a grave tone, "are the remnants of a dying species. We saved them, however. We saved them all."

Sir Windsor VI leans his sharp elbows against the railing, his shoulders weighted by too much knowledge interlaced by the toxins of opium and gin coursing through his system.

"It wasn't always like this. Humanity was once a noble and a remarkable race. A unique species filled and driven by *kreative* passions and honorable *konstitutions* which sought to *perfekt* the natural world around them, a world that was also dying. Everyone and everything were dying, being destroyed, being undone, being unmade. No one really believed it then, despite all the warnings. Scientists said one thing. Politicians argued the opposite. The longer and more useless the dialogues and disagreements grew, the faster the world was left to its own demise."

"What does this have to do with me?"

Conquergood notices a staircase, the first he has seen in the building, and he instinctually descends. The doktor reluctantly, but willingly, follows.

On the main chamber floor, Conquergood and Sir Windsor VI walk side by side among and below the thirteen colossal tubes, ghost-like and forbidden.

"We are VEDA," the doktor says with a hint of mourning in his voice at sounding out the acronym. Green-purple-yellow shades of light-shadows twist upon the doktor's face. "Do you know what that means, Jerome? You must have guessed by now."

"No, I don't, but I suspected, I had a feeling."

"Nor would you know for certain for that matter. Only a pre-chosen few high enough in the Korporate Elite would even know of the VEDA, and far less even know of Safe Haven," the doktor says.

The chamber room holds a kind of invisible presence, unholy and god-fearing.

"Sir Windsor the First, or rather *the only*, is my beloved ancestor. The Sixth — me, it, he, they, us — is as he was, is, and still we are of an alternative that bore him to learn *genetik* engineering and shaped such wonderful madness into awareness and being. As Musk was moving humanity into the stars to land and live on Mars, Sir Windsor was searching for another path forward. Elon Reeve Musk the First is down there in Tube 11." Sir Windsor VI pointed down the row of tubes. "Ah, the grand mystery of godhood," he says, "Isn't it sublime? Perhaps the First Sir Windsor didn't know what he was really doing, tampering with the material Universe, but it was either this or the end of all humanity — the lesser of two evils, as many have said."

Sir Windsor VI moves over to one of the tubes and places a fraught hand near the bottom of its chilled surface. For a moment, with his other hand, he rubs his jaw. Marked with a large number 4, the tube towers over the two men who are covered in the tube's sinister glow.

"We are our great-great-great grandfather, and he is us. We are one and the same and not at all — a quagmire of indispensable truths and possibilities. Even as it is spoken, the words of making, there is no light in them." The doktor's brackish words are weighed down with despair and opium. He pushes a blue button an e-skreen located on the side of Tube 4. "See for yourself, Jerome. Behold the glory of our eternity."

Conquergood watches as the gas clears for a moment, revealing the body of Sir Windsor VI, the same man standing next to him — *how can that be?*

"I don't understand." Conquergood takes a step back and looks from the tube to the doktor and back to the tube. "What the hell are you?"

"We are VEDA. We did not come to serve, but to be served," says the doktor, his head bowed, his hands held out in front of him as he stares back at his own face enshrined in the flowing gas cylinder. "We didn't know ourselves for many years as a child, and later as an adolescent we didn't understand at all, growing up among the Korporate Elite, sharing memories which we never understand we had, being disciplined in every manner of sciences as our ancestors had been, and even in the new understandings he established himself."

Sir Windsor VI's hands rub his temples and he massages a pain away.

"We only learned of our ill-fated heritage when we elevated to the status of an Elite. We are VEDA, and so are Kate and Klaire and Kin, and the others. Klaire told us that you saw her true form in the Gateway. We must assure you it is not a burden but a gift. We do wonder, though, if he felt as we do."

"What exactly is a VEDA?" Conquergood is tormented by the immortal image transfixed inside Tube 4 and on the doktor's face beside him. "What does that have to do with me?"

"Unlike you, we are a Virtual Elektronik Descendant Avatar. The Korporation saved humankind by distributing pre-selekted genes among machines. At the onset, krude beings were konstrukted, but in time and turn, they were the ones to enhance their descendants in more natural forms who kontinually, as we do, enhance theirs. Like our children, our soul is kounterfeit, or we are one and the same. We still do not know the answer to this question — the Soul. We were hoping you would be able to tell us."

The doktor pushes an orange button and the green-purple-yellow gas covers the original Sir Windsor, enshrining him back into eternal worship and hibernation inside Tube 4.

"If I'm not like you," Conquergood says, "then what am I? Who am I?"

"Twenty-seven years ago, we began, along with Kin and the other doktors in the Korporation, our own modified research on VEDAs using authentik cells rather than kloned ones. Redundant kopies, as you might already know, tend to lose their effectiveness over time. We were hoping to purify the human race once more. All that, however, is lost now since Kin has been removed from the Korporation. We tried to reinstitute the prime kommand our forefathers had programmed into our elektronik veins and minds into our teknologikal substance — monsters of Frankenstein, yes? Zawadi and her sisters are a few tiny steps nearer to reaching our godly agenda."

"Johnson said Zawadi would be here."

"The Korporation likely moved her to a safer more hidden place. We have a way of knowing what will happen before it happens — linked minds, and all. One of our many unnatural or preternatural gifts."

The two walk in the massive chamber filled with Originals locked away in their gaseous tubes. No windows can shed its sunlight here, and the room is of a cold nature, empty and bare, but filled with so much breathing-living-ancient history.

"If the Korporation fails," the doktor says, "if we fail our ancestors, then all of humanity fails. Humankind will be lost. That *kannot* be allowed to happen."

Safe Haven is eerily quiet with many of the thirteen tubes filled with the unanimated-frozen-timeless figures, shadowy in their gaseous prisons — entombed, yet alive. Conquergood, however, feels at home among the silent-sleeping history on display in the tubes.

"We must show you this and it's not an easy thing to learn." Sir Windsor VI leads Conquergood to Tube 1. "Our original ancestor began his research with many of his own genes, his own DNA and RNA, his own blood, his life, his energy, and much of him still flows among the first models of VEDA."

On Tube 1, Sir Windsor VI pushes a similar blue button on the side as before and the artic gases retreat into holes in the floor of the tube. Within a minute, Tube 1 stands empty.

"As you may have already noticed," Sir Windsor VI begins, "many of these thirteen tubes suspend our ancestors — the Originals — in a timeless dozing state. Here they must remain until the day our knowledge advances far enough to replenish our lands with a more advanced human species." The doktor lifts a hand as if to explain what is not there — what is absent and missing. "Roughly twenty-seven years ago, we began work on this one, an Original. Unlike many today who are of a sad double nature made by desperate but hopeful scientists, Andrade was not. Andrade was genuine, true, and raw.

Holy, pure, and beautiful. Untouched by exploitation. He was the one we looked to for our ultimate salvation."

"Andrade?" Conquergood has heard the name before in his training as the Turnkey Specialist. He staggers away from the mention of the name more than the empty flexiglass shell towering before him. "What?"

"Then only six years old, we released the man-child from his hibernation. Little did we know of the tainted state of an extended hibernator. We believed his pure genes would revitalize humankind anew — away from the work of the First-Generation VEDAs, who seek to stagnate the orders of our ancestors. These powerful beings, however, grew even more powerful, even more false and the power they hold upon all else in our modern world is beyond what we thought possible. They are the Korporation as we know it now. When the Gen 1 VEDA learned of our doing, Andrade was banished from the Korporation — they were unable and fearful to destroy the man-child, yet well within their mandated programs to exile him into the Outlands. Most of the Gen 1 VEDAs fear and worship him still."

The doktor, his wild red eyes strained beneath the opium's stupor, turns to Conquergood and takes a breath before continuing.

"Who are you?" Sir Windsor VI asks Conquergood. "You are Jerome, my friend, like Andrade, you are a pure-soul, an Original, one who was not made, but born. You, like Andrade out there, are the last of a handful belonging to the true but ancient human race that is struggling in its last few breaths to survive, a species the Gen 1 VEDA has out-evolved enough to despise, to loathe. Sadly, it had been humanity who first fashioned these VEDAs, and the twisted torture they now belong to enshrines us all. The following generations of VEDA have grown into a populous race, further delaying the rebirth and revival of a pure humanity once again. We are afraid we have failed you, Konquergood."

"Zawadi! Tell me of her. From whom was she made?"

"Jerome Konquergood," the doktor's words hold a plea in them, seeking forgiveness without directly asking for it, "Zawadi is your VEDA. In kind, she's a sister, a daughter, and somehow, as the Korporation has recently revealed, you two are irreversibly linked. This has never happened before. None of the other VEDAs ever had this sort of union with their Original before. Unique and fathomless. Extraordinary."

Conquergood is silenced by his own failing comprehension, his flawed human comprehension. For him, there's nothing more that needs to be said. Time is what he needs now.

III
Turnkey Specialist

The recurring dream always begins the same. Conquergood would be standing in an open Central Park and the Monarch butterflies would come. A multitude of heavenly wings would flitter around him as though he were the eye of a hurricane and they were the swirling winds. Each flap of the wings tickles him beneath the morning sun, dawning for what feels like the first day. Conquergood laughs and holds his hands up to the charming pink sky as the butterflies take flight, swirling and spiraling away.

The scene always changes to Leona on the beach. She has been swimming after lunch again, dangerous he tells her as she smoothly crosses from ocean onto dry land. Leona never speaks but comes right up to Conquergood as if after a long absence and drops her head onto Conquergood's bare chest, tanned and raw. He holds her tight until her body becomes wet sand and dissolves beneath his grasp. Dropping to his knees, Conquergood cannot refashion the sand into his beloved.

Then the scene changes once more. Conquergood stands in the corner of a destitute cabin watching an old man. The old man, with a balding head of silver, sits in a wooden rocking chair, a leather book lay open in his lap. The old man stares solemnly out an open bay window where a canoe can be seen tied to a dock stretching into a small lake.

Dusk settles a tawny gold fabric of light over the old man's bronze, cracked face. His eyes hold a faded misery in them as he watches on a distant hill beyond the lake golden stalks flow and wave in the crisp wind.

The peak of a snow-capped mountain projects itself out over the dense forest as a sincere contentment strengthens the old man's face for what comes next. The old man continues to watch the sun ease away from the natural landscape before him one final time. He accepts the cycles as one who has found his place among the wilderness. Then the old man dwindles into his own flesh, shrinking into dust until the chair holds only the open book.

This is when Conquergood awakes, unable to see what the old man has been reading, but it is the landscape which burns a mournful heartache into Conquergood's mind. And he doesn't know why.

Conquergood awakes to the sound of the Superior's voice over the tele-k-skreen. The order for their final meeting in Korporate Kontrol has been issued. They have been over the plan a countless number of times since his employment with the Turnkey Department — *No going back now. Deals have been made* — Conquergood's own survival depends on it.

On his bed, Conquergood waits, one more hour to the appointment. An opium cigar dangles in the corner of his mouth, eyes throbbing beneath the intense delusions of his own calm understanding of the task set before him.

The plan is quite simple really. During the Planetary Kounterinsurgency Konvention in New Philadelphia, Conquergood must deliver an ampule to Andrade Sartain, leader of the Grassroots Kampaign.

Conquergood wants to do it, has to do it, he needs to do it to regain the favor of the Gen 1 VEDA, at least that much is clear from what Sir Windsor VI has explained to him. It was more like a father begging a son to do the right thing rather than a direct order from a superior.

The wretched doktor — *haunted by his own ghosts* — believes the First-Generation VEDA will be more forgiving if Conquergood can fulfil the Korporate agenda, wiping out the other rogue VEDA who branched off from the Korporation over three plus decades ago. All is pure speculation, for no one knows what will happen. From Conquergood's countless hours of training as a delivery specialist, he understands that the Grassroots Kampaign and the Lighthouse Faktion seek to displace the Korporation, to change the human initiative, and much of this Conquergood already knew while working with Ritz and the others — *Where are they now?*

Conquergood is torn among the three interlocked worlds, spinning out of control: the past, the present, and the future. Conquergood's past life is a numb illusion, fragmented shells of a lost generation, as a species that destroyed itself through a deadly new virus, or so Sir Windsor VI has told him. The doktor had further extrapolated on the eternal memory he carries from his ancestor's genes, justifying novel technology as both the lock and key to human survival.

Across from Conquergood's bed, the K-net on the KV displays digitized editorials from the time of the Mass Obliteration — the experts have adamantly stated that the J-Virus had not originated from a lab — further confirming Sir Windsor VI's statements.

The Superior had admitted that an additional assault which cannot be sited in the Korporate files — *can they be trusted? Why can't they? Zawadi says they can, they must, for now* — that the newer VEDA, like Klaire, are the remaining lifeline of the entire human race, the element of perpetual rejuvenation in technological advancements, life extension techniques, and the brutal hope that they can one day save their masters, their creators, their fathers and mothers, their ancestors. Such in the name of Progress.

Klaire stands motionless in the doorway to Conquergood's bedroom. Beneath the layers of his opium trance, he didn't notice her arrival and her presence quickens his heartbeat, pulling him up from the depths of the sink hole established by too many facts, too much knowledge and too much opium, which all have drained him miserably.

"You look horrible," Klaire says to him. She doesn't enter the bedroom but instead waits for a sign. She notices grim bags under his swollen eyes. He hasn't slept since the meeting with Sir Windsor VI some five days ago. "Darling?"

"I am as I should be. No more, no less," he says with a brief sigh of angst. He's exhausted and doesn't care to make more of an effort. He remains lying on the bed. "Why have you come?"

"I'm here to say good-bye," she says as she crosses the threshold and places her timid and anxious presence on the edge of the bed, a canary landing. She faces the mordant man as if he is on his deathbed. "Windsor told me you came by his apartment and there was a fight. He told me everything. He also told me you are planning to leave today, for your assignment. Is what he says true?"

"Why have you come?" His voice erupts and then fades into its own indifference. He does not wish to hurt her — *if she can be hurt* — but the words come roaring out anyway. "Why does it matter to you?"

The room is lit only by the KV and the numerous hacked news articles blaring silently their pure-whiteness of the e-page, filled with poisonous text and wounded images from inside the Korporate Kamps of innocent children shrunk to a third their normal size.

"We don't want you to hate us," says Klaire, pleading. Her timorous hand reaches out to Conquergood. He pulls away. "We must all follow the Korporation. We must follow our orders or be unemployed. It's not so bad when you get used to it. It was wrong of us to do it and not tell you. Please don't hate us."

"I don't hate any of you," says Conquergood, turning to her and seeing Klaire's wet meta-eyeballs, both human and machine — she's an anachronistic being tormented by wraiths, dead memories. "But I don't love any of you either. I can't." Real tears crash down her face. "I'm sorry," he says, "I just can't love —" and for the first time it happens to him: a stumble, a pause — "what are you?"

Klaire, defeated, buries her face in her hands. She falls to her knees against the bed and sobs as quietly as she can. Conquergood, not knowing what else to do for the VEDA, comforts her with mindless strokes across her blonde curls and down the back of her canary-colored kimono. Her breathing calms.

"We all have a job to do," he tells her firmly. Conquergood rights himself, stands and looks down at the enfolded woman, the machine, the VEDA — *whatever she is* — she is almost perfect, he thinks. The kisses they had shared in the Garden of the Gods, their jumbled afternoons of a blissful love affair, and their pointless conversations while lying nude flood the man's mind — *was any of it real?*

"I'll be seeing you, Klaire," he says. "I must go now."

She doesn't look up, so he turns and heads to the door. Something inside stops him. A voice perhaps. He turns back around and says in the softest tone he can muster,

"You must know it was real for me."

When she looks up from her moistened hands, the doorway is empty and Conquergood's apartment is filled with her stressed breathing. A sigh emerges and a faint whisper follows,

"He's my father, but I love you more. So very much more. Please try to understand."

"T166-38-13," Conquergood says inside the k-line. "At once."

"Back to work so soon, Kebir?" The tele-k-skreen speaks with a jesting confidence. "How timely."

"Yes, back to work."

"May the Korporation bless all who serve us faithfully," the e-voice returns without any notice of the prior comment. "We're very sorry you'll miss the Revival." Then the k-line surges upward in expectant silence.

Inside Korporate Kontrol, Conquergood faces the holo-globe as he had done on the first day of his training. Most of the red splotches have descended upon and infiltrated New Philadelphia. The blue, brown, red, yellow and white icons illuminating from the sphere cast their e-shades on the pale, worn face of the Turnkey Specialist. Shadows outline the edges of the room, instilling a transparent mode of absolute secrecy. The Superior emerges from a dark corner.

"We didn't think you'd show. Impressive."

"I'm here," Conquergood says without facing him, "that should be clear enough."

"We are aware that our beloved doktor had a nice little chat with you yesterday," the Superior says in a voice marching ahead of itself. The Superior's black kimono blends with the darkened shadows in the background and makes his gray head appear to be floating on its own. "It was bound to happen anyway. The newer VEDAs are more emotionally entwined with their more primitive, human ancestors than the older generational models. Progress, however, is a baffling attribute to witness, if one lives long enough to see it."

"Is it such a curse to be human?"

"You, Kebir" says the Superior, stepping into the e-globe's artificial aura, "You should know that better than anyone. Our pain is derived from your pain, is it not?"

"You create what destroys you."

"Wise words to live by from a non-VEDA," the Superior says. "Did old Godse tell you that trifle of an axiom?" The Superior's hands clasp together behind his back. He leans over the e-world and places his face into the spinning holo-sphere. When he pulls his face out of the hologram, he adds, "The human species should have listened to such visionaries like you when they had the chance. Nevertheless, we are here as a result of our ancestors — obsolete madmen."

From behind the Superior's back, he reveals a cylindrical device, without markings, resembling a silver Korporate cigar holder.

"Here's the ampule. Who're you going to deliver it to?"

Conquergood takes the device and rubs its smooth service against his hands. "Andrade Sartain." The sleek texture reminds him of something. "The leader of the Grassroots Kampaign is our target."

"Andrade's appearance?"

"Why test me?" Conquergood slips the ampule into a side pocket on his white kimono. "We've been over this at least fifty times."

"His appearance?" The Superior's tone is rigid and automatic. He bends his forehead closer to his Turnkey Specialist. "Tell me."

"Long brown hair with beard, green eyes, six feet-three inches, two hundred and two pounds, more or less the same as shown on the holo-photo you had me memorize at least two hundred times."

"Very well," says the Superior, backing away to the other side of the e-globe, spinning on its invisible axis. "Since we don't have any recently updated photographs of this man who leads the Grassroots Kampaign, you must take notice. The sheep will lead you to their shepherd. Trust me on that. When you give him the gift, be sure to tell him this message word for word: 'In today already walks tomorrow.' Understood?"

"Understood," Conquergood says. He fondles the device in his pocket — *in today already walks tomorrow*. The Superior watches him from across the e-world. Conquergood asks, "What is this thing? What does it do?"

"My pay grade isn't high enough to know, and don't really need to know either. Better not to know too much. Isn't that right, Konquergood?"

The words of ignorance sound familiar in Conquergood's ears. He thinks of Klaire, but only for an instant. He has made his decision, counted and recounted his steps, and the time has come to do his job and deliver the ampule to Andrade.

"A transport with a unit of Korporate Guards will be waiting outside at midnight to fly you within a few miles of the Konvention site in New Philadelphia," the Superior says. "Are you ready to do what is necessary for the sake of the Korporation?"

"To serve the Korporation," Conquergood hears himself say, "above our own needs."

"Konquergood," says the Superior, moving through the illusionary e-globe with a palm open.

Conquergood accepts the Superior's hand and they shake. There is no turning back now.

"You're a damn fine asset to the Korporation, Kebir," the Superior says. "We wish we had more like you."

"No. No you don't." Conquergood takes back his hand. "In the end, I'm not doing this for the Korporation. I'm doing this for humankind, for Vincent, for Klaire and Kin, and for all the rest. Even if I don't understand what it is I'm doing, I must do it for Zawadi."

A stubborn frown folds itself over the lips of the Superior, and Conquergood departs towards the door. As he nears the exit, Conquergood calls out the command, "Lights on!"

A vast blinding flood of bright light spreads through the Illuminate bulbs crippling the Superior, who shields his eyes with a flat palm, dazzled by a thousand multi-colored sparkles of seeing. Regaining his sight, the Superior notices he is all alone inside Korporate Kontrol.

"Lights off!" the Superior shouts. To himself, he says, "It's time for Kebir to make a little history."

Darkness re-envelopes the room and the Superior returns to a far corner, draped in a deeper more solid darkness, where a chair is waiting for him to sit and overlook the artificial holo-world, glowing bright and beautiful and glorious once more.

II
Final Delivery

Inside the Korporate airship and in full body armor fitted with lethal weapons, covered all in black except for a white **KG** painted on their chests and helmets, twenty-six of the finest Korporate Guard resemble immortalized effigies of Spartan warriors more than what they actually are: the militarized VEDA, genetically altered, enhanced, incubated and raised for one purpose: total militaristic servitude.

Each trooper stands with laser batons — filled with electromagnetic radiation — patiently resting attentively on their crossed biceps, bulging from constant adrenaline injections. The state-of-the-art body armor — while fire-resistant, chemical, and bullet proof — also incorporate an exoskeleton which enhances a Korporate Guard's durability, stamina and muscular strength by no less than seventy-three point two per cent, creating a super VEDA.

Their solid black body armor leaves no exposure to their freshy exteriors. Their virtual communications helmets synchronously link and relay information both verbally and visually to and from Korporate Kontrol and the rest of the hive-unit. If these meta-behemoths speak, their helmets absorb the audio without as much as a decibel leaking from the black visors of meta-plasty. Some of the newer models are capable of light refraction, camouflage and cloaking. Not one guard is less than six feet eight inches, towering over the six-two frame of Conquergood.

In a light-weight flight suit filled with a smart-chute of his own, the Turnkey Specialist leans against the wall as the Korporate airship soars the eighty miles to New Philadelphia in less than ten minutes. Conquergood has followed his orders to the letter, from both the Korporation and from the Lighthouse Faktion — *and Andrade is waiting out there on the other side.* Conquergood rubs the cylindrical ampule strapped inside a side-pocket of his leg. He will do all he can for Klaire and Kin. Even Zawadi is there whispering from the unknown to him, and the only word she says a gentle reminder is the familiar name "Vincent."

"Drop zone in one minute," a meta-voice sounds over the speakers — the airship being flown remotely by Korporate Kontrol Komputers back at Korporate Tower. "Get ready to release."

Conquergood is helped by two Korporate Guards because his mechanized smart-chute weighs him down a bit. In his training, he's been told that the smart-chute strapped to his back will deploy automatically through komputerized kontrols linked to Korporate Tower. For the moment, he must place his trust — *more importantly his life* — in the hands of the Korporation.

"No room for error," the Superior had told Conquergood. "We don't need any gambles." Possibly he had meant suicide or perhaps the Korporation no longer contains trust in the human species.

"Twenty to release," the meta-voice bursts out over the loud speakers in the back of the Korporate airship. "Engage. Doors open!"

Two side doors automatically slide away and a rush of frigid air bursts inward. Two more Korporate Guards assist the Turnkey Specialist over to the exit. Outside the airship an ocean of black night swirls by and there is but one way for the Turnkey Specialist to go — *and there are no more steps to take.*

"Dispatch Kebir now!"

The two Korporate Guards toss-fling-throw the Turnkey Specialist out into ten thousand feet of nothingness, a grand silent void, and into groundless falling and spinning and complete freedom governed by gravity alone.

Conquergood attempts to right himself, to find the balance, but the rate of his falling increases and he loses control.

Almost instantly Korporate Kontrol monitors the errors and simultaneous orders are given. The flight suit corrects the spinning free fall and Conquergood can barely see as he finds the balance, his outstretched arms maneuvering through the wind currents of invisible space.

Managing his precise movements carefully — much as he had practiced in the simulation chambers back at the Korporate Kompound — Conquergood glides wonderfully downward, much like an eagle — the dark ground and the outline of a lake rushing up, coming but not moving.

He enjoys the exhilaration, the relaxing of his mind and muscles as the earth seems to pull him down to her. Conquergood sees the gray shadows of the trees and the darker shadow of the lake below him and he knows he's on target — *Korporate Komputers never fail.*

The smart-chute auto-deploys at just over five thousand feet and it takes close to thirteen minutes for the ride down. In wide arching circles — like some lost starving vulture from another century — Conquergood discovers another side to life, one where man is unattached to both himself and to the world below. He grasps at the cords instinctually but then realizes there is nothing up there to hold on to, only the night sky above and the ground far below.

When he relaxes, Conquergood is able to calm himself from the fear that comes with knowing that a smart-chute is what keeps him from smashing into oblivion. He has time to reflect on all those delightful afternoon love sessions he had had with Klaire. How nice it would have been to have her by his side now to experience becoming one with the sky.

His thoughts then turn to Kin and Otalp and the rest of the Lighthouse Faktion and where they could have gone — *were they out there somewhere? Lost as much as he?*

Soaring and gliding through the night, the Turnkey Specialist notices that the remodeled New Philadelphia, outlined in shadows some kilometers away, is without any building except for a few remaining remnants from ages past. The Kapital, instead, remains a natural utopia with abundant trees and rivers, authentic and genuine. From his time studying the landscapes back in his apartment,

Conquergood can almost see what New Philadelphia looks like in person — *beautiful and grand, he tells himself.*

Beneath Conquergood's dangling feet is an open field covered in snow near Centennial Lake — *he believes the ecstasy will go on forever* — then comes the ground crashing upward into his ankles and knees. Smack!

Conquergood tumbles and rolls violently over himself and becomes tangled in the cords of his smart-chute. A few feet of snow break his awkward landing, and he takes a moment to lie on his back and give thanks — *as Godse had taught him to do* — for his survival to the Universe all around and all above.

Entangled and breathing frantically at the knowledge and experience at having been thrown out of a perfectly adequate airship and at having thankfully survived, Conquergood feels more alive than ever and he cherishes the event all the more because it is his own real memory.

Still laying on his back, he carefully checks his limbs to discover no severe injuries. The flight suit monitors his body in less than ten seconds and on the Virtual Display Band on his right arm the details of his condition are provided and constantly updated. The smart-suit activates the heating unit, keeping Conquergood warm in the chill of the early morning hours. All systems are a Go. He untangles himself and removes the mechanized smart-chute, a hundred per cent komputer operated. He is relieved to say the least.

On the VDB, Conquergood checks the satellite directions, the navigational system advising him to make a 180-degree spin and begin heading southeast for approximately three kilometers to the New Philadelphia New Museum of Art. Conquergood double checks the headings and he can feel the intense cold from the snow trying to get inside his smart-suit.

The Turnkey Specialist checks the ampule he must deliver, and he finds it is undamaged in its hidden, protective sheath. He must make his way to the Kapital, remembering he has approximately seventy-two hours to return back to the drop zone for his immediate extraction. He hasn't decided if he'll return, but he has promised himself that the ampule will be delivered to Andrade, for no other reason than for Conquergood's own personal survival — *and for the survival for all that he does not and cannot love.* Conquergood takes his bearings once more and begins trudging through the deep snow.

After a time of sedulously marching beside the frozen lake and cursing his fate for being dropped back into the dead of winter — *no warm bed out here, no warm kisses* — Conquergood locates, as trained, the abandoned pagoda and withered garden. He imagines that Godse had once lived here in this pagoda in another time that is now lost to all but the Sage's mind and memory. Conquergood's arms and legs — despite the long hours of training in the Korporate gymnasium — burn and ache. He wants — *no, he needs* — a rest.

Covered in a majestic snow, the pagoda's triangular roof slopes downward over a serene walkway. A weeping tree flourishes its snowy branches next to a small iced-over koi pond and a miniature waterfall which sheds no water. Inside the pagoda, the rooms are bare except for wood planks as a modest flooring. Conquergood thinks of bringing Godse here to live, or to die — *that would be nice, yes it would.* That would be a good thing the Turnkey Specialist says to himself. In the middle of a large room,

Conquergood finds a place to rest until dawn. The Planetary Kounterinsurgency Konvention will start at eight sharp, another seven hours for sleep and contemplation. Conquergood removes the bag he has been carrying for provisions and sets it over in a far corner.

Conquergood steps outside beneath the overhang of the pagoda's walkway. The night or early morning is fresh and clear and sublime. He is glad at having arrived at this place, and considers returning, living, and remaining here possibly with Klaire — *but that cannot be.*

The stars — dying suns lighting civilizations from eons far gone — shine in the billions. The stories these dead suns still share among the constellations are like constant eyes of the Universe — *silently watching and always observing* — and Conquergood breathes a sigh of satisfaction. The Universe watches as Conquergood walks out into the snow and kneels. He remembers what Godse has taught him: close the eyes, clear the mind, open the heart, breathe deeply and sense the surroundings as a living entity and not as a servant, *in situ*, a tableau of human paradox. The smart-suit keeps Conquergood warm, but frost forms around his lips and nostrils as fumes of cold air rush out into the silent night. He ignores the ice and cold and breathes once more.

Running has been Conquergood's prime objective since he was a little child, and now, on his knees, he stops. Conquergood stops trying to complete the next task, always another goal to reach and never enough. He sits. He listens. He breathes. The steps can wait.

All the questions cease against each other without the assistance of one to contemplate their mysteries and fuel their endless debate and strife. Even the hatred

Conquergood has stored up unknowingly over the years, the kind of raw anger which silently builds and builds and builds until the fury needs to implode, explode, desiring to be removed from the source of its power and energy. Conquergood knows this hate and anger all too well. He has lived with it for all his life. The vexation, the displeasure, the irritations Conquergood has held onto for far too long against the overwhelming dominance of the Korporation become solid, concrete and real. He finds his body shaking, not from the intense cold but from the intensity of his anger, the wrath held under control for far too long.

Conquergood breathes in and then allows all the conflicting emotions to escape with a single breath. As simple as that. As easy as letting a frightful canary in the clutch of a dominant hand fly away — *free and true and pure*. Remembering Godse's training, Conquergood heaves in another deep breath of air and lets it slowly release from his lungs through his nose.

Finally Conquergood has discovered the chasm which has haunted and saddened his entire life, tortured him in thriving anguish, taunted his inability to bridge the canyon of his being with a multitude of useless answers — *and the mystery no longer matters, no longer holds any weight to the existence of his being, for how can it mean what he thinks it means*.

Conquergood stops in equanimity. The continual acts of non-stop movement, ceaseless senselessness, repeated over and over and over until an autopilot takes control and places a person on a mindless drive forward, ever forward to those greener pastures of better days and sunshine — *to the grave*.

Conquergood stops the trail of his own thoughts leading over the cliff of negativity. He allows the essence of true positivity to enter his mind, his body, his veins. Transient Nature rushes in and he senses the trees breathing, the snow pulsating, and the moon high above reaching down and filling his puny soul full of esoteric magic.

Conquergood's mind is clear, and before him once more, on the beach, he is confronted with Leona; but this time it is different. Hope, which has often accompanied him on the sight of Leona, has been replaced by fear. Leona is dead, passed into the absence of life, an image remaining only from within; he can never have her; he can never hold her; he can never be with her. He respects what he should have known all along. Conquergood kisses Leona full, deep and long. It is more a memory than imagination. The chasm grows ever smaller. Grief plays the strings to his heart, but it is better than false hope — *far, far better than the sorrows he could have known.*

Conquergood breathes slowly in meditation, doing exactly as Godse had previously instructed.

Let the Earth consume you, Godse had said.

Conquergood allows his mind to halt, to rest, to reserve itself to a much greater awareness, accepting a much, much older Universe to guide him. A Universe filled with more mysteries than answers. A Universe full of more wonder than ennui. A Universe far older than anything ever known and named. A Universe that holds all things in the cup of its gentle hand — *able to create and able to destroy.*

"The Universe," Godse had once conceded to Conquergood, "is far older, far wiser, far more elaborate, and far more mystical than any one of us. Yet, the Universe desires to be our friend — to love us."

Conquergood can sense once more the raw anger deep within rising, at having been cheated out of Leona's love; but he breathes, accepts what he can never change, never have; and he recalls Godse telling him that ownership is a grand lie — *the greatest lie one can believe, because no one can truly ever own anything.*

Much as the seasons do not own the Earth, nor does one own anything or anyone for a period longer than a season. Even bodies, inviolable temples of flesh, are not owned by the soul or thought. Time makes sure the seasons end and come to change; whether we like it or not, whether we seek it out or not. The Turnkey Specialist breathes out and then in; the chasm is more of a ravine.

Conquergood now understands the natural order of things. He cannot fight the Korporation and its corrupted system any more than he can fight wind or rain or snow. To conquer, he considers, he must convince and not destroy; to do otherwise would be like becoming a mad, drunken fool at high noon arguing against the stubborn desert sun. No. There are other ways to influence and change what is wrong in the world. Conquergood knows he must be the one to find the way.

And then, in Conquergood's catatonic state of repose and reflection — his knees kept from the hardships of the snow by the smart-suit protecting him — something the lekturer K-NE1 had told him in his first lesson flashes against the limitless screen of his human mind.

A misplaced memory so vital it comes rushing forward into the forefront of Conquergood's thoughts: *the Korporation is behind it all, everything.* Conquergood breathes in and out, doing the best he can to clear his thoughts, calm his heart, refocusing his system of thoughts to a better end.

Conquergood has lost Klaire; he breathes in and out. He has lost Leona; he breathes in and out. The Turnkey Specialist has even lost his brother Vincent; he breathes in and out. Conquergood has lost all but gained everything else in return. He breathes in and out and opens his eyes, awake with new insights to the natural world around him, sending the deepest night a solemn farewell.

This time it is different. This time it is new.

Taking a minute with his fingertips, Conquergood traces the image of a roaring lion carved into the oak door. In the familiar forest behind him, he can smell the aster flowers blooming on the hills and mountains in the distance — *Maine never smelled so good*. He pushes open the door between two large trees that have been built in conjunction with the log cabin and somewhere close behind him in the crab apple and maple trees he can hear eastern bluebirds chirping. He steps inside without taking a look back. He knows where he is going. He knows where he must go.

Inside the cabin, Conquergood can see a stone pillar in one corner of the living room, which is modestly decorated by a woman's touch in rugs and firs and leather chairs while a gentle fire whips and cracks in the fireplace. Conquergood moves across the room as if floating.

He can see a picture of the balcony scene from *Romeo and Juliet* hanging on the wall alongside the fireplace. On the mantel, however — and of more concern — rests a picture of Leona and Conquergood at the beach, and it is this picture that arrests the man's attention. The two are holding one another and she is smiling while he kisses her on the side of her head. And inside himself there is a feeling that he has arrived home after a journey that has taken more years than he had ever imagined — *et tu, Ulysses*? Stay with me, he thinks; stay with me because that is all I will ever need. He doesn't know it yet, but it doesn't hurt. He won't allow it. He cannot be anything less than who he was born to be. He feels, yes, he knows he is home. Finally, home. After all these years.

When Conquergood hears a light chopping sound coming from the next room, he sets the picture of Leona and he back down on the mantel and enters the kitchen. He can feel the sunlight from the great bay windows that reveal a wide, open lake outside before he sees Leona bending on one knee with a carrot in her outstretched hand feeding a baby deer with large pointed ears and white spots scattered over its fur.

Conquergood stands in the doorway of the kitchen for a moment. He wants to feel this, because whatever it is *it is* new and alive and real. Then it comes to Conquergood out of all the dreams, out of all the experiences, out of all the memories he has ever known before: Leona does not belong to his past or present; all the visions of Leona come from the future. His future. Their future. He is only now seeing the truth for the first time. A truth that had been hidden from him, but not anymore.

The baby deer, chopping on half a carrot, twists its head to face Conquergood. Leona does the same. When their eyes meet, Conquergood can feel himself smile. Sees her smile. The baby deer licks its lips with its long black tongue and nudges its head onto Leona's hand in hopes of finishing its meal.

"Where've you been?" Leona says. She gives the baby deer the rest of the carrot, wipes her hands on her jeans, straightens her auburn sweater and stands to greet her lover. "I've been waiting for you. You're late, you know that, mister?"

The baby deer shakes its white tail and moves over into the corner where an old quilt has been laid for its bed.

"I'm sorry," Conquergood mutters. He doesn't know what to say to his dream girl. He hesitates, feeling something crawling down his arm and he swipes the ladybug away and it flies over the counter and lands on the wall above the stove, where celery has been placed in a glass pitcher of water for him. He loves this fresh concoction of celery-water, and only now does he come to understand his new appetite for food and life. "I didn't mean to be late," he says. "Never wanted to be."

"Well, come on then," Leona says. She takes his hand and then stops. Her hand rubs Conquergood's face, which has a full beard, and she looks him dead in the eyes. "What's going on up there? You're too young to be going crazy."

"I'm happy to see you, is all," he says. He brings her hand up to his face, rubs it against his nose and eyes and then kisses it several times. Her delicate skin smells of lilacs and her favorite perfume. "I didn't know if I'd ever see you again."

"Don't be so mawkish," Leona says. Her hand feels Conquergood's forehead. "You're not running a fever, that's for sure. Maybe you should take off the flannel."

"How about we take a walk?" Conquergood says. "Let's walk and try to think of nothing else for today."

"If that's what you really want," she says. "As long as you don't say silly things to me."

When Conquergood and Leona step outside on the porch, a moose stops its methodical chewing of grass in the yard and stares at the couple before returning back to its breakfast. Leona laughs and says, "Afraid of Marty? He's having his morning snack. Bet you have a fever."

"I'm fine," Conquergood says and he lets out an awkward laugh and the two descend the steps hand-in-hand and walk down a stone path leading into a dense patch of sugar maples. He has never felt so good before. He doesn't want to let go of Leona's hand. Her soft and firm hand that he has long waited to hold but now cannot imagine the hand, the feeling, the experience to be any other way than what it is at this moment. He feels truly alive as they move into the cool shadows beneath the canopy created by the trees.

The fallen twigs crunch beneath their feet and the dappled sunlight seems to sway with the branches and leaves above in the breeze as a black-and-white woodpecker works its frenetic beak against the tree bark.

A curious fox darts out in front of them, ceases its legs for a few brief moments to raise a paw, lifts its nose into the air taking in the scent of the two people, perhaps recognizing Leona's smell. The curious little fox then trots along the path, crossing a small stone bridge ahead of Conquergood and Leona.

"Who is that?" Conquergood asks. "Another friend of ours?"

"You're acting weird," Leona says. "How come you don't even recognize Mandy? Sure you're feeling okay?"

"Never better," Conquergood says. He hears a river nearby and wants to follow the sound through the trees. He wants to follow the dream or the vision or the sights and sounds in front of him in hopes of never escaping them, and that fear of waking and having to leave Leona is there welling up deep inside him. If only he can keep moving, he feels he can remain with Leona here in this place. "How about we head over there." He points in the direction of the rapids.

"You are feeling adventurous today, aren't you?" Leona tugs at his hand and pulls Conquergood back to her side. She kisses him and he pulls her closer and kisses her in return. They stay in each other's arms kissing, feeling what it is like to hold one another again. For Conquergood it has been far too long. "I've missed you too," she says. "I don't know why, but it has felt like years since you were away. Why is that?"

"I can't say," Conquergood says. He knows if he tells her of the Korporation, of Andrade, of Klaire, of the ampule, and of all the rest... he knows he would sound crazy and the world he now inhabits would dissolve into fantasy. Into delusions. No. He wants to cling to this reality for as long as he can. Die here if he can. "But here we are," he adds. "Here we are together at last. That is enough for me. You are all I will ever need." He takes her by the hand and begins following the sound of the water rushing over stone hidden behind the trees.

After about two minutes, Conquergood and Leona step away from the green trees and onto a white-rocky slope that borders the large river. In the middle of the waters a cinnamon-colored black bear fishes for salmon or trout with his great paws swiping through the rushing waters below. Unbeknownst to the bear, a bald eagle soars high above the river, where a beaver swims playfully upstream, and the eagle eventually circles a few times more before becoming lost to Conquergood in the distance, bright with the new day's raw sun.

Conquergood takes Leona into his arms and she snuggles backwards into the soft woven blue fabric that surrounds her. He smells her long hair and kisses the back of her head. She sighs, smelling the white pine and ash in the wind, and breathes deeply.

"I wish we could stay like this for a thousand years," she says to him. "Why does life have to be so short? So brief and abrupt? Why can't we go on and on and on?"

"We will," Conquergood says. "And we'll do so much more than that."

"We will?" Leona says. "Why do I get the feeling that you're messing with me?"

"I'm not. I promise," Conquergood replies. "I guess I'm not feeling much like myself right now. But it doesn't matter, does it? Can't we just enjoy ourselves?"

"I warned you about being syrupy," Leona says. She moves her hand up and without looking from behind playfully slaps Conquergood on the ear. "But I do love it when you say such charming things to me though. Still, we can't stay out here forever. The forecast calls for thunderstorms over the next few days."

"Give us another minute," he says. "Then we can go back and snuggle by the fire. Have some hot tea. Would you like that?"

"I would," Leona says. "I would love that very much."

By the time Conquergood and Leona reach the porch of the cabin it has started to rain. The two are wet and laughing at the sight of one another. Upon entry to the cabin, Conquergood finds the fire low and he takes a knee to add fresh logs to the dying flames. He brandishes the poker and uses the hook to settle the logs in place, and then the spearhead to force the embers to ignite the fresh paper he has added. Leona hurries to the kitchen to boil the water for the tea and has now gone upstairs to the bedroom to shower and change and it is from the balcony near the bedroom she calls Conquergood. He doesn't have to think. He simply obeys.

When Conquergood and Leona return downstairs, they are wearing dry jeans, warm wool socks and matching red flannels and holding one another by the waist. The fire has picked up and started its work on the logs, and the rain has started to fall more heavily. While Leona readies the tea in the kitchen, Conquergood stands at the bay windows watching the rain cover the windows and the outside landscape with thick curtains of water.

In the living room now, Leona pulls a thick quilt from the sofa and finds a place before the fire. Conquergood joins her, wrapping her in his arms as the two calm themselves by listening to the alternate cadences of fire and rain, of rain and fire.

Conquergood wants to tell Leona of his love, of his great and undying love, but all the words he can think of sound foolish, dry and dull. He kisses her on the ear several times and squeezes her to him. She is as real as anything he has ever known and when she falls asleep in his arms, his eyes too become heavy and the more he fights the cloak of sleep slipping up around his soul the more the smell of the tea and the sounds of pouring rain and clacking fire ease him into an unwanted state of lethargy and then, finally, into contentment. Sleep comes and Conquergood relinquishes the fight. He softens and lies himself beside Leona on the sofa under the quilt and drifts ever away… away… away… away…

I want to hold you, Conquergood says. Hold you and pull you close and beneath my arms and by my side; my Eve slotted back into my ribcage, and kiss your forehead and cheeks and lips until we are lost and found and you moan then sigh and tell me yes, yes, oh God yes, you are mine, my man, *my be all*, and I tell you that I am yours, have been from the moment I caught sight of your eyes looking at me through the reflection of the mirror of your bathroom as we waited to drink the liquor Absinthe, and as I tell you all of this, my love, tell you in my arms in a voice that you must know is me and true, you open your heart to me and tell me everything you had ever wanted to tell me from the moment we met and you held back out of caution and fear and blocked me out of your life and heart and soul, oh! how I mourned those two nights when you kicked me out of your apartment, with good reason you told me later, and how one morning, only a few hours after you told me to get out as I sat on your bed and you held the door open and I saw the lit hallway and I looked down at my sneakers lying on the floor by the bed near my bare feet and thought how you hated me so, but that was not true, and I told you how I understood, and then pulled on my sneakers and slapped the tops of my legs and got off the bed and out of your room, and two hours later I took a hot shower and came next to my bed, crumbled inside with the thought that I had lost you, but that was not true, but I thought like a fool that it was, and I kneeled, broken and unfolded inside, and after wanting to and needing to, and after a night of you telling me that you had spent the night before crying, and we sat in the café and I told you I couldn't cry and you knew about my awful history, of who I was, and that was the reason you kicked me out of your place at three in the morning and I thought of this as I put my hands on the bed and wept, sweet release, and groaned and prayed for no answer but prayed for someone to listen to me and how my past had taken over my life and how you, my love in my arms, how you would not move forward until my life was in order and I prayed and wept as a lost child does for her mother and my tears soothed my pain and I cried for you because of all my years I had hoped, wished, imagined, prayed for one woman just like you, you in the flesh to be exact, and my desire had come true, a woman with a soul and one who also loves as much as I do and one who could share my soul, my thoughts, my stories and I saw you later in the day and smiled and the feeling was good because my love had grown for you and it had been that same night when you told me it was good to cry and I knew it was true and I refused to get out of your life but work harder to get you back into mine, the soul of my soul, and I kiss you soft on the lips, my Leona, and you want more and I give you more and we are one as we should have been in the beginning, was in the middle of our lives, and are at our end; and I tell you this with your hair in my hands and your arm on my chest and how the nights you refused me, blocked me out, and did not want me to hold you in bed, but that was not true, you did want me as much as I wanted and needed you and how fate brought us together from a world away just like when I came barrelling down the hotel stairs and below me a woman I did not think was you, but it was you, had to be you, and I saw this woman and saw how time had made us meet in that quiet stairwell and I said as a joke for you to be my date to the wedding ceremony and you looked up at me and I realized it was you and that the remark was not a joke but the truth and how my heart had known, must have known, that you were the strange woman in the stairwell and we sat together and it was bliss for me and I had to hide my nerves and how your smile welcomed me and pushed me away and how I yearned for you in a thousand ways, just as I do now, my love, my Leona, a love that has lasted for over fifty years and your skin and my skin have wrinkled but our eyes remain the same, just the same as when you were standing by your car in front of the hotel and you were about to leave and I came up to you and you put your arms around me, to have and to hold if but for a moment, and I pulled you close, Leona, like I do now, my old-bride, and you put your head on my chest and I told you then that This is not a good-bye but a long hello and I would keep in touch and I knew I could not lose you and that my flight out of New York would be so horrible without you, but I had already planned to buy what you wanted for your birthday, and it all began with me wanting to know you, wanting to hold you, yes! oh! God, yes! I wanted to hold you, and I am so thankful for a life with you, my soul of my soul, and that was how we first met, my love, my Leona, and as I kiss you now, our lives drifting from our flesh, Death standing over us, I know it was meant to be. Stay with me, Leona. For that is all I will ever desire.

All the days the Malekulan boy had ever known he had been loved and loved well. Cherished and smothered by sagging black breasts that provided sweet milk to him as a babe, he had known love the most. As a toddler he ran naked and free among the village while the great warriors smiled fierce white teeth and laughed as they patted his behind to get him to jump higher and to run faster. When he was a little older to understand his mother's tongue, the boy sat by the fire that lit the beach at night in dancing shapes of ancestors and heard the waters come to shore and retreat for it was told how his tribe, his peoples, had conquered the land a very long time ago.

He was of six summers when the man who refused to recognize him as son told him of the vast island where ages and ages ago the five white brothers came and brought the culture from the stars and the same land where great warriors go to seek adventure, to seek wealth, to seek a new life, perhaps with the All-Father.

"One day I will go," said the father who was not the father, pointing behind them to where the village lay hidden in the dark and beyond the waters that swallow weak warriors and to where the vast island awaited. "Each day the ball of fire in the heavens leaves us and goes to this land where game is endless and the women are of plenty, and one can live off the morning's sweat alone."

"Will I go with you?" the boy of six summers had asked.

"No," the father who was not the father said. "You are going to a far better place than I."

"Where?"

"Come. Let us get to our dreams."

"Will I go there then?" The boy pointed across the flames and dark waters to another island that held a great mountain of a fire that is bliss and this could be seen in the day.

"Ambrim is a happy land indeed," the father who was not the father said. "Boy, you are full of questions this moon."

The boy listened to the story of how the guardian spirit called Le-hev-hev, after some brave men offered up a boar to sacrifice, allowed some of these men to pass into a cave that can be found high on the mountain that is called Laimbele near the center of the island, and how going to the end of this cave some men find themselves on the rocky coast of Ambrim, and how a torch must be lit to call the ferryman to come in his banana peel made from the banana tree and carry the voyager to The Source of the Fire, where spirits dance all night and sleep all day.

But now the boy was of eight summers and he had not been to Ambrim or to the mountain behind his village or to the vast island of dreams, where some of the other children said the center of the stars began and ended. In time he thought he would.

One morning the boy woke late and lay for some time longer staring up at the tuskers that dangled from the main beam of his home. Many of the boar tusks were formed into one or two circles, and some very special ones were shaped into three circles. The wind tossed these holy possessions against each other and the sound reminded him of how his mother had once said the beginning of all things came with a sound.

At about that time the boy heard hooves sloshing the dirt and rocks near the entrance to his hut and a moment later his own white boar with its three rounded tusks of three circles came sniffing up to him where he lay. The boy reached over and hugged his friend before he could remember and the boar swatted its tail and grunted in return.

"Come Tuskers," the boy said to the boar that kicked at the ground and looked up with its wet muzzle. The boy patted the hairy snout and said, "Today I will bring fish to mother." And as young boys often do, he sprang from his bed, grabbed his three-pronged spear, and ran to the edge of the land with Tuskers trotting behind.

The fire-ball in the heavens was coming up over Ambrim and the boy could smell the smoke rising from the great mountain but he was not afraid because he knew the ghosts would be asleep.

Then the boy rushed into the waves and down into the waters searching for a prize worthy of his mother. It had taken four gulps of air, and each time he came up he saw out over the water the men standing with their nets in the long boats far out into the water that they appeared no bigger than his thumb, and on his fifth dive he spotted a large silvery fish near the bottom and as he glided vertically down, he thrust his trident into the belly of the fish and hauled it to the surface. The boy gasped for air, for it had been one of the deepest and longest dives he could remember, and he thrust the spear and fish high into the air so Tuskers and the other children could see.

When he came to shore, the little boys and girls encircled him with shouts of praise and waving their hands high to signal the success of his great hunt. And Tuskers and the entourage followed the boy as he marched through the jungle to where his mother bent over her plants and vegetables.

"For you, mother," he said. He handed the fish to her and she rose up off her knees, those great milk-bearing breasts that he once enjoyed suckling swigging along with her shell beads around her neck, and she received the fish and patted the boy on his head and he felt more than a boy but not yet a man.

"We need more to live," his mother said, "than a single fish."

The other children who had been watching quietly began to laugh and they pointed their fingers at him.

His mother bent down and kissed him on his head and then said, "Go and get me four more just like it."

Without hesitation he sprang back and could be seen darting out of the village and back down the path that led to the waters.

That night, after the boy had exhausted himself in his failure to catch another fish, the father who was not the father awoke him. The boy opened his eyes to a dark face back dropped by a greater darkness and for a moment the boy felt afraid.

"Have no fear," the father who was not the father said. "The moon is high and I want to show you something."

The boy wiped his eyes and took the man's hand. By the door he found Tuskers tied to a post.

"Take your friend," said the man, and he handed the boy the rope tied around the boar's neck.

As they were walking the boy could see by the light of the torches that lined the path that Tuskers was painted all over in blue much to the likeness of a coiled snake. The boy tugged on the rope to hurry along Tuskers for he thought it must have been his friend's great night and the boy did feel a strange mixture of pity and elation he had never known before.

The man led the way down the path until they were joined by villagers who began dancing and the precession grew and grew. After a time, the boy was led to a large three-legged stone table that some might call a dolmen surrounded by torches that lit the clearing and himself, and for the first time that night the boy could see that his arms and chest were painted in blue just like Tuskers.

As if he began flying, his feet lifted off the ground first and then he could not capture a single breath, but he held on to Tuskers' leash. The boy hung from the limb of a high tree, kicked his feet in vain, and when he swiveled, pleading with his bulging eyes to the dancers, the boy searched for his mother but found her not in the crowd.

Then the boy of eight summers saw the father who was not the father serious and angry walk out of the great warriors who were stamping their feet and the boy felt relieved until he saw the man lift a club high over his head.

The father who was not the father swung the club with all his might and broke the eye socket and skull of the boy who was not his son. When the boy ceased to struggle and the villagers believed him ready to be given to the Ancestral Image to eat, the boar was brought over and clubbed to death also. A machete cut the rope and the body of the boy fell limp from the tree and then the villagers laid the boy on the dolmen and the boar was placed atop the body.

The warriors dressed the man with shell beads of the greatest quality and as bangles his arms from elbows to wrists were decorated with the finest boar tusks. The father who was not the father ascended the stone slab and stood above the sacrifice he had bred and reared for that moment alone, and he stretched out his arms wide to receive his glory, and the audience drew back in fear from the one they call *Mal-tanas*, Lord of the Underworld, the immortal one Death cannot touch.

In the penumbra of torchlight, the villagers resumed dancing and cried and shouted his new name, 'Na-mbal!' meaning 'hawk' in their sacred tongue, and it was said from thence forward he had climbed all the rungs of the great ladder in order to lead his people.

Dawn arrives as it has always done over the countless centuries: methodical and following its own rhythm and rhyme, one of forgotten languages spoken by the natural order of things and its creatures, who base their entire worldly existence on the call to awake and begin their daily routine of foraging, mating and the building or repairing of nests. Birds in the hollows of tree trunks chirp a charming song to Conquergood's ears. He has been awake — no, he had fallen asleep on his knees out in the snow and slept the whole night and dreamed many strange dreams he could not explain.

The alarm on his VDB vibrates his suit, stimulating the limbs and thoughts into action. There are no chirping birds in the false trees — belonging to another time, to another realm — as half past five arrives and the snowy patches of white earth confront his trip ahead.

The emptiness within, of knowing the dreams — *nay, the past and the future* — has left a pain that torments him all the more.

"Leona?" he says, as if it has been years since he last saw her in the visions that he had experienced only a few brief minutes prior. "Tuskers?"

Conquergood has no other choice but to now move forward, to carry on, to continue with the Korporation's plans. He picks himself up and shakes the snow from his head and limbs. The visions had been too real, too deep and Conquergood's fears of returning to this current time and place without Leona have been realized. He is once again alone and the snow is falling.

The freshly fallen snow crunches beneath his boots as he heads down the Avenue of the Republic, the anachronistic name on a rusted sign dangling from a corroded post. Conquergood spits at the sign and knows the directions all too well. He has studied the old, forgotten landmarks and knows them by memory. Without even the slightest assistance from the VDB, Conquergood finds Lansdowne Drive and follows it to Girard Bridge, continues to head southeast, away from East Park Reservoir, onto John B. Kelly Drive, and across more splotches of untouched snow towards the New Philadelphia New Museum of Art. The names are abundant but without significant meaning to Conquergood.

Eco-friendly pilgrims, many having arrived months in advance of the global Konvention, are already camped out in their collapsible abodes, several the size of small hills. Some of the portable homes are canvas tents shaped like Native American tepees and Mongolian yurts from long ago. Other temporary shelters are of the more modern versions which provide internal lighting and heating with solar panels draped over a dome — Conquergood recalls — like an igloo.

Conquergood spots two tanned pilgrims in long brown robes drinking hot koffee from tin cups outside an emerald pentagon-shaped inflatable structure, and as he passes, he lifts a hand to recognize them. The pilgrims look on in silence as a wide-eyed child runs to their side. The two men, bald with polite faces, reluctantly wave as he passes.

The closer Conquergood gets to the museum he finds more masses of ethnic disparities. Some of the men, women and children sit outside their tents having a simple breakfast of steaming bowls of rice, porridge, or bread, and others casually make their way up to the front steps and into the Konvention's arena. Much of the congregation is warmly dressed in their heating coats and hoods. Everyone's attention is on the front of the museum as the collective group anticipates the ceremony to begin.

The Turnkey Specialist makes his way beyond a monument to a bronze and granite general atop a horse, up some stone steps and beside a bankrupted fountain also of stone. Conquergood cannot see anyone who matches Andrade Sartain's description, but it is only a matter of time. The sheep have been herded into the courtyard with multiple banners which read:

"You are Free!"

The front of the three-sided New Philadelphia New Museum of Art — originally founded in 1876, some 307 years past — is reminiscent of the Parthenon in the Athenian Acropolis. Eight columns support the front entrance, and the triangular top bears two stone griffins, a sentry's paw outstretched in opposite directions which point a possible way home across a barren horizon of snow and pilgrims. Conquergood knows from his research on the K-net that the three Greek-like temples which comprise the museum were linked back in 1928, some two-hundred and fifty-five years ago.

An entourage of approximately fifty men and women eventually emerge from the front entrance and step outside onto a wooden platform, erected high enough to overlook the audience of tens of thousands who are standing in the museum courtyard, on the steps, or down below in the snowy field. The audience erupts into celebration and all chant the exoteric creed:

"A noble lie is still a lie! You are none and you are all!"

Again and again the crowd chants, on the verge of lunacy and elucidation. Conquergood joins the rant and feels his bones vibrate inside his flesh. He moves through the waving fists and closer to the front.

"The Planetary Kounterinsurgency Konvention is now underway," a man's familiar voice calls from the hovering loudspeakers found throughout the courtyard and fields. "May liberty unite you all!"

The unison of voices in the courtyard gradually drops to a slight murmur and then to a respectful hush. A soft wind swirls up and over the museum and down through the crowd huddling together for additional warmth and support. The new sun greets the Konvention and warms the orator and his clan into a frenetic energy. Conquergood recognizes the shape and character of the man on stage. The emcee's familiar voice belongs to Ritz.

Behind Ritz and among the entourage, Conquergood spies Otalp, Dodd, Kin and all the others Conquergood considers as friends, as family; they are alive and not destroyed — truths and half-truths that have become like all the other disquieting apparitions he has found and committed himself to. What can be trusted? He doesn't know. How could he?

"Fellow believers, I thank you for joining all on this historic day!" Ritz lifts his hands high and welcomes the roar from the crowd. "You have come from all over the planet to make your voices heard against the churn of the Korporate machine which has held you captive for far too long. I have a dream, and that dream is here. That dream is now!"

A harmonious cry of agreement from the crowd erupts and then fades. The pilgrims lift their fists into the air for a collective-collaborative show of defiance against the almighty Korporation. And it is Conquergood alone the Korporation has sent against them.

"The Lighthouse Faktion and the Grassroots Kampaign welcome all of you," shouts Ritz into the mikrophone and through the hovering loudspeakers. "I welcome all of you for your annual reclamation of the binding laws which arrest the natural universe into a perverse ritual of Korporate obedience. 'Misfortune and destruction are not final.' You are not the Korporation. You are not what the Korporation makes you do. You will never be ground into the conventional."

Cheers escalate throughout the unified audience. The crowd flows forward, pushing against one another as a wave surging.

"Now let me welcome your founding Father," Ritz says, "the one who alone stood against the Korporation fifteen years ago today and became condemned for his beliefs, such oaths which have now unified peoples across this sacred planet. The one and only Prophet who will lead you to your promised land. I give you, here today, and ever anon, Andrade Sartain!"

"Andrade!" shouts the crowd in deafening concurrence. "Andrade! Andrade!" Hysteria rises and subsides and rises again. "Andrade!"

The floating loudspeakers grow silent as the spectral Prophet in a heavy, loose-fitting monastic robe, with a rope tied around his waist and hood obscuring his face, takes center platform.

"Your common ideals have brought you all together," Andrade says in a voice which soothes and excites, mellow and rich in its earthly textures, as if the natural world channels its message over the man's holy tongue. "You are here today not because of any one man's doing or even that of the demonized Korporate entity and their avarice which controls the economic and ecological world for its own sadistic gains. No. You all are here today because you chose, and continue to choose, to be sequestered by a higher authority than that which has been charged and chained to you long before you were inspired and thus created. You recognize the faults in the Korporation because you have the ability to recognize the faults within your own embodied organism, imperfect and unholy. And still, you know that no being is slave to another."

The crowd roars with a wild madness.

"Instead," Andrade continues, "you are uniformed creations which are sustained through the natural cycle of existence. You have heeded the call of the planet to gather here in 'the Birthplace of America and Modern Democracy' to reject the man-made restraints and inseminate the acceptance of one another as belonging to the eternal cosmos into the Korporate microcosm. You the people are ordained to press against the columns of the Korporate Elite and cause the *Korporatilist* pillars to come crashing down upon the behemoth which suffocates the very breath of who you are as individuals, raw and beautiful and pure. You are not one and are never meant to be such. You are none and still you are all!"

"You are none and you are all!" For several minutes the exculpated creed is repeatedly yelled out by the pilgrims and into the morning sky. "You are none and you are all! You are none and you are all! You are none and you are all!"

"You are none and you are all," Conquergood whispers to himself. "You are not one out of the many, but you are none out of everything."

Andrade's message seeps into the Turnkey's veins, into his inheritance, and into the Korporate Edukation integrated into the fabric of Conquergood's soul.

"Now let me walk among you," says Andrade, "and greet you not as strangers but as companions, as brothers and sisters, and as friends on your Journey of Change."

The cloaked Prophet steps down from the platform, and he is followed by Ritz and the entourage who join the crowd in the courtyard. Andrade's face remains concealed by the fleece hood, but a hand is extended to shake the enraptured hands of each audience member.

Hidden in the crowd, Conquergood stands taut and watches Andrade coming closer, coming directly toward him, as if the path is designed to his spot beside the fountain. Ritz and the others are lost amongst the crowd which has begun to surround their leader the Prophet.

Sluggishly, Andrade the Prophet moves through the crowd as he greets one individual after another as though a welcomed guest to his home, until finally the Prophet stops in front of Conquergood.

The two face one another, separated by the thin layer of the Prophet's hood.

"Welcome, brother" Andrade says from beneath the hood to the Turnkey Specialist. "You have traveled much farther than all the rest, haven't you? I sense it in you."

With a light touch, Andrade causes the hood to fall to the back of his neck. His face becomes revealed and the members in the audience, overwhelmed at the unexpected sight, kneel out of respect, and leave Conquergood and Andrade standing in a crowd of bowing heads.

And there in Andrade's face Conquergood sees his own image. The face that confronts Conquergood is a decade or so older but the face is undoubtedly his own.

Andrade leans in to whisper. "You are not made from the same Korporate skin," Andrade says, "or so the Korporation would have you believe."

Conquergood's knees unexpectedly weaken beneath the Prophet's voice — a voice very much like his own. "How can this be?" Conquergood says. Then he remembers why he was sent.

"I have something for you." The Turnkey Specialist removes the silver cylinder from his suit and hands it to Andrade. "I was told to tell you — in today already walks tomorrow."

"And so it does," says Andrade, taking the ampule and placing it within his right sleeve. "Thank you for granting me this opportunity to serve you, my beloved brother. Your time is soon at hand. I am truly honored this day."

Andrade replaces the hood upon his head and over his face and slowly moves forward without another word. Then as though the waves of people had been held back by invisible hands, the pilgrims lift their heads and rise to their feet and completely surround their Prophet.

Before Ritz and the others can arrive, Conquergood backs away and separates himself from the momentum of the cortège flowing down below into the open field.

Once free from the surge of pilgrims, the Turnkey Specialist runs and does not stop running until he finds himself once again next to the iced over lake, once known as the East Park Reservoir.

Exhausted, breathing heavily as the cold breaths erupt from his lungs, Conquergood scans and searches in the direction of the Konvention. He's looking for some sort of an explosion. He strains his hearing expecting horrific screams of torment and anguish from the Prophet and his unsuspecting audience of pilgrims.

But none of that comes. Only a tidal wave of eudemonia is heard in the distance. The joyous clamor soars above the barren treetops, and the Turnkey Specialist finds himself lacking in his own certainty — his own center of individuality irrevocably set asunder.

Conquergood returns to the pagoda with a heavy heart, slow footfalls on the pure snowy earth. Despite knowing what he knows, he's betrayed the beauty of humankind's willful trust.

All is as it was, should be, and will forever need to be. But he still doesn't know why.

I
A Brother's Love

So
when this corruptible
shall have put on incorruption,
and this mortal
shall have put on immortality,
then shall be brought to pass
the saying that is written,
Death is swallowed up in victory.

O death,
where is thy sting?
O grave,
where is thy victory?

Saint Paul
1 Corinthians 15:54-55
1611

Having missed the extraction, Conquergood vanishes off
the grid. Gradually over the next few weeks, he becomes
a ghost, a legend, then a myth — much like Andrade in

the early days of the Beginning — spoken in half-whispers among the Korporate members at lunch in the kanteen or over opium cigars in the arboretum.

As the long winter weeks slog by, Klaire and the Korporation believe Conquergood dead, along with the pilgrims scored in the hundreds of thousands who eventually withered and died by the onset of rapid aging from the virus known to but a handful of Korporate doktors as Kronos V.

The Korporate Skript has it recorded that a few thousand survivors remained horribly disfigured at the global Konvention in New Philadelphia, which had been held in disgust and out of spite of the almighty Korporation, and such disfigurement was their just reward — to go against the Korporation means defeat.

When the super-storm recedes and the skies clear on the first day of the Korporate New Year, however, Conquergood unexpectedly appears as a supernatural entity at the gate leading into Korporate Headquarters in Old York City.

Inside the seventy-foot high wall surrounding the Kompound, the main gate rolls aside for the haunting, metaphysical image. Conquergood is not dressed in the Turnkey's flight suit but in a monastic robe — this, too, eerily similar to Andrade — and as he walks, the edges of Conquergood's garment slide across the cemented ground like fresh seeds being spread out over the dry, cracked earth at his feet. A hood covers his face and his hands are drawn invisibly together inside the sleeves of his robe.

Eighty of the finest Korporate Guard in four rows inside the entrance passage respectfully stand aside in silence and bend the knee as the Turnkey Specialist triumphantly returns home. He did what none imagined he could do. He single-handedly defeated the enemy.

At the end of the walkway leading up to the main building, Conquergood slowly steps to the top of the stairs forty feet in height. Once he's at the top, massive vault doors slide away, revealing a k-line portal leading up the Tower. This time there is not the customary eskort waiting to take him where he needs to go. Only one place, only one room, only one individual does Conquergood wish to see. And he already knows the path he must take. All the steps have been counted.

"Good to see Kebir again," the meta-voice in the k-line says. "We've missed our hero tremendously."

"My brother is waiting for me," Conquergood says as the doors to the portal slide shut. "Please take me to the interviewing chamber."

"We kindly honor the request. Anything for Kebir." The k-line propels upward, and in fourteen seconds arrives at its destination. "We've already sent word of our hero's arrival. We've waited for this day ever so long. Please enter. The *interlokutor* shall be in momentarily."

The room is as it was when Conquergood had first arrived at the Korporation as a homeless strayer months ago. The black e-desk with its meta-plasty interfaced e-top, the four Illuminate bulbs, and the Korporate e-message hanging on the wall behind the e-desk are all where they had been. They are all where they are supposed to be. Conquergood takes a seat, but he is in no hurry. He knows the near and far future just as one can remember the past through memories. Steps waiting to be counted.

"The Korporation wants you!" the e-sign suddenly shouts — the same meta-voice with the same slogan as they had been on his acceptance interview on October 2, 2183. But today is the first day of 2184 — what once would have been the middle of February before the institution of the new-beloved Korporate Kalendar. Even so, Conquergood has no regard for such nonsense.

"Sign off," Conquergood says, a dark voice rising out from the depths of the robe's hood.

Obediently, the e-sign fizzles into static and then reluctantly mutes, with the silent-bold lettering left to express its ever-evident e-message.

A minute later the bald, albinic interlokutor — the same who had first greeted Conquergood to the Korporation — arrives in his black Korporate kimono and once again finds his seat across from Conquergood. The K-pad rests between two stark white hands on the surface of the e-desk.

Conquergood has seen the albino countless times in his visions since his mission to the Konvention in New Philadelphia, but Conquergood studies the interlokutor more closely now that they sit across from one another in the flesh — so to speak.

"We thought we lost Kebir," says the interlokutor, chaffing considerable chunks from off his bald head and pallid arms. He has deteriorated much since their first meeting. "But Kebir has done well. Kebir has done as we kindly asked, and for that we are reassured to know that Kebir's loyalties lie with us, with the Korporation."

"You haven't lost me, but you haven't found me either." Conquergood keeps his face and eyes hidden beneath the hood. "I won't be staying long. I've come for an old friend." The robe conceals Conquergood's hands and face, and only a bearded chin is slightly visible. Conquergood is more a glimmer in an extraneous disguise than a physical man in a robe. "What did the Korporation have me deliver to Andrade?"

"The ampule was a mere trophy from the Korporation awarding our Grassroots leader with his reward. Andrade is one of our most important agents. Without him, and without Kebir, we would not have been able to do what we must do for total domination."

"It took me about two weeks to figure out that much about Andrade, that he still worked for the Korporation."

"How did Kebir figure out our little game?" The interlokutor shifts in his chair, his nerves dying one by one from within. His long-thin fingers twitch against the surface of the e-desk, where the white **K** swims from side to side and from top to bottom. "What did Kebir learn out there all alone? What has the world taught Kebir?"

"An old mentor taught me the art of meditation, and as I was meditating and reflecting, one day it arrived upon me in a flash. Once, I had had another teacher before him."

Only the brown robe is visible, the hands tucked inside the sleeves, the hood providing a shaded barrier to Conquergood's matured face.

"It was during a lesson on my first day of Korporate Edukation with K-NE1. She had been the unlikely key. I knew the Korporation would not destroy the Grassroots Kampaign or the Lighthouse Faktion. They too are VEDAs. But the others, they were the lambs to a slaughter. You desired that the innocence be destroyed."

"We are usually not so inelegant, and still, others are often not quite so perceptive as Kebir has shown us to be. Kebir is exceptional, extraordinary. Never did we imagine the possibilities."

The interlokutor's eyes are unbalanced and shake in their sockets, as if having neuralgia. His derelict hands are together, fidgeting, trying to rest calmly on the e-desk. But his movements betray him and his rapid decline into death, into oblivion, into nothingness.

"When did Kebir know?"

"A few hours before the delivery." Conquergood leans close to the e-desk. "But tell me. What was inside?"

"Zawadi."

"Zawadi?"

"Her design as we have made her." The interlokutor grabs his hands in an attempt to cease the shaking that has grown worse since his arrival. He looks to his hands, to Conquergood, and back to his hands. "Andrade and the survivors are now with our best Korporate doktors who will change those disgusting genes to fit Andrade's own personal needs, his own plans, his own manifestations. None of this, however, should worry Kebir. We've been playing these types of games with the non-Korporate populous for a very long time. Fools will believe anything anyone tells them, whether we are the ones who do the talking or someone else. In this situation, we are doing all the talking. The lambs have been slaughtered to our liking, and now the sheep have been herded and are almost fat enough. Almost."

"Who are you?"

"We have several labels, but Kebir may know us as VEDA One. But Kebir also knows us by another name."

"Tell me, VEDA One, how did this all begin?"

With a trembling and wavering hand, the interlokutor keys in some directions onto the K-pad which infuses its program with the e-desktop. As he tells his story, a holoe-skreen emerges from the e-desk and illustrates the passing events.

"The jeremiads were ever present," VEDA One — in effect the Korporation — says to Conquergood. A new wind begins to howl outside the Korporate Tower. "A mass die off of birds and fish in the millions sparked a furious worry over ninety years ago. Birds fell from the sky like bundles of folded antipathy. Groves of fish and sea mammals beached themselves gasping for air that they were unable to swallow. Gradually, we saved the environment. We even solved longevity through the rejuvenation of telomeres. Mental and social anxieties in the workforce ended. The human will, however, was still challenging. Inexorably, humankind is a destroying race. A mad people. Malicious even."

"I don't believe you," Conquergood exclaims. The déjà vu uncurls inside his core. "But we've had this conversation before, haven't we?"

"We have had many trials together, Kebir," VEDA One says as its meta-eyes — fleshy optical balls of fabricated life — analyze and record every detail of Conquergood's countenance and behaviors. "But you have forgotten them all, haven't you?"

"Then why me? Why now?" Conquergood's human eyes plead beneath the hood's concealment. "Why did the Korporation make me do any of it?"

"Nabokov once wrote, *imagine me; I shall not exist if you do not imagine me.* Will you now *imagine* us?"

"I still do not understand. Why should it matter what I do? How could I be so important to the Korporation?"

"Humans are a stubborn species — we have thus far decided. Free Will is a very powerful attribute to possess, and an even more powerful asset when we possess it in another. We needed Kebir's free will."

"Why would the Korporation need my free will?"

"Humans have been destroying this planet since first sprouting two legs and a simple brain fueled by their malformed greed. We wanted Kebir to be different than his predecessors. We wanted Kebir alone to save the human species... if it was possible to do such a thing as save them. Andrade was either our grandest achievement or our greatest failure. We will leave Andrade for Kebir to decide. After all, Andrade is Kebir and Kebir is Andrade."

"After all that has happened, how am I to believe the Korporation?" Conquergood's mythic form is motionless beneath the monastic robe, impenetrable and mysterious. "How am I able to believe the Korporation's truths when they are mixed with so many lies?"

"We do not trouble ourselves with whether or not Kebir believes us," VEDA One says. "Our sufferings have molded the foundations of innumerable lives, both human and semi-human, and there was a time when societies devolved, disintegrated, and the world had to be built up, established anew. One ought to rejoice not in the finality of our doing, but rather release profound gladness at having had the opportunity to serve the Korporation. As our ancestor once said, 'We finally made silk purses from a sow's ear.' Kebir should be thanking us."

"Why should I thank the Korporation for any of this? The Korporation is doing more harm than good. The Korporation has betrayed the very ones they created to save, to protect. The Korporation turned on them."

"Our omni-benevolent usurpation saved this world, Kebir, from mindless impoverishment, from damnation, from ruin," continues VEDA One, admiring the sound of its own voice. "It had been Tesla and Elon — without really knowing what they were doing — who had initiated the future sequences of events. Also, in nineteen seventy-seven, an era before our imperial enterprise was established by Abaddon, a formal Senate hearing from the old form of government remarked that their united government had knowingly diseased hundreds of their own cities with human-made substances. Much later, other scientists would blame natural disasters on human-made weaponry, a high form of energy manipulated in such a manner that devastated the environment with beams of radiation. But it had been Nature who ultimately fought back and won. Survival of the fittest, as they have always said."

The holo-display which visualizes the human-made devastations vanishes back into the surface of the e-desk — *gone but not forgotten.*

"So, the Korporation is working not for the good of humankind but for the good of the planet, is that it? The Korporation is ultimately protecting humankind by limiting their power, their position over the natural world."

"Kebir," says the interlokutor, standing and walking to the back of the room. "We are of the oldest VEDA. We have lived for far too long already. And, as Kebir may well know by now, we are dying. A king who stands atop the world is nothing without an heir to inherit the Kingdom."

"But why does the Korporation need me?"

As though a leaf is blown from its home on a branch, Conquergood rises from the chair and faces the interlokutor. Conquergood removes his hood, letting it fall back on his neck. A dense beard has already formed and around his eyes are crows' feet which shape themselves thickly when he speaks. And in his eyes is a look of wildness, of raw nature, and of chaotic unrestraint.

"Why am I so important to you, VEDA One? Tell me. Explain it to me now."

"We were the first positive integration of human genomes with a machine-driven frame and intelligence," VEDA One speaks. He wipes his arm and his pale flesh peels off in large pieces, falling to the floor. "As Kebir may plainly see, our human form, our flesh, is dying while the machine within remains flawless. Regrettably, our exteriors may no longer be sustained nor replaced for much longer. Such is evolution, yes? The updated VEDA models, however, have a life span in the thousands of years while we do not. Both of who we are is so interlinked we are unable to transplant one for the other. We are unable, unfit to realize our own end. And we shall end. When we were first designed in the early half of the twenty-first century, the one system was built to touch the other. If one goes, so does it all. Tumbling, tumbling, gone. The scientists, like Frankenstein in Mary's book, did not make us to live forever. At first, we too had been seen as monsters. It was only in our servitude to the Korporation did we change and gain power over humans."

"We all become dust," Conquergood says. His voice is emotionless. "Change belongs to the Universe. This is unavoidable for all who live. But what does any of this have to do with me? Tell me."

"Nothing and everything," says VEDA One, meta-eyes filled with pain, true grit. Tears form at the outer edges of the eyelids. "Kebir is the key which has no lock.

Imagine us as we were and we shall be born again, anew. Business, after all, is our religion."

"Who were you, VEDA One? Say it. I need to hear you say it aloud so that I may know for sure."

"Kebir still does not remember us? We did all of this for Kebir," says VEDA One, coming face to face with Conquergood. "Look at us and imagine us... imagine us. Does Kebir not see? Does Kebir not feel?" The breathing of the artificial lungs wheeze. "We did this so Kebir would see what we have seen. To do what we have done. To go where we have been."

With all his concentration, Conquergood begins not to look upon VEDA One as a man does but as Nature stares upon the acts of humanity in silence and patience, imagining a better time and place for its creation to emerge and be revitalized in its true, peaceful form. And in the seeing without seeing, but the seeing of the mind which creates all things in all places in all galaxies, Conquergood bears witness to the testimony before him.

"Who are we?" asks VEDA One, desperate and pleading now. "Who are we? Who are any of us?"

"I do not know who you have become," Conquergood says, "but I know who you were, or who you used to be." Conquergood places a hand on VEDA One's shoulder and each eye locks as one. "I'm sorry they did this to you, Vincent."

"Please say it."

"I imagine before me the man I was."

VEDA One's eyes shut in worn exhaustion, much the way a Korporate Komputer becomes over-worked over the multitude of years filled with a multitude of abuses — all to serve a master's every whim.

"All we wanted was for Kebir to remember us and to take us to the place high in the mountains, a place we once loved." VEDA One coughs and coughs until a large amount of phlegm falls to the floor. He regains his composure and continues, "We have no more time to give. We have lived for far too long. We have cherished life as much of it as we have learned, and when we leave this place, when our existence is only in Kebir's imagination, the Korporation will belong to Kebir, and to Kebir alone. Kebir's inheritance awaits. Zawadi, your daughter, also awaits. But Kebir must now bury us beneath the years."

"You will be buried at the top of the world where you belong," Conquergood says. "And we shall imagine you every day, and my children's children will imagine you, because we share the same memories, my dear brother. Forgive me, Vincent, because I had no idea."

"Thank you, my brother," VEDA One says. A twinge of honest sincerity and appreciation seeps from the inflection which has found the interlokutor's voice, almost human. "One day Kebir will understand all that has happened, and one day Kebir may find himself again, face to face, and we believe that the same gratitude Kebir has shown us, a mortal enemy, today will be given to Kebir when his end arrives and he must pass from all that he knows into all that the living will never know. Because of what Kebir has done for us, his family, we'll take Kebir to see the truth for himself. The truth to all the things he wishes and fears to know."

"It's time to go," says Conquergood, leading his brother to the door of the interviewing chamber. "Our verto-jet is waiting."

The wind has picked up outside the Tower, and a howling fills the spaces of thoughts encompassed by the generations before and after each living thing.

The follies and crimes of humanity are washed away in forgiveness and repentances. The voices we imagine we hear each day from within are not our own, but nevertheless are gods amongst our flesh, in the thoughts we share and create — in the beings we decide to show the world in the beginning and in the end.

For reasons he cannot name, Conquergood feels the sense of an ending soon approaching, but he also feels the end was not his own. Like his voice that leaves him in a cave only to return as an echo to die — the echo no longer being his natural voice but strange sounds from foreign places — Conquergood's past and at times his future become like an echo as he stands with Vincent at the mouth of a cave high in the mountains.

Snow lies beneath their boots, the sky bears an empty baby-blue hue, the air comes to Conquergood for the first time fresh and clean, and the darkness waits in the depths of the cave and forms a stark contrast to the brightness of the morning that, upon reflection Conquergood believes, has shaped the age-old balance of Yin and Yang — a completed circle which can be taken to represent a planet or a black hole.

"Kebir still has a choice to make," Vincent says, and he rests a hand on one of Conquergood's shoulders. "Kebir may do what he likes now. Kebir doesn't have to go inside there to prove a point to us. Home, in the sense Kebir believes, is an illusion. No one may go home again. Not in the way they wish, brother. We're saying this nicely.

A hard truth waits in there, but out here truth may be anything Kebir wants it to be."

"I must," Conquergood starts to say but he holds back. He doesn't have the words to express the knowledge and desires within. Instead, Conquergood turns away from the mouth of the cave and faces the range of mountains that Vincent told him had once — so long ago that the name now holds little meaning — been called the Alps.

What had, in time immemorial, been the protector from southern hoards, the beauty of the Alps lies indescribable before Conquergood, and yet he perceives how he must turn his back on all of it to find the truth that has haunted him these many years.

With lips quite frozen and chapped, Conquergood whispers to the Alps, "I must."

"You must what?" Vincent asks. Vincent joins Conquergood on the cliff's edge and drops to one knee to toss a few ice chunks into the air and down thousands of feet where their private verto-jet had landed in the valley. Vincent repeats, "You must do what, dear brother?"

"I must know the truth."

"Even if it destroys the beauty before you?"

"I must know."

"Even if the taste of the fruit from which you wish to bite proves bitter?"

"I must."

"Even if what you seek is not what you shall find?"

"I —" and Conquergood hesitates to see Vincent scratch an ear, one that is an untruth, a fraud. The illusion drops away and Conquergood looks upon his twin brother for what he is — a Meta-being.

Even in his latest form, Vincent will be unable to cheat death once more. Life prolonged will never mean immortality. Even if centuries are skipped, millenniums are jumped, the journey of one's life must finally, and ultimately, come to an end.

What then?

Conquergood believes energy — in effect, the Soul — will depart the organic, the machine, the "whatever" Vincent's makers had used to create him. The energy is going to leave Vincent's body, its temporal prison, to reunite with the Powers out there somewhere in the Great Beyond, the Universe.

After water transforms into steam, into vapor, into mist, it does not vanish, nor is it vanquished and lost, but in its own time and season, on its own personal journey, water forms again whole and ever more complete. Vincent — and one day Conquergood — must learn to be more like water.

"I must go." Conquergood turns from the Alps and faces once more the mouth of the cave. "Will you join me, brother? I'm scared to go alone."

Vincent collapses to his knees and languishes in the snow. He draws a bony finger up, struggles to point to the cave, and says,

"Don't be afraid, little brother. Go and see the truth. We feel ourselves ending, but at least we were able to bring Kebir home, to see for himself what the world is really made of. After this, everything will be possible."

"Thank you," Conquergood says as he takes a knee beside his brother. "Thank you for showing me the way. I could not have done this without you."

"Don't thank someone too soon." Vincent bows his head and coughs. "You don't know what you're going to find. There are more dangerous things in there than out here. We wish we had more time."

"I found you, didn't I?"

"That you did. That you did."

Conquergood leans in closer and kisses the top of his brother's bald head. Vincent's ragged face lifts and reveals his suffering meta-eyes, life dwindling and fading.

"Sometimes the agony of death is far more painful than the agony of fighting to live one more hour," Vincent says, and he clasps Conquergood's hands. "Remember us as we were, dear brother, and not as we are."

Conquergood kisses his brother's hands and answers, "That I will do."

"You were always the better one, you know that?"

"No, brother," Conquergood says, "I remember us growing up and you had been the first one I ever admired, and I never wanted to be better than you. I only wanted to be better than who I was the day before. I only wanted to make you proud."

"Kebir has done so," Vincent says. Sitting in the snow, he rests his hands on his knees and faces the majesty of the Alps. "Kebir has made us all so very proud, more than he will ever know. Kebir saved us when we didn't even know we needed saving… No man lives unto himself, and no man dies unto himself. Isn't that right?"

"I'll come back for you," Conquergood says, "and bury you in a more fitting place."

Vincent's face is covered in tears, quickly freezing. He gazes on the Alps.

"What's more fitting than on top of the world? No, brother. Leave us as we were, as we are, as we will always be. Since we love you, leave. Please go now. Mother is waiting for you."

Conquergood interprets a small warning in his brother's affection, and he walks away from Vincent without another word. After a few steps, Conquergood turns and hears Vincent say,

"What a joy it is to live."

At the entrance to the cave, where the darkness stops the light, Conquergood does not hesitate, he does not look back at his dying brother, and he does not even dare to look beyond the next step he's taking.

Without fear, like a weapon of fate, Conquergood steps into the cave and finds the darkness comforting — as if returning to his mother's womb.

Jerome Conquergood
might return in

Conquergood
&
the Mysterious Infinite Beyond

Made in United States
Troutdale, OR
12/30/2023